WINGS OF THE MORNING

WINGS OF THE MORNING

Beryl Matthews

This first hardcover edition published in Great Britain 2004 by
SEVERN HOUSE PUBLISHERS LTD of
9–15 High Street, Sutton, Surrey SM1 1DF,
by arrangement with Penguin Books Ltd.
This title first published in the USA 2005 by
SEVERN HOUSE PUBLISHERS INC of
595 Madison Avenue, New York, N.Y. 10022.

British Library Cataloguing in Publication Data

Matthews, Beryl
   Wings of the morning
   1. World War, 1939-1945 - Great Britain - Fiction
   2. Great Britain - Social life and customs - Fiction
   I.   Title
   823.9'2 [F]

ISBN 0-7278-6143-3

Printed and bound in Great Britain by
MPG Books Ltd., Bodmin, Cornwall.

With thanks for all the help and support I have received from Carole Blake my agent, Harriet Evans my editor, and the Forest Writers Group.

Whither shall I go from thy spirit?
Or whither shall I flee from thy presence?
If I ascend up into heaven, thou art there:
If I make my bed in hell, behold, thou art there.
If I take the wings of the morning, and dwell in the
uttermost parts of the sea;
Even there shall thy hand lead me, and thy right hand
shall hold me.

Psalm 139: 7–10

I

3 September 1939

So it had started!

The months of speculation were over and they were at war again.

Annie Webster turned off the wireless and walked into the garden, needing to be alone for a few moments. The tension of waiting for this announcement, knowing it must surely come, had been unbearable. There wasn't a sound anywhere and the streets were empty. A lone dog gave one short bark and stopped, as if it too sensed the enormity of the news. It seemed as if the whole country was holding its breath, wondering what the future would bring. The silence was eerie and rather frightening.

She closed her eyes briefly in an attempt to stop the tears that were threatening to spill over. She had tried so hard to dismiss the talk and hold to the belief that this would never happen, but she couldn't do that any more. The war was a reality now and she would have to face up to it just like everyone else. An overwhelming feeling of sadness swept over her, and for a brief moment her shoulders slumped. Then she straightened up again. This was not the time to indulge in despair and self-pity, because if the last war was anything to go by then there was a long hard struggle in front of them.

She lifted her face to the warmth of the sun and felt it

caress her. The air was clear and almost sparkling without a cloud in the sky. How could this perfect day be marred by such terrible news? With a deep sigh, she opened her eyes again as she heard her family coming out of the house. No one spoke, they were each lost in their own thoughts.

An unearthly wailing cut through the stillness and made them look at each other in alarm.

'Air-raid sirens,' Bill, her brother-in-law, told them.

Still they didn't move, but everyone's face was tilted up towards the sky. Watching, waiting. They scanned the clear sky, looking and listening for any sight or sound of aeroplanes, but nothing happened. In a short time the all clear sounded.

'Just trying them out, I expect,' her mother said softly.

Then all was quiet again and Annie let her thoughts drift. How good life had been in the last sixteen years since they had moved out of the slums of London into these two lovely houses in Roehampton, designed by Bill. The hardship and poverty they had endured seemed like a bad dream now.

'Two wars in our lifetime,' her mother whispered. 'I never thought it would happen again.'

Those few spoken words, cutting through their thoughts, seemed to snap them out of their daze. Her sister Rose bent down and scooped up her youngest child; a beautiful little girl now three years old.

'Why does everyone look so sad, Mummy?' she asked, reaching out for the comforting arms of her father.

'Nothing for you to worry about, Kate.' Rose gave her daughter a kiss and handed her over to her husband, while their ten-year-old son, James, stood by his mother, silent for a change.

'Let's all go inside and have a nice cup of tea.' Her mother turned and walked briskly towards the kitchen.

Annie smiled for the first time that day. A cup of tea was her mother's remedy for all ills – the kettle was constantly on the boil. They trooped after her dutifully, knowing it was useless to refuse.

'Where's Paul these days?' Annie's mother asked her, obviously trying to steer the conversation on to normal lines. 'Have you broken up with him?'

'No, he's been away for the past couple of months.'

'What doing?' Bill asked.

'I've no idea. He was very secretive about it, but he said he'd be back soon.'

'Why don't you marry the poor bloke?' Charlie, her brother, asked.

'I don't want to. I know I'm twenty-eight, but I'm waiting for the right man.' She loved Will and Charlie, her two brothers, dearly, but they still considered her the baby of the family and were always trying to give her advice.

Rose laughed. 'You're a fine one to talk about marriage, Charlie. You're twenty-nine and Will's thirty-two, and neither of you is showing any signs of settling down yet. You like your freedom too much.' She looked pointedly at her two brothers and rolled her eyes, making everyone laugh.

It was a good sound on such a gloomy day.

Annie slipped her arm through her brother-in-law's, and grinned. 'I'm still looking for someone like Bill.'

'Ah, then you're out of luck. He's the only one in existence,' Rose said.

Annie watched the way her sister's dark eyes lingered on her husband. Rose and Bill had a blissful marriage, and Annie wanted one like it and wouldn't settle for anything less.

At that moment there was a brief knock on the kitchen door and Paul strode in. The shock of seeing him hit Annie with such force that she leapt to her feet with uncharacteristic clumsiness and nearly sent her cup flying. He was in air force uniform and sporting a pair of wings on his chest.

She opened her mouth but nothing came out.

Paul laughed. 'Not like you to be lost for words, Annie.'

'Well, what the blazes do you expect?' she managed to say at last. 'You might have told me what you were up to.'

'You haven't wasted any time, Paul,' Annie's mother remarked.

'Well, it was clear that the war was coming, and as I already had my commercial pilot's licence it seemed the sensible thing to do.'

'Sensible?' Annie couldn't believe she was hearing this. She'd met Paul at a dance in Richmond four years ago and she knew he could be impulsive, but she hadn't expected him to do this. 'Why couldn't you wait until war had actually been declared before joining up?'

'The country is going to need pilots and I want to be in at the beginning,' Paul ran his fingers gently down her face. 'I can't sit on the sidelines, you must see that.'

4

'I do,' she admitted, as the shock began to recede. This was typical of Paul and she should have expected it. He had been totally absorbed in his flying lessons over the last year, but she'd put that down to the fact that his older brother, Reid, was already a pilot. She had never met him but from the snippets of information she'd been given he appeared to be a steadying influence on Paul. She thought too about Paul's parents. They were a lovely couple and she knew it would upset them terribly to have him going to war. However, it was done now. She tipped her head on one side and studied the cut of his uniform. 'You look very dashing.'

He gave a self-conscious grin and shuffled uncomfortably at her compliment, then he turned his attention to Bill, who was still holding his daughter in his arms. 'You were in the navy last time, weren't you? A captain, I believe?'

Bill nodded grimly.

'They'll be after you – '

'No!' Rose said sharply. 'He's too old this time.'

Annie watched a rare moment of panic flit across her sister's face. She tried to propel Paul out of the kitchen but he wasn't going to move. It was not the time to discuss this. They all needed a few hours to let it sink in that they were at war again. Decisions had to be made, but not until they'd had time to adjust and absorb the implications. Over the last few weeks many people had declared that Germany didn't want war with Britain, and she'd tried to believe them, but if you looked at the turmoil in Europe it was hard to delude yourself.

'How old are you?' Paul persisted.

'Forty-seven in December.'

'That won't matter. They'll be desperate for men with your experience —'

Annie tugged at Paul's arm, anxious to get him away. She could almost hear the thoughts of the people sitting around the table – troubled thoughts – things they would rather not face at the moment. They were well aware that their lives were going to change dramatically, and seeing Paul in his uniform was bringing home to them what this war would mean for their family. Will and Charlie, her brothers, were young enough to fight, and Bill . . . well, he shouldn't have to go through that again. The Great War had claimed a generation of young men and she didn't dare think about the horrors this one would inflict on them.

'Come on, let's go out somewhere.' She dragged Paul through the door before he could stir things up any more. He was a charming but immature young man, and seemed quite oblivious of everyone's concern. The prospect of another conflict was not something to look forward to, and the awful thing was that men like her brother-in-law would be dragged in to fight for the second time in their lives.

'I wanted to talk to Bill,' he complained as she hustled him towards the car.

'Paul Lascells,' she said sharply, 'you were upsetting everyone, especially my sister, with all your talk about Bill going back in the navy.'

'Rose?' he exclaimed. 'You can't upset her; she'll be rolling up her sleeves and getting stuck in. She'll be in the thick of it.'

Annie shook her head sadly. She was very fond of Paul but he seemed more like ten years younger than her,

6

instead of two. Was it any wonder she knew she didn't want to marry him?

'My sister loves Bill very much,' she explained patiently as Paul started the car and headed for Richmond Park. 'Rose does have feelings, you know.'

'You two are more like mother and daughter instead of sisters,' Paul remarked drily. 'I've never been able to work out why you're so close.'

Annie thought back to their childhood; her sister, being the eldest, had shouldered the whole burden of the family. Rose was very intelligent and had been made to leave school at eleven because they couldn't teach her any more. Although she had won a scholarship to a secondary school, she hadn't been able to take it up because they were so poor. That was when her old teacher Grace Trenchard and her husband, John, had taken over the job of her education in their spare time. A smile of remembrance touched Annie's face as she thought of those two dear people. Thank heavens they had moved out of London to Yorkshire a short time ago. They should be safer there.

She turned her attention back to Paul, who was waiting patiently for her to speak. 'I was a very sickly baby, and Mum was too busy with a large family to be able to give me much time. I wouldn't be alive today if Rose hadn't looked after me,' she explained quietly. 'I owe her more than I could ever repay. We all do.'

Paul shot her a sideways glance. 'I didn't know that. I've obviously misjudged her.'

'Everyone does. On the surface she appears tough and emotionless, but that's merely a façade, she can be hurt just like anyone else.'

7

He reached across and took hold of her hand. 'I'm sorry. I know you had a tough time when you were a child but you've never told me much about it.'

That was true enough, she hadn't, and perhaps it was time she did. 'Well, we came from the roughest street in Bermondsey. As a child Rose fought and studied until she was able to get into university. It was a very hard time for her but she never gave up, and eventually qualified as a solicitor.'

'Ah, now I'm beginning to understand the love and respect you all have for her, but to be honest I find her rather frightening at times. She is a formidable character,' Paul said, as he drove through the gates of Richmond Park. He slowed down so they could enjoy the beauty of the open parkland.

'Good job she is like that,' Annie told him with a hint of sadness in her voice. Her sister hadn't had any doubt that there was going to be another war and was already training with the Women's Voluntary Service, ready to help when necessary. 'We're going to need people like her if we are to survive another war.'

'I'm sure you're right. What are you going to do?' he asked, changing the subject. 'There won't be much call for a fashion editor until this lot's over.'

'No, you're right.' She sighed deeply, hating the prospect of leaving the job she loved. She'd started on a popular women's magazine at the age of sixteen and had worked her way up over the years, and she found her work as fashion editor interesting and fulfilling. Rose had tried hard to persuade her to go to university but Annie hadn't wanted that. She didn't have her sister's passion for learning and had been more interested in going out to work. She had always been good at art, English and languages, so when her application for a job with the magazine had been successful, she'd jumped at the chance. Rose had argued that Annie should make the most of her talents by continuing her education; but she wouldn't be swayed, and she was glad she hadn't because her time with the magazine had been very happy. It was going to be an awful wrench if she had to leave all her friends, especially Chantal Dean. Chantal came from Paris and, after marrying an Englishman, had made her home in London; and when he'd died suddenly she had stayed on. Annie smiled when she thought about the friendship she'd formed with Chantal; they spoke French all the time, and Annie had spent her annual holidays in France with Chantal for the last five years. Now all that was going to change; like Paul she doubted if she could stand on the sidelines either.

'Join the WAAF,' he suggested. 'The school you went to in Roehampton was excellent, and with your aptitude for languages you should be able to get an interesting job. You never know, we might be able to wangle a posting to the same place.' He grinned boyishly. 'It could all be jolly good fun.'

He doesn't know what he's talking about, she thought wearily, but said nothing. Let him keep his enthusiasm for a while longer. Reality would catch up with him soon enough. But he was right and her grasp of French and German might be useful. Because of Chantal her French was fluent and she spoke it as easily as English; her German was quite good because she'd loved languages and her teacher had encouraged her enthusiasm, but she didn't speak it nearly as well as French. All she needed was some practice, though . . .

Paul stopped the car in a spot where the tranquil scene of Richmond Park was laid out before them, the magnificent trees casting shade for the deer to rest under or munch contentedly on the lush grass. He turned and took her face in his hands. 'Before we get swept up in this conflict, will you marry me?'

This was the third time he'd asked her, but her answer was always the same. 'No, I'm sorry.'

He looked crestfallen. 'I hoped you might change your mind now things are different.'

She took hold of one of his hands. 'I wouldn't marry you just because you're going to fight in this war. I like you and enjoy being with you, but in all honesty I can't say I'm madly in love with you. I've never let you believe I feel anything but friendship for you,' she reminded him.

'I know but I keep hoping you'll change your mind.'

'Please don't hold on to false hopes,' she told him gently. 'I wouldn't dream of marrying unless I felt sure it would last.'

He sighed sadly. 'You are the kindest, most gentle girl I've ever met and I love you very much, but I know you don't feel the same way about me.'

'I'm sorry, Paul.' Oh, Lord, how she hated hurting him like this, but she knew in her heart that it just wouldn't work. In fairness to him she had tried to finish their relationship several times, but he wouldn't hear of it and just kept coming back.

'Hey! Don't look so upset,' he exclaimed, kissing her on the nose. 'I understand, but I'm going to keep on trying. In the meantime will you still be my girl? I'll need a glamorous picture to stick up by my bunk,' he joked, obviously trying to hide his disappointment.

'I'll get our fashion photographer to do a special one for you.' He looked so pleased with that suggestion, and this was one small thing she could do for him.

'Great.' He started the car again and headed out of the park.

'What does your brother think about you joining the air force?' she asked, changing the subject.

'He wasn't too pleased. He's joined up himself and I think he was hoping I'd run the family engineering business while he's away.' He drove slowly through the gates and then accelerated towards London. 'But I'm not going to let him have all the fun!'

She wondered how it was possible for two people to look at the prospect of war so differently. She was sad, apprehensive and worried about the future. So apprehensive in fact that she'd rushed out still wearing the old blue cotton frock she wore around the house, but he sounded as if he was looking forward to it.

'You're back early.'

Wally, her stepfather, was alone in the kitchen, a cigarette smouldering in the ashtray and a newspaper spread out on the table. 'Where's Mum?' Annie asked as she came in.

'She's babysitting for Rose. Bill's taken her out for the evening. I think they want a bit of time alone together.' He folded the paper up and tossed it on to a spare chair.

'Do you think Bill will get called up again?' She didn't

know why she was asking that; he would be one of the first to go. Her insides clenched with worry. This family, like every other one in the country, was about to be torn apart.

'Well, he's in the reserves and I think he was contacted a few weeks ago, but he hasn't said anything to Rose. He was hoping this war would never happen, I expect.'

'So were we all, but we were fooling ourselves.' Annie sat down and shook her head sadly. 'Why did this have to happen again, Wally? We've been so happy but now our lives are going to be disrupted, and all because of one man's lust for power.'

'It's crazy, I know, but we're in it whether we like it or not.'

She smiled sadly and patted his hand. 'At least you'll be safe this time.'

'I'm not sure any of us are going to be safe, Annie. This is going to be a very different war.' He dredged up a smile. 'Anyway, why are you back so soon?'

'We ended up in London, and Paul's all excited, but I'm afraid I couldn't share his enthusiasm.' They'd gone to Piccadilly and it had been crowded with people discussing the outbreak of war. Paul had caused a great deal of interest in his uniform but she knew that very soon it would be a normal sight.

'Thought he might be.' Wally looked at her speculatively. 'You going to marry him?'

'No. He's asked me to again but I just don't feel it's right.'

Her stepfather lit another cigarette. 'He's a good boy, but I think you need a stronger man, otherwise you'll lead him a merry dance.'

Annie gave him a playful swipe. 'Are you saying I'm difficult to live with?'

'Not at all,' he laughed, ducking as she aimed another gentle blow at him. 'I just mean you wouldn't be happy with a man unless he was strong-willed and decisive. Any man you marry will have to have a firm hand.'

'Meaning?' She propped her elbows on the table, rested her chin in her hands and looked at him thoughtfully.

'Well, you've got more of Rose in you than you realize, and you know what trouble Bill had with her . . .' He stopped and began to chuckle.

'You're digging yourself into a hole, aren't you?'

'Don't look so innocent,' he said laughing, 'you know darned well what I'm talking about. Let's change the subject, before I get myself into real trouble.'

Annie laughed, reached across and gave him a hug. He'd been a good stepfather to all of them and she loved him very much.

'When's Paul going back?'

'Tonight.' Annie's smile was wry. That was the first time Paul had ever been eager to leave her. He hadn't been able to contain his impatience to get back to his beloved aeroplane – a Hurricane, she thought he'd said.

'He's got a brother, hasn't he?'

'Yes, Reid, he's about three years older than Paul.'

'What's he like?' Wally asked.

'I've never met him, but Paul seems to be in awe of him, and I suspect that's the reason he wanted to learn to fly.' Reid had always been out working or away when Annie had visited the Lascellses' home, so she couldn't help being a little curious about him.

'He's a pilot as well then, is he?'

'Yes. He's got his own aeroplane he uses for business. One of those Lysanders.'

'I feel sorry for his family having both sons as pilots. They'll be just like we were last time, eager to get into it, and convinced it won't last long.'

'And will it, do you think?' All the talk in London had been about a short war, but she didn't believe that. Gas masks had been issued, plans to evacuate children were well under way already, and the government wouldn't be doing that if they didn't believe there was danger.

'I'm not a fortune teller,' he grimaced, 'but Hitler's a powerful man and Germany has been rearming for years.'

'Are we prepared?' she asked.

'Nowhere near. When Chamberlain came back from his visit with Hitler and waved that bit of paper saying there wouldn't be a war, it lulled some into a false sense of security.'

'When you look back you can see that it was unwise to believe anything Hitler said, or signed, wasn't it?' She for one had held on to any slight indication of hope. She knew there were many like her.

'It's easy to be wise with hindsight but I think there are a few politicians who never trusted Hitler's word.'

'It wasn't worth the paper it was written on, was it?'

'No.' Her stepfather gave a tired smile. 'Let's hope they don't attack too soon. We need time to get ourselves sorted out.'

Her mother walked in just then and the expression on her face was troubled.

'Has Bill been recalled, Marj?' Wally asked his wife.

She merely nodded and poured herself a cup of tea.

'Bill has asked George to leave his London home and live

14

with Rose and the children while he's away. He'll be happier knowing Rose's father is there to look after them.'

'That should liven things up having them both living in the same house.' Wally said and chuckled.

Annie couldn't hold back her own smile of amusement. Rose was George Gresham's illegitimate daughter and had inherited his explosive temper; he loved her and his grandchildren dearly. He wouldn't need much persuading to come and live here. Annie admired her mother so much for the way she had forgiven Sir George Gresham. She'd been in service to the Gresham family as a young girl and George had taken advantage of her. When Marj had become pregnant she had been thrown out and ended up in Garrett Street with Tom, the man who took her in. It must have been a terrible choice for her mother but the only alternative had been the workhouse. Tom was a brute and Rose took the brunt of his drunken rages in an effort to protect the younger children. When he'd been killed in the last war none of the children he'd had with Marj were very sorry, including herself. Then just after the war, Wally had moved in as a lodger, and about a year later Wally and her mother had married. It was a good marriage and they were still happy together.

Annie went to bed then, her mind churning away. What was this conflict going to mean to her and those she loved? Her two brothers Charlie and Will were bound to join up, but what about her sisters, Flo and Nancy? They didn't see them very often now as they had families of their own and had drifted away, but they were in London. There was also another brother, Bob, but Annie hardly remembered him. He'd run away to sea when she was little and ended up in Australia. They had a couple of letters a year from him, but she doubted she'd ever see him again.

Thoughts of the war crowded her mind again. What were Hitler's plans, and would this country be given the time it needed to mobilize and arm properly? These were all questions no one could answer at this time.

2

December 1939

Annie shivered and pulled her collar up to shield herself against the cold wind. They had been at war for three months and nothing much was happening. Many were calling it the phoney war, but there wasn't anything *phoney* about it for the poor devils now under Nazi rule.

She shivered again, not caused by the cold this time, but because, as she turned the corner and saw the outline of their house in the gloom, she'd had a brief vision of Germans marching along the road. It was a frightening thought but it couldn't possibly happen, she told herself sternly; they had won the last war against all the odds and they would do the same again. They had to!

When she thought about the terrible losses suffered in the Great War it made her feel sick. Of course, she had only been little but she had still been aware of the grief and terrible loss of young lives. Pray God that this one would not be so bad.

The Germans seemed to be an unstoppable force, but they *had* to be stopped, and that was going to need a supreme effort from everyone, including herself, so she was going to have to make a decision soon.

She opened the back door, pushed aside the blackout curtain and stepped quickly inside. Then she stopped in surprise; it was empty. The kitchen was always alive with activity at this time in the evening, and her mother would normally have a cup of tea ready for her as soon as she walked through the door. This was an unusual break in the routine so it was obvious something had happened. Without a moment's hesitation she hurried into the garden and through the special gate in the fence. She knew where they would be.

Her mother, Wally, George and her brothers were in Rose and Bill's kitchen; when she saw their serious faces her insides clenched with apprehension. 'What's happened?'

Annie's mother handed her a cup of tea. 'Will has enlisted in the Fleet Air Arm.'

'And I'm going into the RAF,' Charlie told her proudly.

Annie gave her brothers a startled look. It wasn't like them to be parted, they were more like twins than brothers. 'Why aren't you going into the same service?'

'No way!' Charlie held his hands up in horror. 'I don't like the sea, I want to keep my feet firmly on solid ground. We're both going to be aircraft mechanics but I will be on an airfield while Will is tossing about on an aircraft carrier.'

'But why didn't you wait until you were called up, like Bill did?'

'If we'd done that, Annie,' Will explained patiently, 'we wouldn't have had a choice. You know how mad we've always been about engines, and by volunteering we've been able to go into the branch of the service we want. I wouldn't have been able to get into the navy if I'd left it much longer.'

They were right, of course, and it was time she made

her own mind up about what she was going to do. 'When are you leaving?'

'We're all going at the end of the week,' Bill told her quietly.

This was it, then. Bill and Will in the navy and Charlie in the air force. Nothing was ever going to be the same again. Annie went and slipped her arms around Bill's waist, gave him a hug, then did the same to her brothers.

'You all take care,' she whispered.

Bill smiled. 'We will, and you never know I might be given a nice desk somewhere.'

Annie looked up at him hopefully. 'Is there any chance of that?'

His smile was wry. 'There's always a chance.'

Annie sat down, not sure that her legs would hold her much longer. She knew, as well as Bill did, that the chances of him being given a shore job were remote. This was a triple blow. She had known it was going to happen but had clung on to the foolish hope that her family would be spared. She looked into Rose's eyes, but they told her nothing. Her sister would accept the inevitable and fight for her family, as she had done all her life, but she would not let anyone see her fears.

'Hey! Why the long faces,' Charlie reprimanded. 'The sooner we all get stuck into this war, the sooner it will be over.'

'Quite right.' Bill put his arm around his wife's shoulders and grinned. 'We don't know where any of us will be at Christmas, so I suggest we have one hell of a party before we leave.'

There was a chorus of approval and everyone roused themselves from their gloomy contemplation of the future. By the time they'd finished their planning it was clear that this was going to be the best party they'd ever thrown, even if the reason behind it all was a sad one.

'Rosie.' Annie looked into the kitchen. It was two weeks since the men had joined up but Rose was obviously preparing for Christmas as if everyone was going to be there. 'Are you busy?'

'No, come in. I've just got to put the last two puddings on to boil.'

Annie sniffed appreciatively. 'It smells wonderful in here.'

'This will be the last chance to have proper Christmas puddings, I think.'

Rose adjusted the gas under the saucepan, and then sat down. 'Once our store cupboards are empty there won't be any more treats.'

'Have you heard from Bill?'

'Yes, had a letter this morning, but he didn't tell me what he was doing. I don't suppose it's allowed.' Rose gave a slight shrug and changed the subject. 'Have you heard from Paul?'

'Had three letters all at once, but I haven't a clue where he is. He might not even be in this country.' The letters had been unusually subdued for Paul, but that was probably because he knew they would be censored before they were sent on to their destination.

'Let's hope some of them can get home for Christmas.' Rose got up and put the kettle on. 'We'll have a cup of tea and some biscuits. You look as if you've got something on your mind.'

Annie laughed. 'You know me too well.'

'Right, tell me what's troubling you.' Rose placed a cup in front of Annie, opened the tin of biscuits, and then settled down again and waited.

'I've left my job.' It had been a wrench but Annie knew it had to be done. A lot of the people she'd worked with over the years had already joined the forces and the magazine was being produced with a skeleton staff. Chantal had already left to stay with her husband's relatives in Edinburgh.

Rose dunked a biscuit and nodded. 'I thought you would. What are you going to do?'

'That's what I want to talk about. I was thinking of joining the WAAF.' She stirred her tea thoughtfully; it wasn't an easy decision to make. 'What do you think?'

'If that's what you want to do, then go ahead, you don't have to get my approval, you know. You're a grown woman now, Annie.'

'I know,' she grinned at her sister, 'but it's hard to break the habit of a lifetime.'

'Why the WAAF? Are you hoping to stay near Paul?'

'No, now he's in the RAF I'm hoping he will meet someone else. He won't take no for an answer, but no amount of persistence will make me change my mind.'

'You're wise to wait, Annie, don't take second best.' Rose poured them another cup of tea. 'So tell me then, why the WAAF?'

'Well, I've been down to the recruitment office and they were very interested in my languages, and besides . . .' She cast Rose a sheepish glance. 'I like the colour of the uniform best. Air force blue is much nicer than khaki.'

'Ah, well, that settles it, then,' Rose joked, her eyes crinkling at the corners, obviously amused.

Annie knew it was a shallow reason, but she really hadn't known what to do. She'd agonized over it night after night, trying to decide what would be the right thing for her. She changed the subject. 'Are you going to evacuate the children, Rosie?'

'Not at the moment, things are pretty quiet and we're not in the heart of London this time. I'd rather wait and see what happens.'

'Bill told me to make sure you send the children to a safe place if things get rough,' Rose raised an eyebrow and Annie laughed. 'I know, you won't take any notice of me but think about Bill. You don't want him worrying while he's away, do you?'

'That's sneaky,' Rose scolded. 'But you're right, and I promise to take the children away if it becomes necessary. Dad's bought a house in Wales and he's there now getting it ready. Bill said it's got four bedrooms so we should be able to cram the lot of us in if necessary, and it should be out of the firing line.'

'Let's hope it is,' Annie thought of Rose's father, George Gresham, with affection. He would make sure Rose and his grandchildren were safe. After their first explosive meeting when Rose had been about sixteen, George had been welcomed into the family. Father and daughter were both strong characters and often clashed but the love and respect between them was obvious.

'Of course I've had a terrible row with Dad about it. He's been rushing around the country looking for a place for us to hide in!' Rose was clearly exasperated. 'We're

22

not right in London, for heaven's sake, and he's very much mistaken if he thinks I'm leaving here!'

'George only wants you and the children to be safe,' Annie pointed out gently.

'I know, and I will want the kids out of danger if things turn nasty, but I've told him he's got to use it as a refuge for others and not just the family.' A slight smile touched Rose's mouth. 'He exploded and said he'd call it "The Haven", and did that suit me?'

'And does it?' Annie asked.

'It has to; he's already bought the bloody place. That father of mine's got more money than sense!'

Annie knew that her sister had never accepted a penny from her father, although he was a wealthy man. Money for money's sake had never interested Rose, it was a commodity to be used to make a better life for her family and others. She had never lost her desire to help those in need, and Annie knew that she would hate to think money was being wasted on something unnecessary.

They fell silent and each thoughtfully dunked another biscuit in their tea just as their neighbour Joyce looked in the kitchen door.

'Rose! The Seascape fishmonger's got fish!'

Annie watched in astonishment as Rose grabbed her purse and ran out of the door, leaving her tea untouched. She began to laugh at the absurdity of it all, but with shortages already beginning to be felt you had to be quick on your feet to get any treats. Her sister had told her that she'd been in a queue the other day and after about half an hour the woman behind her asked what they were queuing for. It seemed that people jumped on the end of any line they saw.

*

Reid Lascells wandered into his brother's room at Tangmere airfield. He'd had a few hours to kill before going to see his brother so he'd borrowed a truck and headed for Bognor. It had been bitterly cold but he'd enjoyed the invigorating tang of sea air before heading for the West Sussex airfield. He picked up a photograph and studied it intently. The girl was quite lovely but the artificial pose wasn't right, it didn't seem to suit her somehow. Not that he'd ever met her, of course.

'Hey! Big brother.' Paul strode into the room, shrugged out of his flying jacket and collapsed on to the bed. 'Keep your lecherous eyes off my girl.'

'It's a bloody awful picture. Who took it?'

Paul removed the photo from his brother's hand and frowned. 'What's wrong with it? I'll have you know that this was taken by one of the top photographers at her magazine.'

'The glamorous pose doesn't suit her. Who is she?'

'Annie, and I think she's beautiful.' Paul looked offended.

'Oh, she's lovely enough, I grant you that, but she'd look better in something more natural.'

Paul fished in his pocket and produced a dog-eared picture. 'Like this?'

'Hmm, that's much better.' Annie was sitting on a fallen tree and laughing as the wind whipped at her hair. Then Reid turned his attention to the other woman in the picture and whistled through his teeth in approval. 'Who's the impressive woman she's with?'

'That's her eldest sister, Rose.' Paul laughed. 'But the word I'd use to describe her is formidable.'

'Yes, I can see that from the photo, but what a beauty!'

'Forget it, Reid,' Paul chided. 'She's a happily married woman with two children.'

'Pity, I'd have made you introduce me.' He handed the picture back, wondering if Rose was as stunning in the flesh as she was in the picture. 'Annie doesn't look like her.'

'Different fathers, I understand. Rose is the eldest of nine children, and Annie's next to youngest.' Paul tucked the picture into his pocket again. 'What are you doing here, anyway?'

'Heard you were back and as I've got a weekend pass I thought I'd come and see you. How was France?'

Paul shrugged. 'All right, but I couldn't understand a word they said.'

'You should have paid more attention to your lessons at university.'

'Nah.' He grinned boyishly. 'I leave all that stuff to Annie, she speaks the language fluently.'

Reid didn't pursue the subject. His brother would never change, and with the situation they were in it didn't seem important any more. Things might be quiet enough at the moment but he had a very nasty feeling that wasn't going to last. 'Have you got time for a drink?'

'Sure.' Paul sprang to his feet. 'Where are you stationed now?'

'Kenley.' This was close to London; Reid knew that if things started to get rough they would be right in the thick of it.

'Hey, I'm going to Biggin Hill in Kent next week. They're not far from each other and we might be able to meet up now and again. I'll try and get Annie down here and then you can meet her.'

Reid noted his brother's jaunty stride and smiled to himself. 'Are you going to marry her?'

'Of course I am. The only trouble is, she doesn't know it yet.'

'Haven't you asked her?'

'Yes, three times, but it will be fourth time lucky,' Paul stated confidently.

Reid didn't comment but he couldn't help wondering about the two women in the photo. Annie was fair and delicate looking and Rose tall, dark and magnificent. He regretted not having taken much notice of Paul's babbling about his girl. They looked an intriguing pair.

'Can you get leave for Christmas, Reid?'

'No. What about you?'

'Yes, I've managed to wangle two days. I'll spend one with Mum and Dad and the other with Annie and her family.'

'Wish I could join you.' And he really meant that. Christmas at the base would be lively enough but he'd rather be with his parents. They were going to be lonely this year without both of them there, and it was tempting to tell his brother to spend the two days with them, but he didn't. Paul would naturally want to see his girl.

'Never mind.' Paul held open the door of the bar and grinned at his brother. 'It will be all over by next Christmas, and we'll get drunk for a week.'

Reid nodded, but said nothing again. There wasn't any point in squashing Paul's enthusiasm, but he was certain that this war was going to last a lot longer than anyone was prepared to admit. And, as fighter pilots, they were going to be in the thick of things when it really started.

He was glad he'd been given a Spitfire; it was fast and handled like a dream.

'Right, everyone sit down,' Rose ordered.

There was an excited scramble for the table, made festive with Annie's artistic flair. This was the first Christmas of the war and she was determined to make a real show this year to cheer the family up.

When they were all seated, Annie looked at the happy faces, and if a brief flash of sadness flitted across her face it was soon gone. There was much to be grateful about. Rose's children, James and Kate, were still at home, her brothers Will and Charlie had a two-day pass each, and Paul had turned up unexpectedly. George had tried to persuade them to spend the holiday in Wales, but Rose had insisted on staying at home. After much arguing Rose had managed to convince George that they should spend Christmas at Roehampton, and delay the move to Wales until they knew how things were going to work out. He'd agreed reluctantly, as he was clearly excited about the house he'd bought and was eager to get everyone there.

The only person missing was Bill, and Annie knew her sister was disappointed about that, although you would never know by looking at her. But she couldn't fool Annie; she never had been able to. She only had to look deep into Rose's eyes to glimpse her innermost feelings.

For a moment her mind went back to their years living in that disgusting hovel in London. She'd watched her big sister fight with grim tenacity to improve their lot. Rose had taken beatings from the old man and suffered all manner of abuse and bitter disappointment; she had never flinched in her determination to drag herself and her family out of Garrett Street.

'Annie?'

Rose's call snapped her out of her reverie.

'You were miles away. What were you thinking about?'

'Garrett Street,' she admitted.

Rose visibly shuddered, and without a word continued with the Christmas dinner. Annie didn't miss the flash of distress on George's face at the mention of that street; she knew that he still felt guilty about his daughter growing up in such squalor because of his callous action as a young man.

'Auntie Annie, where's Garrett Street?' James asked.

'It's where we used to live, but it doesn't exist any more because your mum got it knocked down.'

'Did you, Mum?' he asked, searching her face with enquiring dark eyes, so like her own.

Not for the first time, Annie marvelled at just how much James resembled his mother, in looks, intelligence and intolerance. He was only ten but he did not suffer fools gladly, and that didn't make him an easy child to deal with.

'She certainly did.' Wally started to explain to James how dreadful conditions had been, and the struggle his mother had had to get the council to demolish the place. Annie was pleased that Wally didn't go into too much detail about the vermin, dirt and violence. It would be enough to put everyone off their Christmas dinner. James's eyes glittered with pride as he listened. 'I'm going to be just like Mum when I grow up.'

Rose turned round from the stove and grinned at him.

'Don't be too much like me, my boy.'

'Why not? You've done lots of good things.'

'Maybe, but I've also been difficult to live with, and I hope and pray you've inherited some of your father's gentleness.'

'Where's Daddy?' Kate interrupted, her bottom lip quivering. 'Why isn't he here?'

'I am here, sweetheart,' a soft voice said from the doorway.

Ignoring the squeals of delight, Bill threw his bag down and reached for his wife, holding her in a rocking embrace, and giving a heartfelt sigh of relief. Then he released her and bent down to scoop his children into his arms.

Annie watched with tears of emotion clouding her vision. What an impressive man he was, and his gentleness did not detract from his masculinity. Of course, he'd needed both gentleness and strength to take on her sister.

Bill rose to his feet, standing more than six feet tall, and smiled at everyone. 'Is there room for one more?'

James dragged another chair up to the table so his father could sit next to him, and Kate, who was now standing on tip-toe gazing at him, said in a hushed whisper, 'Don't you look lovely.'

After a few moments' silence, Rose, Bill and Annie burst into laughter.

'That's exactly what Annie said when she saw him in uniform just after the last war,' Rose explained.

Annie grinned affectionately at her brother-in-law. 'But I do believe you've got more gold braid this time.'

'Yes, and the uniform's a better fit,' he joked. 'Now, how about this dinner, I'm starving.'

Bill had clearly changed the subject, so Annie helped

Rose serve everyone, and then they joined the family around the table.

The talk was lively and never once touched on the subject of the war but Annie could feel Paul's impatience to ask questions so she whispered in his ear, 'Don't you dare ask Bill what he's going to do, he won't say anything until he's had a chance to talk to Rose.'

'But I want to know,' he complained. 'They haven't given him all that decoration to sail a desk.'

Dear God! She hoped he was wrong. Bill had been at Jutland in the last war, and later had lost his ship and most of the crew; then spent days adrift in an open boat watching the remaining few die before his eyes. She could only guess how dreadful the prospect of facing something like that again might be.

'You've got to admit it, Annie; they are going to give him a ship. He's an experienced, professional sailor, and his father was an admiral, for heaven's sake. Do you think for one moment they are going to let talent and experience like that go to waste?'

'I'm not a fool, Paul.' He was so tactless and it irritated her. 'I know we need men like Bill but can't you let us enjoy our dinner in peace. And if you can't contain your curiosity you can leave right now.'

'What!' he exclaimed, 'and miss Rose's cooking?' He smiled and took hold of her hand. 'Stop worrying so much about everyone, by this time next year it will be all over.'

She gaped in disbelief and studied his face. He really believed that. But at least he dropped the subject then and allowed them all to enjoy the festive meal without any more talk of the war.

After they'd finished, Marj and Wally insisted on washing up, so the rest of them retired to the front room and handed out the presents. When the children were absorbed with their gifts, Annie watched Bill take hold of Rose's hand and lead her from the room. He was about to tell her if he was going back to sea or not. Please God, let it be not, she prayed, but deep in her heart she knew it was a hopeless plea.

Fifteen minutes later they were back and joining in the fun, but Annie couldn't glean anything from their expressions.

Wally came in carrying a tray of drinks, whisky for the men and sherry for the women. 'I think we ought to drink to the fact that we've all managed to have Christmas dinner together, don't you?'

There were nods of approval, and they took a glass and raised it to toast the occasion. Annie studied her stepfather with affection, and wondered how many precious bottles of drink he'd managed to squirrel away before the war, because he always managed to produce something for a celebration. He was quiet, even tempered, and not at all like her own father who'd been killed in the last war. Her mother had had a wretched time with him, and it was lovely to see her and Wally still happy after twenty years of marriage.

'How are things going, Bill?' Paul asked, and yelped when Annie kicked his shin. 'What did you do that for?' he whispered.

'I told you not to ask questions,' she hissed at him. It was such a job to stop him when he wanted to know something; she didn't want Bill pestered with questions just yet. He would tell them what was happening when he was ready.

'It's all right, Annie,' Bill laughed. 'I've told Rose now.'

James had been watching with curious eyes, taking in every small detail, and clearly picking up on the tensions. He left his train set and went and stood by his father, then asked the question everyone wanted to know and had been wary of asking. 'Have they given you a ship, Daddy?'

'Yes, James, I'm on active service.'

'Gosh!' The boy jumped up and down. 'What is it?'

'I'm afraid I can't tell you that.'

His eyes opened wide. 'When are you going to fight the Germans?'

'I haven't received my sailing orders yet but I expect I'll get them as soon as I've finished a spot of retraining.'

'Why have you got to do that?' his son asked, clearly puzzled. 'You're used to boats.'

'It's nearly twenty years since I took command of a ship and things have changed a bit in that time.'

'Oh, I wish I was old enough.'

James looked crestfallen and went back to play with his toys again, so he didn't hear his father murmur, 'I thank the Lord that you are too young.'

3

February 1940

'What a day,' Ruth, one of the girls in Annie's hut, moaned. 'We've been marched here and there, stripped, examined, had needles stuck in us, then issued with these.' She held up a brassiere with one finger and grimaced in disgust.

'And what about these?' howled Kath, holding a pair of blue winter knickers in front of her.

Annie was crying with laughter. In her job as a fashion editor she'd dealt with elegant clothes and she hadn't been aware that such abominations existed. She'd never seen so many pretty faces with expressions of pure horror on them. Not only were the underclothes and lisle stockings dreadful, most of the uniforms were ill-fitting. Skirts were too big or too small around the waist; one girl couldn't even fasten her jacket without taking a deep breath in and holding it. They were going to have to find someone in their hut who could sew!

'We can't wear these,' wailed another girl. 'Even my granny's don't come past her knees with elastic in them.'

'They will keep us warm.' Annie put her hand on the stove and found it practically cold. The West Drayton camp in Middlesex was lacking all the home comforts they'd been used to. Some of the girls had been horrified to find they would be sleeping in huts, but it was only what Annie had expected. 'It's freezing in here and that bucket of coke isn't going to last long.'

'We'll soon see about that!' Dora, a rough-and-ready Londoner, stated. 'I spotted a wooden fence just around the back, I'll get some of that.'

'Put your knickers on,' roared Kath, 'it's freezing out there, as well.'

'I'll come with you.' Annie stood up, put on her peaked hat at a jaunty angle – at least that fitted properly – struck a model-like pose and slowly lifted her skirt. 'I'm already prepared.'

There was uproar as the entire hut of girls started to stamp their feet and whistle, with varying degrees of success.

Dora came and stood beside her, copied her pose and also lifted her skirt. The noise was deafening as the two girls rushed out of the hut, doubled over with laughter, and headed for the fence Dora had seen.

'You're something to do with fashion, aren't you?' she asked, as they made their way over the icy ground. Annie nodded. 'Yes, I was fashion editor for a women's magazine.'

'Where do you live, then?' Dora asked.

'Roehampton.'

'Ah, I thought you was posh.'

'I haven't always lived there,' Annie said. 'I grew up in Bermondsey, in Garrett Street.'

The girl stopped and spun to face her. 'Wow! I've heard about that place. My gran said it was a filthy hole and so rough that the police had to go down there in threes for safety.'

Dora started to walk again, but this time she slipped

34

Annie's hand through her arm in a gesture of respect and comradeship. 'If I remember rightly, some woman got the place condemned and knocked down. Can't remember her name though.'

'Rose Freeman,' Annie told her with pride. She never ceased to be amazed how much Rose was remembered after all these years. 'She's my eldest sister.'

'Bloody hell,' Dora gasped, 'I had you worked out all wrong. When I first saw you I thought you was some snooty bitch.' She gave an evil leer. 'Until you showed your knickers.'

'Where's your home?' Annie asked, wanting to know more about this friendly girl.

'I come from Stepney and it's a bit rough in our street, but not as bad as the one you came from, if my gran's stories are right.' Dora rubbed her hands together and grinned at Annie. 'I'm glad to be out of there though, and even if it is bloody cold here, this place is still better than Stepney. I hope I'm sent somewhere in the country when we've done our basic training. I'd love to be surrounded by open fields instead of concrete.'

Annie knew just how Dora was feeling. She remembered how she'd felt the first time Bill had taken her and Rose to Richmond Park and then on to the terraces with the River Thames winding its majestic way in the sunshine. It was hard to believe such places existed when all you saw were buildings day in and day out.

'You'll love the countryside in the spring,' Annie remarked.

'Can't wait. I'm going to find myself a bluebell field and run through it with bare feet.' Dora chuckled at the thought.

By this time they'd reached the fence. It was just the other side of the camp's perimeter and already broken down in places, so they reached through the wire to collect all the loose bits, then hurried back to the hut. They didn't want to be accused of stealing on their first day.

The girls fell on the wood as soon as they staggered in, and started feeding it into the stove. It soon made a lovely blaze. Two other girls had been foraging while they'd been out. One had cadged some bread and margarine from the cookhouse, and another produced a tin of cocoa and some powdered milk. They were obviously going to be an enterprising bunch.

The water was just coming to the boil when Kath erupted through the door clutching a jar of jam.

'Where'd you get that?' Ruth wanted to know.

'From the NAAFI.' Kath waved the jar in triumph.

Ruth looked puzzled. 'What's that?'

'The Navy, Army and Air Force Institutes,' Dora explained. 'It's a shop, canteen and a place to meet and have fun.'

It was a happy feast of toast and a welcome hot drink, and if the cocoa was rather watery no one complained. They had survived the first day and were happy.

At lights out, Annie slipped into her bunk. It had been so hard to leave her job at the magazine, and even harder to leave her family. She'd felt that the only choice she had was in deciding which branch of the services to join, but after today she felt this was the right one. She was going to miss her family dreadfully, of course, but everyone had to make sacrifices now. She smiled in the darkness; things were going to be all right. She'd had doubts about signing the final papers but now she was glad she had.

'What do you think think this is all about?' Kath asked Annie, as they filed into the room.

'I haven't got a clue. Another lecture, I expect.'

'Whatever it is, it's better than square-bashing,' Dora collapsed on to a chair with a groan. 'I don't think my blasted feet can stand any more, the last three weeks have been purgatory.'

Annie ignored her friend's exaggeration. The basic training had been tough at times, but they'd had fun as well. They had been confined to camp most of the time, but they had been able to get out occasionally, and they'd been to a lively dance in the NAAFI canteen one night. Once she'd got used to living in a hut with lots of other girls Annie enjoyed the whole experience.

At that moment two RAF officers came in and the girls leapt to attention. They had soon discovered that it was wise to move sharply, and if in any doubt about the rank, to salute. They had made some blunders at first, much to the hilarity of the men, but it was better to be safe than sorry. You could be put on a charge for any small misdemeanour, regardless of how new you were.

'I've never seen those badges before,' Dora whispered. 'The design looks like lightning.'

'At ease, and be seated,' the most senior of the officers ordered. When they were settled he nodded to his fellow officer who uncovered a machine and started to tap out Morse code.

Annie was fascinated and sat forward in her seat, listening intently. When he had finished she looked up and found the officer watching her. She felt slightly uncomfortable under his piercing blue gaze, but refused to be the first to break the contact. A slight smile touched his mouth but was quickly controlled, and Annie was shocked at how much she felt drawn to him. Some people you took to immediately and some you disliked at once, but she had a strong feeling that this man was special. She gave a mental shrug; all that square-bashing must have gone to her head.

He looked away and turned his attention back to the whole room. 'You have now finished your basic training and will soon be shipped to new camps, but first we have to decide the best way to use your talents.' A snicker rippled round the room, which he ignored. 'You all know what you've been listening to, I presume?'

'Oh, yes,' Dora spoke up. 'Messages can be sent and received like that, though how anyone can understand that jumble of bleeps is a mystery to me.'

Dora always spoke her mind and Annie expected the officer to reprimand her, but much to her surprise he merely smiled. He looked a very calm man and not at all like some they'd met since they'd joined up. She'd never believed people could have such loud voices.

'Well, let's see just how many of you can distinguish between the dots and the dashes, shall we?'

Annie found the next hour intriguing. First they had a short lecture, then had to listen to each sound and note down what they thought it was. Right at the end they had to try to decipher a very short burst.

After that there was a fifteen-minute wait while the men went through the results.

'Ann Webster,' the officer said suddenly.

Annie sprang to her feet. 'Sir!'

He gave a satisfied smile. 'You stay, the rest of you can go.'

'Oh, oh.' Dora whispered in her ear. 'I knew he was after you; he's been staring at you ever since we came in. You know the golden rule – never volunteer for anything. Whatever he wants, say no.' She gave the tall, elegant man a studied glance. 'On second thoughts . . .'

Annie gave Dora a push to send her on her way and looked down to hide her smile. She was incorrigible, but they got on well together and had laughed a great deal during basic training. Even when they'd been tired and fed up Dora could still make the girls smile. She was a great asset.

As the door closed behind the others Annie looked up again, eager to know what this was all about.

The officer had perched himself casually on the edge of the desk and pointed to a chair in front of him. 'My name's Graham. Sit there, please.'

She obeyed, eyeing him surreptitiously. Dora was right; he was dishy but not as young as she had first thought. He must be like her brother-in-law and have some special qualifications.

'You had a pass rate of ninety-five per cent in that test,' he told her.

Her eyes opened wide in surprise. She'd loved doing it but had no idea she'd got that much right.

'Don't look so startled,' he told her. 'It was the very result I was hoping for. I have been reading all the new recruits' records and decided that you were just what we were looking for, but we had to find out if you had an ear for Morse code.' He smiled warmly. 'And you most certainly do.'

He picked up a folder from the desk and started to read it. 'I see that you didn't go on to university but the grades from your secondary school are excellent, with art and languages your strong points.'

'Yes, I was lucky with my tutor. He said I had a good ear for languages, and he used to set me extra lessons.'

He continued reading her records and Annie waited patiently. When he spoke again it was in German, which threw her for a moment, but she quickly gathered herself together and answered in the same language. There was no doubt he was testing her for something and she became tense with excitement. What was this leading to?

He then reverted to English and started talking about films and books, and everyday things. When he switched to French, a language she was very much at home with, she talked for a while, and then could stand it no longer.

'Will you tell me what this grilling is for . . . sir?' It was always best to tack that word on the end.

He threw the folder down, folded his arms and grinned with pleasure. 'We need wireless operators, and your languages could be useful as well. Your concentration is good and your German, though a bit rusty, is adequate; but your French is excellent. Where did you learn to speak it so fluently?'

Annie explained about Chantal and watched him scribble notes in her file.

'We would like to train you for this, but I must warn you that it is a very secret occupation; the work will be arduous and the hours long at times.'

'I understand.' Annie couldn't contain her excitement. 'When do I start my training?'

'At once. We are in desperate need of operators. You will have to learn not only to receive and send in Morse code, but you will also have to be able to repair your machine should anything go wrong with it.'

'And how long will this take?' she asked.

'In normal times it's a lengthy process, but you will have to become proficient in just six months. Quite a daunting task, I admit, but I believe you are capable of doing it.'

'Where will I be going?' Annie was bursting with excitement and many questions. She had never imagined she would be asked to do anything like this.

'Your training will take place at Compton Bassett in Wiltshire.'

'And after that?'

'You will be told when the time is right and not before.' There's a lot of hard work in front of you.' He smiled again and looked at his watch. 'You have thirty minutes to pack your kit and meet us outside.'

'Er . . . I thought we were due some leave now?'

'Not you, I'm afraid. We have to start your training immediately.'

Annie ran back to the hut and found all the girls waiting anxiously for her. She was too excited to be disappointed about having her leave cancelled.

'What happened?' Dora asked as soon as she was through the door. 'Does he want you for that tap tap stuff?'

'Yes, I've got six months' training ahead of me and I have to start at once.' She grabbed her bag and began stuffing her possessions in it without bothering to fold the clothes properly. 'I never thought I'd get such an exciting job.'

'How did you do in the test?' Kath wanted to know.

'Ninety-five per cent correct.'

'Wow! No wonder he wanted you.' Dora looked sad. 'This means we'll all be splitting up.'

'I'm afraid so, but it has been fun and we must try to keep in touch.' Annie would be sorry to lose Dora's companionship. 'What will you be doing, Dora?'

'I've signed on as a clerk because I thought it would help me get a better job after the war. I don't want to go back into a factory after this.'

'That's a good idea. My sister learnt to type in the WAAC during the last war, and it was very useful to her.'

'Ah, well, I've definitely done the right thing. Don't forget you promised to introduce me to her some time.'

'I won't forget.' Annie laughed at Dora's eagerness.

'What's everyone else doing?' she asked.

While Annie continued to pack, the girls spent the next half an hour talking about their various jobs and postings, then they said goodbye, and one or two tears were spilt. After that, Annie headed for the truck waiting to take her to her new posting.

Officer Graham was standing by the vehicle, talking quietly to another man, and when she hurried up he looked at his watch. 'Right on time.'

He threw her bag in the back of the lorry, then the three of them clambered in the front and set off. As the countryside sped by her Annie couldn't help wondering what she was heading into.

'Hello, Rose,' Annie popped her head around the kitchen door and grinned at her big sister, who was sitting at the kitchen table with a book in front of her, as usual. She'd been away from home for nearly four months and it was so lovely to see Rose again. She was wearing a dark red frock, which suited her beautifully; a shaft of the warm May sunshine was resting on her hair, making it shimmer blue-black.

Rose looked up from the book she was reading, smiled broadly and stood up to hug her young sister. 'When did you get home?'

'Just arrived. I've got a seven-day pass.' Annie did a graceful pirouette. 'What do you think?' She'd managed to have some alterations done to the tunic and now it fitted a treat; of course, the stockings and heavy shoes were unflattering, but with the complete uniform it wasn't too bad. The air force blue suited her as well.

'Very smart.' Her sister stood up and put the kettle on the stove. 'I'll make some tea and you can tell me how you're getting on.'

Annie sat down and picked up the book Rose had been reading. It was the Bible her sister had won at the age of eleven for coming top of the school.

'You still read it, then?' she asked, as Rose sat beside her.

'Oh, yes, and I'm still trying to understand it.'

'So I see,' Annie laughed, looking at the dog-eared, well-worn book in front of her. There was hardly a margin where Rose hadn't scribbled a comment or two. She remembered when she'd been very little finding her sister studying well into the night, with this book never far from her hand. The fact that she was reading it now

43

alerted Annie. 'You're worried about something. Is Bill back at sea?'

'I'm afraid so. I knew it was going to happen, of course, but I couldn't help hoping the navy would change their mind and give him a shore job. He went through enough last time, and I've got a nasty feeling this could be even worse.'

Annie wanted to reach out and hug her big sister, but she knew Rose didn't like to be fussed over, so she picked up the Bible again. 'We'll pray for everyone's safety. What were you underlining when I came in?'

'That.' Rose pointed to a psalm.

Annie read the sections marked in red ink.

Whither shall I go from thy spirit?
Or whither shall I flee from thy presence?
If I ascend up into heaven, thou art there:
If I make my bed in hell, behold, thou art there.
If I take the wings of the morning, and dwell in the uttermost
        parts of the sea;
Even there shall thy hand lead me, and thy right hand shall
        hold me.

'Oh, that's lovely,' Annie said when she'd finished reading, 'and so appropriate.'

'Yes, it's one of my favourite passages. Now,' Rose settled back in her chair, 'tell me all your news; you haven't said much in your letters. We expected you home sooner than this.'

'I should have been, but when I'd finished my basic training I was posted immediately. I've hardly had time to draw breath since then.'

44

'What kind of a job have they given you?'

'Wireless operator.' Annie grinned and started to tap out Morse code on the table. 'Seems I've got an ear for it. I'm only halfway through my training, but when I start as a qualified operator I won't be able to talk about the work.'

'I understand. How are you finding things in general?'

'All right.' Annie then started to tell her sister about their first day at camp and the awful underclothes; the mess they'd got into when first on parade, all turning in different directions until the sergeant had been almost crying with frustration. She went through everything in great detail, and by the time she'd finished they were both roaring with laughter.

'Oh, you've cheered me up no end.' Rose wiped her eyes.

'I could hear you laughing from my kitchen.' Annie's mother walked in and kissed her, holding on as if she didn't want to let her go. 'It's so wonderful to see you. Sorry I wasn't here when you arrived. How long are you home for?'

'Seven days.'

'Oh, lovely, you look tired though. A few days relaxing in the garden will bring the colour back to your face.' Marj smiled happily at her daughter, sat down and poured herself a cup of tea. 'I had a letter from Charlie yesterday, and he seems happy enough in the air force, but I haven't heard from Will for some time. I wish he hadn't gone into the navy, but he was sure that was what he wanted.'

'They'll be all right, Mum,' Annie assured her.

Wally came in then. 'Annie!' he exclaimed. 'Good to see you again, we've missed you. Now, I don't suppose you've got a pitchfork or an old sword, or anything I can use as a weapon?'

'What on earth would we be doing with such things?' Marj asked her husband. 'What are you up to?'

'I'm going to join the Local Defence Volunteers, and they haven't got any guns yet, so we've got to improvise.'

'The LDV? You?'

Wally sat back with a huge grin on his face. 'You only have to be capable of free movement to join. And I'll have you know, my dear wife, that many of the men volunteering are a lot older than me, but as long as we hold our parades within easy walking distance of the pub we should be all right.'

Annie and Rose started to chuckle as their mother muttered, 'God help us!'

Just then James tumbled through the kitchen door, flushed with excitement.

'What are you doing home?' Rose asked. 'I thought you were spending the day on the river with John's father?'

'He's had to take the boat somewhere. It's been comm . . . comm . . . taken over by the navy. There's hundreds of them all going up the Thames!' He was jumping up and down with excitement.

'The word you're looking for is "commandeered",' his mother corrected, standing up quickly.

'What would the navy want with a load of small boats?' Wally asked with a worried frown.

'I don't know, but I'm going to find out.' Rose swept out of the house with a determined look on her face.

'John and me wanted to go with his dad but he wouldn't let us. He said he didn't know what it was all

46

about and it might take some time.' James scowled in frustration. 'It's rotten being a kid, you get stopped from doing anything exciting, and no one tells you anything.'

Annie hid a smile and stood up. How like Rose her nephew was, always wanting to know, always looking for answers to his unstoppable questions. 'I'll just go and unpack my bag.'

She had no sooner reached her room than she heard Wally calling.

'Annie! Rose's back and she's got some news.'

She didn't like the tone of urgency in his voice. She had not been taking a great deal of notice of James's excitement, putting it down to childish exaggeration, but now she was worried. She ran across the garden and into Rose's house, looked at her grim expression and sat down, waiting for her sister to tell them what she'd found out.

'It's bad, I'm afraid.' Rose paced the room. 'I've had a hell of a job prising information out of people, but fortunately I've still got some good contacts. Our army is trapped on the beaches at Dunkirk. Mum, will you look after the children for me?'

'Of course, but where are you going?'

'Dover.' Rose was already pinning her WVS badge on to her coat. 'They're going to need all the help they can get when they start bringing the poor buggers home.'

Annie stood up, all thought of a leisurely few days disappearing. 'I'll come with you.'

4

Reid Lascells sat down and looked at the meal in front of him. He was so damned tired! He had been promoted to squadron leader only last week when Dan Holdsworth had been shot down and killed over France. It was a hell of a way to gain promotion, and it gave him no pleasure to try to fill that fine man's shoes in this way. He picked up his knife and fork just as the sound of the bell to scramble jangled through his head. He was on his feet and running, leaving his breakfast untouched on the table. They weren't even having time to eat, and he couldn't remember when he'd had more than three hours' sleep at a time, but the fatigue was forgotten as he hurtled towards his Spitfire. Those poor devils on the beaches were undoubtedly more tired than he was.

'All ready for you, sir.' The ground crew sprang into action as he reached the plane. 'We've repaired the damage and she's as good as new.'

'Thanks.' They strapped him in and he cast them a quick smile; he didn't know what they'd do without these men. They were totally dedicated to keeping the planes flying, and he knew they waited anxiously to see if *their* pilot returned after a sortie.

He climbed, and as tired as he was he felt the usual exhilaration as the sweet Merlin engine responded to his touch. After checking that the squadron was airborne, trying to ignore the blank spaces of those they'd lost, they banked and headed for the Calais–Dunkirk patrol.

'Hell! Look at that,' came through Reid's headset. The airways began to crackle with voices.

'They're not going to try and take them off the beaches in those, surely?'

'They're pleasure boats.'

'And barges.'

'Where's the navy?'

'On fire! Look to your left.'

'Oh, hell, what a mess.'

'Hey they're shooting at us!'

'Blue leader here, climb! climb!' Reid commanded.

When they had regrouped above the clouds, one pilot swore, 'Christ, don't they know the difference between us and the MEs?'

'I'd be shooting at everything if I was down there,' muttered another pilot understandingly.

'OK, shut up, everyone,' Reid ordered.

'Bandits! Three o'clock!'

In the mêlée that followed, Reid shot down two ME 109s, and saw one Spitfire blown apart and, just for a split second, he wondered where his brother was, but it was foolhardy to let your concentration wander when some swine was trying to kill you.

Kenley airfield was a welcome sight, and so were the ground crew who rushed up to help him out. 'How many missing?' he asked, as soon as his feet touched the ground.'

'Three, sir, but there's always the chance they've landed somewhere else.'

He knew that for sure one of them was gone, and he

started to walk towards the debriefing hut, trying not to wonder who he wasn't going to see again.

'Sir, what's it like over there?' One of the ground crew looked at him anxiously. 'We'll be in a mess if we lose our army.'

Reid summoned up a smile; though he was so damned tired he wasn't sure if it came out as a grimace. 'You don't have to worry, lads, the navy will get them home.'

''Course they will.' The men gathered around him nodded in agreement.

'Did you make a kill today, sir?'

'Yes, two definite.'

The men cheered, and then started to clamber all over the plane to check for damage.

Reid walked across the grass deep in thought and cursing under his breath. He hoped they did manage to rescue the troops because they were losing quite a few planes in this operation, and worse still was the loss of the pilots. Many of them didn't look much more than kids. They hadn't had any experience of life before they were shot out of the skies.

They flew sortie after sortie that day, until they were exhausted. Their day started about three in the morning and continued until dusk, and he decided that if he survived this he was going to sleep for a week.

He was in the air again just as dawn was creeping over the horizon, and they were in battle as soon as they crossed the French coast.

'On your tail, Skip!'

Reid dived, then climbed and turned, trying to shake off the German fighter. The Spitfire didn't let him down and the position was soon reversed. He was just lining up for the kill when he heard a thud and the plane shuddered.

'You're trailing smoke!' someone yelled. 'Bail out!'

But Reid was too far inland so he banked and headed for the coast. He knew he was risking his life by staying in the air but the last thing he wanted was to land behind enemy lines and end up as a prisoner for the rest of the war. As soon as he saw the smoking ruins of Dunkirk in the distance he searched for a suitable landing place. He couldn't bail out now, he was too low, so he made for a small field just below him. The thought of dying never occurred to him, his main worry as he headed for the field was capture. That possibility made his insides clench in apprehension . . .

As he hit the ground his undercarriage collapsed; he crashed through a fence and came to rest on a dirt road. His head smacked against the side of the cockpit, knocking the breath out of him. For a split-second he didn't move, but as the smoke began to billow in front of him he shot back the canopy and slithered to the ground.

He stood there dazed and disorientated. The air was full of different smells, smoke, burning oil, and something else. He frowned and licked his lips, tasting blood, and then he turned his head and was staring straight into the eyes of a doleful-looking cow, busily chewing. In his befuddled state he thought its expression was accusing.

'I'm sorry,' he said, reaching out to stroke its velvet face. 'Have I made a mess of your field?'

The animal burped noisily and Reid started to laugh.

'I should have spoken in French.'

A strange noise coming from the Spitfire brought him

back to his senses. My God! He was standing here as if he was on a casual day out in the country, *and* talking to a cow.

At that moment three men came running through the gap in the fence waving their arms frantically and yelling at the tops of their voices. Two of them grabbed hold of the cow and started to tow it back into its field, the other one didn't stop running but caught hold of Reid and dragged him away from the plane. They had just made it when the Spitfire exploded and knocked them to the ground.

Reid was horrified. What was the matter with him? He should have been running for his life as soon as he'd got out of the plane, instead he'd been trying to have a conversation with a cow! That knock on the head must have scrambled his brains.

'You must get to Dunkirk,' he was urged. 'The Germans will be here soon.'

A young boy came hurtling towards him on a bike, and when he reached Reid he leapt off and thrust the bicycle at him. 'You go, quickly. That way.'

Reid was off and pedalling as fast as he could. It was an obstacle course, the road was littered with abandoned trucks, tanks, cars, dead bodies and animals, but he ignored the scenes of devastation, and pedalled like a man possessed. The irony of the situation did not escape him; he was going to end up on the beach they had been trying so desperately to protect. What chance of survival there? About fifty-fifty, he assessed, but it was his only hope, and he wanted to live so very much. Every time he went into battle, never knowing if he was going to survive had made him realize how precious life was.

He hadn't gone far when the bike had a puncture, but he kept riding, the rim of the wheel screeching as it spun on the road. It was either this or walk, and that would take him hours.

'That won't get you far,' a cultured English voice said.

Reid was gasping for breath by now, and looked up to see a motorbike idling along beside him. It contained an army officer and a bedraggled soldier of indistinguishable rank on the pillion.

'Hop on,' said the officer.

'But there isn't room.'

''Course there is, mate, I'll move up a bit.' The soldier patted a couple of spare inches behind him. 'You should be able to get your backside on there all right. I shouldn't hang about 'cos Jerry's right on our tail.'

He didn't argue; it would be better than the pedal bike, and quicker. Tucking his legs up, he hung on grimly to the man in front of him, and the bike sped off towards the clouds of billowing smoke that was the remains of Dunkirk.

An hour later he fell off the bike, thanked the unknown driver who had probably saved his life, and ran on to the beach. As he collapsed on the sand in exhaustion he became aware that his head was pounding and he could feel dried blood all over his face. Strange, but in the urgent dash to reach Dunkirk he hadn't been aware of his injuries.

'Blimey! The air force has arrived, at last,' a voice shouted scornfully. 'Where you been, mate?'

Reid dragged himself to his knees and stared at the sea

of hostile faces around him. He pointed to the sky. 'Up there, fighting like bloody maniacs.'

'You could have fooled us, mate,' another man jeered.

Reid was now on his feet, bristling with anger. 'I've lost half my squadron trying to protect you. Planes and pilots we're going to need to defend Britain since you couldn't bloody well keep the Germans out of France.'

'We did our best,' one soldier told him defensively.

Reid dropped wearily to his knees again; this was stupid. 'I know you did, and so have we.'

'Sorry, mate, we're just frustrated trying to get off this bleeding beach.' The man, who was a sergeant, knelt beside him. 'There's no need to take it out on you, though. That's a nasty gash you've got there. Dave!' he yelled, 'see if you can find a medic.'

'What did you do, bail out?' another soldier asked.

'No, I had to land in a field. The locals got me away just before she blew up.' There was no way he was going to tell them that they had found him talking to a cow!

'Christ!' the soldier muttered.

'Sorry, Sergeant.' The corporal returned. 'They're all busy.'

Reid waved his hand. 'It doesn't matter.'

'Here they come again!' the shout went up.

The two soldiers grabbed hold of Reid and dragged him towards a large crater. The next few minutes were sheer bedlam, screaming fighters strafing the beach, bombs falling, men shouting and cursing. And then, suddenly, it was all over and the only sound was an irate seagull screeching above their heads. Gradually Reid became aware of the moans and cries for help coming from the injured. If there was such a place as hell, then

54

it must be like this. He lifted his head, looked at the sergeant and swore with ferocity, 'I'd rather be in a Spitfire, at least I can shoot back.'

The man held his hand out. 'My name's Ron.'

'Reid.' He shook his hand.

'Well, Squadron Leader, we'd better see if we can get you on a ship, because you're right, we are going to need you in the months to come.'

'Hey, Sergeant, that destroyer's coming back.'

The beach was suddenly alive with activity, and Reid was impressed with the way the men behaved. Every one of them must be frantic to get off the beach, but they were taking orders from their officers and forming orderly queues. The men started to walk into the sea and wait for the few remaining small boats to pick them up and ferry them to the large ship. It was an impressive sight but Reid didn't miss the anxious glances at the sky as they waited for the German planes to return again. Reid didn't rate his chances of getting on a boat very high.

'There's another small boat over there, Sergeant,' the corporal shouted. 'Let's get the Air Commodore on that.'

Reid grinned, but felt like weeping. These men had been here for God knows how long, but even in a situation as desperate as this, they could still joke.

He was hoisted into the boat and he reached out to give them a hand up.

'Not me, mate, I've still got some of my men on the beach, but the corp will come with you.'

'I'm staying.' The corporal grabbed hold of another man and tossed him into the boat.

Ron nodded, as if this was only what he'd expected,

and then they began to help others into the small vessel until it was dangerously overloaded. The sea was only inches from the top and one more passenger would have made it pour in and sink them.

As they headed towards the destroyer, Reid swallowed a lump in his throat as he wondered if those men would survive. He hoped to God they did. And what was going to happen to Britain now with only the strip of Channel between them and the might of the Germans?

The destroyer was in a dreadful state. She had obviously taken a real pounding, and he wondered how many trips she had made. It was quite a few by the look of the damage.

The men scrambling aboard were a mixture of British, French, civilians and sailors from ships that had been sunk, but as far as he could see he was the only pilot.

When she was full to capacity, the vessel headed out to sea, and all eyes were fixed on the horizon, waiting for the first glimpse of Dover.

'Sir?'

Reid turned to the sailor who had appeared beside him.

'The captain asks if you would like to come to the bridge?'

They pushed their way through the crowds of men and up a flight of steps. The man who greeted him was above average height, greying slightly at the temples, with deep lines of fatigue etched on his face. But there was a calmness about him that was balm to Reid's jangled nerves. As dangerous as flying was, he would rather be up there than down in this hell.

'You looked out of place with all the khaki.'

Reid grinned, taking an instant liking to the tall, impressive man. 'I'm surprised I wasn't thrown overboard. Some of them seem to think the RAF hasn't done much to protect them.'

'That's just their anger talking. Any fool knows that you couldn't provide continuous air cover. Do you know what the losses are to date?'

'I don't know the exact figures, but it's far too many.'

The captain grimaced. 'We've lost ships as well, but thank God we've been able to get a lot of the troops off the beach.'

'The soldiers seemed to recognize you. How many trips have you made?'

'Four, but we were damaged on the last run . . .'

'Captain Freeman!'

The sailor who had just come on the bridge was covered in oil and dirt, and dripping wet, but he still had a wry smile on his face.

'We've sprung another leak, sir. The pumps are coping but we'll need a repair crew as soon as we dock, or we won't be able to do another run.'

The captain nodded. 'I'll see that it's arranged. In the meantime, can you make a temporary repair?'

'Yes, sir.' The dripping sailor's face broke into a grin. 'We'll stick our fingers in the holes if necessary.'

'Have you got enough men for that?' the captain asked drily.

'Oh, I expect we could persuade the army to help us. We ain't got enough lifeboats for this lot, and I'm damned sure they won't want to swim home.'

Reid watched this light-hearted exchange and had a

vivid picture of the pilots diving into action, the courage of the soldiers on the beach, and now the crew of this battered destroyer. He was seeing a different side to his fellow man, and it was awe-inspiring. And at that moment he knew that no matter how desperate the plight of the country there was no way they could lose this war. A lot of them wouldn't see the end, of course, but they would win!

He walked forward and gazed out to sea for a while, then turned and watched Captain Freeman issuing orders in a quiet, unruffled manner. That his crew respected him was very clear, and his placid nature by no means hid the strength of the man.

'I'm sorry we can't offer you something stronger.' A sailor carrying a tray of steaming cups thrust a mug of tea into his hand. Reid curled his fingers around it gratefully. 'Thanks. This will do just fine.'

'Why don't you sit down?' The captain pointed to his own chair. 'You look just about done in.'

'I am. God what a day!' Reid sat and rubbed his hand over his eyes, then started to gently probe the injury to his temple.

'There will be nurses to take care of you when we dock.' Captain Freeman turned away to deal with the business of getting his ship back to Dover.

Reid watched the captain and officers on the bridge spring into action as another crisis erupted. But he took little notice of it as reaction was beginning to set in, and his mind started to shut down. He had survived and was going home, that's all that mattered at the moment. And the ship wasn't going to sink, the captain had said so, and he believed him.

58

He wasn't aware of the passing of time as he sat there, the mug was replaced with a fresh one every so often, and the activity all around him was just so much background noise. He watched the sea, noting the different colours and shades, his mind drifting and thinking of nothing in particular . . .

He was roused out of his stupor when the destroyer's guns shattered the quiet. Rushing to the front of the bridge, he looked up into the sky and eagerly grabbed the binoculars being held out to him. It took him only a few seconds to identify the planes as German, but there, just above them . . . 'Stop shooting,' he yelled, 'those are our fighters coming to intercept them.'

Orders were quickly given and the guns fell silent. Reid breathed a sigh of relief, walked back to the chair and almost collapsed on to it. 'Bloody hell,' he muttered, 'we're going to have to do better at identification than this.'

'I agree,' the captain said. 'And I can assure you, Squadron Leader, that my men will get a refresher course as a matter of urgency.'

'It wasn't their fault,' Reid admitted. 'If our planes were there they would be high and coming out of the sun, so I knew where to look.'

Captain Freeman nodded. 'I'm glad you were here, and your planes, of course, have just saved us from serious damage. This poor old ship can't take much more.'

And neither can the crew, Reid thought, as he saw the strain on their faces. But he said nothing and sat back to wait out the rest of the journey. He was filled with a sense of gratitude for the courage of these men around him. Without the soldiers on the beach and the crew of this ship he would still be stuck in France.

It didn't seem any time at all after that when he heard cheering, and there in front of him was Dover. It was the most beautiful sight he'd ever seen! The injured were taken off first, followed by the relieved soldiers. Reid thanked the captain and his officers, and then made his way ashore.

The quay was crowded with doctors, nurses and civilians, all helping the returning troops. He stood there for a while, wondering how he could get a lift back to Kenley, when he saw Captain Freeman striding along, then stopping in front of a woman and holding her close for a few moments, then kissing another girl on the cheek. He couldn't see who they were because of the crowds milling around them, but he was glad the captain had someone waiting for him.

'Let me see to your head, sir.' A military nurse began to lead him towards a building.

After he was cleaned up, had stitches and a dressing put on the gash, and been given something to eat he went outside again looking for any kind of transport heading towards his airfield. There was a blast on a ship's horn, and he saw the destroyer making her way out to sea. Dear God, they were going back again already. He prayed that they had been able to stop the leaks.

The journey back to Kenley was long and tiring. He'd spent more time looking for lifts than he had actually travelling. He'd had umpteen modes of transport and all equally uncomfortable, but the help had been willingly given. He finally reached the airfield at four in the morning.

He was greeted enthusiastically by everyone, and after a short debriefing he staggered into his hut.

'Reid! Where the blazes have you been? Couldn't you have let us know you were all right?'

He glanced at his brother's angry and worried expression, and then gave a lopsided grin. Paul must have driven over from Biggin Hill. 'It's good to see you, as well, little brother.'

Then he threw himself on his bed and was instantly asleep.

5

Annie rushed through the gate at Compton Bassett and sighed in relief; she'd only just made it in time after spending longer than she should have with Rose. Her sister had refused to leave Dover until she saw Bill come back again, so she'd stayed with her. Annie smiled to herself. How wonderful it had been to see him return, and now he had some leave while repairs were carried out to his ship.

As an officer approached she saluted smartly. She remembered the pilot she had caught a glimpse of on the dock. For a brief moment she had thought it was Paul but he had been taller and his hair darker. She hadn't been able to see all of his face for caked blood down one side, but there had been something about him that had drawn her. Before she could go over and offer him some help a nurse had led him away. Rose had put her WVS training to good use and Annie had taken her orders from her sister. It had been a relief to see the ships come in and the men pouring off them. At least they had managed to rescue a lot of men . . .

'Hey! Annie,' someone called. 'Show us your knickers!'

She spun round, a smile of delight on her face. 'Dora!' They hugged each other, laughing.

'What are you doing here?'

'I've been posted here and I'm working in the office.'

Dora grinned. 'It's better than that awful factory I was in, and I'm getting to mix with some smashing blokes. I'm hoping to get promotion when I've finished my training.'

Annie fought back a smile. 'So I hope you're not going to get me into trouble while you're here.'

'Who me, now would I do that?' Dora put on an offended expression.

Both girls burst into laughter, remembering the escapades they'd been involved in while doing their basic training.

'Anyway . . .' Dora composed herself. 'Where have you been, I arrived three days ago and not a sign of you.'

'I've been with my sister, helping with the troops coming back from Dunkirk, but they're nearly all home now, thank heavens.' Annie shuddered inwardly when she thought of the perilous situation this country was now in. Getting the troops off the beaches had been a massive operation by the navy and a flotilla of little boats all manned by civilians. These men had shown remarkable bravery and disregard for their own lives in their determination to rescue the soldiers. The army had been plucked off the beaches, but all the military equipment – trucks, guns, tanks – had been left behind. What a mess! This was Hitler's chance to walk right in . . .

She glanced at her watch and gasped. 'I must drop off my kit and report back for duty.'

'There's a dance at the NAAFI this evening.' Dora grabbed Annie's arm to stop her running away. 'Can you come?'

'Wouldn't miss it.'

'Smashing. I'll see you later then.'

Annie hurried away. It would be fun to relax and have a laugh tonight, and that was always guaranteed when Dora was around. It might help to dull the distress of Dunkirk and the worries about the future. This country was alone now and vulnerable!

The afternoon was exam time to see how much they had learned in the last three months, so Annie grabbed a cup of tea and skimmed through her notes. There wasn't time to do more than that, but she felt confident of passing. Then it would be into the last three months of training, and she was determined to do well because she couldn't wait to start doing the job for real. She could already send and receive messages quite well with few mistakes, but the next stage would be learning to maintain their wireless sets and doing their own repairs. She smiled to herself; the work as a fashion editor had not prepared her for using soldering irons, or whatever it was they were going to have to do, but she loved the idea of it.

'Would you like to dance?'

Annie smiled at Officer Graham who was standing in front of her and felt the same surge of empathy she'd experienced when she'd first met him. 'I'd love to.'

He was an excellent dancer and Annie relaxed, lost in the floating music and the smooth movements of her partner.

The floor was crowded and as he marked time when they were surrounded and unable to move forward he smiled down at her. 'And how have you been getting on, Ann Webster?'

'Fine, thank you, sir. I love what I'm doing.'

'Good. And we're off duty now, so my name is Jack.' And everyone calls me Annie.'

He swept her off again as a space appeared. 'What do you like to do in your spare time, Annie?'

'Well, now that the weather is warming up, I like to get out in the countryside and just walk. I love the peace and quiet, and Wiltshire is a beautiful county.'

'So do I. Perhaps we could spend some time together? There are some good walks around here and I know of a very nice tearoom.'

'Oh, I'd like that.' Annie had taken to this man from the moment they'd met. He was so like her brother-in-law. But no, that wasn't true; her feelings for Jack Graham were different from those she felt for Bill. It was amazing that this was only the second time they'd met, and yet it seemed as if she'd always known him . . . .

'Before you accept so readily,' his deep voice interrupted her thoughts, 'I must tell you that I'm married and have two children. I'm looking for companionship, that's all.' He shook his head. 'That sounds insulting. It isn't that I don't find you attractive. I do, but I'll behave myself.'

'Do you think that's possible at the moment when everything's so uncertain?' she asked drily, knowing instinctively that it was all right to joke with him.

'Difficult, I agree.' He held her away from him and looked down into her upturned face. 'Will you still come out with me?'

'I'd love to.'

'Thank you, Annie. I shall be stationed here for a while, so just let me know when you have some free time.'

The dance ended and he led her back to her seat, his fingers lingering on hers for slightly longer than necessary, before smiling again, and then leaving her.

'Ah!' Dora said with satisfaction as they watched him walk away. 'I thought he wouldn't be far away.'

'That's the first time I've seen him since he recruited me.'

'Go on?' Dora clearly didn't believe that.

The expression on her friend's face was too much for Annie and she dug her in the ribs. 'And what have you been up to since I last saw you?'

'Having fun. And if you think I'm going to tell you all about my sordid past, then you're in for a big disappointment.'

'I don't think I want to know.' Annie feigned a look of horror. 'I don't think my chaste little ears could stand it.'

Dora allowed herself to be dragged on to the dance floor by an exuberant sergeant before she'd had a chance to reply, but from the expression on her face it was clear she'd had a snappy answer ready for Annie.

Annie didn't see Jack again until the last waltz, which he claimed, and then walked her back to her billet. He kissed her hand gallantly, sighed deeply, and walked away. There was no sign of Dora.

'Don't you ever get any time off?' Dora complained, a week later.

'Not much,' Annie admitted. 'I've got less than three months of training to go and I must be expert by then.'

'Do you know where they're sending you after that?'

'No.' Annie stirred her tea thoughtfully. 'About time off, I have got tomorrow afternoon free, but —'

'Oh, that's no good, I'm on duty until the weekend.'

'Never mind. If we can fiddle a couple of days together I could take you home to meet my family.'

'Wow! Annie, would you?'

'Of course.' She laughed. Dora had such an open expression and didn't try to hide her pleasure at the idea of meeting Annie's family. They would like her, she was sure.

Her friend started to flip through a diary. 'I'll go and make eyes at the sergeant in the office. So, what are you going to do on your own?'

'I won't be on my own. I'm going out with Jack.'

'Who's Jack?' Dora looked intrigued. 'I didn't know you'd found yourself another bloke, you've got this pilot, Paul, haven't you?'

Annie sighed. 'Yes, he thinks so.'

'Ah.' Dora pulled her chair closer so they wouldn't be overheard in the crowded mess. 'Tell me all.'

Realizing that she wasn't going to get any peace until Dora knew the facts, Annie bowed to the inevitable and explained about Paul.

'Why don't you just tell him that you don't want to see him any more?' Dora said when she'd finished the story.

'I can't do that, he's a nice boy and I wouldn't want to hurt him. Especially now.'

'Annie, you're too soft,' Dora told her gently. 'Have you got a picture of him?'

'Yes.' Annie took a letter out of her pocket and removed the photo Paul had sent her the other day.

Dora took it and whistled. 'Nice-looking bloke.'

'He is, and at the moment he needs me. I think he's

realized that being a fighter pilot isn't the fun he thought it was going to be.'

'Bloody dangerous, if you ask me.'

Annie agreed with that! 'So you see, I don't like it, but I don't see what else I can do at the moment.'

'Don't worry, it will all work out. Right, now you haven't answered my first question. Who's Jack?'

'He was the one who recruited me. He was at the dance, don't you remember?'

'What, you mean, *Sir*?' Dora squeaked. 'But . . . hold on a minute, mate, he must be about forty, and that means he's most likely married.'

'He is, but we're just going to be friends. He only wants some companionship.' Annie was well aware how ridiculous that sounded, yet somehow she believed Jack Graham. She knew she was being naive but he didn't appear to be a man who would lie to her. She trusted him.

Dora's mouth opened in disbelief. 'Oh, come on, Annie, you don't believe that, surely?'

'Of course I do. He's been absolutely honest with me.'

'Worse and worse,' her friend groaned. 'Never trust a man who's being *honest*.'

'Why on earth not?'

'My God! We've got a babe in arms here. I know you look like an untouched angel but you can't be that green.' She leaned towards Annie urgently. 'When a man says, I want to be honest with you, then it's time to run for your life.'

'You're wrong.' Annie laughed. 'He's so like my brother-in-law.'

'And you sleep with him, do you?'

'No, I don't. I love Bill, but not in that way. Anyway, Rose would kill any woman who tried to take him from her, even me!'

Dora's grin was evil. 'I bet she would. So where are you going with *Sir*, then?'

'Just for a walk.'

'Any cornfields on the route,' she asked drily.

'Oh, you're impossible,' Annie said and laughed. 'You've got only one thing on your mind.'

'Is there something else, then?' Dora sat back and pretended she was puzzled.

Annie glanced at her watch and got hurriedly to her feet. 'I've got to get back. And you needn't worry about me, I know what I'm doing.'

She left Dora muttering fiercely, 'Too bloody innocent for her own good.'

It was a lovely June afternoon. The sky was clear, the sun warm, and just for a few hours they could relax and pretend that everything was well with their world. When Churchill had been made Prime Minister, and given his first speech to the House of Commons on the 13th of May, he'd said, 'I have nothing to offer but blood, toil, tears and sweat.' They all knew this was true as they waited for Hitler to invade – for he must surely come now.

Annie smiled at the man walking beside her. 'What do you do, Jack, apart from finding people with an ear for Morse code?'

'Whatever I'm asked to do. Oh, look, there's a green woodpecker!' He pointed towards a clump of trees. 'On that lower branch.'

'Yes, I see. Isn't he lovely? Oh, he's flown away now.'

Jack started to talk about the different kinds of birds, which was a subject he was very interested in, and Annie knew he wasn't going to tell her about his work. She'd been asking a question he obviously couldn't answer. Though that made her even more curious. There was an air of mystery about him and that intrigued her. The attraction between them was very strong so she must not forget that he was a married man!

'Sorry,' she apologized, 'I shouldn't be asking you questions about your work, should I?'

He wrapped his long fingers around her hand and sighed. 'Let's not spoil this afternoon with talk about the war.'

They walked down country lanes, admiring quaint little cottages and open farmlands, sometimes talking and at other times quiet. The war seemed a long way away in this tranquil setting, and Annie sensed that Jack needed to unwind. He held her hand. Every so often she could feel the tension in him, then it would go and he'd smile again.

After over an hour of strolling along they came to a tearoom where in normal times they would have been selling cream teas. The thought made Annie's mouth water, but she knew they would be lucky just to get a pot of tea now.

They sat at a table near the window overlooking a picture-postcard scene of sheep grazing contentedly in a field. Annie sighed at such a peaceful scene in these violent and troubled times.

'This is blissful,' she told Jack. 'You could almost believe we weren't at war.'

'Hello, my dears.' An elderly lady, with grey hair and a round smile, came up to them. 'What would you like?'

'A huge cream tea,' Annie said, laughing.

'Ah, I wish I could.' The lady joined in the joke and her smile became even broader. 'I can let you have a pot of tea and a piece of home-made carrot cake.'

'That would be lovely,' Jack said, and watched her bustle away with her smile still firmly in place.

'There's a dance at Chippenham Town Hall tonight, Annie. Would you like to go?'

'Oh, I'd love to!'

'That's right, my dears, you enjoy yourselves.' The woman was back with their tea and had obviously overheard their conversation. 'There now, you'll find that cake quite tasty, though nothing like the ones I used to make. Famous for my fruit cake, I was.'

'I'm sure it's lovely.' Annie smiled and watched her walk away, her spotless and highly starched apron rustling as she moved.

They spent an hour over their tea and then walked back. As soon as the Compton Bassett camp came into view they were back in the real world, but it had been a lovely interlude of peace.

'I'll meet you at the gate at seven,' Jack said, and strode off after giving her hand a gentle squeeze.

It was only when she was having dinner with Dora, and thought about the afternoon, that Annie realized she'd told Jack a great deal about herself but had learned practically nothing about him.

The dance at Chippenham was crowded with service personnel determined to have a good night out. Jack was a wonderful dancer, but the dance Annie liked most of all was the foxtrot, and they swept around the floor as if they'd been partners for years. That was why she was amazed when after being there for about two hours Jack stepped away from her in the middle of the dance floor and swore fiercely under his breath.

'What's the matter?' she asked, alarmed by his action. They'd been dancing and laughing, completely at ease in each other's company, and suddenly he looked angry.

'This wasn't a good idea!' He turned and walked out of the room.

Annie's mind was racing – what had she done? She'd never seen him so disturbed; he was such a quiet, controlled man. She ran after him and caught him up just as he stepped out into the fresh air. 'Jack?'

'I'll take you back to camp,' was all he said.

Now she was getting cross. 'Not until you've explained!'

'I'm sorry. I thought we could just be friends,' he grimaced, 'but I was wrong. Being close to you and not being able to make love to you is agony.'

Annie saw his jaw clench in frustration and understood, for she felt the same, but this relationship couldn't be anything but a friendship. And if that was all she could have from him then she didn't want to let it go. 'We won't come dancing again but we can still see each other, can't we? Still go for walks?'

'Do you think that's a good idea?' He looked angry. 'If I can't control what I feel for you, will you sleep with me?'

'Oh, Jack.' She was dismayed by this conversation;

how she wished she could say yes. 'If you were free . . . but you're married, Jack.'

'Exactly! And you're not the kind of girl who could ignore that.' He ran the back of his hand down her cheek in a gentle gesture. 'I really am sorry.'

She caught hold of his hand and held on firmly. The thought of losing him was upsetting, and she wondered how on earth she'd become so attached to a man after only meeting him about three times. 'Let's try and be friends, please.'

Jack sighed and gazed into space for a moment with a deep frown on his face, and then he looked back with a smile. 'OK, Annie, we'll see how it goes, shall we?'

Over the next couple of weeks they spent every spare moment together, and he behaved like the perfect gentleman. It was as if the incident at the dance had never happened; he was back in complete control of himself again. Yet Annie's feelings were in turmoil. The more time she spent with Jack the more she liked him – or was it love? He was a quietly spoken man, but there was a strength about him that was obvious to her. They had much in common, the same music, a love of the countryside whatever the season, and their outlook on life seemed to dovetail without any seams showing. He had every quality she loved in a man, and at the end of each outing she couldn't wait to see him again. The attraction between them was very strong and if this was love then she didn't allow herself to admit it; he was a married man and she would never let herself be the cause of a breakdown in anyone's marriage.

One day they were returning from another walk and

were a short distance from the camp when Jack led her towards a large oak tree. He turned her to face him. There was an expression on his face Annie had never seen before and it took her breath away. This was not the warm, affectionate Jack Graham she had come to know; it was as if he'd switched something off inside himself. But one thing she was sure of, he was about to tell her something she didn't want to hear.

'Annie, I won't be able to see you again, I'm going away.'

'Oh.' Dismay ran through her. She didn't want to lose him, even if they did have to keep a tight rein on their feelings for each other. It wasn't easy, of course . . . If only he wasn't married! 'Are you being posted somewhere else?'

He nodded.

'Then we can keep in touch,' she suggested.

'I'm sorry but I won't be able to do that.'

She looked away from his face, sad that he was ending their time together like this. They got on so well and she would never have made any demands on him.

He kissed her gently on the lips. 'I would stay here for ever with you if I could but I have to go away. I shall be leaving tonight. I'll write if I can, but I can't promise anything.'

'I'm going to miss you, Jack.' It was difficult to keep her voice steady; this had come as a shock. He hadn't given the slightest hint that he was being moved and she was upset that he hadn't mentioned it before. 'Will you be coming back here after this posting?'

'Not before you've been sent somewhere else.' He brought her fingers up to his lips and kissed each one in

74

turn. 'Thank you for this lovely couple of weeks; it has meant a great deal to me.'

She hugged him and knew that he was saying goodbye. That realization hurt very much, but she wasn't going to make a fuss, even if she couldn't understand why this sounded so final. When she was moved to another post he would still be able to contact her, surely? But from the shuttered expression on his face she knew he was cutting her out of his life.

'I hope we meet again.' Annie struggled to keep her tone bright.

He didn't comment on that. 'You take care of yourself, Annie Webster. You are a very special person.'

Then he turned and strode away, walking out of her life, she was sure.

6

The need to refuel and rearm was urgent. Reid had already stayed up longer than he should have done, but the fight had been desperate so he'd left it to the very last minute before breaking off. Now he had to get down, and quickly. He cast an anxious glance at his gauges and put the Spitfire into a steep dive. He was close to Biggin Hill and headed for that, determined to make the airfield. He didn't want to land in some farmer's field as that would put his plane out of the fight and every single aircraft was badly needed.

He made it and the plane spluttered her way towards the hangars. 'Can you refuel and rearm her?' he asked, as he hauled himself out of the cockpit.

The ground crew sprang into action just as a truck skidded to a halt beside him.

'Hop in, sir. I'll take you to the mess so you can get a cuppa.'

'Thanks.' Reid got in and the driver hurtled towards a group of buildings at great speed. 'My brother's stationed here,' he told the sergeant, hanging on grimly and wondering if this was a frustrated would-be fighter pilot. 'I'm hoping I'll be able to see him.'

'Ah, well, they're all up, sir. It's a busy day.' He cast a quick sideways glance towards Reid, 'Not that I need to tell you that. It's turning out to be a bugger of an August, isn't it?'

'It certainly is.' He couldn't argue with that! By nightfall each day he was surprised to be still alive.

'Here you are, sir.' The airman disgorged his passenger and sped off in a cloud of dust.

Reid got himself a mug of tea, then wandered outside where there was an assortment of chairs. He sat down, closed his eyes and turned his face to the warm summer sun. Over the last few weeks he had learned to grab any quiet moment for a catnap, but any call to scramble and he was instantly awake and alert. He'd always been good at athletics during his days at university but he was sure his sprinting speed had improved lately.

The sound of aircraft had him on his feet and scanning the sky. Hurricanes and Spitfires were returning, and he watched each pilot as he jumped out of the plane. Then he saw Paul and, smiling, went to meet him.

'Reid!' He greeted his brother with enthusiasm. 'What are you doing here?'

'Ran out of fuel and ammo.'

'Well, we've chased them off for a while; so let me report in and then we'll get something to eat. I'm starving.'

Reid laughed. 'You always are. I'll wait inside for you.'

Fifteen minutes later they were both tucking into a large plate of sausage and mash. The wartime sausages had more bread in them than anything else, and just for a moment Reid remembered the succulent bangers his mother used to cook for them, but immediately dismissed the mouth-watering thought.

77

The brothers were ravenous after their time in the air and finished their meal in silence.

'Have you managed to get that girl of yours to agree to marry you?' Reid asked as they enjoyed a cup of tea after their meal.

Paul stirred another spoon of sugar into his tea and then smiled at his brother. 'No, she's busy training as a wireless operator and we are forever chasing the Luftwaffe, but I talk to her on the phone now and again.'

Reid studied his brother intently; Paul seemed to have a strange relationship with this girl and he hadn't been able to work it out yet. 'Have you changed your mind?'

'No, I'll never do that. I love her very much, but she's a very kind person, Reid, and I could probably persuade her to marry me, given the circumstances we find ourselves in, but it wouldn't be right to put that kind of pressure on her.' He sat back and sighed. 'And anyway, I wouldn't like to make her a widow so young.'

Reid didn't like to hear his brother voice his fear of leaving Annie a widow if they married, though he knew every pilot wondered if they were going to survive this fight. Of course they all believed it wouldn't happen to them but reality had a knack of creeping under your mental guard now and again.

'She's always been honest with me, and I know she doesn't love me the way I do her, but I can't seem to let her go.' Paul grimaced. 'I keep hoping she will change her mind but I know it's a forlorn hope.'

'I should leave it until the war's over; she might feel differently by then. This isn't the time to make serious commitments, just keep in touch and enjoy the friendship,' Reid told him.

78

'Sound advice as usual, Reid, and I do know a very accommodating girl in the village, so I'm not being deprived of comfort.' He winked at his brother then became serious again. 'But it's Annie I want for my wife, and always will.'

'Squadron Leader?' A WAAF was standing beside their table. 'Your plane's ready for you now.'

Reid hauled himself to his feet. Paul walked out with him, and when they reached his plane Reid clasped his brother to him for a brief moment. How he wished this brother of his hadn't followed in his footsteps and become a pilot, but there was no point in agonizing over it now. It was done and they had to make the best of things. 'Take care, and watch your tail, Paul.'

'And you do the same.'

Reid slid into the cockpit. He was glad he'd landed here, it had given him a chance to see Paul and get some idea of how he was coping, but he clearly hadn't needed to worry – his brother was handling the situation very well by the look of him.

'Hey!' Paul called. 'That's the first time you haven't called me "little brother".'

'Doesn't apply any more. All I can see is a man.' With a last wave to his proud-looking brother, Reid took off.

Annie put the last stitch in the badge and examined it with pride. She was now a fully trained wireless operator. It had been six months of hard and intensive training but she'd come through and was now qualified to start doing some proper work. When Jack had picked her out for this work August had seemed a long way off, but the time had flown by. The thought of Jack Graham caused the usual pain. Where was he now; what was he doing? How she would love to let him see that she hadn't let him down . . .

Dora came in and threw her bag on the floor and admired the badge. 'Very impressive. You ready? Don't want to miss our train.'

Annie grinned at her friend who was having a job to contain her excitement. She had been talking for days about going home with her.

'You sure your family won't mind me coming?' Dora looked uncertain.

'Of course they won't. We've got plenty of spare room now the boys are away.'

They managed to get a lift to the station and were soon on the train heading home. Annie's sigh was one of contentment. It was heaven to get away for a while and just relax.

'You heard anything from Sir?' Dora asked when they were settled in their seats.

'Not a word.'

'That's not very kind. You'd think he could write.' Annie shrugged, trying to make light of her disappointment. 'Well, I don't suppose I'll hear from him again. It was just a pleasant interlude for him, I expect.'

'Men!'

'One of these days you're going to meet a man who will knock you sideways, and you won't have a cynical thought in your head,' Annie told her with a grin.

'Huh! That'll be the day.'

When they reached the station there was an RAF lorry outside, and with very little persuasion they managed to get a lift to Annie's house. The vehicle was crowded, and they laughed all the way to Roehampton. The men were discussing William Joyce, or Lord Haw-Haw as he'd been nicknamed. His broadcasts beginning with 'Germany calling, Germany calling' were the cause of much hilarity. Although a lot of the information was accurate, much of it was absolute nonsense, and his upper-class British accent made him sound ridiculous.

After waving goodbye to the truckload of airmen, and knowing where everyone would be, Annie took Dora round the back and into the kitchen.

'Annie,' her mother said in delight. 'What a lovely surprise.'

'Hello, Mum, I hope you don't mind but I've brought Dora home with me.'

Marj smiled at the girl standing uncertainly in the doorway. 'You're very welcome, Dora. Come on in, and I'll make us all a nice cup of tea. Wally's out with his Home Guard lot, but should be back soon.'

'I'm already here.' Wally gave Annie a hug. 'Oh, it's good to see you, the house seems empty these days.'

She kissed his cheek. 'Well, I've brought someone with me this time. Dora, this is Wally, my stepfather.'

'And I'm her brother,' said another voice from behind her.

Annie spun round and squeaked in delight. 'Will, I didn't know you were home.'

'Arrived yesterday. Aren't you going to introduce me to your friend?'

'Sorry. Dora, this is my brother Will.'

'I'm pleased to meet you, Dora. Are you girls staying long?'

'Three days,' Annie told him.

'Good. Don't arrange anything for tomorrow night, we can all go dancing in Richmond.'

When they were settled down with cups of Marj's famous tea in front of them, Annie studied her brother. He really was a very attractive man, and he looked smashing in his navy uniform. She also noticed Dora gazing at him with a very interested expression on her face.

After spending some time swapping stories about their service experiences, Will glanced at his watch and stood up. 'I've got to go, I'm meeting some mates at four.' When he'd gone, Marj said, 'Dora can share your room. I keep the beds made up in case any of you turn up unexpectedly.'

'Thanks, Mum. Come on, Dora, we can stow our gear later. I'll take you to meet Rose.'

Annie opened the kitchen door of Rose's house and found her in a tussle with her daughter. It wasn't unusual, as Kate had a stubborn streak and mother and daughter often clashed.

'You'll do as you're told, my girl.'

'Won't go!'

Rose sighed and looked up. 'Come in, Annie.'

'This is Dora,' she introduced.

'Hello, Dora, welcome to bedlam.'

'What's all this about?' Annie asked her sister.

'I want Kate and James to go and stay with Dad in Wales. James is happy enough, but this little miss refuses to leave home.'

'Why?' Annie asked the little girl. 'You like Grandpa George, don't you?'

Kate nodded and a large tear trickled down her chin.

'I can't go. What if Daddy comes home and I'm not here? I'll never see him!'

'I've told you umpteen times that we'll come to Wales.' Rose was clearly exasperated.

'No, you won't.' Kate hiccuped and wailed in earnest. 'Daddy's gone away. I don't want him gone away. He don't love me any more.'

'Oh, that isn't true.' Dora was on her knees in front of the distraught child. 'How could he not love a beautiful daughter like you?'

Kate hiccuped again and stared at her with interest. 'Why's he gone away, then?'

'There's a nasty man who wants to come and take over our country,' Dora explained, wiping Kate's tears with her own hanky. 'Your daddy's gone to stop him.'

Kate thought about this for a while, and then gave a watery smile. 'He'll do it.'

'Of course he will.'

'Can't go away, though.' Kate obviously wasn't going to give way on this important point and her mouth settled in a determined line.

'Why not, sweetheart?' George Gresham strolled in and tossed his bag down. 'I've just come back from Wales and the house is all ready now. I've had to have a lot done to it because it's old, but everything's cosy now.'

Rose stood with her hands on her hips and sighed again. 'Thank goodness you're here, Dad, try and talk some sense into her, will you?'

George sat down and pulled Kate on to his knees. 'It's a pretty house and there's a farm next door with lots of animals. It's near a place called Pontypool and we won't get any bombs there.'

Kate looked unimpressed. 'No bombs here.'

'Not yet, but they're getting terribly close, my precious, and London is bound to be attacked soon.'

'We've got a shelter in the garden. Daddy dug it,' the girl pointed out.

Rose was about to say something but George silenced her with a look.

'You and James will be much safer with me. One of the farm dogs has just had puppies. You can choose one for your own.'

This caused a spark of interest, and although the little girl was fighting it, the mention of animals was too much for her. 'How many puppies?'

'Six, and they've got two donkeys as well. The farmer's very nice and he said you can help to look after them if you want to.'

Kate shoved her thumb into her mouth and sucked on it thoughtfully.

Annie and Dora walked over to Rose, who was shaking her head in disbelief.

'My God, look at her; she's weighing the whole thing up. That girl will never make a hasty decision in her life.'

The three of them watched the scene being played out, with the little girl firmly in charge.

Kate's thumb slipped out of her mouth and she looked up at her grandfather. 'What colour are these puppies?'

'Black and white, they're sheepdogs.'

'Hmm.' The thumb shot back and two feet waved about in concentration. 'You got pussy cats, as well?'

'Yes, one, and she likes to sit on my lap in the evening.'

The little girl screwed her face up as she imagined

that, and ran her hand over her knees as if there was an imaginary cat there.

'Come on, Kate,' Rose muttered. 'You're not going to get a better offer than that.'

The girl had now moved her hand away from her mouth and was studying the sucked thumb carefully. 'My Daddy won't be able to find me.'

'Yes, he will, sweetheart, he came with me when I bought the house. We got it so that you could come and live there with me and be safe from the bombs.'

Annie watched George with great interest. He was not a man known for his tolerance, but he showed infinite patience with the children. He loved them very much and nothing was too much trouble where they were concerned.

'Hmm.' Kate squirmed around and looked at her mother. 'You bring Daddy to see me?'

'I promise, Kate.'

She wriggled back and looked at her grandpa. 'Can I choose my own puppy?'

George nodded, struggling to hide a smile of triumph. 'All right,' she said on a sigh, 'I'll go,' then slid down and trotted out into the garden, leaving them all convulsed with laughter.

'I hope you can deliver on your promises, Dad,' Rose exclaimed, 'because if you can't she'll have you bringing her back straight away.'

George chuckled proudly. 'I know my granddaughter, Rose, she'll remember every word of that conversation and check it all out before she even unpacks her bag.'

'Dora,' Rose said, 'thank you for talking to Kate like

that. She idolizes her father and just can't understand why he isn't here.'

'Oh, I love kids, and she's adorable. She's got your lovely black hair, and those huge brown eyes . . .,' Dora chortled. 'What a beauty she's going to be.'

Suddenly there was a loud squeal and they all rushed into the garden. Rose was running to the side gate where Kate was frantically pounding on it with her small hands and trying to climb over the securely locked gate. There was a tall sailor there in a captain's uniform. Bill!

Annie watched as Bill plucked his daughter off the gate and comforted her as she cried for joy on his shoulder. She blew her brother-in-law a kiss and told him she'd see him later, then turned to Dora. 'We'll leave them alone for a while.'

'Wow,' Dora exclaimed, when they were in Annie's bedroom. 'This is some family you've got here.'

'Special, eh?'

'I'll say! And I know you said that Sir reminds you of your brother-in-law, but' – she gave Annie a wide-eyed look – 'that man over there is stunning. No wonder Kate adores him.'

'We all do, and if anything happens to him this family will be devastated.'

Dora nodded, then smiled sheepishly. 'I pray every night that all my friends and family will survive this mess. I'll add yours to the list if you like?'

'Thanks, Dora.' Annie's respect for her was growing all the time. There was a lot more to her than the brash, worldly wise girl you saw on the surface. She was beginning to suspect that that was only a front. 'What did you think of Rose?'

'She's wonderful, and so beautiful. I never expected her to look like that.' Dora hesitated. 'There's something I don't understand, though. Rose called George, father, but didn't your dad die in the last war?'

'Yes, but he wasn't Rose's father. That's why she's so dark and me and my brothers are fair.' The contrast in their colouring was always being talked about, but when you saw Rose and George together there could be no doubt whose daughter she was.

'Your mother was married to George?' Dora looked puzzled.

'No. Mum was seduced when she was in service with the Greshams and so Rose is Sir George's daughter.'

'Sir George?' Dora asked, her eyes wide with astonishment.

'That's right. It was a stormy relationship, but they eventually became friends. It's a long story and when we've got a week to spare I'll tell you all about it.'

'But doesn't your mother mind him being part of the family now?' Dora was still having trouble grasping the situation.

'No, once she was happily married to Wally and George apologized for his disgraceful conduct towards her – he blamed it on his wild youth – she forgave him. They made their peace with each other a long time ago, and Rose is his pride and joy. He hasn't any other family so he's become a loved member of ours.'

Dora gazed at her friend in wonder. 'Doesn't Wally object to him being here?'

Annie smiled at the thought of her stepfather being angry about anything. 'He's accepted the situation and he really likes George. There isn't any conflict or jealousy between them.'

'My God, what a family!'

'And you haven't met all of them, yet,' Annie pointed out, laughing.

7

Annie was getting ready to go dancing with Will and Dora when Marj called up the stairs that there was someone to see her.

Annie was surprised to see Paul. 'Have you managed to get some time off?'

He kissed her gently and shook his head. 'No, I'm on stand-down for a few hours, that's all. When I phoned I was told you were on leave, so I came on the off-chance that we could spend a little time together.'

At that moment Will and Dora came into the room wearing their best uniforms.

'Paul, it's good to see you.' Will shook his hand and Annie introduced Dora.

'Ah.' Paul looked crestfallen. 'You look as if you're all going out.'

'Dancing,' Will told him. 'Why don't you come with us?'

'Well, I was hoping for some time alone with Annie,' he admitted.

Annie had been looking forward to going out with her brother and Dora, but Paul had driven to see her when he could have been resting, and he appeared strained. She didn't hesitate. 'We'll go for a quiet drink somewhere, shall we?'

Paul smiled happily at her. 'That would be lovely.'

'Do you mind if I don't come dancing?' she asked her friend.

'Of course I don't, I'm sure I'll be safe with Will.' Dora cast him an amused look.

'I can't promise that,' he joked, 'but we'll have a good time.'

Dora slipped her hand through his arm and raised her eyebrows. 'What more can I ask?'

Then, both laughing, they left.

'They look happy together,' Paul remarked.

'Yes, they do, don't they? Now, where do you want to go?'

'The nearest pub is only a couple of miles down the road, so we'll go there.' He held the door open for her. 'I've borrowed a car from another pilot because I haven't got much time.'

The pub was busy when they arrived so they went into the saloon bar where it was less crowded. Paul bought them both a half pint of beer then sat back, closing his eyes for a brief moment before opening them again and smiling affectionately at her.

'This is nice.' He reached out and took her hand in his. 'You look lovely in your uniform, Annie, and I hope I haven't spoilt your evening by turning up like this?'

'You haven't.' She squeezed his hand; she was glad he'd come tonight. He really did looked drained and a few hours relaxing and talking would do him good. 'I'm very pleased to see you.'

'I'm sorry it can't be for longer.' He consulted his watch. 'I'll have to leave in about three hours, I'm afraid. It seems they can't do without me,' he joked.

She was dismayed. On the surface Paul looked the

same as always but there was something different about him, and she couldn't work out what it was. Then, when she looked deep into his eyes, she knew – he had grown up. But dear Lord, what a way to do it. Dunkirk was behind them, and the pilots were now fighting fiercely to stop the Luftwaffe from gaining superiority in the air. It was a desperate battle with these tired, overstretched men in the air from dawn until dusk. The responsibility on them was enormous, because they knew, only too well, that if they failed then the Germans would be pouring across the Channel. She was sure each pilot was fully aware of the awesome task, and she often wondered how they felt each time they took to the air, knowing that it could be the end of their lives. Paul never mentioned it and nor, she suspected, did the others, but each one of them must have their own inner battle to win.

'I'm glad you came,' she told him brightly, and knew that if he asked her to marry him again she would agree this time. She was aware that couples were falling into hasty marriages; with the future so uncertain people were grabbing at happiness with little thought of the consequences. She had vowed not to do that but . . .

'So am I. Now, do you think the landlord would rustle us up something to eat. I'm starving.'

'You always are,' she teased, glad to see the boyish grin back in place.

'That's what Reid says.'

'How is your brother?' she asked. She guessed he was still alive because Paul would have told her immediately if anything had happened to him.

'He's a squadron leader now,' he told her with pride, 'and gaining quite a reputation as an ace.'

'I expect you both are.' She put her head on one side and looked at him. 'With both Lascells brothers in the fight, I shouldn't think Hitler stands a chance.'

'He doesn't. Believe me, we won't let him win.'

A man with a mission, Annie thought, as she watched him walk over to the bar. There had been a look of cold determination in his eyes, and she guessed that all the fighter pilots were like that.

When he returned, she launched into a few funny stories about the girls, and a while later the landlady put two steaming plates of food in front of them.

'My goodness,' Annie exclaimed. 'How did you manage that?'

The landlady smiled. 'You'll find more veg than meat in the pie but it's tasty and filling.'

Paul picked up his knife and fork. 'It looks smashing.'

'Well, nothing's too good for our pilots.' The woman patted his shoulder affectionately, and then walked away.

Paul looked up and winked at Annie. 'Wear a pair of wings and you can get almost anything.'

She laughed at his expression. 'And I see you're not too proud to take advantage of that.'

'Of course not; just lately we've hardly had time to grab a sandwich, so this is a real treat.'

After they had cleared their plates, Paul sat back and gave a contented smile. 'It's lovely to be able to relax like this, even if it is only for a few hours. Do you know where you're going now you've finished your training?'

'Yes, I have been told.'

'Can you tell me where?'

'No, but send your letters to Compton Bassett as usual

and they will reach me. I'll get out and phone you as soon as I can.'

'I hope it isn't in London.'

'It's near Stoke-on-Trent, and that's all I'm allowed to say.'

'Ah, Cheadle, the RAF intercept station.' He gave a knowing wink and laughed when Annie grimaced.

'It's supposed to be a secret place,' she told him, glancing round to make sure no one had heard them.

He laughed again. 'Annie, we're pilots and there isn't much we don't know.'

'Paul, you're in the front line,' she said, changing the subject, 'so how bad do you think things are going to get?'

'Very bad, Annie.' He took her hand in his again, his face suddenly serious. 'The Luftwaffe expected to break us in a few weeks after Dunkirk, but they haven't managed to do it. We think it won't be long before he starts to attack civilian targets, especially London, in an effort to demoralize the population.'

'He won't do that.' Annie spoke with conviction. 'No matter what he throws at us, I can't see anyone – man or woman – allowing the Germans to take over our country. They'll have to get past the Home Guard first.' A smile flashed across her face as she remembered some of the hilarious tales Wally had told them.

Paul chuckled. 'Don't put the Home Guard down, Annie. They're doing a grand job picking up German pilots who have been shot down. They even charged up to one of my mates as he parachuted down and tried to arrest him.'

'What happened?'

'Once they knew who he was they insisted on taking him back to the airfield, after he'd been escorted to the pub for a pint of beer first.'

'Oh, I can just picture the scene,' she said laughing.

At that moment a crowd of soldiers came into the saloon bar, putting an end to their quiet chat.

Paul glanced at his watch. 'I'd better make a move. Come on, my darling, I'll take you home.'

They were quiet on their way back. Paul didn't seem to want to talk any more and she left him in peace. He stopped outside her house and walked her to the door. 'I won't come in, Annie; I've got to get back. I shall be flying again at dawn.'

'You take care,' she told him gently.

'I will.' He turned her face up so he could gaze into her eyes. 'Hey! Don't look so glum. I know our survival rate isn't too hot but I'm an experienced pilot and that increases my chances.'

His kiss was nothing like the ones he had given her in the past; this one was full of passion, love and need, and she gasped when he pulled away.

'I expect you're wondering why I haven't asked you to marry me,' he joked.

She put her head on one side. 'You've changed your mind?'

'No, I'll never do that, but this is not the time.' He held her away from him. 'But as soon as this bloody war's over, I'm not going to take no for an answer. Is that clear?'

Annie saluted smartly. 'Yes, sir!'

'Good.' He kissed her again, then turned on his heel and walked away.

There wasn't anyone around when she went indoors, and she guessed that they were all with Rose and Bill. It was eleven o'clock and she was tired, so she went to bed.

Her mind went over every moment of her evening with Paul. He wasn't the same person who had first joined up, and she liked this more mature man. But liking wasn't love! She sighed deeply and drifted off to sleep.

It was about one in the morning when Annie was woken by a giggle and some whispering going on outside her door. She smiled to herself; it sounded as if Will and Dora had enjoyed themselves. Will was tall and slim and he looked really good in his bell-bottom trousers; she knew her friend had noticed that as well. She was just dozing off again when there was a gentle knock on her door and it opened a crack.

'Annie, are you awake?'

'Of course.' She sat up and blinked when the light went on, and her friend came and sat on the other bed.

'Did you have a good time?' she asked, plumping up a pillow behind her so she could sit up.

'Smashing. How did your evening go with Paul?'

'Very enjoyable.'

'Did he ask you to marry him again?' Dora asked.

'No, he said he wouldn't until the war is over, but do you know, Dora, if he had asked me tonight I would have accepted.' Annie sighed. 'But I'm glad he didn't because it wouldn't have been right. He's such a nice man but I don't feel any passion for him.' Annie rubbed her temple. 'I wish I could feel more, I would love to make him happy.'

'Why didn't you just go to bed with him, then? I'm sure that would have made him happy.'

'He didn't have time, but I think I would even have done that tonight if he'd asked.' Annie laid her head back and closed her eyes. 'I'm confused. This flaming war has a lot to answer for.'

'I know this is none of my business, and you can tell me to sod off, but have you ever slept with him?' Dora raised an eyebrow in query.

'No.'

'Anyone?'

'No.'

'Ah, just as I always thought, an innocent babe.' Annie sat up. 'How many have you been to bed with?'

'Only one, and don't look so surprised. I might be a flirt but that doesn't mean they get more than a goodnight kiss. Well, not much more. If the groping gets out of hand, I put a stop to it.'

'Did Will's groping get too urgent?' Annie asked with a grin.

'You can mind your own bloody business, that's between me and Will.' Dora rolled her eyes and began to undress for the night.

Annie held her hands up in mock surrender. 'All right, tell me what happened to your boyfriend. Do you still see him?'

'No, he got killed in an accident at the docks before the war started.'

'Oh, I'm so sorry.'

'Yes, it was a shame. We'd known each other since kids and it was taken for granted that we'd marry some day.' Dora slipped into her bed. 'It was a long time ago. Now, I'd better let you get some sleep.'

'Night.' Dora's hand hovered on the bedside light

96

before switching it off. 'Er . . . Annie, Will's asked me to write to him; do you mind?'

'Of course I don't, I think that's lovely. You seem to get on well together.'

'We do. Thanks, Annie.'

After their leave Annie and Dora returned to camp. It was two days later when Annie collected the details of her new posting and went in search of Dora to say goodbye. They were both sad to be splitting up again, but this was a fact of war.

Annie hugged Dora. 'You keep in touch now, and behave yourself.'

'I'll write every week, but I'm not sure about behaving myself,' her friend joked. 'Without your steadying influence, there's no telling what I'll get up to.'

'It's been fun,' Annie told her, 'and I really hope we'll meet up again at some time in the future.'

'Bound to, you're not getting rid of me that easy.'

They hugged each other again and Annie headed back to her hut, packed her bag and hitched a lift to the railway station. All she knew was that she had to go to Stoke-on-Trent, where someone would be waiting to take her to her new posting in Cheadle.

She had plenty of time to think during the journey and was excited at the prospect of doing the work for real, but also apprehensive, hoping she was good enough. Six months had been a very short time to learn everything about being a wireless operator, and mastering Morse code, and she hoped she wouldn't make any blunders. It was going to be strange not having Dora around, but she'd soon make friends with the girls already at Cheadle.

And there was another good thing about her posting; the journey from Cheadle to Wales should be fairly easy. She hadn't seen the house yet, but it sounded cosy.

As promised there was a truck waiting for her at the station. Annie was too excited to take much notice where they were going but she'd studied a map beforehand and she knew there was moorland not far away. As she loved walking there would be plenty of interesting places to discover in her spare time. Papers were checked as they arrived at the camp, and she was escorted to a hut. She unpacked her bag and looked around. It was rather spartan like most of the billets but it would be comfortable enough.

She had stowed away her things in a tall cupboard by the bed, and was wondering what she should do next when a pretty WAAF walked into the hut, checked Annie's badge, and held her hand out.

'I'm Jean. Welcome to Cheadle Intercept Station. If you're ready, I'll take you to the ops room. I've been ordered to take you there as soon as you arrive.' Jean gave Annie a curious look. 'They've been waiting for you. Are you someone special?'

'Me?' Annie was surprised. 'You must be mistaken.'

'No, they've been anxious for you to get here.' Jean led her to the operations room and Annie gazed around wide-eyed with excitement. It was a large room and filled with men and women, headphones clamped over their ears. No one looked up as Annie came in; they were all concentrating on the job they were doing. The officer-in-charge introduced himself as Group Captain Jones, and then led Annie to an empty place.

She looked up at him, awaiting instructions.

'Each day you will be given a certain frequency to work on.' He wrote something down on the pad in front of her. 'This is yours for today. Take down any Morse code messages you hear, then ring the bell and someone will take it from you to be deciphered.'

She took a deep breath. 'I understand, sir.'

He held out the headset to her. 'We have received good reports about your abilities, and I hope to God that's correct because we badly need you.'

'I won't let you down,' she said quietly. Praying that she was right to sound so confident. This was her first time doing the job for real; her heart was fluttering badly. She told herself that she must remember her training and concentrate as hard as she could.

He nodded grimly and strode away.

It wasn't until Annie was relieved four hours later that she realized just how hungry she was. She took the headphones off and smiled, feeling elated. She had managed to pick up several messages. She had no idea what was in them, of course, as everything was in code, but it was interesting work, and there was always the excitement of wondering if it was something really important.

Jean was waiting outside the door for her. 'I'll take you to the mess.'

'Thanks.' Annie smiled at the girl. 'Are you a wireless operator as well?'

'No,' she said and laughed. 'I'm not clever enough for that; my job's in the office and running errands.'

Annie fell into step beside her. 'Do you know a cipher officer by the name of Graham?'

Jean shook her head. 'The name's familiar, but I don't think he's here.'

Annie was disappointed; she had thought there was a good chance of Jack being stationed here, and she would love to see him again. She'd missed him dreadfully; the fact that she hadn't had a letter or phone call from him had been upsetting. He'd said he wouldn't be able to contact her, but that was hard to believe. It was obvious that he had cut her out of his life, and that hurt.

'Hello, Sam,' Jean said, as they sat opposite him. 'This is Annie, and she's asking about a cipher officer called Graham.'

Sam shook hands with her. He was a striking-looking man; around thirty or more, she guessed. His hair was a sandy colour and eyes a deep grey.

'What's his first name?'

'Jack, Jack Graham.'

His gaze held hers but it was hooded, blank. 'Sorry, never heard of him.'

He was lying, but why? However, a lot of these people were engaged in very secret work, so she didn't probe any further. She knew there was another place called Bletchley because they'd considered sending her there, but changed their minds at the last minute. She'd heard it referred to as Station X. Very cryptic, but Jack was most likely there.

'Never mind.' She smiled. 'He recruited me, that's all, and I thought he might be here.'

'She's special.' Jean winked at Sam. 'They've been on tenterhooks waiting for her to arrive.'

Sam's cup clattered back into the saucer and he

straightened up. 'Of course, you must be Ann Webster, I should have realized . . .'

'I wish someone would tell me what this is all about.' She was becoming rattled by now. What was going on?

The man on the other side of the table studied her intently, and then gave a very slight shake of his head. 'You look too delicate —'

'I'm stronger than I look, but what's that got to do with my job? And you haven't answered my question.' She understood the need for secrecy but someone should tell her what this was all about!

'Ah, yes, why have we been waiting for you? Well, the answer to that is simple. You speak French and German, and you are a good operator; we are short of people with your qualifications. We are delighted to have you here, Ann Webster.' He smiled, stood up and walked away, effectively putting an end to the conversation.

Annie watched him in disbelief. The man wasn't telling the truth, of that she was sure. However, half an hour later she was back on duty with no time to ponder the mystery, and it was midnight before she finished. They were on eight-hour shifts and they'd put her to work as soon as she'd arrived, not giving her a chance to settle in. Good job Jean had been there to show her around or she would have been wandering about lost. As she crawled into bed she was exhausted but quite pleased with herself. She felt as if she was doing something positive at last.

Her mind raced around for a while, denying her much needed sleep, but eventually she began to relax, listening to the other nine girls in the hut fidgeting. One right down the other end was snoring, but the sounds didn't disturb her. It was surprising how quickly she had become used to sharing a barren hut with lots of girls she'd never met before. She often remembered the fun they'd had on their first day in the WAAF when she had met Dora. What a good friend she had turned out to be.

As she drifted off to sleep, her thoughts lingered on her family, as they always did at the end of each day, and she prayed silently for Bill, Charlie, Will, Paul and all the pilots, not forgetting every other member of her family. Her loved ones were scattered around fighting for their freedom. It was clear now that Germany hadn't invaded because they were trying to destroy the air defences first. If they succeeded then God knows what awaited this country and its people.

In the seconds before sleep claimed her she thought about the man she'd met today. He was strange and she had been shocked when Jean had spoken to him in that casual way. You salute a group captain, not plonk yourself down at his table and call him Sam! It was unbelievable, but he hadn't seemed at all perturbed. He was clearly right when he'd told her they needed operators, so perhaps she had made more of their conversation than she should have.

She smiled to herself as she remembered her silly suspicions. Sam, whoever he was, had no reason to lie to her.

8

'Look at that, do you see them?'

'There's hundreds of the sods!'

'I see them,' Reid said, estimating that they were outnumbered by at least ten to one, and there wasn't anything in the manual to cover this situation.

Someone gave a tight laugh. 'Where do we start?'

Reid took a deep breath. Oh what the hell! 'They're all yours, lads,' he called, then shot through the middle of the formation, firing all the time. He hit one Dornier, then banked, missing another by feet, and hurtled out the other side. Turning, he saw one going down, two more on fire, and a Spitfire with smoke pouring out of it; the pilot was already floating down. The planes of his squadron were buzzing in and out of the German bombers like pesky flies; ones with a deadly sting.

It was a wild battle, the third one that day. Reid, like the rest of his squadron, was numb with fatigue but determined to inflict as much damage as they could, whatever the cost.

His ground crew were waiting for him as usual when he landed, and set to work immediately to get the Spitfire ready to fly again.

Reid watched the planes straggle back. One was coming in without the undercarriage down, and a gaping hole in the fuselage. It shaved the trees, leapfrogged over a fuel truck and hit the field, tearing along sideways. He jumped on to a lorry heading for the plane. When they reached it he leapt on the wing before it had even stopped. Another man joined him and they wrenched open the canopy, dragging the pilot free.

Reid swore fluently. 'Bouncer! I might have known it was you.'

His friend grinned. 'Wow! That was what you'd call a bumpy landing,' he exclaimed, wiping oil and dirt from his streaked face.

'You crazy bastard, why didn't you bail out?'

'Wanted to save something of the plane if I could.' He pointed to the fitters now swarming over it. 'See, they're already after it for spares.'

'You're more valuable than a few spare parts,' he exploded.

'That's jolly decent of you to say so, Reid, but you know how I feel about throwing myself out of a plane with only a scrap of silk between me and the ground.' He shuddered.

'You're going to get yourself killed one day,' Reid muttered.

Bouncer shrugged and looked totally unconcerned. 'If Jerry keeps this up for too long, I think we all will.'

Someone shouted and Reid looked up to see one plane coming in on fire, and they watched helplessly as it exploded before it hit the ground. Neither man said anything; they would find out soon enough who it had been. There was now another gap in their ranks, and another family to mourn the loss of a son or husband. Dear God, he prayed, please don't let this misery be in vain. Make something good come out of the sacrifices.

They hardly had time to grab a cup of tea before they

were scrambled again. Two hours later, Reid slumped on his bed.

'I've brought you a sandwich and a mug of tea, sir.' The orderly was standing beside the bed.

'Put it on the table,' he muttered, and closed his eyes.

'Take your boots off, sir. You'll be more comfortable.'

'Might have to scramble again.'

'That's unlikely, sir. It's nine o'clock and the light's failing.'

'Good Lord, is it?' Reid opened one eye. 'What's the date today?'

'August 15th, sir.'

'Ah, one to remember, eh?' Then he was asleep.

Annie stepped out into the night air and took a deep breath.

'Hard day?' asked someone beside her.

She started. 'Oh, I didn't see you there, Sam?'

'Just come out for a breath myself.'

'I've been so busy I haven't heard any news today, though I know something has been going on.' The airwaves had been buzzing all day. 'Do you have any details?'

'Jerry's been coming over in waves, but he's suffered heavy losses.'

'What about us?' she asked anxiously.

'Quite a few fighters have been shot down. I don't have the exact figure yet, but it isn't nearly as bad as the Germans. So they tell us.' Sam sounded sceptical.

Annie's insides tightened at this news. Everyone was doubtful about the figures announced every night on the nine o'clock news. Our losses were always less than the Germans, but how accurate were they?' 'I've got a friend who's a fighter pilot,' she told him. 'I hope he's all right.'

'What's his name and where is he stationed?'

'Pilot Officer Paul Lascells, and he's stationed at Biggin Hill.'

Sam ground out his cigarette with the toe of his shoe. 'Stay here, I'll go and see what I can find out. Won't be long.'

As he disappeared back inside she couldn't help wondering, once again, who this man was? He was clearly a man with secrets, and expert at keeping them. He had a quiet air of authority about him and he was indeed an officer. But she hadn't found out what he did or how he fitted into the set-up here. His attitude to everyone was very informal and friendly.

He soon returned, but didn't speak until he had lit another fag, then he drew deeply on it and smiled at her. 'You can stop worrying; he's all right.'

'Thank heavens for that!' She felt herself relax. 'Thank you for checking.'

'No trouble.' He gave her a studied look, his eyes glinting in the gloom. 'Means a lot to you, does he?'

'Yes, I've known him a long time and he's a nice man.'

'Nice? That doesn't sound like a lover talking.'

'We're friends, Sam,' she said, surprised. It wasn't like him to start asking personal questions.

'Ah, no big romance, then?'

'Not on my part.' Annie tried to see his expression but his face was in shadow, and his voice gave nothing away. The questions were being thrown at her in a casual way, but she had the feeling that this wasn't idle conversation.

In fact, she was certain that Sam never did or said anything unless he had a good reason for it.

He nodded as if satisfied with her answer. 'I was told there are two Lascellses, and one is a squadron leader.'

'That's Paul's elder brother, Reid. Is he all right?' she asked quickly, feeling guilty for not enquiring about him sooner. She didn't know him but he was loved and respected by Paul.

'Yes, he's survived this day as well, but they've had a tough time, and I fear this is only the build up for a more intensified attack on the country.'

'A prelude to invasion?' she asked.

'Hard to say, but if the air force can hold out . . .' He shrugged. 'Who knows?'

'And can they, do you think?' She didn't know why but she felt she could talk to Sam; the fact that he was an officer didn't seem to matter. She wouldn't dream of being this familiar with any of the others, men or women. This man was an enigma and she was deeply curious about him.

He drew on his cigarette again, watching the smoke curling past his face. 'I believe they can if this kind of intensive attack doesn't last too long.'

Annie's heart reached out to all the pilots. They were in a frantic fight but they were giving the army time to regroup and rearm after Dunkirk. All the heavy equipment had been left behind on the beaches. All that stood between this country and the Germans were the exhausted pilots. 'They must be so weary.'

'No doubt.'

'I heard that Croydon was bombed today; is that true?'

'Yes, quite a few casualties, I believe.'

'Do you think London will be next?' It was her turn to quiz him; he was obviously well informed.

'Yes, I think it will.' Sam stubbed out his fag. 'What time are you on duty again?'

'Six hundred hours.'

'Then I suggest you grab a few hours' sleep, because I don't think any of us are going to get much rest during the next few weeks.'

Annie yawned. 'You're right. Goodnight, Sam, thank you for checking on the Lascellses for me.'

A light flared briefly as he lit another cigarette. 'Night. And by the way, you are doing a good job.'

'Thank you.' She started to walk away, then stopped and turned to face him. 'Why does everyone call you Sam?'

'That's my name.'

She gave an exasperated sigh. 'I know that, but I've never heard anyone call you sir, and yet you are an officer. And you seem to know a great deal, so just who are you?'

'No one you need be concerned about, Ann Webster. Yet.'

Information was a precious commodity, and in a quiet way the wireless operators were in the front line as well. Annie's hours on duty were long, and although she was fully aware of the seriousness of the war she was rather insulated in her operations room. There hadn't been time for leave or even a night out at the local pub. When she did finally get to leave her post all she wanted to do was sleep. She'd hardly had time to see Jean, who had become a firm friend, but they did manage to grab a meal together now and again.

Annie decided to make one more sweep of her frequency for that day when something came through her headset. It was very faint and interference from a radio station made it even more difficult, so she pressed her headset close to her ears in an effort to hear. The message started to come through but she could only get part of it. Damn!

Sitting back, she snatched off the headset and rang the bell. 'I couldn't get it all, there was too much interference,' she apologized to the officer who collected it from her, ready to be sent with the next despatch rider to the deciphering unit.

Annie put the headphones back on and settled down again, hoping she was going to be relieved soon. She was dying for a cup of tea and her ears were ringing. Even when she took the headphones off she could still hear the bleeping of Morse code in her head.

It was lunchtime the next day when Sam came and sat beside her. 'We want you to see if you can pick up another message from the sender you found last night. Do you think you can find him again?'

'Yes, if he transmits, I'm sure I can. Was it something important?'

'Maybe. We can only wait until he sends again, and then, hopefully, we can find out who it is.'

Annie knew she wouldn't be told anything else. It was frustrating not to know what the messages said when they picked them up, but everything was in code, and that was the job. 'That sounds exciting.'

'You like a bit of excitement, do you?' Sam asked.

'I've never thought about it, but I suppose I must.' She was beginning to uncover emotions in herself she hadn't known were there.

'Hmm.' Sam stood up. 'Well, you've earned a break, so do you think a meal in the mess with me would be exciting enough for the moment?'

She placed a hand over her heart. 'I don't know if I could stand that much excitement.'

'Come on then,' he chuckled, 'I'll catch you if you faint.'

'Er . . .?' She looked around for Group Captain Jones. 'I'm not sure if I can leave my post.'

'Yes, you can.' He signalled to the group captain. 'We're going to get something to eat.'

He simply nodded his agreement and went back to what he was doing.

Annie walked beside Sam, puzzled. 'You act as if you outrank the other officers.'

'Well, I don't. I have a special expertise, and can help them out quite often.'

'Can I ask what it is?'

He bent his head and whispered in her ear. 'I'm a spy.'

'Ours or theirs?' she asked drily, not believing a word he said. He was more relaxed with her now, and she felt able to joke with him.

'Ours, of course.' He looked offended, but the twitch at the corners of his mouth showed he was teasing her.

Annie searched in vain for the rest of the day but the mystery sender never came through. 'I'm sorry, Sam, I don't think he is going to transmit.'

'Never mind, you've done well. Now all we can do is leave it and hope he tries again.'

'Who do you think it was?'

He gave an expressive shrug. 'We're not sure, but we've managed to decipher a part of the message and whoever he is we need to catch him.'

She knew she couldn't ask any more questions, so she nodded and returned to her work.

It was the early hours of the 18th of August when Annie was summoned to the ops room. Sam was waiting for her, a huge smile on his face.

'We've got lucky. A concerned neighbour reported some strange sounds coming from next door, and it turned out to be our mystery sender. He was working for the Germans.'

'Oh, that's wonderful.' She was elated.

'It's even better than that. He was careless and so confident he hadn't even made an attempt to hide anything.'

Annie looked at him and laughed. 'Now I know what you do.'

'And what's that?' he asked.

'You're a spy catcher.'

'Ah, my cover has been blown,' he said in mock despair. 'Now I shall have to retire and go back to tending my chickens.'

She didn't believe him but joined in the fun anyway.

'And where are your chickens?'

'I expect the Germans have eaten them by now.'

Her mouth dropped open as realization dawned. Why hadn't she guessed?

'That's right, Ann Webster, I'm French.'

'But you haven't a trace of an accent,' she gasped, 'and you don't wear that on your uniform.'

'It's on my dress uniform only and I seldom wear that. And I speak English well because I was educated in this country,' he told her in French.

He asked her many questions about her life, making her answer him in French. He kept her there for about half an hour; she didn't mind though, he was an intriguing man to talk to. He probed deeply into her family life, but did it in such a way that she found herself answering his questions without hesitation. When she'd joined up they had been interested in her languages, but she hadn't used them at all, and that was rather disappointing. She'd had visions of being asked to translate captured German documents. She smiled inwardly at her fanciful notions.

Eventually Sam sat back and reverted to English. 'You have a slight accent but it's hardly noticeable. Where did you learn to speak so fluently?'

'I studied it hard at school, because I loved the language, and then when I went to work on a women's magazine I made friends with Chantal who came from Paris. She was the chief editor and more than ten years older than me, but we became firm friends. We used to speak French all the time we were together, and I often went home with her for my holidays.'

'What about the German?'

'That was only at school. I was lucky enough to have a teacher who took an interest in me. He said I had a natural ability with languages, and to be honest I found it quite easy and great fun.'

Sam rubbed his chin thoughtfully. 'What kind of training did you have when you joined up?'

'The usual basic training of square-bashing and PT. Why?' More questions. It was almost as if he was gradually building up a picture of her.

'I have an insatiable curiosity. Go and get some breakfast now, you're not on duty until eleven. And thank you for helping us to catch a spy.'

'I wish I could have got more of the message.'

He picked up a pile of papers and began to look through them. She had clearly been dismissed.

After she had eaten she went for a walk in the grounds. It was a beautiful day and she lifted her face to the sun, feeling its rays warm and relax her. This was just the kind of weather the Germans liked to launch an attack in; she prayed that they would stay away for a while, allowing pilots and ground crew a rest. She strode out, giving her legs a chance to stretch and move, knowing that she would be sitting at her desk for most of the day. She was enjoying this beautiful weather, but the pilots must view it with misgiving . . .

'Annie!' Jean came running towards her, puffing badly. 'I've been searching for you everywhere.'

'Why? What's the matter?' Annie asked.

'Don't know, but something's happening, and you're to report for duty immediately.'

Annie didn't even say goodbye as she started running.

The Kenley airfield had taken the most terrible pounding. Reid propped himself up with two hands on the tail of his Spitfire and gazed at the devastation around him. He bowed his head, took a deep breath and wondered how many of them were going to survive this day. It would surely go down as the day the Luftwaffe tried to crush their air defences once and for all.

'Don't worry, sir, we'll get her operational again.'

He dragged his eyes open and saw his ground crew were as battered as his Spitfire. Ted had a filthy bandage around his head and John could hardly walk but they were working like men possessed.

Standing up straight, he ran a shaking hand through his tangled hair. Thank God the sun was going down. If he went up one more time he would be asleep at the controls.

'The mess has been flattened,' Ted told him in a matter-of-fact tone of voice, 'but there's a mobile canteen over by the ops room. Why don't you go and get yourself a mug of hot, sweet tea, sir. We'll have her ready to go again in no time at all.'

'Thanks.' Reid picked his way through the rubble and looked at the row of bodies covered with blankets. Some were obviously female and he hoped that Paul's girl was safe somewhere. And the thing that was worrying him the most was, had his brother survived this horrendous day?

'Reid.'

He looked up and saw the station commander with two young boys, no more than nineteen or twenty, he assessed.

'Two new pilots for you, Barrett and Johnson, and we've put you all in the house just outside the gates. The accommodation took a direct hit, I'm afraid, but the people in the village are offering beds until we can sort something out.' He gave his squadron leader a sympathetic look. 'Debriefing won't take long, then go and get some rest.'

'You've had a bloody awful time down here,' Reid remarked wearily.

'Yes, but we managed to get the airfield operational again in time for you to be able to get down,' he stated proudly.

'Do you know what state Biggin Hill is in?'

'They've taken a pasting as well, but I don't have the details yet.' The officer smiled grimly. 'The Germans were attacked so fiercely by you lads that they eventually split up and ran for home.'

Reid nodded towards the destroyed hangar. 'Have we got any planes left?'

'Replacements are already on their way.'

'What about pilots?' he asked quietly, knowing that the loss of experienced men was high.

'We've pinched some from the Fleet Air Arm, and a few Canadians arrived yesterday.' He sighed and walked away.

There was a wealth of meaning in that heartfelt sigh. Reid knew he was saying that things were bad. And there wasn't a pilot who didn't know that to be true.

Reid made the recruits wait for him while he went to report in, then took them to the house just outside the gates that was serving as makeshift accommodation. He chatted away to them on the walk over, trying to put them at their ease, but they were clearly nervous.

When they walked in they were greeted with the cry, 'They've blown the bloody roof off the pub, the bastards!'

Reid grinned at the outraged expression on Timber Woods's face. 'Has the cellar survived intact?'

'It has.' The landlord of the Crown staggered in carrying a tray loaded with pints of beer. 'Here you are, lads, have these on the house – what's left of it.'

Hands shot out and whipped glasses from the tray. Reid did the same and downed the liquid almost without it touching the sides of his mouth. The two new boys watched wide-eyed as the glasses were emptied in one swallow and placed back on the tray.

Timber slapped the landlord on the back. 'By God, we needed that, Harry.'

'Thought you might. Er . . .' He looked anxiously around the room. 'Where's Lofty?'

'Bought it,' was the only comment from one of the pilots.

'I'm sorry about that.' His sigh was one of deep regret. 'The wife will be upset, she liked that boy.'

Just then the door opened and a dishevelled pilot came in, reeking of fuel and smoke.

Reid peered at him, trying to see through the thick layer of oil and soot. 'Bouncer?'

116

'That's right.' He pounced on the last remaining pint, and all that could be seen was his bobbing Adam's apple as the glass emptied.

'Hey!' Timber shouted, thumping the sleeve of Bouncer's flying jacket, 'you're still smouldering, you silly sod.'

'I know,' Reid said in a resigned voice, 'you thought you'd save the plane instead of bailing out.'

White teeth shone through the grime. 'That was the idea but she went up as soon as I landed.'

'What did you do, then?' asked one of the new boys, staring in disbelief at the apparition in front of him.

'Ran, old boy, what else would one do?' Bouncer asked innocently, not appearing at all perturbed by his narrow escape.

'You're a maniac, do you know that?' Reid told him.

Bouncer shrugged. 'It helps.' Then he looked around the room, counting under his breath. 'Have any of the others returned?'

'Not unless they've landed at other airfields or bailed out,' Reid told him, knowing there wasn't much chance for the other three. He'd seen two go down himself and there hadn't been a sign of parachutes.

There was a brief moment of silence, as they each remembered their friends who were no longer with them. It was something the survivors faced every day but they kept their emotions to themselves, knowing they would be up there again the next day, and it might well be them missing or killed. But of course it wouldn't happen to *them*.

Bouncer turned his attention to the new boys who were clutching their untouched glasses of beer. 'Are you going to drink those or make love to them?' he wanted to know.

One of them held his out with a slight tremor of the hand.

'Thanks.' It disappeared in a few seconds, and Bouncer looked pointedly at the other glass. This was also thrust at him and suffered the same fate.

'Ah, that's better, I feel almost human now.'

Timber snorted. 'You could have fooled me. You look as if you've just risen from the fiery depths of the earth.'

The white teeth flashed again. 'Just as hot up there today, old boy.'

'Are you injured under all that mess?' Reid asked.

'Nah.' Bouncer examined his ruined jacket. 'Just scorched around the edges, that's all. Now,' he turned to the two boys, 'are you our replacements?'

They nodded, clearly speechless by now, and someone in the background muttered, 'Christ!'

'Well, welcome to Kenley, though you're not seeing it at its best,' Bouncer joked.

Reid introduced the boys as Barrett and Johnson to the rest of the exhausted pilots, then asked, 'How many hours have you flown in Spits?'

'Ten, sir,' Johnson said.

'Ei . . . ght, sir,' Barrett informed him.

There was another muttered expletive in the background.

Reid tried not to let his dismay show. 'When we've had something to eat, and Bouncer has cleaned himself up, you are going to be given some lessons on how to fight, then if Jerry will give us an hour's peace at dawn we're going to take you up and put you through your paces.'

'Thank you, sir,' they said, a spark of enthusiasm in their eyes at last.

At that moment the cooks arrived and everything stopped while they demolished the food.

Reid stood up when they'd finished and headed for the door. 'I'm just going to see if I can contact my brother. I won't be long.'

'That might be difficult,' Timber told him. 'The last I heard all the land lines were down.'

'I know. I tried as soon as I landed, but I'll have another go.'

Then the door opened and Paul limped in, leaning heavily on a stick. 'Ah,' Reid smiled in relief, 'I was just going to have a go at phoning you again.'

'Hi, Paul,' Bouncer called. 'I'm afraid we've drunk all the beer.'

'I'll bet you have,' he laughed. 'What happened to you?'

'Well, there was this bloody-minded German, and he insisted on shooting at me.' Bouncer looked scandalized.

Paul tutted. 'Do you know they did the same to me? One bullet went straight through my leg. Can't think what we've done to upset them,' he added drily.

'We keep hurtling towards them with guns firing and spoiling their fun,' Timber chortled.

'Come into the other room, Paul,' Reid said, 'and we can talk in peace there.'

Both men slumped into armchairs and Reid asked, 'How badly are you hurt?'

'Oh, it's only a scratch and I'll be flying again in a

couple of days.' Paul held the leg out in front of him and flexed it. 'See, no problem.'

Reid looked at his brother's tired face and was pleased that he would have a short break. 'Are you going to see your girl now you've got time off?'

'No, she can't get any leave at the moment.' He leant forward and smiled. 'Guess what? I was so badly shot up that I had to land at Tangmere and Annie's brother Charlie is there. He's a mechanic, and a good one, I was told. Will and Charlie always were a whizz with engines.'

Reid stifled a yawn, not really interested in this family, his brother seemed to think the world of. 'How did you get back here?'

'After the medic had bandaged me up, I hitched a lift.' He grinned. 'A female ferry pilot was delivering a trainer, so she dropped me off here.'

'Did you enjoy the ride?' he grinned.

'Not much, but she was quite competent. I offered to sit on her lap and fly the thing myself,' he joked, 'but she wouldn't hear of it.'

'I don't blame her,' Reid remarked wryly. 'So, will you go home for a couple of days?'

'No, I'm going to stay on the base. I want to get back in the air as soon as possible.' Paul gazed thoughtfully into space, then back at his brother. 'This has been the hardest day, hasn't it?'

'Yes.' Reid didn't add anything else, they were only too aware of the gravity of the situation, but he knew every pilot was determined to keep fighting. The thought of losing this battle was not something they were pre-pared to consider.

'Reid, can I ask a favour? If anything happens to me, will you look after Annie for me?'

'What makes you think I'm going to survive and you're not?' Reid asked, studying his brother intently, rather alarmed at the strange request.

He shrugged. 'I don't know what's going to happen, or if either of us will come out of this alive . . .'

'Good God!' Reid exclaimed, in horror. 'Don't even give that a thought. If that happens the parents will never forgive us.'

They both laughed, then Paul became serious again. 'I mean it about Annie.'

'Surely she's old enough to look after herself?' Reid didn't like the way this conversation was going. If his brother began to believe he wasn't going to make it, then he could start getting careless. He *mustn't* do that!

'I know what you're thinking, big brother, and you're wrong. Today has made me take stock of my life and I'll be happier if I know Annie is going to be all right should the worst happen.'

'What makes you think she needs a protector?' Reid asked, not willing to commit himself to such a promise. 'She's got a large family, you told me, and I'm sure she wouldn't want a stranger interfering in her life,' he pointed out.

Paul sighed. 'You don't understand. She's special, and if I'm not here to watch over her then I want you to do it. Is that too much to ask, Reid?'

There was such an intense look of concern on Paul's face that he knew he couldn't refuse. At least he could put his brother's mind at rest. He would never have to carry out this task, anyway, so there wasn't any harm in agreeing. 'No, it isn't too much to ask. If that's what you want, I'll see that Annie is all right.'

'Thanks.' Paul smiled and relaxed. 'That makes me feel a whole lot better. Have you got anyone special?'

'No.' Reid grinned, relieved his brother had dropped the subject of Annie. 'So that lets you off, you won't have to go looking after a girl for me.'

'Damn!' Paul remarked in mock dismay.

The brothers started to reminisce, laughing at the fun they'd had while growing up. They'd always been close and the three years between them had never made any difference to their friendship. Paul had always followed Reid's girlfriends around with wide-eyed admiration for his brother's pulling power.

'Seriously, though, Reid,' Paul said after a couple of minutes, 'you ought to have a special girl. You're not getting any younger,' he mocked, and then his look became dreamy. 'You find yourself someone like Annie. In fact, if I don't make it you can marry her yourself. I'd like that.'

Reid tipped his head back and laughed at the ridiculous notion. 'I don't think that will be necessary. I'll be very happy with her as a sister-in-law.'

'Yes.' Paul brightened up, his earlier gloom disappearing. 'We'll get married as soon as possible. In fact I think I'll ask her next time I see her, and you can be best man.'

'That's a date.' Reid stood up, pleased to see his brother back to his normal self. 'Let's go and get a pint. They've only blown the roof off the pub.'

*

When Paul had left and the rest of the pilots were flaked out, Reid and Bouncer, now somewhat cleaner, gave the new boys a lecture on how to attack and, hopefully, stay alive.

After snatching a few hours' sleep they went to the airfield just as dawn was breaking. Reid was determined that these young men were going to survive. Too many of them were dying within the first two weeks of combat, and that was terrible.

'Try to remember everything we told you last night,' he said. 'Once we're airborne we'll take you through a mock battle sequence.'

Barrett and Johnson nodded eagerly.

'And just one more piece of advice. Fly and fight like Bouncer, but whatever you do, don't land like him.'

They looked puzzled.

'He isn't called Bouncer for nothing,' Reid added drily.

'If you get into any trouble, for heaven's sake bale out.' Bouncer shuddered and Reid despaired of his friend. He was a fearless pilot and fought like a tiger, but the thought of jumping out of an aeroplane sent him into a panic. Reid knew he wouldn't hesitate, especially if the damned thing was on fire.

'Sir?' Barrett, the younger, asked, 'we've heard that the Germans shoot at pilots on parachutes.'

'Some do, the bastards,' Bouncer growled. 'They know that if we land safely we will live to fight another day.'

'Nevertheless, you are a valuable asset,' Reid pointed out firmly, 'and we need you alive. The planes can be replaced, but experienced pilots are a necessity, and the only way you can become experienced is to stay alive.'

*

And they did. Reid watched over them for the next few days, and saw them quickly change from nervous boys into confident, efficient pilots. And whenever they received more new recruits he and Bouncer tried to find the time to give them some training before they actually had to face the enemy. It wasn't always possible and there were always some who didn't survive for long. Reid found that hard to take but he continued to nurture and instruct his pilots whenever he had the chance.

IO

September 1940

'Have you heard the awful news?' Jean sat opposite Annie in the mess and wiped tears from her eyes.

'I've only just come off duty.' She reached out and took hold of her friend's hand in concern. 'What's happened?'

'The Germans have sunk a ship carrying children.' She looked up, her face stricken. 'How could they do a thing like that?'

Annie's heart lurched. Thank goodness Bill had vetoed the idea of James joining that scheme to evacuate children to Canada and elsewhere. His son had been keen to go but Bill and Rose wouldn't hear of it.

Jean blew her nose. 'The thought of all those terrified little ones in the sea is too dreadful for words. There's been an awful loss of life.'

'When did this happen?' Annie was surprised she hadn't heard about it earlier, but then she'd hardly left her post over the last few days.

'Two days ago, the 17th of September.' Jean grimaced and wiped away another tear. 'The *City of Benares*, I think it was called, and they sailed on Friday the thirteenth. How's that for a bad omen? This isn't a war of armies, is it?' Jean remarked with sadness. 'Innocent civilians are in the thick of it now. Look at poor old London, being bombed night after night.'

'Yes, it's terrible, and I'm relieved that my family are in Wales with George for a while, all except Rose, and she refuses to leave. She's working with the Women's Voluntary Service in London, and it's damned dangerous. I'm worried sick about her but she insists on doing something now the children are safe.' Annie gave a little dry laugh. 'Bill will be furious when he comes home and discovers what she's been doing. If anyone can send her packing to Wales, then it's him.'

'Annie?'

She looked up at the tall figure standing beside their table and leapt to her feet, nearly knocking over the chair in her haste. 'Jack!' It was four months since he'd walked away from her, but she was so pleased to see him. Her smile faded as she took in his appearance. He had deep lines across his forehead and around his mouth, and dark smudges under his eyes, which looked sunken in and haunted. There was also a lot more grey hair than she remembered. He had aged almost beyond recognition.

'Dear God!' she breathed. 'What have you been up to?'

'I need to see you, Annie. Have you got some spare time?' he asked, touching her arm.

'Yes, I'm off duty until six in the morning.' She'd planned to go to the pub with Jean, so she gave her friend an apologetic look, and nodded in relief when Jean indicated that she could forget their outing.

They walked out of the mess in silence, and Annie could hear Jack drawing in deep breaths of the early evening air, as if trying to revive himself. He was clasping her hand tightly; she knew that something traumatic

126

must have happened to him but she didn't speak, sensing that he needed time to gather his thoughts together.

He stopped just outside the camp and leaned against a tree, pulling her into his arms and burying his face in her hair. 'I hope you don't mind me coming to you, Annie? I didn't know where else to go.'

'What is it, Jack?' she asked.

'You've heard about the ship with the children on it?' he rasped as if in pain. 'My two boys were on it.'

'Oh, Jack!' She hugged him in sympathy. No wonder he looked devastated. 'I'm so sorry. Do you know if they're safe?'

'Both missing.' He swore in anger. 'I was against this scheme, but my wife went ahead and made all the arrangements while I was away.'

'You mean you didn't know they were going?' she asked in disbelief. How could a father not know that his children were being sent abroad? What kind of a woman would keep that from her husband?

He nodded grimly. 'Alice knew I'd stop her if I found out. When she brought up the subject a while ago, I opposed it, but she didn't listen . . .' His voice broke.

'She shouldn't have done that, Jack, but she must be grief-stricken now.' Annie looked at him with tears in her eyes. 'You should be with her, not here pouring out your sorrow to me.'

'I've been home for the last two days, and she's all right; she's with her family, and I needed to be with you.' He kissed the top of her head. 'Our marriage was rocky before this happened but we stayed together for the children, now there's nothing to hold us together.'

'Oh, please don't feel like that,' Annie pleaded, frightened by the tone of utter despair in his voice. 'They might still be found.'

'Please God they are, but I don't think I can ever forgive her. And I couldn't stay any longer, I have to get back.'

Annie frowned. What could be more urgent than Jack staying with his family at a time like this? 'Back where?'

'France.'

The breath caught in her throat as she realized, for the first time, what he did. What an idiot not to have guessed it before. She'd known that his work must be secret but it had never entered her head that he might be doing something so dangerous. 'You're working behind enemy lines?'

'Didn't you guess that when I left so suddenly and said I wouldn't be able to keep in touch?' he asked.

'No, fool that I am, I thought you didn't want to see me any more.'

'Quite the opposite,' he said, summoning up a ghost of a smile. 'That couple of weeks we spent walking, talking and laughing, was like heaven. I had just returned from a mission and your relaxing company was a godsend to me.'

'Jack?' Annie chewed her lip, deep in thought. 'Are there many people doing what you do?'

'A few, yes.' His tone was guarded.

'Men and women?'

'No, Annie!' He held her at arm's length, his expression fierce. 'I admit that was what I had in mind when I recruited you, but it's out of the question.'

'Why?' she answered with determination. 'My French is fluent.'

'No.' He gave her a gentle shake. 'You're too fragile and far too beautiful. Do you know what the Germans would do to you if they caught you?'

'Shoot me?' she asked.

'Worse than that, and after they'd finished with you they might shoot you, if you were lucky.'

Annie's mouth set in a determined line. 'I still think –'

'Forget it, Annie! I've told Sam that if he tries to persuade you to do this, I'll come back and kill him myself.'

'Sam?' Annie studied his angry expression. 'So that's what he's involved in.'

'Of course, and he's got his eye on you, so if he offers to teach you unarmed combat you tell him to go to hell.'

So many puzzling things were now becoming clear, and her mind began to whirl when she thought about what Jack and others like him were doing.

'Annie,' he growled. 'I don't like the silence. I can practically hear your mind working. Don't even consider it,' he pleaded. 'We need you here – I need you here.'

She looked up sharply. 'What do you mean?'

'I have persuaded Sam to let you become my contact here. I transmit regularly and I need someone I can trust.'

'I'd like to do that,' she agreed eagerly.

'Thank you.' He breathed a sigh of relief. 'Tomorrow you will be given my code name and call sign.'

'Tomorrow? But when are you going back to France?'

He glanced at his watch. 'I'm leaving in six hours.'

Annie almost reeled in shock. He couldn't go at a time like this, and he didn't look fit enough. This was madness!

'But, Jack, what about your children? Suppose they're found and they need you?'

'If there is any news you will be told and can transmit it to me, and if I need to come back they will send a plane for me, if they can.'

'I understand.' Her heart ached for this brave man who was still doing his job, even though he was burdened with a dreadful personal tragedy.

'There's one more thing I would ask of you,' he said softly. 'One of the officers is letting me use his room tonight and I need to get some sleep . . .' – he paused – 'would you . . .' He tailed off.

'What?' Annie wasn't sure what he wanted.

'Stay with me tonight. I'm not going to make love to you, I'm too damned tired, but I can't be alone tonight. If I could just hold you for one night I might be able to get some rest.' He grimaced. 'That sounds ridiculous, and if things were different I would want to love you very much, but a sexual relationship between us would be wrong for you.'

'Because you're married?'

'Among other things, yes.' He kissed her eyes gently. 'I'm too old for you and my life is in a mess. You deserve better and I would never do anything to hurt you, Annie.'

'Oh, Jack.' The tears began to flow down her cheeks.

'If you really wanted me –'

'Shush, don't cry for me, Annie. I don't want your love out of pity.'

'It wouldn't be for that,' she protested, but deep down, she knew he was right. She was desperately sorry for this lovely man and she absolutely adored him. She had never felt so in tune with anyone in her life, and she longed to reach out to comfort and take some of his pain away. 'I do care for you very much.'

'I'm too damned tired to take advantage of your generosity, and I'm glad, because I can leave in a few hours knowing that I haven't done something that will weigh heavily on my mind in the future. Do you understand?'

'Yes,' she whispered, 'and I'll stay with you tonight, Jack.'

When they reached his room, he sat on the bed, kicked his shoes off and held his arms out to her. She also removed her shoes and he pulled her down, nestling her into his arms with a ragged sigh of utter exhaustion. And he was instantly asleep.

Annie listened to his steady breathing for a while, and just before slipping into sleep herself thought, Dora would never believe this!

A movement in the room snapped Annie awake and she sat up, disorientated for the moment, wondering why she wasn't in her own bed.

Jack was in civilian clothes and standing by the window, looking up at the night sky. He turned when he heard her move.

'Are you leaving now?' she whispered.

He nodded. 'The truck has just arrived to take me to the plane.'

'Take care, Jack.' She stood up and wrapped her arms around him. 'I'll be waiting for your messages, and any word about your children will be sent to you as soon as possible.'

He smiled down at her. 'Thank you for staying with me, Annie.'

'Did it help?'

'Oh, yes.' He gave a crooked smile. 'I must be getting old if I can sleep with a beautiful girl and not make love to her.'

She chuckled. 'You're not old, you just needed some rest.'

'And I do feel rested,' he told her with a wry grin. 'It's a shame I've got to leave at this very minute.'

'Do you jump out of the plane?' she asked.

'Yes, but that's not my favourite part of the trip.' He turned her face to the window so he could see her expression clearly. 'And it is something you are never going to do, isn't it?'

'I promise,' she told him, wondering why the thought of parachuting out of a plane was so exciting to her. 'If you need me here, then this is where I'll stay.'

'That makes me feel easier. Now, Annie, I don't want to ruin your reputation, so try not to be seen when you go back to your own hut.'

She gave him an impish smile. 'You haven't done anything to ruin my reputation. I'm sure that sleeping on a bed, fully clothed, doesn't count as a reputation-ruining pastime.'

He groaned. 'Don't remind me. Nevertheless, I don't want people believing that I've taken your virginity.'

'How do you know I am still a virgin?' she asked.

'I just do; you are not worldly wise, and it shows. I believe you will only give yourself to a man you truly love.'

'You're making me sound deadly dull,' she protested.

She felt uncomfortable about the conversation. She knew that the danger and uncertainty of the war was making a lot of people's moral code slip, but she had resolved not to let that happen to her. However, she had been willing to make an exception tonight, but that had been out of pity and compassion for this man she admired so much. All the wrong reasons, in fact, and he had been right to refuse her.

'You are anything but dull, Annie, so you be careful going back.'

'Don't worry. If I'm seen people will just think I've been working late. We are often called out in the night.'

He hugged her again and whispered, 'I must go. Goodbye, Annie.' Then he turned abruptly and left the room.

She waited for about ten minutes after he'd gone, pondering that goodbye. It had sounded as if he was saying that he would never see her again. Then with a sigh she made her way back to her own hut. No one saw her and the other girls were fast asleep so she slipped out of her clothes and crawled into bed, her heart troubled. She could only guess at the things Jack would have to face.

Sam was waiting for her in the ops room at six o'clock that morning. Jack hadn't left Annie until three o'clock and sleep had been impossible through worrying about him. Their meeting had been too brief but it had answered a lot of her questions. She now understood why he had left her so abruptly four months ago. He was such a brave man and if she could have gone in the plane with him then she would have done so.

'Jack explained what you will be doing?' he asked.

'Yes, is there any news of the children?'

'Not yet, I'm afraid.' He sighed. 'Terrible business!'

Annie was desperately disappointed. 'I was hoping to be able to give him some good news. What time will he transmit?'

'Not until twelve hundred hours, but you'll have plenty to do until then. You will still be monitoring other calls for us.'

Annie settled herself down and picked up the headphones.

Sam put his head on one side and studied her face. 'Are you and Jack lovers?'

'No. Not that it's any of your business, Sam,' she told him, annoyed at his blunt question.

'That's where you're wrong. I like Jack, he's a very good agent, and I wouldn't like to see him get careless because of some slip of a girl.'

Annie bristled. 'I object to your tone of voice, and I certainly don't like being referred to in that rude way.'

Sam held his hands up in surrender. 'I'm sorry, my English has let me down. I should have said "young woman".'

She couldn't decide if she liked this man or not. One minute he was friendly and easygoing, and the next probing and insulting. 'You're a liar, Sam whatever your name is, because your English is as good as mine.'

He sat down again, his expression grim. 'This is a very dangerous business, and I don't like any of my operatives to be distracted by personal problems.'

She looked at him in amazement. 'If that's true, then why did you send Jack back when his two children

134

are missing? That is a monumental personal problem, surely?'

'I didn't have any choice, I believe Jack is man enough to handle the situation and not let it interfere with the task he has to do.' He ran a hand through his hair in an agitated manner. 'I didn't want to send him, but he's the only one who can carry out this mission. Jack understood that.'

'But you didn't want him involved in a romantic attachment outside of his marriage?' she asked, not prepared to let the subject drop.

'That's right. Jack's marriage was finished a long time ago, and I didn't want him to fall in love with you.' Sam pulled a rueful face. 'Love scrambles the thinking process and that can have dire consequences when you're behind enemy lines.'

'I assure you that there is nothing romantic or sexual between us, and I know it sounds corny, but we really are only friends.'

Sam stood up again. 'That's what he told me. I think he could fall in love with you quite easily, but he's got too much self-discipline to let that happen. However, I did agree to you becoming his primary contact because I believe it will give him some comfort at this difficult time to know you are here for him.'

'Thank you, Sam.' Annie felt slightly better now. At least Sam had explained, and she could see what a difficult decision it had been for him to send Jack back to France. This was the first time she'd seen uncertainty in Sam's eyes. If anything happened to Jack he wasn't going to be able to forgive himself.

*

135

It was a week later when Sam called her into his office. Before each contact with Jack she'd been praying to have some news for him about his children, but nothing had come through and hope was now fading.

'I've got some good news and some bad news,' he told her. 'They've just found a lifeboat and Jack's elder son, Steven, is alive, but the younger, Peter, has been confirmed dead.'

Annie put a hand over her heart and gave a ragged sigh. 'Well, at least one has survived; that is bound to give Jack some comfort. Is the boy all right?'

'He's been in that small boat for many days but I'm told he has come through the ordeal well.'

'He has some of his father's strength of character, I expect,' she remarked sadly. Annie glanced at her watch. 'He'll be transmitting in half an hour. I'll tell him then.'

'Keep it short,' Sam warned. 'You know he mustn't stay on too long. Don't let him chatter or ask questions.'

'I won't, I know the danger.'

In fact, they needn't have worried. Jack was a trained professional and took the brief news without comment, except for two extra words at the end of his message – *thank you.*

II

December 1940

Annie sat cross-legged on the bunk and eagerly opened the first letter. It was from Paul.

'My darling, I'm being moved to the Midlands for a while to give our squadron a rest. I was hoping for a spot of leave over Christmas so I could see you, but couldn't wangle it, I'm afraid. Still, I'm sure you'll have a great time with your family, and Reid's lot are also being rested, so no doubt we'll be able to amuse ourselves.'

Annie could almost hear his infectious laugh as she read the rest of the letter and put it back in the envelope. She was glad the two of them were being given a break because they had been in the front line for weeks without a rest. Paul never told her anything about the fighting, of course, but she heard stories and worried.

The next letter was from her mother and Wally, and his account of the exploits of the Home Guard had her in fits of laughter. Rose had added a footnote giving her all the news about the children, and how George was having the time of his life with them in Wales. Her sister Rose wasn't very forthcoming about her own activities but Annie knew she was in London almost every night. It frightened her to think what danger she was in. However, when her strong-minded sister made up her mind to do something then no one could sway her, not even George, who was doing his best to get her out of the firing line. Their rows were explosive, her mother and Wally had told her. Annie gave a sigh and looked at her other letters. There were hastily scribbled notes from her brothers Charlie and Will. Charlie didn't say much, except to rave about how much he loved being an air mechanic. She knew he was at Tangmere and the airfields had taken a pounding during the summer but he had come through it unscathed, much to their relief. Will's letter had been written weeks ago; with the strict censorship there was nothing to say where he was. The only one who wasn't mentioned was Bill, and that was because they had no idea where he was. News coming from those at sea was sketchy, and letters few and far between. Separation from loved ones was a fact of life all families were dealing with. With a sigh she put the letters in her bag, hoping she would be lucky enough to see some of them over the holiday.

Jean came in the hut then, all ready for her leave. 'See you in the new year, Annie.'

Annie gave her a hug, knowing she was going to London. 'You dodge those bombs.'

Jean pulled a face. 'I expect we'll spend quite a bit of time down the tube stations. Mum says it's quite lively there.'

After Jean had left Annie finished packing, sped over to Sam's office, and knocked on the door.

'Come.'

'I'm just about to go,' she told him. 'Thank you for arranging ten days' leave for me.'

'You've earned it.' He smiled. 'Have a happy Christmas, Annie, and don't worry about Jack, I'll look after him for you.'

She nodded, her expression sad. 'I wish it had been possible to bring him home so he could see his son.'

'So do I.' Sam twirled a pen around in his fingers. 'But it would have been too dangerous to move him at the moment.'

Annie was well aware of the peril Jack Graham was in, and wished with all her heart that he were back in this country.

'Don't look so sad,' he reprimanded. 'Jack knows what he's doing. Now, forget everything and enjoy your-self.'

It had been a cold journey as the trains were not heated, and Annie was grateful to get a lift from Pontypool station from a friendly local vicar. When he dropped her by the gate with the words The Haven painted on it, she stood looking at the house. George and Bill had certainly picked a beautiful place. There was a gravel path leading up to a solid two-storey house, built in a warm beige stone. It had four bedrooms, she'd been told, with room downstairs to fit in extra beds when needed. On the left was the neighbour's farm with a paddock between. A couple of donkeys munched hay in the doorway of their stable. They looked up briefly as she walked by, then went back to their food. At the back was a fairly large garden where the flowerbeds had been taken over and were now used for growing vegetables. Wally and George were turning into enthusiastic gardeners and were already producing a good supply of things to eat.

There was a chicken run at the end of the garden, next to a derelict brick building that had probably been a stable at some time. She stood for a moment savouring the peace; she was going to enjoy coming here now and again.

'Auntie Annie!' Kate hurtled towards her as soon as she arrived. 'Come and see my puppy.'

She allowed herself to be towed towards the kitchen by her excited niece, only having time to toss her kit into the corner of the hall.

Kate opened the door and peered in, then whispered, 'Is he still asleep, Mummy?'

'Yes.' Rose saw Annie and smiled. 'You found us all right, then.'

'Managed to get a lift from the station,' she told her sister, trying to control a chuckle. 'The Reverend Jenkins, he said his name was, and he seems to know you.'

'Ah, yes.' Rose filled the kettle and put it on the stove. 'We've had a couple of lively discussions.'

Annie burst out laughing, knowing her sister's *discussions* well. 'I'll bet you have. Does he know the Bible as well as you?'

'Just about, but like a lot of people, he takes it far too literally.'

'You mean you disagree on interpretation?'

Rose's grin spread. 'Of course, I've always believed that there's a golden thread running through the Bible, but like all things of value you have to dig for it.'

Annie felt a tug at her sleeve, and looked down at Kate, who had her finger to her lips.

'You'll wake Pirate,' she scolded.

'Sorry,' Annie knelt down to examine the bundle curled

up in a box by the old black-leaded cooking range. 'He's beautiful,' she whispered, 'but why do you call him Pirate?'

'Because he's got a black patch over one eye.' Kate carefully lifted his tail out of the way so Annie could see the animal's face.

The puppy opened one eye, then two, and fastened his gaze on the object of his undying love, and then he clambered to his feet, tail wagging frantically, and jumped on to Kate's lap. The little girl giggled in delight as she tried to ward off an enthusiastic wet tongue. Then she tore out of the kitchen with the puppy in hot pursuit.

'How long have you got?' Rose asked when they were alone.

'Ten days. I don't have to report back until the 2nd of January.'

'That's wonderful. We've seen so little of you,' Rose remarked.

'And I understand from George that the family hasn't seen much of you either,' Annie pointed out.

'Ah, been telling tales, has he?' Rose didn't seem at all worried by this.

'Tell me what it's like in London, Rose.' Annie settled down at the kitchen table and waited. If she could find out exactly what her sister was involved in, then perhaps she might not worry quite so much about her.

'It's terrible.' Rose shook her head in despair. 'The tube stations are packed with families, all sleeping on the platforms, but at least they're fairly safe down there. Up in the streets it's bedlam. I've never seen such fires and those firemen are bloody brave.'

'And what exactly do you do?' Annie prompted when

her sister looked as if she wasn't going to say anything else.

'Anything I can, but most of the time I drive an ambulance taking the injured to hospital or the dead to mortuaries. Quite often we can't get the vehicles through the rubble and when that happens I get out and start digging for survivors or help to clear the road. It's dangerous, but at least I feel as if I'm doing something useful.'

Annie felt cold when she pictured the scenes her sister had described, and knew that the 'something useful' was an understatement.

Their conversation was brought to a halt when the kitchen door burst open and James rushed in, throwing his school bag on to a chair in the corner.

'Auntie Annie,' he exclaimed in delight, 'are you staying for Christmas?'

She nodded and hugged her nephew, much to his discomfort. 'My goodness, you've grown.'

'I'm going to be as tall as Dad.' He straightened up proudly, and then left them to go up to his room.

'They've really changed since I saw them last. Are they happy here?'

'Very, and Dad loves having them,' Rose told her.

'Oh where is George, by the way?'

'Gone to get a Christmas tree and he's taken Mum and Wally with him.'

'Do you know if Bill can get home over Christmas?' Annie asked, knowing there was probably little hope of that happening.

'I doubt it, I haven't heard from him.' Rose began to peel the potatoes for dinner. 'We don't know if Will or

142

Charlie will manage to get here, either, but we are so pleased you could make it.'

At that moment, there was a commotion in the hall, and they went out to investigate. George and Wally were struggling to get a huge tree through the door with Marj giving them the benefit of her advice. It had become stuck and there was much cursing and swearing going on.

'Good heavens, Dad, couldn't you find one smaller than that?' Rose reprimanded as she pitched in to help release one of the branches and haul it into the lounge.

'There!' George stood back and admired it when it was safely in the corner of the room. 'That's perfect.'

Kate and James had arrived as they were struggling with the enormous tree, and were waiting patiently with the box of decorations. Everyone joined in the fun of dressing the tree, even the puppy and the cat.

An hour later, Rose called out, 'Leave that now. Dinner's ready.'

They all tumbled into the dining room, chatting and laughing, already in the holiday mood, in spite of the war. Rose was a master at producing meals out of very little and her cooking was always a treat. Tonight it was slices of spam fried in a light batter, and served with fresh vegetables grown in their own garden. The chickens provided a few precious eggs but these were mostly given to the children.

Annie was listening to James regaling them with tales about his school, which he seemed to love. In the background she could hear George trying, vigorously, to persuade Rose that her place was with the children and she shouldn't go back to London after the holiday.

'The children are safe and happy with you here, Dad,' she told him. 'I've got to do something to help the poor old Londoners. I was born and bred there and I still care what happens to it.'

George's sigh was resigned. 'I know, Rose, but I worry about you.'

The discussion ended when Charlie strode in the room and threw his kitbag on the floor so he could greet everyone. Marj and Wally were overjoyed to have one of their sons home for Christmas. Although Wally was their stepfather the Webster children now all looked upon him as a father. A place was made for Charlie at the table, and a plate heaped with food was quickly placed in front of him.

'How long have you got?' Rose asked her brother, smiling in delight.

'A whole week.' Charlie attacked his meal with obvious pleasure. 'I've managed to scrounge a few tins of food and I'm looking forward to some good home cooking for a change.'

'I only had a letter from you this morning,' Annie told him. 'I thought you couldn't have any leave?'

'Some of the pilots are being given a well-earned rest; the poor blighters are exhausted. The station commander said I was overdue for some leave, so here I am.'

After dinner George produced a precious bottle of whisky to toast Charlie's unexpected and very welcome arrival. Charlie savoured a mouthful of whisky, then smiled in amusement as he watched the children opening his kitbag.

'We'll do your unpacking for you, Uncle Charlie,' James told him, smothering a giggle as Kate let out a

144

whoop of delight and held up two oranges. Their Uncle Charlie was a great favourite and he always managed to bring a few treats with him.

'Good Lord, Charlie, where did you get those?' Wally asked. They were a very rare luxury indeed.

'I won them in a game of cards.' He smiled at the children. 'They're for you.'

Kate handed one to James and said seriously, 'I think we should save them for Christmas Day and we can all have a bit.'

'That's a good idea,' Marj told them with approval.

'Do you want an egg for breakfast, Kate?' Rose asked her daughter the next morning.

The little girl looked up from her task of feeding the animals and nodded. 'Boiled please, Mummy, with a nice runny middle.'

'Aren't we lucky to have our own chickens,' George said, buttering a slice of bread and cutting it into thin strips. 'With soldiers, sweetheart?'

Kate nodded, washed her hands, and then sat at the table. She tackled her egg with obvious enjoyment, dipping the bread soldiers into the yolk, then scraping it out and tipping the shell upside down in the egg cup, making it look like a whole egg again. Then she pushed it towards her grandfather.

'You can have my egg, Grandpa,' she told him with a straight face, then laughed in delight as he tapped the top and it crumbled. 'Fooled you! Did you finish the tree?'

He nodded. 'And we've put the presents round it.'

The girl slipped off her chair and headed for the lounge.

Rose and Annie went with her, followed by the rest of the family.

They watched as Kate checked all the names on the parcels. It wasn't easy to find presents these days for there was so little in the shops. Most of the gifts for this Christmas had been hand-made.

Annie knew that George had been clearing out his storeroom in the London house and had found a train set for James; Wally had been working away in the shed making a doll's cot for Kate.

'No peeking,' George teased, but she didn't take any notice.

'There aren't enough here for Daddy,' she told them with an outraged expression, as she ran over to the bureau and collected her piggy bank.

Annie watched her niece with fascination as she tipped some coins on the floor and started to count them.

'How much have I got, Mummy?' she asked, chewing her lip in concentration.

'Three and sixpence.'

'Hmm. That's not much.'

'What do you want it for?' Rose asked.

'I'm going to get a present for Daddy. He hasn't got enough parcels.' She gave everyone an accusing look, and then counted her money again.

'That's because we've sent them on to him,' Rose pointed out patiently. 'They'll be delivered to his ship,' Kate stood up and gave everyone a beatific smile. 'He might come home and I want to buy him something special.'

'Ever the optimist.' George gazed at his granddaughter with pride.

146

Annie marvelled at the tenderness in George where his grandchildren were concerned, and Wally was nearly as bad. The two men would spoil the children if Rose and Marj didn't keep a sharp eye on them.

Kate looked at the money again, and then she looked up. 'Have I got enough for a present?'

'Yes, plenty,' Rose said.

Annie saw George and Wally both put their hands in their pockets, but Rose stopped them with a fierce glare. Although George was wealthy and the Freemans very well off, Rose would never allow the children to be spoilt, and made sure they knew the value of money.

'Good. Can we go shopping now, Mummy?'

They all decided to have a family outing, so they put on coats and gloves against the cold wind and headed for the bus stop to take them to Pontypool.

Annie relaxed, determined to enjoy this time with her family. The worry about Jack was pushed to the back of her mind, knowing that Sam would contact her if she were needed.

12

Doubled over with laughter, Reid watched the lanky Timber Woods trying to do the tango with a broom for a partner and a drooping chrysanthemum between his teeth. Some of them had been transferred to a Midlands sector station for a short rest, and he was determined the men would have a good time. They'd pushed the tables back in the mess to make a dance floor. Reid had a surprise lined up for them.

'That's disgusting!' Paul roared. 'He took that out of the vase and the water's green with slime.'

'You don't have to worry about that,' Bouncer told them, 'with the amount of booze he's downed he must be well anaesthetized by now.'

'Why don't you speak English?' another pilot chided.

'You mean he's drunk!'

'I thought that was what I said, dear chap?' Bouncer gave a puzzled frown.

At that moment the door of the mess burst open and girls poured in. They were a varied selection – tall, short, blonde, dark and even a redhead or two, and none of them above the age of twenty-two. They had obviously spent a lot of time on their appearance, all were wearing colourful dresses. These were civilians, and it was a treat to see red, green, yellow and pink, instead of the dull colours of uniforms. Some girls appeared hesitant and others quite bold, but they were all gazing at the group of pilots with great interest.

'Wow! Comforts for the weary pilots.' Bouncer rubbed his hands together and grinned at Reid. 'Who managed to get that bevy of lovelies here?'

'I did,' Reid told the wide-eyed pilots, and laughed. 'I paid a visit to a local factory and asked if any of the girls would like to celebrate the new year with us if I sent trucks to transport them back and forth. As you can see I had plenty of volunteers. Well, don't just stand there drooling, take your pick, lads.'

There was a stampede then, and even Timber threw his broom into the corner of the room, spat out the flower, wiped his mouth and joined in the mêlée. It did Reid good to see his men relaxed and enjoying themselves. The horrors of this summer could be forgotten for a while.

Reid watched the scramble with amusement. It was funny how sober they all appeared now, even Timber, who had chosen the shortest girl he could find. The top of her head only reached the wings on his chest.

He waited until the crowd thinned out then walked over to a girl who was standing by the door and looking as if she was going to bolt at any minute. He wasn't surprised. These crazy pilots were enough to frighten any timid girl.

He touched her arm. 'Not thinking of leaving, are you?'

She started, and looked at him with large green eyes, almost the same colour as her dress. 'I . . . I thought . . .'

'I'm Reid.' He smiled, trying to put her at ease. She was

obviously doubtful about the evening, and he couldn't blame her for that. 'What's your name?'

'Hazel.'

'I'm pleased to meet you, Hazel. Would you like a drink?'

She smiled for the first time. 'Yes, please.'

He led her over to the bar and thought he hadn't done too badly. She was no beauty, but she had nice eyes, and a refined air about her. It could turn out to be a pleasant New Year's Eve.

As he handed her a drink, he couldn't help wondering what 1941 would be like. He hoped that it wasn't as frantic as the last few months had been, but he didn't entertain the thought for long. This was a time for enjoyment, and whatever they had to face in the coming year would be dealt with then.

The holiday had flown by for Annie but it had been wonderful to have some time with her family. The house in Wales was a lovely place to relax, and The Haven was an apt name. Her mother, Wally, George and the children were there all the time now as Kate and James had settled into new schools; it was an open house for anyone who wanted to get away from the war for a while. Wally had transferred to another Home Guard unit, and he often had members of his squad lodging there when they were on duty in the area. Rose wouldn't stay though and spent most of her time in London. But that was Rose, and no one expected her to do anything else. George was still very vocal in his objections to her activities but it was a waste of time.

A car pulled up and Annie glanced out of the window.

If that was her lift then he was far too early, she had another two hours yet before her train left. She was about to turn away from the window when the front door burst open and the children erupted through it, giving wild screams of delight.

Annie watched the tall man get out and gasped in delight. Bill! She hurtled down the stairs and joined in the excitement, waiting patiently for her turn to give Bill a hug. He looked very tired and moved slowly, but was laughing and joking with the children, obviously delighted to see them and everyone again, especially Rose, whom he loved deeply. The gentle smile he gave her spoke volumes.

'Dad?' James was studying his father anxiously as he sat wearily on the settee. 'You are limping. Are you all right?'

Bill patted the seat beside him for James to sit down and pulled Kate on to his lap. 'It's nothing. My ship was torpedoed and we spent a few hours in a lifeboat, but someone soon found us.'

Bill gazed over the top of his daughter's head for a few moments as a look of pain crossed his face, then he smiled. 'I can stay here until they find me another ship; hopefully that might take a while.'

Annie was pleased to see the tension gradually leave Bill's face. A few days at home relaxing with his family was just what he needed.

Marj bustled in with a tray of tea and Wally snorted in disgust. 'Good Lord, Bill needs something stronger than that!'

'It's only eleven o'clock in the morning.' Marj was obviously scandalized.

'Tea will do fine.' Bill winked at Wally. 'You can save the stronger stuff for later. Now, tell me what you've all been up to?'

They were chatting away and Annie lost track of time. When she heard a toot on a horn outside she glanced at her watch. 'Oh, I've got to leave.'

After saying goodbye to them all she picked up her bag and hurried out to the waiting car, wishing she could stay for a few more days, but content that Bill was safe for a while.

'Group Captain André Riniou wants to see you urgently,' a WAAF Annie had never seen before told her as soon as she arrived back at Cheadle.

She frowned. 'Who's he?'

'Er . . . I think everyone calls him Sam.'

'Oh, why didn't you say so?' She tossed her bag through the door and watched as it thudded on to her bunk. 'I've never heard his proper name before.'

Without wasting any time she hurried to his office, eager to hear the news about Jack. After knocking on the door, she stepped in and saluted smartly. 'Reporting as ordered, Group Captain Riniou.' The corners of her mouth twitched as he scowled. 'That's a nice name,' she told him. 'Why do they call you Sam?'

'It was chosen for me because it's short and easily identifiable by all the operatives. And I prefer to be called Sam,' he told her sharply.

She curbed her amusement, wondering why addressing him by his real name should have put him in this tense mood.

'Sit down, please.' He gestured to a chair and waited until she was settled.

It was only then she realized that his worried frown had nothing to do with her knowing his name. Something had happened!

'What's wrong?' she asked, feeling her whole body tense as she anticipated bad news.

He threw his pen down, sat back and surveyed her intently. 'Did you enjoy your leave?'

She nodded and waited patiently for him to speak again. He wasn't the slightest bit interested in her time at home. Whatever his news was it was something he didn't want to tell her. She braced herself for something very unpleasant.

'We've lost contact with Jack,' he said suddenly.

The breath caught in her throat and she leant forward. 'When? And what are you doing about it?'

'We've got to find him first, then if he's still alive we'll try and get him out.' He studied her intently for a few moments, and then seemed to come to a decision. 'How well do you know France?'

'Not all that well,' she admitted. 'My friend came from Paris, but she had a holiday home at Dinard in Brittany, and I spent most of my time there.' Annie willed her hands to stay relaxed in her lap, guessing where this was leading, and not wanting to show any sign of agitation. 'I can read a map.'

Sam held her gaze with thoughtful eyes. 'You are familiar with Brittany, though?'

'Yes.' Her heart was thudding, but she spoke clearly and without any nervous haste. 'It's an interesting

153

coastline, and we used to explore along there all the time.'

He stood up, went over to a large map pinned on the wall and stabbed at it with his finger. 'The last message we had from Jack was from here.'

Annie joined him and studied the map. 'That's only about twenty kilometres from Saint-Brieuc. What's he doing there?'

'No idea, but if he's still in that area . . .' – he began to pace the room – 'and we can locate him, we might be able to get him to the coast. We could then send in a motor torpedo boat to pick him up.'

'Suppose they've caught him, Sam?' she asked quietly. It was the question uppermost in her mind, and the thought of Jack Graham in Gestapo hands frightened her.

'I don't think they have. From the little information I've been able to glean there's been some trouble and he might just have gone to ground, afraid to use his wireless . . .' His words tailed off and he shrugged.

'But you're not sure?' They obviously didn't have much information and that was very worrying. Someone should know where he was!

Sam hit the wall with the flat of his hand in frustration. 'No, I can't be sure about anything, but I don't like this continued silence. It isn't like him, and if he's still alive then we've got to get him out.'

'Can you tell me what Jack's mission was in France?'

'He was there to help the Resistance destroy a certain factory. I can't tell you any more than that, but he shouldn't have been anywhere near Saint-Brieuc.'

'Did he succeed?' she asked quietly.

'Reports are coming in that it's been badly damaged.'

154

Sam ran his hand through his hair. 'We've got to find him, Annie. I've been told that his son is pining to see him, and that poor kid has been through enough.'

Annie held her tongue. Sam was experienced and would make a decision when he'd weighed up all the options, but he was obviously reluctant to abandon Jack to his fate. Something she was in complete agreement with.

'I wish I could do this myself but I'd be picked up as soon as I set foot in France.' He continued his restless prowling.

'Why, Sam?'

'Because my picture is plastered all over the place, offering a hefty reward for my capture.' He grimaced. 'I caused havoc with their communication lines and killed quite a few of them. They eventually caught me, but I threw myself off a lorry when we were going over a bridge and leapt into the river. I'm a good swimmer and managed to escape, but they'd love to get hold of me again.'

'Then you can't possibly go back,' she told him sternly. 'It would be far too dangerous!'

He sighed wearily. 'I know. And the added problem is that I've got the whole Resistance network in my head and those animals are experts at squeezing information out of their victims. I couldn't guarantee that I wouldn't talk – no one can.'

'It's out of the question, Sam,' she said gently, touched by his distress. 'You've got to find someone else.' She paused for a fraction of a second. 'I know Jack, and I'm familiar with that area of Brittany – you've got to send me.'

He sat down again and ran a hand over his eyes. 'You are the logical choice, but my God, Annie, Jack will kill me if I send you into such danger.'

'It's my decision and I'm willing to go,' she told him determinedly. 'I'm not a fool, Sam, I know the dangers.'

'Do you think you could jump out of a plane?' he asked.

'I won't know that unless I try, will I?'

He looked at her with renewed respect, hesitated for a few moments, and then surged to his feet. 'Come on, then, let's see what you're really made of, Ann Webster.'

This was the culmination of her brief training, and the part she was dreading the most. She was back at West Drayton where she'd done her basic training just after joining up; instead of square-bashing, she was swaying about in a basket under a balloon! If she could do this then they would fly her out from Croydon airfield. Annie took a deep breath, peered over the edge of the basket and her stomach heaved in terror. It was a long way down. She'd been all bravado when she'd volunteered for this mission, now she was not so sure. This last week had been hell and every limb ached, but this was the end of her very brief training. She drew in large gulps of cold air in an effort to calm herself. All she had to do was keep her mind focused on Jack. He was out there somewhere and obviously in trouble. She had to do this! She was the only one available who knew Jack, except Sam, of course, but that was out of the question. They couldn't waste any more time. Every hour of delay meant it would be harder to find Jack.

Sam eased himself beside her in the cramped conditions and she glanced at him, forcing herself not to show her fear.

'If you can't jump then I'll have to go in your place,' he told her grimly.

She couldn't let that happen. She knew he had already been frantically trying to find another operative to send instead of her but without success. If he went himself he could be signing his own death warrant, and maybe those of many more.

The instructor checked her parachute again, and then smiled encouragingly. 'I'll be right behind you. Come on, sit on the edge and close your eyes if you must, but you'll be missing a marvellous view,' he told her with a wink.

Annie gave him a withering look. This was not the time or place to make smart remarks. She glanced through the hole she was about to launch herself from, sat down and dangled her legs through the gap.

His grin broadened. 'Once you've done this then jumping out of a plane will be easy. Honest, everyone says that throwing yourself out of a balloon basket is the hardest.'

'Now that I do believe!' She was praying that she wasn't going to be sick and disgrace herself.

'When you're ready, jump.'

Forcing herself to keep her eyes open, for she was sure it would be much worse if she shut them, she gritted her teeth and dropped through the hole . . . .

'You blasted fool!' she screamed into the empty air. 'You're going to die!'

Then there was a jerk, her world of terror steadied and she laughed, albeit with more than a touch of hysteria. She'd done it. Gazing up she saw the balloon and two more parachutes coming down – it was a beautiful sight.

But the moment of elation was short-lived as she saw the ground coming towards her with surprising speed. Concentrate on landing safely, she told herself sternly. If you break anything then you'll never be able to go on this mission.

Detached from the earth like this, everything was very clear, she knew that this was something she had to do. She had to find Jack. She would regret it for the rest of her life if she didn't try.

Sam checked Annie's parachute again, his face lined with worry. 'I've managed to get a wireless message through to a Resistance group and they will be waiting for you.'

Annie certainly hoped they were. With a brief nod of her head she walked towards the DC3, its engines already running. It was a cold but clear night, and moonlight was shining on the camouflage colours, giving it an almost ghostly appearance. She forced her legs to keep moving towards the airman waiting by the door for her; this was no time to let her silly imagination run riot.

'My name's Healey,' he told her, 'and the pilot is Group Captain Andrews, one of the best in the business. He'll get you safely to your destination.'

Annie's stomach did an unpleasant somersault. Dear Lord, she hoped so!

He helped her in, and as soon as the door was closed they were hurtling along the runway. Once they were airborne, Annie closed her eyes and laid her head back. It was too late to change her mind now; she would have to deal with her fears. It was too noisy to be able to talk above the roar of the engines and she was glad about that. She found the motion of the plane rather soothing and her mind drifted. Sam had given her every opportunity to chicken out of this mission but she had refused. She wondered what her family would say if they knew she was on her way to parachute into France. They'd be worried sick, just as she was herself.

The time passed without her noticing and she was startled when someone tapped her on the shoulder.

Healey held up five fingers to let her know it was nearly time. She stood up and was horrified to find her legs shaking badly. She had to clench her mouth to stop her teeth chattering. Heavens, she was in a state, and this wouldn't do!

The door had been opened now and she could feel the cold air rushing in. And then a strange thing happened – suddenly she was calm and focused on the task ahead of her. She made her way to the open door, and when Healey shouted 'Go!' she stepped out into space.

Once the chute opened she peered into the gloom and wished the moon would come out again just for a moment so she could see her landing site. The instructor had been wrong – this was much more terrifying than jumping from the balloon in daylight. At least she'd been able to see what was beneath her then, but the moon had chosen this moment to go behind a cloud and it looked just like an empty dark pit beneath her . . .

As she hit the ground every bone in her body was jarred and the breath knocked out of her, but she hadn't injured herself – that had been her greatest fear. Thank heavens she'd missed the trees. It had been a close thing and one part of her parachute was snagged on a lower branch. The plane she had come in had already disappeared and there was darkness and silence everywhere. The drop zone was as close to Saint-Brieuc as possible. She hoped the pilot had found the right field because she couldn't see a damned thing.

Two men and a woman appeared out of the trees and ran towards her, quickly freeing her and rolling the chute into a bundle. They already had a hole dug and it was soon expertly hidden.

'Come, come!' the woman whispered, 'we must hurry.'

The men were barking out orders, and Annie was glad her French was fluent as they were speaking hurriedly and in hushed tones.

Annie didn't have time to ask questions until they reached a secluded farmhouse, then they introduced themselves. The man who was obviously the leader shook her hand.

'My name is Pierre, and this is Marcel and Christine.' She shook their hands. 'Annie.' It had been decided that she should use her own name because if she couldn't find Jack then he might hear it and come to her.

'Welcome, Annie, you must be hungry. Sit down and Christine will give us some food.'

Annie sat at the large kitchen table and hoped she could eat. That jump into the darkness had been terrifying and hadn't done her stomach any good, but common sense made her pick up the spoon and start eating as if she was starving. It wouldn't do to show any sign of weakness. These brave people lived with the danger every

160

day but she would only be here for a short time if all went well.

'You know why I'm here?' she asked.

Pierre nodded. 'We were told you are looking for someone.'

At that moment the door opened and a small man slipped into the room.

'Ah, Pascal, have you had any luck?'

'Maybe.' He eyed Annie suspiciously.

'This is Annie,' Pierre told him. 'She has just arrived. Now tell us what you've found out.'

The man sat down next to Annie, and she instinctively wanted to edge away from him. He wasn't very tall but he looked tough and not at all happy to see her. She couldn't blame him for his caution because she knew that her presence here was a danger to them all. He kept glancing at her and shaking his head as if he couldn't believe what he was seeing. It was obvious from his attitude that he didn't think she was going to be much use, but she was determined to prove him wrong.

'There is a man being hidden in a church not too far from here, but nobody knows who he is or if he is French or English.'

'Why?' Annie asked sharply.

Pascal glared at her. 'He is badly injured and has not been able to speak.'

'What does he look like?' she demanded. This surly man was not going to intimidate her. She was determined to find Jack and would follow up any lead, however tenuous. Sam had only given her a week to find Jack; if she weren't successful in that time she would have to return. Going back without him was something she was not prepared to consider.

'I do not know.' He started to tuck into the bowl of stew Christine had placed before him. 'The place is swarming with SS and I didn't stop to ask questions.'

Annie stood up. 'Tell me where this place is and I'll go there now.'

Pierre placed a hand firmly on her shoulder. 'No, Annie, it is curfew until dawn. You and Christine can go and pray in this church tomorrow. No one will think that suspicious and the priest knows her.'

Annie sat down again. Of course, that was sensible. She mustn't allow her anxiety about Jack to make her careless. These Resistance workers knew what they were doing, and would make sure she didn't do anything stupid. And what good would she be to Jack if she was captured or killed before she found him? The silence from him made it clear that he was in great trouble and she had to find out what had happened.

She held her bowl out for another helping of stew. 'Very well, we will go in the morning.'

It was going to be a long, anxious night.

13

It was eleven o'clock before Annie and Christine reached the church the next morning. It was in a tiny village about twelve kilometres from Saint-Brieuc and, according to Annie's map, another five more kilometres from the coast. The journey had been nerve-racking for her, as she expected a hand on her shoulder at any moment. Annie and Christine were on bicycles and it took every ounce of her willpower not to pedal faster when they passed German soldiers. She became even more worried when she realized they were heading inland all the time, because the man they had come to see was badly injured, and if it was Jack then the journey back to the coast was going to be a long one for a sick man.

They slipped into a pew and Annie bowed her head in prayer. There were two Waffen SS soldiers in the old church and they weren't there to pray. They were standing at the back and watching everyone as they came in and went out. It was frightening, but Annie copied everything her companion did, and pulled the headscarf forward so it covered more of her face.

After about half an hour Christine whispered that if the SS men didn't go soon they would have to abandon any action for today. If they stayed there bowed in prayer for much longer then it would look suspicious.

Annie rested her forehead in her hands, certain that the Germans must be able to hear the thump of her heart, but she was reluctant to leave until she'd found out if it was Jack in the crypt. If it wasn't him then she would have to start searching. She had a rough idea of where his last message came from and that would be the place to start.

She prayed that it wasn't Jack being hidden here, because this church was about twenty kilometres from the coast; that was a long way when you had to move with stealth.

Christine made Annie jump when she touched her arm a few minutes later. 'They've gone. Quickly.'

Annie followed her as she lifted aside a curtain and opened a heavy oak door. This led to a flight of worn stone steps. At the bottom was a dark, bleak room. A makeshift bed had been made up behind a large marble tomb, and the priest, who was bathing a man's face, looked up anxiously.

'You must move him,' he said. 'It is getting too dangerous to keep him here. Two men of the Resistance brought him here; they could do no more for him, and left immediately because they were being hunted. I'm sure the SS are suspicious.'

Annie rushed to the bed and knelt down beside the injured man. It was hard to see his face in the gloom. He had a couple of weeks' growth of beard. She pushed his hair away from his forehead and felt like crying out in panic. She didn't know if it was Jack or not.

'Is it your friend?' Christine asked.

She was about to say that she didn't know when the man opened his eyes and looked directly at her. They glittered with fever and pain but she would have recognized the bright blue anywhere. It *was* Jack Graham.

She bent over and kissed his cheek. He muttered something. He was delirious and clearly didn't know who she was but she whispered, 'I'll get you home, Jack.'

'Come.' Christine pulled her to her feet. 'We will tell the men and they will move him today.'

'But how?'

'We will leave that to them, but now I will take you to the first safe house on the route and they will bring him to you.'

Annie never asked how Pierre and the others managed to spirit Jack out of the crypt right under the noses of the Germans, she was only too relieved they succeeded. Over the next three days they moved from one safe house to another, all the time getting nearer to the coast, but progress was slow and she was so afraid Jack was going to die. She prayed, talked to him and held his hand, refusing to leave his side for more than a couple of minutes at a time. If only he could know she was with him it might give him some comfort; but he didn't appear to know her, and when he did occasionally open his eyes she saw no sign of recognition in them. The only response from him was a moan every time they moved him. He was suffering and it nearly broke Annie's heart but she controlled her distress. These brave Resistance workers were risking their lives to help and she was not going to add to their problems by causing a fuss. As she nursed Jack she felt like screaming – *he's dying*, we must move faster than this. But she didn't.

Annie was heaping more straw around Jack to try to keep him warm when she heard voices – German voices! Her heart crashed against her ribs when the barn door opened and the soldiers came in. Annie lay beside Jack and pulled his head on to her shoulder. She was so frightened. If they came up to the loft then that would be the end for them.

Annie prayed as never before. Jack, she silently urged, be quiet or we shall be discovered. His arm moved around her waist and he became absolutely still, just as if he had picked up her urgent plea. She bit back a sob of relief. Through his delirious pain, did he know she was here? Was he aware of what was happening? She pressed her lips to his hot brow, and listened to the Germans below, hardly daring to breath. Were they looking for them?

The barn door scraped open again and Annie heard the farmer urging the soldiers to come into the house for food and a warm fire. He sounded so friendly and accommodating but Annie knew the Frenchman was only trying to get them away from the barn. The Germans didn't need much persuading and abandoned their search. As they all left, she allowed her rigid, tense body to relax, and sat up. That had been close. They just had to get away from here. But how?

'Annie,' Jack called.

She bent over him, her hope rising that he was coming round. 'I'm here, Jack.' But her hopes were immediately dashed when she saw that he was still delirious. She clasped his hand in hers and could have wept but she couldn't allow herself to fall apart. It was bitterly cold so she lay full length beside him, trying to keep him warm. Jack seemed to settle then and quieten down, so she stayed like that for an hour, until she couldn't stand the waiting any longer.

Scrambling down the rickety ladder in the barn she

166

peered through a small hole. There was no sign of the German soldiers. Annie had always considered herself to have infinite patience but there was little of that in evidence in this situation. Anxiety was making her want to take chances, and that was dangerous. Not only for herself but also for everyone who was helping her. The Resistance workers were too experienced at dodging the Germans to allow her to put this operation in jeopardy.

Annie sat on the floor and tried to calm her agitation, but it was useless. Where was Pierre? It was going to take days to reach the coast at this rate, but she knew she couldn't do this on her own – she needed their help. Then she heard a cart being brought into the yard and breathed a sigh of relief. At last!

With Pascal was a man she didn't know; he hurried in, shinned up the ladder and carried Jack down as if he were nothing more than a child.

'Quickly! The soldiers are relaxed and enjoying a good glass of wine, so we are taking you to the next safe house,' the farmer told her.

'And how far is that?' she asked.

'Five kilometres,' Pascal informed her.

'Is that all! We've got to make better progress than this,' she exploded, forgetting all her good intentions to remain calm.

'It is too dangerous, Annie.' Pierre had arrived. 'We have to go past a checkpoint as it is, so you will have to keep Jack quiet.'

'Can't we go another way?' Annie knew how difficult that was going to be; Jack was delirious and he groaned frequently.

Pierre shook his head. 'The farmer has to deliver the

hay to the next farm and it would be suspicious if he made a longer journey. Be patient.'

Annie bowed her head. She had no right to question the wisdom of these moves, but she was frantic with worry for Jack. He had been badly shot up in the sabotage operation, and although someone had done a good job in patching him up, each day that passed lessened his chances of surviving. He couldn't die like this, far away from his home and family. She wanted him to live so much.

The journey to the next safe house had been dangerous but they'd got through the checkpoint without being challenged. The farmer made this trip several times a week and was known to the guards, so as far as they were concerned it was simply routine.

Annie was relieved to find Christine there when they carried Jack into the house. The elderly woman with her had fresh bandages and some kind of ointment; without a word she set about tending to Jack's injuries. He had at least four gunshot wounds, two of which were obviously not serious, but despair ripped through Annie when she saw the other two. They were infected, and it was no wonder he was delirious.

She spun round, fists clenched, to face Pascal. 'How much longer before we reach the coast?'

'Not long,' he told her. 'You had better send a message now.'

Annie hurried upstairs, set up her wireless and tapped out the signal to Sam. It had been arranged before she'd left England and was only four words – *Wish you were here*. She waited, counting the seconds, because every one that passed put them all in danger. The reply came through quickly, and after deciphering it she went back downstairs.

'A boat will pick us up in two days' time, at two in the morning from a bay ten kilometres north of Saint-Brieuc. Can we make it?' Annie asked anxiously.

'We'll get there in time,' Pierre assured her.

When they reached the coast two days later, Annie was just about at the end of her strength. When the sea came into view and she heard the gentle sound of waves caressing the beach she nearly wept in relief. The sound and smell of the sea was the most wonderful thing in the world to her at that moment. They'd made it, and Jack was still alive, but only just. How he had survived the journey was a miracle.

They scrambled on to the beach and laid Jack in a sheltered spot to protect him from the biting wind. Annie shone the torch on her watch. They'd arrived with half an hour to spare. She walked forward until the water was lapping at her feet and then scanned the sea for any sign of the signal.

An hour later she was still standing in the same place and watching. Had she got the time wrong? Would they be able to come? Was this the right place? Oh, God, suppose she had come to the wrong beach? Doubts assailed her.

'Annie,' Pierre called softly. 'Over to your left.'

There was the flashing light she'd been waiting for. She let out a pent-up breath, returned the signal, then turned to the men who had helped her, and silently hugged them in turn. It was impossible to put her gratitude into words. 'You go now,' she whispered. 'You mustn't get caught here.'

They slipped into the darkness and she was left alone, watching a small rowing boat make its way towards her.

Two men leapt out. 'Where is he, Annie?'

'Over there,' she answered in surprise. 'You shouldn't be here, Sam.'

'Get in the boat,' he ordered. 'We'll argue about it later.'

The motor torpedo boat was a welcome sight and she groaned in relief as Sam tossed her aboard. Willing hands lifted Jack on to the deck and he cried out at the rough handling.

'There's a doctor with us,' Sam told her.

She tried to soothe Jack's pain, talking quietly to him, as she had done throughout this dreadful journey. The boat purred its way out to sea, moving as quietly as it could.

'Let's get him inside,' the doctor ordered.

Annie followed them and watched as they went to work on the dying man.

'How badly hurt is he?' Sam asked the doctor, after they had managed to strip the clothes from their patient.

'He has been shot several times, but someone has made a reasonable job of tending his wounds before he lost too much blood, and that has obviously kept him alive. However, I will need to get him to an operating theatre as soon as possible.'

The boat picked up speed as it left the Brittany coast behind, and Annie knew that England was going to be a very welcome sight. She closed her eyes as utter exhaustion swept through her and didn't protest as someone picked her up and put her on a bunk. Then, with all her responsibilities taken from her, she slept for the first time in days.

There was an ambulance waiting for them at Dover and they sped to the nearest hospital. When they arrived Jack was rushed straight into the operating theatre.

'Drink this.' Sam handed her a mug of black coffee, made by a kindly ward sister.

'Any news yet?' she asked, sipping the piping hot liquid. They'd been here for two hours; what was taking so long?

'No, they are still operating.' Sam sat next to her, studying her pinched and weary face. 'Is it any good telling you to leave?'

She shook her head.

At that moment the doctor came striding down the passage and she jumped to her feet. 'How is he?'

'I've done the best I could but his injuries are severe. If we'd been able to treat him as soon as it happened he *might* have stood a chance.'

Annie's head began to swim and she swayed as the floor seemed to be coming up to meet her. 'What are you saying?'

Sam had a firm grip on her and nodded to the doctor. 'Tell her the truth.'

'Well, he's survived the operation but I'm afraid he will not live more than a few hours.' He gave them a sympathetic look. 'I'm so sorry, but we've done everything we can for him.'

Annie gripped Sam's hand and took deep breaths to

clear her head, determined not to fall apart now. 'Go and get his son; I'll sit with him until you get back.'

The doctor showed them to a side room and when she saw Jack she knew the doctor had been right; he was not going to live. His breathing was distressed and he already had the look of death about him.

'Go! Go!' she told Sam urgently.

He left immediately and Annie settled beside the bed and took hold of Jack's hand. 'Sam's gone to fetch your son, so you've got to hold on a while longer,' she told him firmly. Then she began to tell him about their journey and all the people they'd met along the way who had been willing to risk their lives to get him to safety.

She had just finished telling him what a welcome sight the boat had been, when he squeezed her hand.

'Jack?' She stood up and leaned over him.

'Hello, my lovely,' he whispered. 'Thank you for getting me home.'

'Did you know it was me, then?'

He tried to smile. 'I knew it was you talking to me and soothing my pain. Having you there kept me alive, Annie.'

'So I should think.' She smiled and kissed him gently on the cheek. 'I wouldn't like to have made that trip for nothing, you know. I hope you're not going to kill Sam for sending me?'

'I'll let him off this time.' His voice faltered and he closed his eyes. 'I'm glad I shall be dying at home.'

'Oh, Jack, you're not –'

'Shush, Annie.' He squeezed her hand again. 'I'm not a fool . . .'

'Dad!' A young boy rushed in and Jack held up his arms to greet his son.

Annie stood up and quietly left the room. That gesture to his son had taken the last of Jack's strength, but it comforted her to know he'd been able to see at least one of his sons.

'Who are you?' a woman demanded, following her out into the passage.

Annie turned wearily and glanced at her. She was petite and had probably been quite a beauty, but now her face was lined with worry. This was obviously Jack's wife.

The woman opened her mouth to speak but Sam interrupted. 'This is Annie Webster, and it is only because of her bravery that your husband is still alive.'

It was then that Annie became conscious of the state she was in. She was dirty, smelled of various animals, and still wearing her filthy and torn civilian clothes. She brushed her hair out of her eyes. 'I'm pleased to meet you, Mrs Graham.'

The woman looked uncomfortable. 'Oh, I didn't realize . . .'

'Why don't you go and sit with your husband?' Sam told her firmly.

'He won't want to see me,' Mrs Graham told them miserably.

'Of course he will.' Annie stepped towards her and lied. 'He loves you very much.'

Mrs Graham hesitated for a moment, wiped a tear from her eyes and went in to her husband.

Sam touched Annie's arm. 'Nothing we can do here now. Why don't you let me take you back to base?'

'No, I won't leave him.' Annie sat down again and

dredged up a smile. 'I could do with a nice strong cup of tea.'

In fact, it was three cups of tea and a plate of sandwiches later when the door opened and mother and son came out. The boy came up to her and gave her a self-conscious hug.

'That's from Dad,' he told her seriously. 'He said you had rescued him and I was to thank you.'

'He's a fine man, and I was pleased to be able to do it.'

'He just died,' the boy blurted out, but was quite composed. 'I'm glad I got a chance to see him. My little brother got killed when the boat we were on was sunk and Dad's gone to join him now.'

Annie didn't know what to say, but one thing she knew for sure, it had been worth all the trauma to get Jack home.

'He forgave me in the end,' Mrs Graham told them, wiping tears from her face. 'Will you both come to the funeral?'

'We'll be there,' Sam told her and scribbled a telephone number on a piece of paper for her. 'You can contact me here when you have the date.'

They watched mother and son walk down the corridor and Annie turned to Sam, her mouth trembling: 'That boy was so composed.'

'Yes, he was, but remember, Annie, he must have seen plenty of people die as that ship went down, even his own brother.'

She nodded understandingly. 'What a terrible experience for such a young lad, and now to lose his father . . .' Sam led her out of the hospital and into a waiting car.

'Time to get you cleaned up, a decent meal inside you and then you must rest.'

She nodded. 'I must look a sight.'

'No, you look beautiful.'

14

'And who are you?'

Annie hadn't expected anyone to be at the Roehampton house and was surprised to hear Rose's voice. She must have just arrived. The last she'd heard was that they were all in Wales to celebrate Wally's birthday. They'd just come from Jack's funeral and Sam had insisted that she take some leave, and made sure of it by driving her home. Coming downstairs, she hurried towards the kitchen as she heard her sister interrogating Sam.

'Group Captain André Riniou, madam,' he replied with a pronounced French accent. 'And may I ask who you are?'

'No, you may not!' Rose replied indignantly. 'What are you doing here?'

'Making tea.' He lifted a brow in query. 'Would you like some?'

Annie put her hand over her mouth to stifle a laugh and slid behind the door to listen. If Sam continued to act the polite Frenchman with Rose, then he could soon find himself in trouble. When her sister asked a question she expected a quick reply.

'I can see that, and if you don't give me a straight answer, then I'll box your ears, young man.'

Annie peered round the door. Rose could be very intimidating but Sam didn't look at all worried. He was carefully warming the pot before putting the hot water in.

Rose tapped his shoulder when he continued with his task. 'I still want to know what a Frenchman is doing in my mother's kitchen?'

'I've brought Annie home,' he said without a trace of accent.

'Well, why the devil didn't you say so? Where is she?' Annie stepped out from behind the door and Rose touched her arm gently and smiled a welcome, but Annie knew her sister had noticed just how exhausted she was.

'Right,' Rose said lightly, 'as the tea's made we might as well all have a cup. Sit down, young man, you're making the place look untidy.'

Sam looked hurt. 'I'll have you know, madam, that this is my best dress uniform.'

'Oh, very pretty,' Rose put enough cups on the table.

'Do you take sugar, André?'

'No, thank you, and the name is Sam.'

'And that's as phoney as the fake accent,' Rose declared. He grinned.

Annie was seeing a different side to this enigmatic man, and he was clearly enjoying sparring with Rose.

As the first cup of tea was poured, Rose tutted in disgust. 'That looks like gnats.'

Sam placed elbows on the table and studied the tea for a moment. 'What's gnats?' he asked mildly.

'You know very well what I mean,' Rose scolded. 'That tea is too weak to struggle out of the pot.' She stirred it vigorously, poured another cup and shook her head in disgust.

'Ah, well,' Sam said, his accent reappearing, 'you can't expect a Frenchman to know how to make a proper cup of tea, can you?'

Rose's expression didn't change as she emptied the pot and started again.

'We didn't expect anyone to be here,' Annie said, changing the subject. 'I thought you were all in Wales at the moment.'

'Oh?' Rose popped the cosy on the pot, and gave Sam a questioning look. 'Wanted to be alone, did you?'

'Not for the reason you are implying,' he told her, holding the dark, accusing stare unflinchingly. 'Your sister has had a difficult time and needs rest. I shall be leaving within the hour.'

'I see. Well, I live next door and you're welcome to stay if you wish,' Rose informed him, clearly backing down, which was unusual for her.

And Annie knew that was as close to an apology as he was going to get.

'Thank you, but I have to get back.' His grin broadened. 'Are you not afraid to have a lecherous Frenchman in your house, madam?'

Rose controlled a smile, stirred the pot until the tea was a respectable colour, poured two cups and handed them to Annie and Sam. 'I'm sure I could keep you in line, young man.'

'I don't doubt it.' Sam gave a deep chuckle of amusement.

Sam was at ease with Rose, and her sister had clearly taken to him. Annie couldn't help wondering if he had lost more than his home when the Germans had invaded France. He wasn't much older than her, but he might have had a wife and children.

'And what is your job?' Rose asked, eyeing Sam's uniform with interest.

178

He shrugged expressively. 'Oh, this and that, but my main task is making a nuisance of myself. I'm very good at it.'

'That I can believe,' Rose replied with feeling, and then spoilt the serious expression by grinning.

Annie started to laugh at their antics, but something happened, tears began to stream down her face and she found herself crying in earnest. All the worry, fear, danger and distress had been enclosed within a strongly erected dam, but now it broke. She sobbed as if her heart was breaking.

'I'd like to know what's going on, Sam?' Rose demanded, placing an arm around her sister.

'We have been to a funeral,' he told her. 'It was a much loved and respected colleague.'

Annie gulped and wiped her eyes, thoroughly ashamed of herself for breaking down. 'I'm so sorry.'

'There is no need to be.' Sam reached out and took hold of her hand. 'It is right that we should shed tears for Jack.'

'Have you?' she asked.

'Of course.' He gave a gentle smile. 'We French do not believe in the stiff upper lip; if we need to cry then we do. There is no shame in it, Annie.'

The tears began to flow again and she forgot there was anyone else in the room. This was the first time she had allowed her true feelings to surface and it was painful. She had loved and admired Jack Graham, feeling a closeness to him that she had known with very few outside her own family. It was almost as if she had lost a part of herself. 'I feel as if I failed him, Sam.'

'No, no, it was because of you he died in peace with

179

his family around him, and in his own country. That was not a failure – it was a triumph.'

Annie blew her nose and nodded. 'Yes, of course. I'm sorry, I'm just being silly.'

He squeezed her hand affectionately. 'You are a very brave girl, Ann Webster, and I'm proud to know you.'

'I suppose it's no good asking you what this is all about, is it?' Rose asked again, and looked enquiringly at Sam.

He shook his head. 'I'm afraid not, but I will tell you one thing, your sister has great courage, and when the story can be told you will be as proud of her as we are.'

'We've always been proud of her,' Rose told him. 'Would you like to stay for dinner?'

'No, thank you.' He stood up. 'I must be going.'

He bowed to Rose, and then he lifted Annie's chin. 'You rest now, do you understand?'

'I promise,' she said, and then he was gone.

'Where on earth did you find him?' Rose asked.

Annie felt much better after her bout of tears. 'He just turned up one day.'

Rose sat back, clearly intrigued. 'Tell me about him.'

'All I know is that he was in France when the Germans invaded; he caused a lot of trouble and had to leave quickly. I don't know anything else about him. He never talks about his private life.'

'Hmm, there's a lot of fury simmering behind those eyes.' Rose gazed at her young sister and frowned. 'Do you want to go to bed?'

'Not yet.' Annie sat up straight again. 'It's nice sitting here talking to you like this. And I need to chat about normal, everyday things.'

180

Rose poured them another cup of tea and produced some biscuits. They had spent many hours in the past talking over tea and biscuits, and Annie found it very comforting at this moment.

'Why aren't you in Wales, Rose?'

'I can't stay there all the time, Annie, not when there's so much to do here. You know I love London, and it's taken such a pounding.' She grimaced. 'Talk about a drastic way to clear the slums.'

Annie knew her sister was remembering her battles for better housing when she'd been a young woman.

'You in love with this Sam?' Rose asked her bluntly, changing the subject.

'No.'

'What about this man you've buried today?'

'Jack.' Annie pondered for a few moments. 'We all loved him, he was a fine and brave man.'

Rose stood up. 'You going to have dinner with me?'

'Thanks, that would be nice.'

Rose slipped her coat on. 'Come over at six, then.'

'I'll be there if I can stay awake.' Annie yawned, feeling absolutely drained of energy by now. Jack's funeral had been held in a church near his Kensington home. It had been very emotional for her, and far too ordinary for such a special person he'd been. She'd wanted to tell everyone what a special person he'd been, but of course that hadn't been possible. It was doubtful if anyone there, apart from Sam and herself, had known what he did, or how he had been killed. Even his wife would not have known anything for sure, though she may have had her suspicions.

'This man Jack,' Rose hesitated by the door, 'Sam said

he had been able to die in his own country because of you. You taken a holiday just lately?'

'I took a little trip,' Annie held her sister's gaze and knew she'd worked out what had been going on. She would love to tell her the whole story but knew she couldn't. Perhaps one day . . .

'Thinking of going again?'

'I really don't know.'

'You be careful, Toots,' Rose said gently, using the affectionate nickname she had called Annie when she'd been a tiny child.

'Tea, Annie?'

She dragged her eyes open and sat up in bed. 'Thanks, Rose. How long have I been asleep?'

'You haven't been aware of anything for the last fourteen hours. You missed dinner but you were so tired I didn't bother to wake you.'

Annie stretched, enjoying the comfort of her own bed, then picked up her cup and sipped the steaming brew. When she remembered the uncomfortable places she'd tried to rest on her journey to the Brittany coast, this was pure luxury.

'Paul phoned me yesterday but I told him you couldn't be disturbed. He wasn't best pleased but he knew better than to argue with me.' Rose sat on the edge of the bed. 'You've been crying in your sleep. Do you feel better now?'

'Yes.' Annie rested her head against the headboard and closed her eyes. So her sister had been watching over her during the night; that was just the sort of thing she would do.

182

'Are you going to get up for lunch?'

Annie opened her eyes and smiled at her sister and nodded. 'It's time I got up and tucked into one of your hefty meals.'

'It'll be that,' she laughed. 'I've made a huge suet pudding just for the two of us, as you need something to line your stomach by the look of you.'

'Lovely, I shall enjoy that.' This was a great favourite with all her family, and it was a mystery how Rose was finding enough suet to make it these days. She might have found a substitute for suet; everyone was very inventive with their ingredients in these days of shortages, but if she had, then it wouldn't spoil the taste of the pudding.

'I'll leave you to get up then.' Rose stood up.

Annie watched her sister leave the room and felt like a child again having Rose look after her like this. It was a secure and comforting feeling. She had come back to Roehampton because she'd felt the need for solitude to come to terms with what had happened. Sam hadn't agreed with her about being alone, and he had been right, she was glad her sister was here instead of in Wales.

She went into the bathroom and ran a bath, filling it past the regulation five-inch mark without a pang of guilt. After the deprivation of the French trip she'd earned a little luxury.

As she eased herself into the water her mind replayed the sequence of events. After Jack died Sam had wanted her to take some leave, but she'd refused, feeling that she would cope better if she kept busy. They'd had quite a row about it but once the funeral was over he had insisted, and she'd been too exhausted to argue any more.

183

After a relaxing soak she dried herself and got dressed. When she was brushing her hair she sent up a silent prayer that there was a heaven, and Jack had been reunited with the young son who had been killed in that ship.

She gazed at herself in the mirror, saw the gaunt face with dark shadows under her eyes, and didn't give a damn about her appearance. She had done her very best to get Jack back alive, and she'd succeeded. The fact that he had died afterwards was beyond her control. . .

'Annie!' Rose called up the stairs. 'Lunch is ready.'

'I'm coming.' She turned away from the mirror with a resolute expression on her face. It was time to put the episode behind her. There would be more challenges to face before this war was over, and although she would never forget Jack Graham it was time she got on with her life. He would have wanted that.

They were in the middle of their lunch when there was a sharp knock on the kitchen door and Paul strode in, fixing his eyes on Annie and ignoring Rose.

'Where the blazes have you been?' he demanded. 'I couldn't get hold of you while I was in the Midlands, and when I rejoined my squadron a week ago there wasn't any sign of you.'

'It's good to see you, too,' Annie replied with a touch of sarcasm.

He studied her face and drew in a deep breath. 'Are you ill, my darling?'

'No, I'm fine.'

'You don't look it, you're so thin and —'

'Stop badgering the girl,' Rose ordered sharply. 'All she needs is rest and plenty of good food.'

He looked up quickly. 'Oh, hello, Rose,' he said belatedly. 'I've been so worried about my Annie.'

Annie clicked her tongue in exasperation, and realized in that instant that she had changed. The danger and grief had made her tougher and not quite so ready to put up with this nonsense.

'You don't own me, Paul.'

'Not yet.' He smiled affectionately. 'But I will one day.'

She was about to say something about this when Rose interrupted.

'Sit down, Paul. Do you want some suet pudding and treacle?'

'Yes, please!' He pulled up a chair, his good humour back in place.

Annie raised her eyebrows to her sister, who winked back, piling a plate high with pudding.

Paul would never get over this obsession with her and Annie knew that she was going to have to deal with it one day – but not just at the moment.

15

September 1941

'The CO wants to see you, sir,' Reid eased himself out of the cockpit and jumped down. 'Thanks. I'll just report in first.'

'No, sir, he said you were to go as soon as you landed.' The WAAF smiled, not trying to hide her admiration for the handsome man standing in front of her. 'He was insistent.'

'All right.' Reid sighed, removing his jacket and draping it over his shoulder, then headed for the office. He wondered what the hell could be so urgent. All he wanted to do at the moment was report in and then find himself a large beer.

The office door was wide open in an effort to catch any breath of air. It was unusually hot for September.

'Ah, Reid, come in and shut the door.'

The officer indicated a chair and he sat down, not taking his eyes off the man on the other side of the desk. He was shuffling papers around for no apparent reason and Reid wished he'd get on with it. This was unusual for the commanding officer; he was a brisk, decisive man and he never wasted time. Reid couldn't help wondering what had made him so ill at ease.

Suddenly he looked up. 'I've received some bad news. I'm afraid your brother, Paul, was killed today.'

Reid felt as if he'd been punched in the stomach and his mind started racing. He must be talking about someone else. Paul couldn't be dead. They must be mistaken . . .

'I'm so sorry.'

Slowly Reid's mind began to clear and he looked at the officer, who was obviously unhappy about telling him this terrible news, and took a deep breath. Pilots died every day and they accepted it, but he had never thought his brother wouldn't make it through to the end of the war. A vivid picture of Paul laughing flashed through his mind, and he only just managed to stop himself from doubling over in agony.

'There's no mistake? He hasn't bailed out somewhere?' he asked, clutching at a last thread of hope.

The officer shook his head. 'No, he crashed in a field just after crossing the coast. His body has been recovered and it looks as if he might have been dead before he hit the ground – he was badly shot up.'

Reid felt paralysed with shock. Paul really was dead. It was impossible to grasp; he'd had such enthusiasm for life. And at that moment he would gladly have swapped his life for Paul's.

'I've given you leave,' the officer told him. 'Your family will need you.'

'Do they know?' It didn't sound like his voice as he struggled for control. His parents were going to be beside themselves with grief.

'Yes, and you needn't return until after the funeral. You've earned a rest.'

At least they would be able to give him a proper burial, and Reid knew this would be some comfort to his parents, but it was a small consolation. They'd lost a dearly loved son and he'd lost a brother he'd thought the world of. He stood up, but it was an effort, and a feeling of the utter futility of war swept over him. At that moment he hated Hitler with every fibre of his being. The madman was causing anguish and pain to untold millions of people. He had to be stopped!

'One more thing before you go, I do have some good news for you.'

Reid wondered how anything could be considered good on a day his young brother had died.

'You've been awarded the DFC and promoted to the position of Station Commander at Tangmere. That's if you want it?'

Reid nodded, not really taking in the implications of this change. 'Yes, I do.'

'Good. You take up the post as soon as you return from your leave.' The officer smiled for the first time. 'You deserve this decoration and promotion.'

Reid felt sick. It seemed obscene to be standing here talking about medals and promotion, but somehow he controlled his emotions. The only thing on his mind now was to get home as quickly as possible.

Reid's journey to his parents' house in Thatcham, in Berkshire, was a blur of pain and disbelief. It was so difficult to grasp that he would never see Paul again that he expected him to be in the lounge, with his usual easy smile, as he walked in the house. But that feeling was shattered when he saw his mother prostrate with grief and his father struggling valiantly to hold himself together.

'Oh, it's good to have you home.' He clasped Reid in relief, gazing at his elder son as if he couldn't take his eyes off him in case he too disappeared from their lives.

Reid's mother was on the settee and he went and sat beside her, taking her hands in his.

'Did he suffer?' she asked hoarsely. 'You hear such terrible things . . . fire . . .'

'No,' he said. 'They believe he died at the controls and that was why he crashed.'

She nodded, seeming to draw a little comfort from that news. Then the tears began to flow again as she looked at him with frightened eyes. 'Are we going to lose you as well, darling?' she asked.

'I've just been given a station commander's job,' he told her, relieved that he could at least put her mind at rest in this way. Suddenly it hit him what this was going to mean – he would be leaving his squadron – and that was going to be damned difficult. He'd been too numb when the job was offered to realize this . . .

'Does that mean you won't be flying any more?'

'I expect I'll be too busy.'

'Thank God!' His mother laid her head back and closed her eyes.

'We'll go into the garden,' his father said quietly, 'and let her rest. The mind's a strange thing, you always believe that these things only happen to other people, don't you, and it comes as a terrible shock when it's one of your own.'

Reid agreed, knowing exactly how his parents were feeling, and followed his father. It was a pleasant evening, and they walked in silence, each lost in memories of the boy they had loved so much. After a while they stopped in the rose garden and sat down on an old wooden seat. Reid closed his eyes as the heady perfume from the flowers acted as a balm to his grief. He took in a deep breath.

'Beautiful evening, isn't it?'

'Yes.' Reid knew what his father was thinking; that his younger son would never sit here like this again. He opened his eyes and looked around. He could almost see his brother as a ten-year-old, running wildly across the lawn, and their mother calling for him to mind her precious flowers. Paul had always done everything with such enthusiasm.

His smile was bittersweet as the happy memories flooded in. How they'd loved this old house with its huge gardens. There was also a wooded area with a small stream on the boundary, and many times they'd had a severe telling-off for coming home soaking wet and covered in mud. It had been a happy childhood, and it was sad to know that any children Paul might have had wouldn't –

Reid shot to his feet and cursed fluently.

'What's the matter?' his father asked in alarm.

He swore again. 'Paul's girl, Annie something or other . . .'

'Annie Webster.'

'That's right.' Reid raked his hand through his hair.

'Have you ever met her?'

'Yes, a few times. She's a very nice girl, and Paul adored her.'

'I know he did, and he made me promise that I'd look after her if anything happened to him.' He started to prowl along the rows of bushes, touching one colourful rose after another. Damn, damn! he raged inwardly; he could do without this.

'She seemed a very capable girl, Reid, but Paul always did fuss over her too much. I think that's why she wouldn't marry him.' His father came and stood beside him when he stopped in front of a pale apricot bloom. 'But she must be told, and I'm ashamed to admit that in our shock we never gave her a thought.'

'Neither did I, but I must tell her. I did promise Paul, but I never believed for a moment that I would have to carry out his wishes.' Out of respect for his father, he cursed quietly under his breath. He should never have let Paul talk him into this stupid promise, but he must honour it now.

'Do you know where she is?' His mother had joined them looking much more composed.

'All I know is that she's a wireless operator in the WAAF, so I should be able to track her down all right.'

'Do that as soon as you can.' His mother came up to him and slipped her hand through her son's arm. 'They've been friends for a long time and I expect she'll want to come to the funeral.'

It was the next afternoon before he managed to find out where she was stationed. He decided to go at once. He had no wish to meet this girl his brother had been besotted with but it had to be done.

'Have you got any petrol in your car?' he asked his father.

'Yes, the tank's nearly full and there's a spare gallon in a can.'

'That should be enough to get me to Cheadle and

191

back. Can I borrow it? I'll try to replace the petrol for you.'

'Of course, and you might as well take the car back to base with you. I won't be using it.' The keys were handed over. 'You've found her?'

'Yes, but I had to pull in a couple of favours. This place she's at is very hush-hush, evidently.'

'Ah,' his father said knowingly. 'She always did strike me as a very bright girl. Paul told us she spoke French and German fluently.'

Reid raised his eyebrows and sighed. He was sick and tired of hearing about this paragon of virtue, and as soon as he'd seen her he wouldn't bother with her again. Promise or no promise!

'What's the matter, Reid?' his mother asked, not missing his exasperated expression. 'Don't you like Annie?'

'I've never met her, but from the way Paul went on about her I shall expect to see someone with wings and a halo.'

'He loved her,' his mother reprimanded gently. 'I wish they had married and then we might have had a grandchild to remember him by.'

Her eyes filled with tears and Reid was immediately sorry for his sarcasm. 'I apologize. I'm sure she's a charming girl, and I must tell her before she hears it from someone else.'

'Yes, that wouldn't be right.' His father picked up his son's bag. 'I'll help you get the car started; she hasn't been used for a while and might need a bit of persuasion.'

'When will you be back?' his mother asked anxiously.

'I'll get back tonight if I possibly can. I've been given

permission to go into this place so it shouldn't take long.'

'You will be kind to her, won't you?' she asked. 'It will come as a great shock.'

He bent and kissed her cheek. 'I will do my best.'

At Cheadle his papers were checked carefully before he was allowed to enter.

'I'll wait for her here,' he told the sergeant who was escorting him. When the man looked doubtful Reid said, 'I have some bad news for her and I'd rather see her alone.'

'Very well, sir, but I must ask you not to wander around.'

'I understand.' As the man hurried away, Reid lit a cigarette. He wasn't looking forward to this and felt it might be easier to talk to her in the open. He hoped she wouldn't be long because he wanted this unpleasant task out of the way.

The cigarette was nearly finished when he saw a slim, fair girl come out of a building and head towards him. He ground the cigarette under his foot and waited.

'Annie Webster?'

She saluted. 'Yes, sir.'

She looked puzzled; he knew he bore a slight resemblance to Paul but not enough for people to immediately identify them as brothers. But one thing was abundantly clear – she was quite lovely in a delicate way, and he began to understand Paul's protective feelings towards her. However, there was something his brother had missed – this girl was no weakling. He could see it in her eyes, in the way she stood, and he could feel strength coming from her and touching him. It was almost tan-

193

gible and he couldn't help wondering why Paul had never seen it.

'You wanted to see me?' she asked, breaking the silence between them.

'Yes.' He pulled in a deep, silent breath, steeling himself for this. 'I'm Reid Lascells.'

Surprise flashed across her face and the colour drained from it, but she remained silent, and he guessed she knew what he was going to say. It wasn't very hard to figure out, because there could only be one reason for him being there.

'It is my sad task to tell you that Paul was killed yesterday.' He heard the words as if spoken by someone else, and he cursed himself for breaking the news in this stilted way.

He watched her sway slightly and close her eyes as the shock hit her, then she opened them again and he caught a glimpse of the gentleness and compassion in her.

'I'm so sorry. How did it happen?'

'He was on convoy protection and got shot up badly; he crashed as he crossed the coast. He was nearly home but they think he was dead before he hit the ground.'

She nodded and reached out to touch his sleeve in a gesture of sympathy. 'It's a terrible loss, he was a lovely man.'

Reid narrowed his eyes, perplexed by her composed demeanour. He had the strong feeling that this was not the first loss she had suffered in her life. But he could feel anger building inside him. Apart from that first moment of shock, there wasn't a sign of a tear, and surely his brother warranted some display of grief from the woman he had worshipped? If she was such a caring creature, as

194

he'd been told many times, then where was her sorrow? He took a note from his pocket and handed it to her. 'The funeral is being held here next Thursday and you'll be welcome, if you want to come?'

Her eyes locked on to his and blazed with anger. 'Of course I want to come. Paul was my friend and I loved him.'

'Not enough to marry him, though,' he snapped.

'You are wrong. I loved him too much to condemn him to a marriage that couldn't last.'

'Well, it wouldn't have lasted, would it?' He was boiling now. The death of Paul had finally sunk in, and he was consumed with a raging anger. Just what did his brother see in this heartless creature? 'He died, didn't he?'

She took a step towards him, hesitated, and then moved back again.

My God, he thought, she was going to hit me. He knew he should back away as well, but some devil was driving him and he couldn't move. He was going to let this little madam know exactly what he thought of her.

'Don't pretend you cared for him. He spent his time fretting about you and you couldn't even be bothered to write or answer his calls.'

'That's not true!'

'Oh?' His laugh was humourless. 'What about January? He was beside himself with worry because he couldn't contact you.' He could remember Paul's frantic efforts to phone her when they'd been in the Midlands for a rest from combat, and being fobbed off with the excuse that she couldn't be contacted.

He noted the change in her expression. 'I see that hit home.'

195

'I wasn't in the country then.'

'You don't expect me to believe that, surely? There's a war on, so where would you go?' His voice was laced with contempt. What a ridiculous excuse!

'That's none of your business, and I object to the tone of your voice, Squadron Leader.' She lifted her head defiantly. 'I am not a liar.'

Whatever modicum of decency he had left was telling him to stop this, but he couldn't stem the tide of bitterness from pouring out. 'If you couldn't marry him, why didn't you at least sleep with him?'

She held his gaze firmly, and then spoke softly. 'Because he never asked me.' She turned and walked away.

Those few words made everything clear about Paul and Annie. His brother had put her on such a high pedestal that marriage between them would have been impossible, and this sensitive girl had had the sense to recognize that fact.

'Miss Webster,' he called. 'Annie.' But she didn't look back and soon disappeared from sight.

Reid lit another cigarette and drew on it deeply, trying to calm himself down. Why had he treated her like that? She hadn't deserved to be attacked by him, but there was something about her that riled him. Still, that was no excuse, his conduct had been inexcusable and he was thoroughly ashamed of himself. He would have some apologizing to do next time they met.

'I'm sorry, Paul,' he muttered, as he made his way back to the car. 'I made a terrible mess of that.'

Annie managed to reach her quarters before breaking down. She had been determined not to blubber all over that swine. She would mourn for Paul in her own way – in private.

This was turning out to be a terrible year. First the loss of Jack, and now, eight months later, Paul had been killed. Two men she had loved dearly, in different ways, and they were both gone. It was hard to believe, and there was now a big empty gap in her life. But it was fast being filled with dislike for Reid Lascells. How dare he stand there with that accusing look in his eyes? What had she done to deserve such treatment? How could brothers be so different?

Thankfully the hut was empty and Annie sat on her bunk and allowed the tears to flow unchecked. Perhaps she should have married Paul at the beginning of the war and given him a short time of happiness? But it was useless to agonize over that now – he was dead and nothing could change that. She pulled his photograph out of her bag, clutched it to her and wept.

After about an hour Annie blew her nose and splashed cold water on her face, once more back in control. She had work to do and her sorrow would have to be controlled, then she would write a letter to Paul's parents. They must be devastated.

She sat on the edge of the bed again, giving herself a few more moments before returning to the ops room. So that had been Reid, the arrogant devil. And that wasn't the first time she had seen him. He had been the airman she'd seen during the evacuation of Dunkirk. She hadn't been sure until she'd got close enough to see the scar on his forehead, and that had confirmed he was the same man.

Annie remembered how she had seen him looking

hurt and slightly bewildered on the quay, and had wanted to go and help him, but now she was glad she hadn't.

The objectionable man didn't deserve any help or sympathy.

16

Annie dropped a golden rose on to the coffin as it was being lowered and said a silent, heartbreaking farewell to Paul. It was almost impossible to grasp that she wouldn't see him again. She was going to miss him dreadfully. She felt so guilty that she hadn't been able to love him in the way he'd wanted.

Annie shivered; it was early October and felt more like the middle of winter, with overcast skies and a nasty wind whipping around the graveside. It seemed to have changed from summer to winter in one week, almost as if the weather was as angry and distressed as she felt at the terrible waste of young lives. Paul had loved life . . .

His mother touched her arm. 'Will you come back to the house with us?'

'I'm sorry, Mrs Lascells, but I have to get back and my train leaves in an hour.'

The woman smiled sadly. 'I understand, but thank you for coming, and for the lovely letter you sent us. We drew great comfort from it.'

Annie was relieved to hear that because it had been the most difficult thing she had ever tried to write. It had taken four attempts before she'd felt able to post it, and even then it had seemed so inadequate.

'Yes, we did.' Mr Lascells kissed her on the cheek. 'If you can't stay then let me drive you to the station.'

'No, you have a lot of people to ferry back to the

house, and I can walk.' She dredged up a smile. 'The exercise will do me good.'

Paul's mother seemed reluctant to let her go. 'You will come and see us now and again, won't you, Annie?'

'Of course.' She shook hands with everyone she knew and then stopped in front of Reid. 'Goodbye, Squadron Leader.' She didn't offer her hand or look into his eyes, she just turned and walked out of the churchyard making it clear that she never wanted to see him again. It was puzzling why he should have hurt her so much. She would normally have put such conduct down to grief, but his rudeness and sarcasm had cut deep. It had been totally unwarranted and she didn't know why he'd acted like that towards her. She could understand the anger he must have been feeling caused by the death of his brother, but where had his compassion been for her sorrow? Was he incapable of seeing past his own loss? But no, that didn't sound like the man Paul had loved and respected. Reid Lascells was a fighter pilot and, therefore, no stranger to death and grief. However, his hostile attitude towards her was puzzling. What had she ever done to hurt him?

She hadn't been walking for more than fifteen minutes when it started to rain, that heavy kind of drizzle that can soak you to the skin in no time at all. Blast, she thought as she turned up her collar, a rotten end to an upsetting day.

A car came along beside her and the passenger door was thrown open.

'Get in.'

After glaring at Reid, she put her head down and ignored him.

200

'You're going to get drowned,' he told her sharply. 'It's another mile to the station.'

She walked up to the car and slammed the passenger door with a thud, then continued walking. If he thought she was going to get into a car with *him*, he was very much mistaken. She'd been on the receiving end of his sharp tongue before, and had no intention of repeating the experience. Her emotions were too fragile at the moment and she would either hit him or sob uncontrollably. It was better to be wet than to have to endure another moment of his company.

The car disappeared from her sight and she breathed a sigh of relief; he'd got the message at last. But her satisfaction was short-lived. A door closed and footsteps crunched on the gravel road behind her, then Reid caught her up, shoved his hands in his pockets and started to walk with her, not saying a word.

Annie endured this for some ten minutes and then couldn't stand it any longer. She stopped and spun to face him. 'What the blazes do you think you're doing?'

'I'm walking to the station with you,' he replied mildly.

'What on earth for?'

'Well, this is a very lonely road, so I'm going to make sure you're safe.'

She was incensed. How dare he play the gallant knight after his heartless treatment! 'I'm perfectly safe. I've been trained in unarmed combat, and if you don't go away it will give me a great deal of pleasure to show you just how proficient I am.'

'Now come on, Annie Webster, you don't expect me to believe that, do you? Why would the RAF teach a fragile little thing like you to kill with her bare hands?'

'Believe what you like.' She realized that she shouldn't have given him that piece of information, but he made her fighting mad. He hadn't taken it seriously so it was all right. Anyway, she'd only had one week of intensive training, so she'd have been hard pushed to make good her claim if he challenged her. He was a tall, well-built man and she would have had to take him completely by surprise if she'd wanted to throw him. But, by heavens, she'd like to try!

She started to step out again, and still he came with her. 'Will you please go away?'

He shook his head and the water ran down his face.

'Can't do that. I promised I'd look after you.'

'Are you taking the bloody rise out of me?' Her voice had risen now, and if he wasn't very careful she really would belt him one. At the funeral she'd watched the coffin being lowered and felt as if Paul's death was all her fault. But, of course, that was ridiculous . . .

'Such language from a well-educated girl.' He gave her a disapproving look, but the corner of his mouth twitched.

'Oh, I know a lot worse than that, mate. I grew up in the roughest street in Bermondsey.'

'Well, well, you learn something new every day, don't you? Paul never told me that.' There was softness to his voice as he spoke his brother's name.

At the mention of Paul she stopped again. Her anger melted, leaving a lingering sadness. She pleaded, 'Will you leave me alone?'

'Can't do that.' Reid glanced at his watch. 'And if you don't keep moving you're going to miss your train.'

He was right, damn him. The only thing to do was ignore him.

They walked in silence until the station came in sight, then he stopped and turned her to face him. 'I want to apologize for the way I treated you when we first met. I was hurting badly from losing Paul, but I shouldn't have taken it out on you.'

'No, you shouldn't, but I forgive you. *Now* will you leave me alone?'

'I'll see you on the train.'

Annie tried to wipe the rain away from her face with her sleeve. It was like a soggy sponge; she was going to have a devil of a job getting it dry, and she was in for an uncomfortable journey back to Cheadle. Reid was in the same state. 'Why did you come with me? You could have stayed in the car and kept dry.'

He shrugged. 'I guess I can be as bloody-minded as you.'

A fleeting grin crossed her face. 'That I can believe.'

The train was delayed, which was nothing unusual. Annie was regretting her stubbornness; she was soaked to the skin.

'Ah, there's a mobile canteen over there.' Reid steered her over to it, and as they were both in uniform got them two cups of steaming hot tea.

'You know,' he said as he sipped his drink, 'you don't look a bit like the immaculate WAAF I met for the first time. You resemble a cat who's just been thrown in the river.'

'Thanks! You don't look any better yourself.' She put her head on one side and studied the scar on his temple. 'Anyway, we've seen each other before.'

He frowned and looked at her for a few moments, then shook his head. 'No, I'd have remembered.'

'It was when Dunkirk was being evacuated,' Annie said. 'I saw you on the dock and I was just going to come over and see if I could help you when a very pretty nurse led you away.'

'You were there?' he asked in disbelief.

'Yes, I was on leave and went with my sister, Rose, to see if we could be of any help.'

'Really?' He sat on a platform seat and pulled the wet trousers away from his knees with a grimace. 'What a day that was, I got shot down in France and managed to get on a ship. That captain was bloody brave, in fact all the crew were, but he was a very impressive man. Freeman, his name was.'

'That's my brother-in-law,' she told him proudly. 'He's married to Rose.'

'Good Lord!' Reid's eyes opened wide. 'Were you the two Captain Freeman hugged when he came ashore?' She nodded.

His gaze was intense. 'I think I've badly misjudged you, Annie Webster.'

'You have, and you hurt me very much,' Annie said. 'I was devastated to hear Paul had been killed, and I could have done without a tongue-lashing from you.'

He tried to take hold of her hand, but she pulled away. 'Ah, here's my train, at last. Goodbye, Reid.'

He closed the carriage door and leant through the window. 'Can I see you again?'

'I don't think that would be a good idea.' Definitely not a good idea, she told herself firmly. There was something about this man she couldn't fathom. He appeared to be

204

the complete opposite to his brother. Though perhaps he wasn't as hard and unfeeling as she'd first thought. She'd glimpsed real pain in his eyes during the funeral, and on the way to the station he'd shown a dry sense of humour. She liked that, but one redeeming trait didn't mean he was someone she wanted to get to know.

The train pulled away and she gave him one more glance, then shut the window and sat down. She didn't want any more to do with him, even though she'd had a different view of him today. He was strong, could be aggressive and not the type of man she liked at all. He didn't appear to have any of his brother's gentleness.

When she arrived back at camp it was a relief to get out of her damp clothes, have a bath and put on a dry uniform. She wasn't due back on duty until six hundred hours tomorrow so she headed for the mess and had something to eat.

Sam was sitting on his own reading a newspaper, so she joined him. He looked up and smiled when she sat down. 'How did your day go?'

'Distressing.' Her voice was husky when she spoke.

'Take the day off tomorrow, Annie,' Sam ordered. 'Go for one of those long walks you love so much and clear your head.'

'Thanks, Sam,' she agreed gratefully. 'I'll do that.'

The sun was shining the next morning and Annie cadged sandwiches from the cook, put them with a bottle of water in her bag and set off. She caught a bus for the short ride to open country where she knew there would be some lovely walks. She needed to be alone and Sam had recognized that as soon as he'd seen her. She would find a quiet place, and while she walked she would ease the sorrow by filling her thoughts with memories of the two men she had lost. Happy memories!

17

March 1942

The last year had been sad for Annie as she'd tried to come to terms with the deaths of Jack and Paul, but slowly the pain was easing. There seemed to be no end to the war in sight, but spring was just around the corner and with the lengthening days the sorrow lifted. She had thrown herself into her work, not wanting to go out or socialize. Jean had despaired of her and had dragged her out to a couple of dances or the local pub whenever they could make it. She had been right not to let her brood, and Annie was grateful for her friendship and understanding. She loved her work, though, and the anticipation of finding messages that might be of use to the war effort never diminished. Three weeks ago she'd had seven days' leave and had spent it in Wales. Her family were very supportive, without asking questions, and Wally's quiet love for her had been particularly healing. Her stepfather was not a demonstrative man but he'd always made it clear that he loved them all. She was feeling more like her old self now.

The mess was in uproar. Annie couldn't help grinning as she put her hands over her ears. This birthday party was getting out of hand. In fact there had been a few parties over the last few months. Pearl Harbor on 7 December 1941 had been a dreadful affair, but at least the

Americans were now in the war and Britain was not alone any more. It was nothing short of a miracle that the country had survived. And a complete mystery why Hitler hadn't invaded after Dunkirk when the country had been so vulnerable, but he hadn't, and the brave battle by the RAF had given Britain a chance to regroup. With the Americans now involved, he was going to live to regret that decision.

Sam came to her table, spun a chair round and straddled it, then he reached out and pulled her hands away from her ears so he could talk to her.

He said something she couldn't hear, but at that moment the noise died down as quite a few of them left to go back to their duties, making conversation easier.

'We ought to celebrate the fact that the Americans are in the war with us, and now over here.'

She laughed. 'It's a bit late, Sam, they've been here since the end of January.'

Sam rested his arms on the back of the chair and smiled. 'I know but we were so busy we hardly noticed 1942 arriving. Would you come out with me tonight?'

'I'd love to,' she agreed at once. Jean was on leave and she felt like having a good time.

'Good, I'll borrow some kind of transport and meet you at seven.' He raised a brow in query. 'Will that suit you?'

'Perfectly, thanks, Sam.'

He stood up and swung the chair back into place. 'We'll have fun, Annie Webster, and it's wonderful to hear you laugh again.'

She watched him walk away and nodded to herself.

Last year had been a swine and she had been glad to see the back of it. At one point she had felt so wretched that she'd begged Sam to send her on another mission, but he had refused, and looking back she knew he had been right to veto the idea. He had stayed in the background, watching, waiting, and leaving her to recover in her own time.

He was a wise man, she realized, and she had come to like and respect him.

Glancing at her watch she gulped her tea down and headed for the ops room. She was on duty for another two hours but that would leave her plenty of time. A quick bath and change of uniform and she would be ready. She thought wistfully of the pretty dresses and shoes she had in her wardrobe at home and wondered how long it was going to be before she wore them again. Quite some time, she guessed, as this war still had a long way to go. She sighed as she pictured one of her favourite outfits: a turquoise dress and jacket she'd bought on her last holiday with Chantal in France. Those carefree days seemed like a dream now. She pushed the thoughts away.

Sam had commandeered a truck. When she got to where it was parked outside the mess hall it was full of service men and women. He shrugged and grinned. 'They all want to come.'

'That's fine.' She waved to the boisterous group and climbed in the front with Sam. 'Where are we going?'

'The Jolly Sailor's the nearest pub,' someone shouted from the back.

'I know the place.' Sam headed out the gate at a reckless speed.

Annie grabbed on to the dashboard and gasped. 'Who taught you to drive?'

'No one.' He crashed the gears and looked down, muttering under his breath.

'Sam!' she shouted at him. 'Have you ever driven one of these before?'

'No' – he shot her a sideways grin – 'but I'll soon get the hang of it.'

There was another ominous screeching and a head appeared through the gap at the back of them. 'I say, Sam, it's not a good idea to engage reverse when you're going forward.'

'Ah, is that what I was doing?'

Sam turned round to speak to the man and Annie grabbed the wheel in terror. 'Will you please keep your eyes on the road.'

He grinned again, thoroughly enjoying himself, then after some more crashing and pumping with his feet, he settled back. 'I've figured it out now.'

Annie groaned. 'Thank God! And I hope this pub isn't far because I'm going to walk back.'

Sam tutted. 'I never had you down for a coward, Annie.' He squeezed her hand. 'We're going to have fun tonight, things are on the turn and France will be liberated now we have the troops to do it.'

'You just missed the pub!' came a shout from the back.

Sam jammed on the brakes. 'Where?'

The head came through the gap again. 'You can put her into reverse now, old boy, the Jolly Sailor's about a hundred yards back.'

There wasn't room to turn the big truck around, so

he slapped it into the correct gear and shot back, narrowly missing an American car parked in front of the place.

Annie found that her legs were shaking as they all tumbled into the hostelry. Sam's driving was almost as bad as jumping out of an aeroplane. She hadn't realized he had such a reckless streak.

The place was crowded with British, American, Polish and Australian military personnel; in fact, there seemed to be just about every accent you could think of.

Sam kept Annie firmly in his sights, and made it clear from the moment they walked in that she was with him. Any amorous approach to her, and there were many, was quickly rebuffed; it amused her that he was being so possessive.

The table was soon littered with drinks, the French accent had appeared, and she had never laughed so much in her life. It was wonderful, and after the last traumatic year she revelled in feeling light-hearted and normal.

'You ought to be on the stage,' she chided, after listening to him having a ridiculous conversation with a group of Americans. He had pretended that he couldn't understand what they were saying, and in the end had them completely confused.

'If I didn't know you, I would really believe you couldn't speak English properly.'

He grinned again. 'Ah, would you deny a man a bit of fun with these allies of ours?'

'No,' she giggled, 'but they were trying to be polite and ask you where you lived in France and how you came to be over here, but you tied them up in knots and didn't say a thing they could understand.'

He leant forward until his mouth was touching her

ear. 'You think we should tell them that we are spies?'
Of course not!' She thumped him playfully as he
nibbled her ear. 'Anyway, you might be, but I'm not.'

'Oh, yes you are.' He sat back and pulled a tatty sheet
of paper out of his top pocket, then read it thoughtfully.
'I have your name on my list. ACW Webster, it says here
. . . spy.'

She roared with laughter and made a grab for the
paper, but wasn't quick enough. He stuffed it back in his
pocket before she could get her hands on it. 'Group
Captain André Riniou, you are incorrigible.'

He frowned. 'What does that mean?'

'Don't you start that with me,' she threatened. 'And
my glass is empty; what kind of an escort are you?'

'I don't think I can drink much of this warm English
beer,' he complained, and sighed. 'Oh, to have a bottle
of exquisite French wine . . .'

One of their group tottered up with a tray loaded with
pints. 'Come on, drink up, those Yanks are miles ahead
of us, they've been here for hours.'

Annie smiled as Sam downed a pint in two gulps. He
didn't seem to be having any trouble making do with
the English beer after all. Suddenly she remembered
something. 'I wonder if they've got any chocolate with
them?'

'Oh, no, you don't,' Sam grabbed her as she stood up.
'Do you know what they want for a bar of chocolate?'

'I've no idea,' she told him, trying to look innocent.
Tales were rife about these young men who were pouring
into this country. A lot of the British servicemen resented
them because they had more money, and attracted the
girls with gifts of nylon stockings and chocolate. Over-

paid, oversexed and over here, was the common grumble, but no one could deny that this country was relieved to welcome them into the fight.

'A quick grope around the back of the pub, and more if they can get it.' Sam pulled her back into her seat again.

'What do you want sweets for?'

'I want some for James and Kate.'

Sam's expression softened. 'Ah, Rose's children. Would they like some, do you think?'

'They'd love it.' There was a sweets allowance on the ration, but it was hard to get even that, and usually involved a lot of queuing. When she'd been a child sweets had been a luxury they couldn't afford, but this generation of children just couldn't get them, or very few anyway.

'In that case,' he stood up, 'they shall have some.'

Annie watched him talking animatedly with a group of American soldiers, and after a while he came back and handed her two small bars of chocolate. 'Goodness. How did you manage that?' she asked.

He put his head on one side and studied her intently.

'I can be very persuasive when I need to be.'

She was beginning to believe that was true. If Sam wanted something bad enough he wouldn't be averse to putting on the French charm to get it.

At that moment all conversation was made impossible as a British soldier started thumping out all the favourite tunes on the piano, and everyone started to sing at the tops of their voices. Even the Americans, who appeared to love the pubs and enjoy the beer!

Annie was about to go on duty when she was told to report to Sam. Jean was also waiting to see him when she arrived.

'Do you know what this is about?' Jean asked.

'No.' Annie could understand why Jean looked so puzzled because it wasn't like Sam to be so formal. If he wanted to see you he usually ambled up, said what he had to say, and then strolled away again. To be summoned to his office was very unusual, and intriguing.

The office door opened and Sam looked out. 'Good, you're both here. Come in and shut the door behind you.'

Annie and Jean cast each other amused glances. Sam's door was never closed!

They did as ordered and stood to attention in front of his desk. The corners of his mouth twitched at their military bearing.

'Sit down, I have something to tell you.' He waited until they'd settled. 'You've been given new postings and I want you ready to leave within the hour.'

Annie gasped in surprise, while Jean appeared to be speechless. This was very sudden.

'There's an RAF intercept station called Chicksands Priory, in Bedfordshire,' Sam explained. 'Men have staffed it until now, but they're moving out and WAAF wireless operators are replacing them. I've volunteered the two of you to accompany me.'

'Is this place special?' Annie asked.

'It's going to play an important part in the war effort. And you, Annie, are the most talented operator I've come across. You pick up messages others miss, and you also recognize individual operators by the way they key the Morse transmissions. You're just what they need there.'

Annie was stunned, but pleased with the praise, as she knew Sam didn't say anything unless he meant it.

'But I'm not a wireless operator,' Jean pointed out.

'They need clerical staff as well, and I'm going to need you to handle the paperwork.' He stood up and glanced at his watch. 'I'll meet you outside in forty-five minutes.'

They didn't even have time to say goodbye to everyone as Sam hustled them into a truck to take them to the station. Much to Annie's relief Sam wasn't driving.

There was one thing about being in the forces, Annie thought as the train chugged its way through the country-side, you certainly travelled around. The train was crowded as usual, making conversation impossible, so she gazed out of the window. She was sorry in a way to leave Cheadle as there had been some breathtaking walks in the area, but from the little Sam had told her the new posting sounded exciting.

Annie was shaken from her reverie when the train stopped and women from the Women's Voluntary Service came round with welcome refreshments. She smiled her thanks at the woman who handed her a cup of hot tea and a sandwich. Then they were on their way again. Everyone had the greatest respect for the women of the WVS. They worked tirelessly and often in very dangerous situations, like during the Blitz, but they always had a cheery smile and a joke when you met them. She could understand why Rose had joined them.

The rhythmic clatter of the train lulled Annie into sleep and she wasn't aware of the journey until Jean shook her awake at Bedford station. There was a truck waiting to take them the rest of the way. They drove through the town towards Shefford, and then turned right into a country lane, and another right turn brought them to some gates with a guardroom just inside.

Sam had obviously been there before, because, after their papers were checked, he pointed to some Nissen huts set under trees. 'Annie, you're in the first one, and Jean's in the one next to it. Jean, once you've stowed your gear, report to the offices and I'll meet Annie here in half an hour.'

They hurried off, eager to find out what their new posting was going to be like.

There were sixteen beds in Annie's hut and several were obviously empty, so she chose one about halfway down the hut. It looked as if there were a few girls to come yet, and she hoped they were going to be as nice as most of the others she'd met. Her mouth turned up in a smile as she remembered the first crowd she'd met back in February 1940. She wondered where they all were now. She unpacked her washing things and then looked around. The hut had beds, and that was all, so where on earth was she going to put her clothes? There weren't any cupboards.

'You'll have to keep your knickers in a box under the bed, I'm afraid.'

Annie recognized the voice, spun around and let out a squeal of delight. 'Dora, what are you doing here?'

Her friend grinned at her and tossed a cardboard box on to Annie's bed. 'That's your wardrobe.' She hugged Annie and danced her around the hut. 'Oh, I'm so happy to see you. I got fed up with Compton Bassett, it wasn't so much fun after you left, and when I heard they needed clerical staff for this place I volunteered.'

Annie was so delighted by this unexpected turn of events that she hugged Dora warmly. 'I'm so pleased.'

'Me too. I've been here three weeks, and when I saw all these girls fiddling with wireless sets I hoped they might send you here.'

Annie stuffed her clothes into the box and shoved it under the bed; she'd sort that out later. 'I must introduce you to Jean. She comes from Stepney as well.'

'If she's the bubbly WAAF with blonde hair and baby-blue eyes, then I've already met her. She's in my hut.' Dora glanced at her watch. 'I've promised to show her where the offices are so I must fly. See you later, Annie.'

Annie watched her friend hurtle out the door and then went in search of Sam. He was waiting outside smoking a cigarette, which he stubbed out as she walked towards him.

'Good, that didn't take you long. Now I'll show you where we are going to work.'

She fell into step beside him. 'You obviously know this place, Sam.'

'I've been here quite often, Annie, and when they asked me to transfer, I wanted to bring you with me.'

He gave her a sideways glance. 'I hope you don't mind?'

'Not at all, I liked Cheadle but it does hold some painful memories for me, and once I'd got used to the idea I wasn't too sorry to leave.' Annie knew that a change of location was probably a good thing at this point. The memories of Paul and Jack would always be with her, and she was glad about that, but it was time to move on. There was still a war to be won.

Sam stopped in front of a door, opened it and then they walked down some steps into the operations room. Annie looked around eagerly. There were rows of desks, each one partitioned off into small cubby-holes, and most occupied with WAAFs concentrating on their wireless sets.

'Annie,' Sam said, touching her arm, 'this is Wing Commander Felshaw.'

The wing commander was of medium height with brown hair sprinkled with grey; but the thing that struck her most about him was the shadows of tiredness beneath his brown eyes. The gathering of information was vital, and although they worked quietly in the background the demands on their time and concentration were immense.

'Glad you're here,' he told her. 'Sam's given us a glowing report of your abilities and we badly need experienced operators.'

Sam gave Annie a sly wink and sauntered off, leaving her to settle into her new post.

The wing commander showed her to a vacant desk and sat down beside her. 'I'm sure I don't have to explain the job to you, but I'll run through it anyway. You will be given a radio frequency to work on each day. Write down any messages you pick up, ring the bell and someone will take it to be deciphered.'

'I understand, sir.'

With a brief nod, he hauled himself to his feet. 'I'll leave you to it, then.'

Annie finished her shift by seven that evening, and as there was no sign of Sam she asked directions to the mess and headed there. She heard Dora's laugh as soon as she walked through the door, and found her sitting at a table with Jean. If the laughter was anything to go by, then the two girls were getting along well. She made her way over to them, feeling her spirits rise; it was going to be lovely having both Dora and Jean here.

'Ah, you're free at last.' Dora grabbed a chair from another table for her. 'Get yourself something to eat. They're giving a concert in the old house here, and we're going.'

'What kind of a concert?' she asked. She'd seen some of the ones put on by the troops at Cheadle, and although great fun Annie wasn't sure she wanted to watch amateurs tonight. It had been a long, tiring day.

Dora laughed at her doubtful expression. 'You'll like this; it's classical music. I've seen them before and they're good.'

'In that case I'd love to come.' Annie loved classical music and decided that an evening in the company of friends would be a lovely way to spend her first night.

The airman playing the piano was excellent and his repertoire extensive, from Beethoven to Gershwin. A

WAAF sang some Vera Lynn songs, and a squadron leader thrilled them with music from *Madame Butterfly*. The forces were crammed with talent and this intercept station was clearly no exception.

When the concert ended at eleven o'clock, Annie was ready for bed, but Dora wouldn't hear of it, declaring that they had far too much catching up to do. Although Annie had kept in touch with Dora through letters, they hadn't seen each other since Compton Bassett, so she stifled a yawn and agreed.

The hut Jean and Dora were in was in darkness but Annie's still had lights on, and it sounded as if there was a party going on. So they headed for that, not wanting to disturb the other girls if they were asleep. When they walked in Dora started to chuckle. 'Ah, Annie, this brings back memories, doesn't it?'

It certainly did. More girls had obviously arrived during the evening, and they were all sitting on the bunks, cups in their hands and eating sandwiches.

One tall girl stood and held out her hand. 'I'm Gladys, welcome to Chicksands. Would you like a drink?'

'Thanks.' Annie recognized Gladys as one of the wireless operators she'd seen in the ops room.

There was a scramble to introduce themselves, and then they all sat down again. Cups were thrust into their hands. Annie took a sip, gasped, and everyone in the hut collapsed with roars of laughter.

'What is this?' Annie said hoarsely. She looked across at Dora who was licking her lips in obvious enjoyment.

'Just a dash of bourbon,' Gladys explained.

'What's that?' Annie had recovered a little by now but her voice was husky and her eyes were watering.

220

'It's the Yanks' idea of whisky.' Gladys sat back and crossed her long legs in a provocative pose that reminded Annie of her time as a fashion editor. 'I'm going out with one and they can get anything.'

'Great!' Dora held out her mug. 'I'll have another one of those.'

After that they talked for a couple of hours, and by the time they packed up for the night Annie knew the life history of everyone in the hut. She went to bed late, but happy, and glowing from two slugs of bourbon. It wasn't too bad as long as you tossed it back quickly. She smiled to herself as she settled down for the night; this was going to be a good posting, she was sure.

Two days later Annie was delighted to receive some letters that had been redirected. She had thought it might take a few more days before the post caught up with her, and letters were so important to everyone in these times of long separations. There was one from Rose, with carefully penned notes from James and Kate thanking her for the chocolate that Sam had cadged from the Americans. There was another from her mother and Wally giving her news received from Will somewhere at sea. The last was in a bold hand. Reid! Blast the man, he was turning out to be as stubborn as his brother had been. It must be a family trait.

She searched through her bag and found the pen she was looking for. Perhaps this would get the message through!

Oh, dear, Annie Webster, you're going the wrong way about getting rid of me, Reid thought. As he read the note again he laughed.

'What's amused you?' Bouncer sat beside him and peered at the letter.

Reid held it up. It was written by him, but had been returned with the words *Go away* written in green ink at the bottom. He chuckled again.

'Are you making a nuisance of yourself with someone?' his friend asked, rubbing his left arm.

'Hmm. Is that arm still bothering you?'

'Yes. It's taking too long to heal and this damp autumn weather doesn't help. I hate being grounded.' He glanced at Reid's expression and held up his good hand. 'I know, I should have bailed out.'

'Yes,' Reid told him. 'You've tried that trick once too often.'

Bouncer sighed. 'I really thought I could get down safely.'

'With no rudder control and only one wheel down, not to mention a bloody great hole in the wing?' Reid shook his head in despair. His friend was lucky he hadn't blown himself to bits.

'Underestimated the damage, eh?' Bouncer sat back and grinned.

'Anyway, thanks for getting me transferred to Tangmere. I'd have gone mad at Kenley with nothing to do.'

'I needed someone to help me with the job of station commander, and you are just the man.' Reid managed to keep a straight face, but with considerable difficulty. Bouncer was next to useless on the ground but he was glad to have him around. He found the station commander's job lonely after the camaraderie of the squadron, and it made Bouncer feel useful. And it was keeping his friend out of the air, which was much more important. How Bouncer had survived so far was nothing short of a miracle, as he took unimaginable risks.

'I'm glad to be here, but I can't believe you really need anyone. You're as organized and efficient on the ground as you are in the air. Tangmere is running like clockwork because of you.' Bouncer nodded towards the note. 'You still haven't told me who you're pestering.'

'Annie Webster.'

Bouncer's eyebrows nearly disappeared into his hair.

'Paul's girl?'

'That's the one.' Reid gave a gleeful grin. He didn't completely understand why he kept pursuing her, but in a strange way he was thoroughly enjoying the chase.

'Well, if the vivid green ink is anything to go by I'd say you've really upset her. What did you do?'

'I was rude and shouted at her,' he admitted honestly. 'I was shattered by Paul's death and her composure irritated me.' Reid grimaced in disgust. 'But that's no excuse for the way I treated her.'

'Have you thought about apologizing?' his friend asked with a wry smile.

'I did that after the funeral, and got soaking wet for my trouble. She wouldn't get into the car with me and it was pouring.' 'That walk in the rain amused Reid whenever he thought about it. Annie Webster was a spirited little thing, but he still didn't understand why he hadn't stayed in the car and left her to it. He just hadn't been able to leave the stubborn girl.

A deep chuckle came from Bouncer. 'I'm beginning to like the sound of her, and it doesn't look as if your usual charm had any effect.'

'Oh, she said she forgave me, then more or less told me to get lost.' The corners of Reid's eyes crinkled in amusement. From his brother's description, he'd gained a completely different impression of her but Paul had got it wrong, Annie Webster was not a timid, dependent woman. Behind the gentle façade there was a fire burning, and he'd love to get close enough to feel the heat.

'Then why are you still writing to her?'

'Bugger if I know.'

His friend struggled to strike a match with one hand, and when he had succeeded lit a cigarette and drew on it, his eyes never leaving Reid's face. 'Pretty, is she?'

He opened a drawer and took out the framed photograph Paul had always kept beside his bed. It hurt to look at it when he remembered just how much his brother had adored this girl, and he couldn't understand why he was holding on to it. 'I ought to give this back, I suppose?'

Bouncer took the picture out of his hand and whistled. 'No wonder Paul was crazy about her. I'd like to meet her. Tell you what, let's go and return this now.'

'I've only got a few hours free and, anyway, I've just found out she's been transferred to this hush-hush place, and I don't suppose we could get in.'

'Oh?' Bouncer was clearly intrigued. 'What does she do, for heaven's sake?'

'Wireless operator, and speaks French and German.'

'Does she now?' Bouncer prowled over to the window to watch the planes taking off, then turned and sat on the windowsill. 'I heard about these agents . . . do you think she's one of them?'

Reid tipped his head back and laughed at the ludicrous idea. 'Where on earth did you get that daft notion from?'

'Just a thought.' Bouncer grinned. 'Well, are you going to take me to meet her?'

'I've told you, there isn't time.'

'Reid, I know you've got your Lysander here doing nothing, and the weather isn't too bad, so can't you find somewhere you need to visit urgently – with your second in command?' he added.

'Well . . .' Reid only hesitated for a few moments because the expression on his friend's face decided him. Being grounded was purgatory for Bouncer. Reid knew that every time the Spitfires took off his friend's soul went with them. He stood up and shoved the photo into his pocket. 'Come on then, I've promised to pop in and see the station commander at Duxford to discuss a meeting of top brass we've been ordered to attend.'

'Ah.' Bouncer's eyes gleamed with amusement. 'Want to get your story straight beforehand, do you?'

'We're not sure what it's about but we don't want to be caught out with questions we can't answer. Once that's done with I'm sure he'll let us borrow a car. This place Annie's in is only about an hour or so from there, I think.'

Bouncer wasn't as nimble on his feet as he had been but he beat Reid to the door, and waited impatiently for Reid to obtain permission from Duxford and file his flight plan. 'Where is this place?' he asked when they reached the plane.

'In Bedford, near a place called Shefford.' Reid helped Bouncer into the plane and snapped his harness into place. As well as having badly injured his arm, he had also made a mess of one hip, which made manoeuvring into small places difficult.

'I'll fly,' Bouncer announced, his expression animated.

'No, you won't,' Reid told him. 'You're grounded, remember?'

'Oh, come on, you rotten blighter,' he growled. 'Who's going to know?'

'I'll make a bargain with you.' Reid eased his tall frame into the pilot's seat, well aware that his friend was desperate to get his hands on the controls of any plane again. 'You can fly her, but I insist on landing.'

'You've got yourself a deal.'

It was not the smoothest take-off Reid had ever experienced, and he breathed a sigh of relief as they levelled out. Once they were flying in a straight line he relaxed and listened to Bouncer singing at the top of his voice.

He was only doing this trip for his friend's sake, he told himself. It certainly wasn't because he wanted to see Annie again; he had promised his brother he would see she was all right, hadn't he? He couldn't just abandon her, even if she was more or less telling him to bale out without a parachute. His quiet chuckle of amusement was drowned out by the sound of the engine and Bouncer's happiness.

It didn't take Reid more than thirty minutes to talk over the forthcoming meeting with the station commander at Duxford, Simon Stratton, and he was only too happy to put an air force car at their disposal.

When they arrived at Chicksands their papers were scrutinized, and permission to enter took a while. Bouncer pulled his collar up and shoved his hands into his pockets in an effort to protect himself from the cold wind.

'Good Lord,' he complained. 'What is this place?'

'I told you it was going to be difficult to see her, didn't I?' Reid stamped his feet and blew on his fingers, wishing he were back at base. It had turned much colder since they'd left and he was concerned for Bouncer. This was a crazy idea.

'I thought that uniform you're sporting would get you in anywhere,' his friend muttered.

A sergeant came up to them and saluted. 'Would you follow me, please?'

He led them to a small, sparsely furnished room, which was like an icebox, then left them, closing the door firmly behind him.

'We've been arrested!' Bouncer roared. 'I bet he's locked the door.'

Reid laughed, opened the door and looked out. 'It isn't locked but there is a guard outside.'

'What do they think we're going to do, blow the place up?'

Reid paced the small room. 'I should never have let

you talk me into this crazy scheme. She won't see us, anyway.'

His friend looked astonished. 'So, it's my fault now, is it?'

'I've got to blame someone.' Reid grinned. 'And I'm flying the plane back.'

The stream of colourful language was cut off sharply as the door opened and Annie came in.

She saluted in front of Reid. 'You sent for me, sir?'

He ignored Bouncer's smothered laugh. If that was the way she wanted to play, then he'd go along with it. He took the photo out of his pocket. 'Yes, Webster. Paul always kept this beside his bed and I thought you might like it back.' He handed it to her and moved away. 'But if I'd known you were going to greet his brother so rudely I wouldn't have bothered. You do know how to hold a grudge, don't you?'

As she looked at the photo her military bearing sagged, he saw tears clouding her eyes and she was fighting for control of her emotions. This was the first glimpse he'd seen of how much she had cared for Paul, and seeing the special photograph again had caught her off guard. He had been, and still was, treating this woman in a disgraceful way but he couldn't seem to help himself. There was something about her . . .

'Thank you,' she said quietly.

He reached out to comfort her, but Bouncer stepped in front of him and blocked the gesture.

'It's a beautiful picture,' he told her kindly, 'Paul was always very proud of it, and you.'

She smiled at him. 'He was a good man.'

'And a brave fighter pilot.'

228

'You all are,' she told him with obvious respect.

Bouncer nodded towards Reid, who was sitting on the edge of the table watching his friend turn on the charm. 'And Paul's brother, over there, is one of the finest you could ever know.'

'I'm sure he is.' Annie ran her fingers round the edge of the frame, but didn't look up.

Bouncer tilted her chin up. 'I can hear a "but" there.'

'I don't like him very much,' she admitted, talking to Bouncer as if he was the only one in the room.

'Ah, well, I agree he can be an awkward devil, but he grows on you, if you give him a chance.'

'Will you two stop talking about me as if I wasn't here,' Reid demanded, getting to his feet. 'I don't need you to fight my corner for me, Bouncer.'

'Oh, oh.' Bouncer winked at Annie. 'That's torn it. Is there a pub where we can buy him something to eat and a large beer?' He rubbed his left arm. 'And a huge fire. I swear I'm frozen to the marrow.'

Annie looked at his left arm hanging useless by his side. 'I'm so sorry, they should have found you somewhere warmer to wait.'

Bouncer gave her one of his most beguiling smiles. 'I thought they'd arrested us when they put us in this cell-like room.'

Annie laughed. 'The Red Lion pub always has a log fire, but it's about three miles from here.'

'That's all right, the station commander here has borrowed a car.'

'In that case I'll explain how you get there.'

'I suppose you couldn't come with us, could you?'

Bouncer asked, giving a plaintive sigh. 'I was a friend of Paul's and have always wanted to meet his girl. It would be nice to have a chat. Somewhere warmer than this,' he added, rubbing his hip this time.

'Lying sod,' Reid muttered quietly under his breath. His friend had left a string of broken hearts, and goodness knows what else, he thought wryly, and he was damned if he was going to let him get Annie in his clutches.

'Well' – she looked at her watch – 'I do have a couple of hours, so let me tell them I'm leaving the base, and I'll meet you outside.'

Bouncer treated her to the full smile.

When she'd left, Reid turned on his friend. 'And what the hell do you think you're doing?'

'Digging you out of a hole, old chap. That was about to turn into a slanging match and the poor girl was already upset.'

'I know she was, and I was about to apologize until you stepped in with your phoney charm.'

Bouncer shook his head. 'You don't get it, do you? She can't stand you, and if you'd dared to touch her she'd have floored you.'

'You're exaggerating.' Reid opened the door and waited for his friend to follow.

'What about the unarmed combat you told me she can do?'

Reid laughed. 'You don't believe that nonsense, do you? I don't think she could do me much harm.'

Bouncer's limp was more pronounced now he was cold. 'I think, my friend, that she could do you a great deal of harm.'

'And I think the cold wind has seeped into your brain,'

230

Reid chided as he opened the door of the car. 'Get in before you turn into a gibbering idiot.'

'Ah, here she comes.' Bouncer eased himself into the back of the car. 'She really is very beautiful. I think I might make a play for her myself.'

'Don't you dare,' Reid warned.

When Annie reached them he held open the front passenger door for her, but she ignored him and got in the back with Bouncer. She really knew how to snub a man, he thought, highly amused by her continued hostility. She was wasting her time because it only made him more determined to break through her defences.

On the short journey, Reid decided that he wasn't going to let her get away with this for much longer. Her anger at him was understandable, but he'd apologized, damn it. He thought about his brother and a lump came into his throat. I've made a right mess of my promise to look after your girl, Paul, he said to himself.

The pub had a blazing log fire in the grate so they pulled up a table and chairs and settled down with a drink.

Bouncer held his leg out to the warmth and groaned in relief. 'Oh, that's heaven.'

How did you tell a man like him that he would probably never fly in combat again? Reid thought, his heart aching for his friend. Bouncer was like a fish out of water when he was on the ground and he made no secret that he was determined to get back into the fight.

'Rest your leg on here.' Annie dragged another chair over. 'You might find it more comfortable.'

'Thank you.' Bouncer gave her an approving smile. 'You'd make a good nurse.'

A brief moment of sadness flashed across her face. Reid was curious to know why a casual remark like that should have caused such a reaction. He was beginning to wish he knew more about her.

Bouncer had put a cigarette in his mouth and was trying to light a match with one hand. Annie took it from him, struck the match and held it up so he could light his fag. He nodded his thanks, drew deeply, and blew the smoke up to the ceiling.

Reid was highly amused, because if he'd offered to help he would have been put very firmly in his place with 'I'm not a bloody invalid'. But his friend was certainly playing for full effect now, the crafty devil. Bouncer had a real way with women when he set his mind to it.

He was brought out of his musing when Bouncer asked a question.

'That's right, isn't it, Reid?'

'Sorry. What were you saying?'

'I was telling Annie that I should have baled out.'

'It would have been wise,' he remarked drily.

'The thing is,' Bouncer turned his attention back to Annie again, 'the thought of trusting my life to a flimsy bit of silk terrifies me.'

'Many pilots are alive today because they did just that,' Reid pointed out. He'd lost count of how many times he'd said this to Bouncer. On one occasion he'd even managed to get him up in a DC3 and promised to jump with him, but no amount of urging had made his friend take that step into thin air. He found it quite exhilarating himself, and had made a couple of jumps before the war. He was sure Bouncer only needed to jump once and then he wouldn't mind doing it again, but persuading him had proved an impossible task.

'I know, but they're braver than me.' Bouncer grimaced in self-disgust.

'I don't believe that,' Annie told him. 'Everyone is scared of something and yours just happens to be jumping out of planes.'

'You're right, of course. Have you ever jumped?' Bouncer asked, his face a picture of innocence.

There was a slight hesitation before she spoke, then, 'I jumped out of a balloon once.'

Reid frowned. Was this another tall tale, like the one about being expert in unarmed combat? 'Why would you do that?'

She gave him a cool look. 'To see what it was like, of course.' Then she turned back to Bouncer and smiled. 'It was frightening but I would do it again.'

Reid listened to her telling his friend all about it, heard her soft laugh, and started to reverse his opinion of her.

First impressions were definitely misleading. He narrowed his eyes and tried to see beyond Annie's apparent delicate façade. This was no weakling; there was a formidable strength of character radiating from her. Before the war she had probably been that rare creature, a career woman, or else she would have married before now. And she was clearly intelligent. He also doubted that she would be swayed by anyone else's opinions, and that was why Paul had never been able to persuade her to marry him. She would make her own decisions in life.

He sipped his beer thoughtfully, feeling a stirring of interest.

He liked her!

Annie removed the headphones and stretched her arms above her head, giving a groan of relief. It seemed as if she'd been sitting there for days.

'Come on.' Sam pulled her out of the chair. 'Let's see if they've got any food left in the mess.'

'I jolly well hope they have because I'm starving.' They walked outside and she breathed in deeply, enjoying the cold evening air.

'Looking forward to your leave?' he asked.

'Oh yes, it's an age since I've seen my family. Things have been so hectic we seem to have gone from winter to summer and back to winter without me noticing.'

'Do you even know what year it is?' he asked with obvious amusement.

'I think it's 1942, but the way I'm feeling at the moment, you'd better confirm that,' she joked.

'November 1942, to be exact.' He chuckled at her confusion and opened the mess door for her. 'You've been shut away for too long, Annie, and that's what you get for being so good at your job.'

'Oh, I enjoy it, but I just wish they wouldn't keep dragging me out of bed whenever there's a flap on, except for last night, of course.'

'Yes.' He rubbed his hands together in excitement. 'Montgomery's victory at El Alamein is a real boost to the spirit. This is the turning point, Annie, you can be certain of that.'

'I'm sure you're right.' She yawned. Everyone was so excited by the news that the Germans had been ousted from El Alamein. It was a tremendous boost to morale.

'But I'm so tired, Sam.'

'Well, from tomorrow you can forget everything for seven days and sleep the clock round.'

She sat down, leaving Sam to see what they could get to eat.

He was soon back. 'Spam and chips, all right?'

She grimaced and he chuckled. 'Sorry, they didn't have any rump steak. It'll be about ten minutes.'

'Have they got anything for pudding?' she asked, dreaming of a succulent steak and some of Rose's gorgeous trifle with real cream. Those days of plenty seemed like a dream now.

'Rice, made with powdered milk, of course.'

'Oh, well,' she said in a resigned voice, 'that will fill me up a bit.'

'I don't know how you do it, Annie, there's nothing of you and yet you can eat more than me.'

'Blame it on a deprived childhood,' she told him, moving her arms from the table so that the plate could be put in front of her.

'I don't believe that!' he told her, pinching one of her chips and popping it in his mouth.

She gestured with her knife. 'Get your hands off my chips, you've got more than me, anyway.'

He nicked another one and laughed when she scowled at him.

'You can have my rice pudding, I can't stand the stuff,' he said.

'In that case' – she speared a piece of spam with her fork and held it out to him – 'you can have a bit of this.'

Sam was tremendously cheered by the news lately, and Annie knew he was longing for the day when France would be liberated. Every defeat the Germans suffered made him more animated.

'Oh, no!' he told her in mock horror, 'I couldn't take that, you've had a *deprived* childhood.'

'You don't believe me?' Annie ate the piece of spam, tipped her head to one side and studied the man sitting opposite her. They had an easy rapport with each other now and she enjoyed fighting with him in this light-hearted way. 'Well, next time you see my Rosie, you ask her, she'll tell you what our childhood was like.'

'Are you going to see the magnificent Rose on your leave?' Sam asked.

'Yes.' Annie laughed at his description of her sister. 'They're all back at Roehampton at the moment.'

'I'll drive you there, if you like.'

She gave him a horrified look, remembering the last time she'd been in a truck with him.

'I've been having lessons,' he assured her, his eyes gleaming with mischief.

'Er . . . how many?'

'A couple.'

'No thanks!' She went back to her food. 'I think it would be safer on the train.'

He watched in disbelief as she polished off her spam and two plates of rice pudding.

Annie sat back with a sigh. 'Will you go home when

236

the war's over, or stay in this country?' she asked. She had come to know him quite well, and although he controlled his feelings well she knew he loved his own country. But what would he have to go back to?

'I don't suppose my home is still standing, but yes, I will try to rebuild my life there.'

'What about your family?' He'd never mentioned anyone but Annie was used to having a large and boisterous family, and was curious.

His expression changed to one of simmering anger. 'They were shot. All except my sister. I shall try to find her, if she's still alive.'

'I'm so sorry,' Annie placed her hand over his clenched fist. This was the first indication he'd given about the trauma of his escape from France, and she instinctively reached out to comfort him.

His fingers uncurled and wrapped around hers, the fury leaving his face, and he smiled. 'I can understand something of why Jack found you so comforting. There's an inner peace about you that reaches out and touches other people.'

Annie pulled a face. 'You make me sound more like Florence Nightingale than an ordinary woman.'

'Oh, no, that is not true. You are very beautiful and desirable, and I will not try to fool you, Annie, if I could take you back with me once my country is free, then I would.'

She hadn't missed the sadness in his voice when he spoke about his home. 'What will be waiting for you when you get back?'

'Very little, I suspect, but the land will still be there and I shall enjoy building myself a new home in a free

France. There is much to look forward to. And when I believe that the invasion is imminent, I shall return home' – he gave a boyish grin, his earlier fury gone – 'and cause some mayhem of my own.'

'You'll need a good wireless operator,' she suggested.

'Hmm.' He narrowed his eyes as he looked at her. 'We shall have to see, Ann Webster. Anyway, that is all in the future,' he told her, clearly dismissing the subject. 'I have managed to get more chocolate for the children; you can take it with you. They will be pleased, hmm?'

'Very.' She grinned. 'I had to send the other through the post, but I received the most enthusiastic thanks from both of them.'

Annie hesitated for a moment, and then decided. This man had lost everything, so surely she could share her family with him? 'You must have leave due you.'

'I have, but there seems little point in taking it.'

'Why don't you come home with me, and then you can give the children the chocolate yourself? There's plenty of spare room,' she told him quickly.

'Oh, I would like that very much, but are you sure it would be all right?' he asked, looking eager but doubtful.

'Positive. My friend Dora's coming as well, but we'll go on the train,' she added, the tone of her voice daring him to argue. 'There's one at nine-thirty in the morning, so be ready.'

Dora came over to their table, flushed with excitement. 'Annie, the Americans are having a dance at their base tonight and are sending trucks to collect us. Put your make-up on because we're going.'

Sam sat back and grinned. 'That should be interesting.'

'You can't come,' Dora told him. 'They only want the girls.'

'Now why doesn't that surprise me?' He stood up. 'Behave yourselves, and I'll see you in the morning.'

Jean rushed over looking as excited as Dora. 'Hurry up. The trucks will be here in an hour.'

'I've heard about this base, but how far is it away from here?' Annie asked.

Dora pulled a face. 'My God, I don't think you know what's going on in the outside world. I think all that Morse code bleeping in your ears is scrambling your brains. It's less than fifteen minutes in the truck, especially the way the Yanks drive.'

Annie laughed at her friends as they towed her out of the mess to get ready for the evening.

Annie couldn't believe her eyes. The tables at the end of the room were laden with food, ham, chicken, salmon and all manner of cakes. Things they hadn't seen for the duration of the war. 'Wow! Is that real cream?'

'It certainly is, ma'am,' an American pilot told them. 'Why don't you just tuck in and enjoy yourselves.'

They didn't need any more urging, and nor did the rest of the girls from Chicksands, as they all grabbed a plate. It was a difficult choice but most of them took just a small portion of everything, not wishing to appear greedy.

'Better take it easy,' Dora cautioned. 'Our stomachs aren't used to rich food any more.'

'Quite right.' Annie bit into a pastry and groaned in ecstasy as cream oozed out. She licked her fingers, not wishing to waste a precious drop of this luxury. At that moment a big military band burst into life with Glenn Miller's 'In The Mood', and the dance floor became a seething mass of gyrating bodies. The music was so uplifting it made everyone in the room smile and determined to enjoy themselves. Gladys was here with her boyfriend, and that probably meant another bottle of bourbon for them to enjoy. It was always shared out between the sixteen in their hut, and Dora and Jean who had become honorary members of their group.

It was a glorious evening and Annie even managed to jive with some of the Americans. They had all been very polite, and seemed to have fun teaching them how to do their dance. At eleven o'clock they were all in the trucks again, tired but happy after such an unexpected treat, and on their way back to camp.

The next day, the two houses in Roehampton were already full when Annie, Dora and Sam arrived. There were Rose, Wally, Marj, James, Kate and George, who loved the children so much he wouldn't let them out of his sight. Charlie had made it as well, and was still wildly enthusiastic about being a mechanic in the air force. It would have been even better if Bill and Will could have been there but they were both at sea and you never knew when they might turn up. This was a fact of life for everyone now and it was accepted without comment.

'It is very good of you to let me stay,' Sam told Rose, dropping his bag on the floor with a thud. He stooped down to open it and produced tins of fruit, corned beef, powdered egg and milk, and a few other treats.

'Where did you get all that?' Rose gasped, as the food was put on to the table.

240

'While the girls were dancing at the American base I slipped into the kitchens, and they were very generous to a poor homeless Frenchman.' He gave a dramatic sigh.

'You crafty thing,' Annie chided. 'Why didn't you let us know you were there?'

'Oh, they wouldn't let me in the dance hall, they wanted to keep all the girls to themselves.' He made a pretence of searching the bag. 'Now what else have I got here?'

'I should think you've brought quite enough,' Marj told him, eyeing the row of tins and packets in wonder.

'No, no, I'm sure there's something else.' He was on his knees and rummaging in the bag. 'Ah!' he exclaimed, pulling out two bars of chocolate and handing one to each child.

'Wow!' James couldn't seem to believe his eyes, and turned the bar over and over in his hands. 'Thanks, Sam.'

Kate threw her arms around his neck and kissed him on the cheek.

'Don't eat it all at once,' Rose admonished her children.

'We won't, Mum. We'll put it away until tomorrow.' James looked at his sister who was clearly tempted to start on the chocolate at once. 'Come on, Kate, let's leave it in our bedrooms.'

They both headed up the stairs, clutching their precious gifts.

Sam started to help Rose put the tins in a cupboard. 'And what have you been doing with yourself since I last saw you, madam?' he asked with a strong French accent.

'Not as much mischief as you have, I'll be bound,' Rose teased.

'She was in London during the worst of the Blitz,'

George interrupted. 'When she couldn't get the ambulance through the rubble, she got out and started digging for survivors.' His tone was exasperated, but he couldn't hide the pride in his voice.

'Well, you don't need to worry any more, Dad,' she told him. 'The worst seems to be over, and I'm only an air raid warden now.'

'Only!' George threw his hands up in a gesture of defeat. 'The raids on London might have eased, but the Luftwaffe is picking on our historic cities now. Exeter, Bath, York, places like that, and when Jerry's finished with those he'll most likely start on London again.'

'Pessimist.' Rose grinned at her father. 'You worry too much, Dad.' She finished packing the food away and then spotted a packet of biscuits on the table. 'Where did those come from?'

'I brought them.' Dora held out two packets of tea and a bag of carrots. 'I thought you might like these as well. I went and made eyes at the cook.'

'Well done,' Marj complimented her and picked up a packet of tea. 'I think this calls for a nice cuppa, don't you? And while we drink it we can decide who is going to sleep where.'

It was eleven o'clock before Annie wandered downstairs the next day. The rain was pounding on the windows and she'd been so comfortable in her own bed that she had just turned over and gone back to sleep.

She stuck her head round the kitchen door and saw only her mother and Rose in there. 'Do you need any help?'

'Ah, you've surfaced at last, have you? What have you

been doing to get so worn out?' Her mother handed her a cup of tea.

'Working.' Annie walked in and leant on the sink. 'What can I do?'

'Nothing.' Rose hustled her towards the door. 'Go and join the others in the front room, we've got everything under control here.'

They clearly didn't need her so she went to find the rest of them.

Sam was sprawled on the floor playing snakes and ladders with Kate; Wally and George were immersed in a game of draughts and everyone else was reading. Pirate was standing on the back of an armchair watching the rain and giving a ratty grumble from time to time.

Annie was greeted when she came in, then they all went back to what they had been doing. She sat in an armchair, sipped her tea and gazed into the fire. This is lovely, she thought with a satisfied smile on her face. No straining to pick up Morse code under atmospherics, no jumping to attention, or rushed meals. It was only when she was away from the base that she realized how tiring the work was. It took total concentration, but she still loved it and wouldn't want to do anything else.

Suddenly Charlie surged to his feet. 'Come on, Dora, let's put our coats on and take Pirate to Barnes Common for a run.'

The dog's ears shot up at the mention of his name, and he jumped down straight away and started to tear around in excitement.

Dora tossed her book aside and stood up. 'That's a good idea. Do you want to come, Annie?'

243

She shook her head and yawned again. 'No thanks, I'll stay by the fire.'

Charlie ruffled her hair as he walked past. 'Try and wake up by tonight, because Sam and me are taking you girls out dancing in Richmond. We want to see if you can do the jive.'

'What's that?' Annie pretended she was puzzled. Charlie didn't know they'd been taught by the Yanks, and she did love to tease him.

Her brother frowned at Sam. 'Where do you keep her, in a cage?'

Sam shook the dice in his hand and grinned. 'Something like that.'

Pirate had obviously had enough of this delay and dropped his lead at Charlie's feet.

'Oops! We'd better go. We'll show you tonight, Annie.'

The next three days were the most relaxed Annie had spent for some time. It stopped raining, they took long walks in Richmond Park, went to a dance and the pictures.

They returned on the fourth day after an invigorating walk to find an air force truck parked outside the house.

'Looks like trouble,' Sam said, striding into the kitchen, where the driver was enjoying a cup of tea.

He jumped to his feet when he saw Sam, and handed him a sealed envelope.

Sam slit it open and read in silence for a while, then said, 'I have to leave.' He looked at Rose and Marj. 'I have enjoyed myself immensely.'

'You are welcome any time,' Rose told him.

He smiled and headed for the stairs. It only took

him five minutes to get his kit together, and after a quick goodbye to everyone, he hurried out to the truck.

'Sam!' Annie caught him at the gate. 'You're not going to do anything dangerous, are you?'

He bent and touched his lips to her cheek in a fleeting kiss. 'It is just another boat trip.'

She knew how dangerous that could be.

It was ten o'clock the next morning before Annie dragged herself out of bed, and as it was raining she played games with the children or read a book and dozed by the fire. Outwardly she was relaxed and enjoying her rest, but her mind was racing. Where was Sam now? But she wasn't allowed to dwell on this too much, as Kate and James dragged her into dealing the cards for a game of snap.

There was a knock on the front door, and James listened to the sound of voices, and then leapt to his feet. 'More visitors,' he exclaimed and shot out of the door, closely followed by his sister.

Annie, finding herself alone, stood up. She had better go and see who had arrived.

Her mother was making tea, as usual; James was standing in front of two tall airmen, gazing at them in worship, and Kate was surveying them from the other side of the table, a rapt expression on her face. And what Dora was thinking was anyone's guess, but Annie knew she would find out after their visitors had left. Her friend was studying the pilots and would no doubt have some comments to make.

'Hello, Bouncer.' Annie spoke quietly and waited for

him to turn, relieved to see he could move with more ease than the last time she'd seen him.

'Annie!' He reached out with his good arm and pulled her towards him for a kiss on the cheek. 'We didn't know you'd be here. Have they let you loose for a few days?'

'Yes, I'm on leave. They think they can do without me for a while,' she joked. Annie had only met Bouncer once but he seemed like an old friend. 'How are you?'

'I'm fine, but the station commander here still won't let me fly.' Bouncer glared at his friend. 'Says he can't do without my help, but he's lying, of course.'

These two men were obviously great friends and Annie suspected that Reid was concerned about Bouncer, and was trying to keep him out of combat as long as he could. Reid, who hadn't taken his eyes off Annie, smiled. 'You're looking well, Webster.'

She snapped to attention and gave a sloppy salute, although she was out of uniform and wearing a pair of slacks and a jumper. Reid had an amused glint in his eyes and Annie had a job to keep a straight face. He really was quite handsome. 'Thank you, sir.'

'At ease.' Reid started to chuckle as he gazed at her casual outfit, his eyes lingering on her curves.

The look he'd just given her told her, quite plainly, that he liked what he saw. Reid Lascells was a vital, physical man and she was beginning to feel drawn to him. That was dangerous . . .

Bouncer groaned and raised his eyebrows, looking around at everyone. 'They haven't been in the same room for more than two minutes and they're at it again. As soon as they see each other they fight.'

Annie laughed with everyone else and pulled a chair

out for Bouncer. 'Sit down, both of you, and tell us what you're doing here.'

'Reid came to thank me for the letters I've been writing to his parents.' Marj said and poured them all a cup of tea. She smiled with pleasure as Bouncer slid her a packet of the precious brew. 'Oh, thank you so much, that was very thoughtful of you.' Bouncer received a kiss on the cheek for that.

'How are they?' Annie asked Reid. 'I meant to get over and see them, but I've been so busy.'

'They understand, and the letters they've received from you and your mother have been much appreciated. Losing Paul has been a terrible blow, but they're coming to terms with it, slowly.'

'I'm glad.' Annie knew it was going to take his parents a long time, and Paul would never be forgotten by any of them.

'Would you stay for lunch?' Marj asked them.

'Thank you, but we must get back.' Reid stood up. 'This was only a fleeting visit as we were in the area.'

After they'd gone, Annie went back to her reading, but couldn't concentrate. They'd only refused lunch because it wasn't the done thing to take other people's rations. If you knew you were going to eat at someone's house you took food with you, just as Sam and Dora had done. Still, she was glad they hadn't stayed as her nerves were too strung out from worrying about Sam, without having to put up with Reid's disturbing presence.

Dora came into the lounge and sat beside Annie. 'Well, well, so that was Reid Lascells. Wow!'

'I'm not denying that he's gorgeous' – Annie looked over the top of her book – 'but he's an awkward devil.'

'Yeah, I'll bet he is!'

Dora grinned at her, so Annie went back to her reading, feeling it was better to cut this conversation off right now!

21

'It was a shame Will couldn't get home,' Annie told Dora, when they were on the train going back to Chicksands. 'But did you enjoy yourself?'

'Of course I did, Annie. You know I adore your family.' Dora cast her friend a sideways glance. 'Fancy Paul's brother and his mate turning up like that.'

'Just fancy.' Annie gave a snort of disbelief. She'd managed to fend off Dora's talk about Reid for the rest of their leave, but now they were on the train there wouldn't be any escape from her opinions. 'Bouncer didn't know I would be there, his surprise was genuine, but I'll bet Reid did. He's always writing, and sometimes I get the feeling the blasted man is following me.'

'No.' Dora shook her head. 'I'm sure he didn't know – and anyway, what have you got against the poor man?'

Annie had never spoken about Reid's rudeness when he'd come to tell her about Paul. It had upset her too much at the time, and still did, she had to admit. She didn't normally harbour a grudge or take offence so easily, but the circumstances had been distressing, and she couldn't seem to let go of it. Taking a deep breath, she started to tell her friend what had happened, allowing the hurt to see the light of day for the first time. And she was surprised at the intensity of her feelings for him. It was a confusing mixture of dislike and admiration. He really was a most disturbing man!

249

'Oh, Annie.' Dora patted her arm in sympathy. 'That's no reason to be so hostile towards him. I expect he was devastated by his brother's death and lashed out at the nearest person he could. Everyone reacts to grief in a different way. He's obviously sorry for the way he acted, you ought to understand that and forgive him.'

'You're quite right, but there's something about him . . .'

'He's too handsome?' Dora asked.

'Hmm.' Annie's mouth turned up at the corners in amusement. 'He is a bit of a stunner, isn't he?'

'There's a very kind man lurking under that abrupt exterior, and I can't help thinking he would make you a gorgeous husband.'

Dora roared with laughter, drawing curious stares from the packed train. 'You sounded just like Rose then.'

Annie stared at her friend in astonishment. 'Now you're delving into the realms of fantasy.'

'Have you fallen for Sam?'

'I'll take that as a compliment,' she told her.

'It was meant as one.' Dora studied Annie carefully.

'I like him and he is attractive.' Annie stared out of the train window, trying to decide how she really felt. 'But I don't think it's more than that.'

'If you don't love him, Annie, then let him know, because I think he's attracted to you. He's had enough sorrow in his life, hasn't he?'

'Yes, he has, and it isn't going to be easy for him when he returns to France.' How would someone recover from being thrown out of their country and losing all their family? Britain had suffered death, destruction and a shortage of food, but they hadn't had to deal with a conquering force walking the streets.

'Then leave him alone, my friend.' Dora smiled. 'If you're not sure if you love him, then I can tell you that you *don't*.'

'Oh, how can you tell?' Annie frowned. She'd heard girls talking about being in love, and listened to their raptures as they explained that they couldn't live without a certain person, but quite honestly she'd never felt so bowled over. She was fond of a lot of men, but each time she'd asked herself if this was the one man for her she hadn't been able to give an affirmative answer. This being in love was a mystery to her.

'You just know when it's right. That's all I can tell you.'

Annie settled back in her seat. 'Do you know what you feel for Will?'

'I'm in love with him. Do you mind?'

'Not at all.' Annie grinned. 'Welcome to the Webster family, Dora.'

'Oh, don't be hasty.' She held her hands up in horror. 'Will hasn't said he loves me yet, but I'm hopeful.' Dora looked curiously at her friend. 'You've changed since we first met, do you know that?'

'So you told me once before, but a lot has happened, and I'm sure none of us will come out of this war unscathed.' Annie shrugged. 'I hope you don't think I've changed for the worse?'

'No, I think I like the new Annie Webster better, but be careful you keep your gentleness. I'm not sure exactly what you've been doing, but I know that it's something quite traumatic, and you're starting to bury your feelings.'

251

That remark, from someone she trusted so much, shook Annie. She had seen her sister Rose do exactly the same thing when she'd been about twenty-one and remembered how worried they'd all felt. She mustn't do the same thing. She'd send Reid a letter of apology – as soon as she had time.

'Hi, Annie,' Sam greeted her as she walked into his office.

'Did you enjoy the rest of your holiday?'

'Yes, thanks. How did your trip go?'

'Weather was rough, but we didn't have to swim back.'

He grinned. 'But it was a successful exercise.'

She didn't ask what the emergency had been, knowing Sam wouldn't give her an answer. She was surrounded by secrecy in her job and you were only told what was necessary. She headed for her desk, feeling refreshed and ready to start work again after her leave.

She was soon totally absorbed in what she was doing and jumped when she was tapped on the shoulder.

'There's someone here to see you, so take an hour's break,' the officer told her. 'He's waiting outside.'

Annie was alarmed to see her brother Charlie waiting for her, and pacing up and down in a very agitated way. She'd only seen him this morning as they'd all prepared to return to their bases. It looked as if he'd thrown his air force uniform on in a hurry; if an officer saw him with buttons undone and tie badly knotted he would be put on a charge. A sense of dread gripped her.

'What's happened?' she asked, rushing up to him.

His face was ashen and he was close to tears, but he just gazed at her without speaking.

'Charlie! Tell me,' she exclaimed.

252

Her brother took a deep breath and blurted out, 'Will's missing.'

Stunned, Annie hugged her brother, and a strange thing happened. She was back in the scullery of the Garrett Street house during the First World War, the day they'd received the telegram saying that their father was missing. It was as if Rose was standing beside her again saying, *Missing doesn't mean he's dead.*'

'When did the news arrive?' Her mind was racing, searching for some way to comfort him. The brothers had always been close, and she knew this would hit Charlie very hard, as it would every member of the Webster family.

'This morning, after you'd gone.' He gulped, trying to control his emotions. 'I rushed to the station to catch you but the train had already left.'

'How is everyone coping?'

He lifted his shoulders in a helpless gesture. 'We're all worried, of course, but Mum is holding up quite well, and Rose is being positive.' A brief smile flashed across his face at the mention of their sister. 'She's trying to get information out of the Admiralty with not much success at the moment.'

Annie was relieved to see her brother more in control. Worry and fear gnawed away at her but she was determined to hold herself together. If she broke down now it would upset Charlie even more.

'Thanks, Sis, I feel better for talking with you.' He gave her another hug.

'Are you going back home?' she asked.

'No, I've got to return to base at once.' A worried frown appeared. 'Tell Dora. I've gathered from Will's letters that they have a romance going, albeit from a distance.'

'I'll do it right away.' She watched her brother jump into a truck and drive away, and then she went to look for Dora. This wasn't going to be easy, and she wanted to get it over with.

Annie found her friend in the mess, taking a break.

'Ah, come up for air at last, have you?' Dora pushed her a cup of tea across the table. 'Here, you look as if you need this, I'll get another one.'

'Sit down again, Dora, I've something to tell you.'

'What is it?' Her friend touched her hand in sympathy. 'You look upset.'

'There isn't any easy way to do this.' Annie's eyes clouded with tears and she wiped them away with her hand. She now had an inkling of how Reid must have felt when he'd had to tell her about Paul.

'Tell it straight, Annie.' Dora's mouth set in a straight line.

'Will's been reported missing. His ship was torpedoed, but that's all we know at the moment.'

Annie's friend let out a ragged sigh. 'I thought you were going to tell me he was dead, but missing doesn't sound so final.'

'You're needed back on duty, Annie.' Sam was standing next to their table.

She squeezed Dora's hand, and then stood up, wishing she could stay a while longer, not only to help Dora but also to deal with her own emotions. However, they had all learned that you had to keep going, whatever was happening in your own life. 'I'll let you know the moment there's any news.'

254

As she headed for the door, Sam fell into step beside her. 'Trouble?'

'My brother Will is missing. Dora's been writing to him and I think they are serious about each other.'

Sam stopped suddenly and swore in two languages. 'If I'd known I wouldn't have dragged you back to work.'

'That's all right, I'd rather be busy.' She gave a tired smile. 'You know that's how I cope with grief. When is it all going to end?' she asked wearily.

'Not for a while yet, I'm afraid.'

Annie straightened up and marched along with a determined stride. Let's hope 1943 will be a better year, she thought.

Over the next three days Annie phoned her sister a couple of times a day, and after each call felt weighed down with worry and disappointment. On the fourth day after she'd heard about Will she tried again and prayed for some good news this time.

'Rose!' The line was bad and she had to shout down the phone. 'Have you heard anything yet?'

'Nothing yet, but it's only been a few days.'

'How's Mum bearing up?'

'She's all right, Annie. She's no stranger to trouble, as you know, and all we can do is wait.'

'It's hard though,' Annie grumbled. 'Anything else been happening?'

'We're all getting ready to go to Wales for Christmas, and Reid came round with some sweets for the children.'

Reid! Blast, she'd forgotten all about her apology. 'That was kind of him.'

Rose's laugh echoed down the distorted line. 'He's a handsome beast, isn't he?'

'I agree with . . .' Annie was talking to herself and it wasn't worth trying to get reconnected. She'd phoned for news of Will, but there wasn't any.

Annie wandered back to her hut and wrote to Reid, before it slipped her mind again.

'What are you looking so pensive about?' Bouncer eased himself into a chair.

Reid glanced up from the letter he was reading. 'Hmm?'

'I asked why the deep frown, old boy?' Who's the letter from?' Bouncer leaned forward to get a closer look. 'It isn't in green ink, so it can't be Annie.'

'Yes, it is, but she only uses that when she's being rude to me.' Reid watched his friend light a cigarette, using both hands quite freely. 'It's a sort of an apology. She says she's sorry for insulting me whenever we've met.'

'That's nice.' Bouncer took a deep drag on his fag, watching his friend through a cloud of smoke.

'Then she ends by saying that she would appreciate it if I would stop pestering her with letters.'

'Ah, that sounds more like our Annie. I was getting worried there for a minute.'

'So was I.' Reid grimaced and fanned away the smoke drifting towards his face. 'What the blazes are you smoking?'

'Got them from a Yank.' Bouncer grinned as he waved the cigarette under Reid's nose. 'Do you want one, they're not bad.'

'No thanks.'

'So, why do you think Annie suddenly decided to apologize?'

Reid folded the letter and put it back in the envelope. 'She's probably feeling down at the moment; her brother Will has been reported missing.'

'Hell, I'm sorry about that. Air force, is he?'

'Fleet Air Arm, and I expect they're all worried sick.'

'Yeah.' Bouncer lit another American cigarette and fished in his pocket for a Players Navy Cut, then handed that to Reid. 'They're a nice family, and what do you think of Rose? If she wasn't a happily married woman, I'd like to take her on. What a beauty!'

Reid laughed at his friend's expression. 'You'd have a job in your state of health.'

'I'm nearly back to full strength, but you, my friend, are looking frayed around the edges. How long is it since you've had some fun? And more to the point, how long is it since you've bedded a woman?'

'Let me see.' Reid blew smoke rings in the air, his brow furrowed in thought. 'Bugger if I can remember.'

'Right! That settles it.' Bouncer dragged Reid out of the chair. 'We're going out on the town tonight to find ourselves a couple of girls.'

Reid opened a drawer and shunted the paperwork into it. He'd deal with that tomorrow.

'What do you think of those?' Bouncer nudged Reid so hard his beer slopped on to the table.

He peered through the smoke-filled bar. 'Too young.'

'Hmm. Perhaps you're right. Drink up and I'll get the next round in.'

Reid watched his friend weave towards the bar, and

then studied the dregs in the bottom of his glass. This hadn't been such a good idea. He was restless, unsettled and drinking himself senseless wasn't going to help.

A soldier started to pound on the piano and the bar erupted into 'Roll Out the Barrel'. The table Reid was leaning on actually shook as everyone sang at the tops of their voices.

Bouncer arrived back carrying a tray full of pints of beer. 'Thought I'd get a few reserves in, it was like a rugby scrum trying to reach the bar.' He shouted above the racket.

'Let's go in there,' Reid yelled, pointing to the door of the saloon bar.

They fought their way into the quieter room and closed the door behind them. They could still hear the noise from the other bar, but at least it was muffled now.

'Are you sober enough to have a serious talk?' Bouncer asked, when they'd settled themselves at a table in the corner of the bar.

Reid eyed the four pints lined up in front of him and tried to remember how many he had had already, 'You'd better talk now, because by the time I've polished off those, I'll be incapable of doing anything.'

'I've put in a request to return to my squadron,' Bouncer announced.

'Ah, I thought it wouldn't be long; you've made a remarkable recovery. And to tell you the truth, Bouncer, I've been considering the same thing myself.' He couldn't remember when he'd been so restless, and had wondered if flying regularly again would help. The only thing stopping him was the distress he knew it would cause his parents. They thought he was safe on the ground for the duration of the war, running the Tangmere airbase. If he took to the air again they would be in constant fear of him being killed, and after losing Paul he didn't want to put them through that.

'You mustn't do that, old boy. You're a first class administrator.' Bouncer emptied his glass and pulled another one towards him. 'You've been used to running the family business. What do you make?'

'Nut and bolts.'

'That's right, and very useful too. Well, as I was saying, you've been used to working for a living and you're making a damned good job of station commander . . .' Another pint vanished. 'But I've come from the idle rich and the only useful thing I've ever done in my life is fly, and being grounded is driving me round the bend.'

'I know how you feel.' Reid drank two pints in quick succession. He was a bit out of practice with this drinking lark, but he'd soon get back into it again . . . with Bouncer's help.

Bouncer watched and grinned. 'Now you're getting the hang of it. Have you had enough booze to make you forget the desirable Annie?'

'Who's she?' Reid finished off his last pint and heaved himself on to his feet. 'I don't think those two girls were that young, do you?'

'Nope.' Bouncer staggered upright. 'Perfect age, I would say.'

'Come on, then. Let's have some fun.' Reid draped an arm over Bouncer's shoulder and the pair of them lurched back into the public bar, singing 'White Cliffs of Dover'.

Annie was so excited. What a way to start the new year! The last few weeks had been terrible as they'd waited for news of Will, and to make matters worse they hadn't heard from Bill for weeks. She knew Rose fretted in her own quiet way, but kept her fears to herself. However, George had finally won the battle he'd been having with Rose and had persuaded her that it was time she joined them in Wales. James and Kate were living there most of the time and they didn't see enough of her. She had agreed in the end to move there and was no doubt immersed in her beloved books again. Her sister had never lost her thirst for knowledge; it was part of her character. She was still in the WVS and had taken over the library books in a convalescent hospital for injured servicemen. Rose would enjoy that. Annie remembered how concerned her sister had been for the ex-servicemen after the last war. She had done all she could for them and would want to help again.

She walked into Dora's hut and found her sitting on the bunk gazing at a photo of a tall sailor.

'Get your coat,' Annie ordered, 'we're going down the pub for a drink.'

'Oh, I don't think – '

'It's no good you arguing. You're coming whether you

want to or not.' Annie's heart went out to her friend. The long wait without any news had been agonizing.

'Come on, Dora,' she coaxed. 'It will do us both good.'

'You're right.' The photo was tucked back into a bag and Dora sighed. 'Life goes on, eh?'

''Course it does. Everything's going to be all right, you'll see.'

She gave Annie a suspicious look. 'You seem very bright; have you been at the booze already?'

'No, but I'm certainly going to have a few tonight.'

'Well, if that's how you feel, what are we hanging around here for?' Dora shivered as a blast of cold wind hit them on the way to the gate. 'Damned cold tonight, have you got your knickers on?'

Annie stopped and lifted her skirt a little to show the hated air force issue.

Dora smirked. 'I can't help remembering when we saw these dreadful bloomers for the first time.'

'They're warm though, but I draw the line at wearing those awful brassieres.' Annie signalled the driver of a truck. 'You going near the Red Lion pub?'

'Sure. Jump in.'

The place was crowded as usual, and Annie stood in the doorway, searching the faces. At that moment she saw him and her face broke into a brilliant smile. 'Look over there,' she told her friend.

With a cry of joy, Dora shot across the room into the waiting arms of Will. He kissed Dora, then lifted his head and smiled at his sister, drawing her into his embrace.

'Annie!' Dora was crying. 'Why didn't you tell me?'

'He just walked in earlier. No one told us he was all right and on his way home.'

'I asked Annie to keep it a secret.' He kissed Dora again. 'I wanted to surprise you.'

'You've done that all right!'

'Hey, mate, that's a bit greedy, hugging two gorgeous women at once.'

Annie could just make out the figure of an Australian soldier through her tear-clouded vision.

Will laughed. 'This is Dora, and that's Annie.'

'Good grief!' the Australian exclaimed. 'That's never little Annie?'

Annie rubbed her eyes so she could see better, and studied the man. He was talking as if he knew her, but she was sure she'd never seen him before.

'Don't you recognize him, Annie?' Will asked, looking highly amused. 'This is Bob.'

'Bob?' She gazed at him in bewilderment. There was something vaguely familiar about the man.

'Take a closer look. It's our long lost brother.'

'Bob?' she cried, then threw her arms around him and received a bear hug in return. 'We didn't think we'd ever see you again. Have you seen Mum?'

'Yes, and Rose.' He grimaced. 'You should have heard what she called me.'

'I can imagine, and you deserve all you get from her,' Annie pointed out, as she remembered the upset Bob had caused when he'd run away to sea as a young boy. He'd been a rebellious child, nasty, bad-tempered, and always fighting with Rose who did her best to control him. It was only after he'd run away that they'd realized how unhappy he had been, and how he'd hated life in Garrett Street.

'I know, and I'm sorry I hurt everyone, but I couldn't take it any more. I just had to get out of that dreadful hovel. Mum said she understands.'

Annie nodded. 'We all managed to get out eventually, and it's all thanks to Rose and Bill.'

Bob shook his head in disbelief. 'I've heard the whole story and it's hard to believe the things Rose has done, and without her our family would have ended up in the workhouse. I still remember that terrible beating she took from the old man as she tried to get the rent money back from him. She's still as fierce, though.' He gave a deep chuckle. 'When I saw her glaring at me with those black eyes, I nearly turned tail and got out of there quick. But I would have known her anywhere.'

'Sit down everyone.' Will pinched another chair from the next table. 'We've got a lot of catching up to do.'

'I'll get a round of drinks in first,' Bob said.

Annie watched him make his way through the crowd, absolutely astonished by this turn of events. There had been sporadic letters from him over the years, but they had been brief, giving little indication of his life in Australia, except to assure them that he was all right. When he'd written to let them know that he was getting married, their mother had been upset because she couldn't be there to see her son on his special day. 'He's an officer, Will.'

'Yeah, who'd have believed it, and he's attached to a British unit here. He's doing all right for himself, and when you look at him now it's hard to believe he was once a rebellious tearaway.'

263

Dora was holding on to Will's arm and appeared to be speechless with happiness. Annie had never seen her friend so quiet before.

'What happened to you?' Annie asked Will when Bob returned with the drinks.

'I was on my way back from America when the troop-ship I was on was so badly damaged by a U-boat attack that we had to take to the lifeboats. The weather was appalling and we were scattered all over the ocean so it took some time to find us.'

'What on earth were you doing in America?' Dora asked, finding her voice at last.

'I'd been working in one of their factories, learning about the American engines. A merchant ship eventually picked us up, which was a damned risky thing to do. Then we went straight into battle again, and the radio room was damaged. Fortunately for us a destroyer came back to look for the straggler and saved us from further damage.'

Annie understood why they hadn't had any news before. Her brother was making light of it but things must have been dangerous.

'When I turned up it caused quite a rumpus, but not as much as when Bob walked in an hour later.' He gave a deep chuckle. 'Mum didn't know whether to hit him or hug him.'

'Rose knew what she wanted to do, though,' said Bob grinning. 'She would have liked to shake me until my teeth rattled.'

'And she could do it,' Dora said and laughed.

'You don't have to remind me what she's capable of.' Bob took some photos out of his pocket and gave them to Annie. 'That's my wife and daughter, Sara, with baby Emma.'

'Ah, they're lovely, Bob.' She touched her brother's hand, pleased to see he had such a lovely family. 'Are you happy in Australia?'

'I was until this bloody war started. I've got a sheep farm and love the wide open spaces; after Bermondsey it's paradise.'

Now Dora had got over the shock of seeing Will again she was bursting with curiosity. 'Would someone tell me what's going on? I didn't know you had another brother, Annie?'

'Bob ran away to sea when I was only little,' Annie explained, 'and this is the first time we've seen him since he disappeared.'

'Wow! What a night this is turning out to be!' Dora smiled happily and clung on to Will's arm even tighter.

'Did you enjoy yourself in America?' Annie asked her brother.

'I'll say. But do you know they don't have a tea break in their factories?' He looked scandalized. 'They've got these machines and you can get drinks from them, but we weren't going to have that. We bought a small camping stove, a saucepan to boil the water in, tea, milk, sugar and biscuits, but we couldn't get a teapot anywhere so we had to use a coffee pot.'

Annie was laughing. She could just imagine a group of British sailors wanting their tea break, and she wondered if they put a tot of rum in it as well. She wouldn't put it past them. 'And what did you do then?'

'We sat on boxes, lit the stove and brewed up in

265

the middle of the factory floor.' He shook his head in amusement. '"The Yanks thought it was hilarious and used to call out "Having a tea party, boys?"'

There was so much news to catch up on that the evening flew by, and all the time they drank steadily. Annie didn't know how much she'd had, but she was too happy to keep count. This was a night to enjoy and blast the consequences!

As she reached out to pick up another glass, it was whipped out of her way. 'You're not going to be fit for anything in the morning.'

She peered at the man standing beside the table. 'Hello, Sam, I didn't know you were here.'

'I've been sitting no more than six feet from you all evening, watching you trying to get drunk.'

'I think I've made quite a good job of it,' Annie giggled. 'Sam, meet my brothers. Will has just been rescued from the sea, and the last time I saw Bob I was no taller than knee-high.'

'Ah.' Sam shook hands with the men. 'I see the reason for the celebration, but I'm afraid I need Annie sharp and alert tomorrow.'

'He's my boss,' Annie informed them from behind her hand, and then fell about laughing as if it was the funniest thing she'd ever said.

Bob was grinning. 'It's a bit late for that, mate. She's plastered; you'd better take her back now.'

Dora whispered in Annie's ear. 'Go back with Sam. I'm staying with Will tonight.'

'Right.' She managed to stand up by holding on to the table. 'What are you going to do now, Bob?'

'I've got a room here for the night, the same as Will,

266

and in the morning I'm going to Wales with Mum and Wally to meet Rose's kids.' He stood up and smiled ruefully. 'I'm told I'll also see Rose's real father, Sir George Gresham. That was a turn-up for the book, wasn't it?'

'You'll like him, Bob,' Will said. 'That's where Rose gets her fiery temperament from.'

'I can't wait.' Bob wiped his brow in mock fear.

Annie hugged both her brothers, and being in a very emotional state shed a few tears, before being helped out of the pub by Sam.

'Jush you and me, then, Sam.' The cold air had a strange effect on her and she gave a lopsided smile. 'I'm so happy.'

'I can see that.' He held her around the waist to keep her upright. 'Wish I'd brought the truck with me.'

Annie staggered as she shook her head. 'Noo, rather walk.'

He chuckled. 'Still don't trust my driving, then?'

'I'm not that drunk.' She tried to prove the point by pushing him away and walking in a straight line – without any success at all.

'Really? You could have fooled me.' He grabbed hold of her again as she staggered dangerously, then they headed up the road towards Chicksands.

They had almost reached her hut when she stopped and threw her arms around Sam's neck. 'Kiss me.'

He did, but it was a gentle, teasing embrace.

'You're not taking this seriously,' she complained. 'I think I could fall in love with you.'

'I don't want you to do that, Annie, but I wouldn't mind some uncontrollable lust.'

She leant against him and sighed. 'I think I can manage that.'

Annie opened one eye and groaned. She had to be on duty in an hour and she didn't think she could move.

'Here, drink this.' Dora thrust a glass of something fizzy at her.

Without asking what it was Annie emptied the glass and then shuddered. 'Hell, that is the first and last time I ever get drunk.'

Dora sat on the edge of the bed. 'You'll feel better when you get moving.'

'You sure?' Annie was finding that hard to believe. There was a notice on the wall opposite her and she could swear it was sliding up and down of its own accord. Her friend nodded and grinned. 'You're not used to drinking and you really overdid it last night.'

'Well, I've learnt my lesson. Never again!' She looked at Dora's happy expression. 'You seem cheerful enough. Had a good night, did you?'

'Wonderful! Annie, me and Will are getting married.'

'Oh, that's marvellous,' Annie exclaimed, throwing her arms around Dora in delight. 'When?'

'As soon as we can.' Dora hugged her back, and then glanced at her watch. 'I'll tell you all about it later, but you'd better hurry or Sam will be furious with you.'

Sam! The way she had behaved last night came rushing into her thoughts, and she coloured in embarrassment. 'Oh, my God!'

'That look of horror tells me you've been up to something. What have you and the delectable Sam been doing?'

'I remember getting back here, and then I tried to seduce him.' Annie buried her head in her hands. 'After that my mind's a blank.'

'You've made it then.' Sam studied her face carefully.

'You look awful; are you all right?'

'That's what I need you to tell me.'

'Ah' – he was clearly fighting to keep a straight face – 'you can't remember our night of passion.'

She took a deep breath. 'Tell me what I missed.'

'After you threw yourself into my arms and begged me to make love to you . . .' He paused.

'Begged?' Lord, but she'd really made a fool of herself this time.

Sam nodded. 'Definitely *begged*.'

'What happened then?' she asked with a resigned air.

'You passed out.'

'And?' She had to know the whole sordid truth.

'Annie,' Sam laughed, 'I didn't want to make love to a senseless woman. I expect the girl I'm with to join in with enthusiasm, or it's no fun. I put you to bed – your bed. I had to do it myself because the place was deserted – not a damned female in sight when you need one,' he complained.

Annie sagged in relief. 'So nothing happened?'

'Well, I wouldn't say that.' He raised his eyebrows. 'I did have the pleasure of undressing you, but that's all.' He sighed. 'I managed to control myself, but it was damned frustrating. Still, those terrible military issue knickers did help to cool my ardour a little.'

Annie blushed. 'I was wearing them because it was so

cold. I'm sorry for my disgraceful conduct. And I'm never going to get drunk again.'

'It would be wise,' he told her. 'Drink obviously makes you amorous, and the next man you try that with might not have my self-control. Can you remember anything?'

'Yes.' Her head came up and her gaze locked on to his eyes. 'You told me you didn't want me to fall in love with you. Why?'

'I would find it impossible to place you in danger again, and I can't afford that kind of emotional baggage. It clouds the judgement, as you well know, and I don't know what awaits me when this war is finally over.'

'Are you going to send me to France again, Sam?' she asked quietly.

'Once the invasion is imminent, then I might not have any choice. We're going to need as many operatives as possible to help the Resistance disrupt German communications.'

The hangover was forgotten and she smiled. 'I wouldn't mind doing another parachute jump.'

'Hmm. You like a bit of excitement. Is that why you never married your pilot friend? Was he too tame for you?'

Annie chewed her lip, deep in thought. That had never occurred to her before. 'There's nothing like a war to make you realize what you really are, is there?'

'I agree, and our true nature comes as a shock, eh?' She changed the subject. 'When the invasion does start, what are you going to do?'

'Go home and help to kick the bastards out of France.' There was a look of grim determination on his face. Annie hoped she was there to see him get his revenge.

23

Dora and Will were married at Caxton Hall in London at the beginning of February; they were in uniform, but it was obvious that her friend didn't mind not having a grand wedding, for she was too much in love to care. And it didn't matter because Will looked splendid in his naval uniform and Dora radiant in air force blue. Annie tried not to cry as the ceremony came to a close. Will and Dora were now husband and wife. She was so happy for them.

There was a large turnout. Dora's family were there, and Charlie had managed to get home just in time to act as best man. Bob went as well, and had been welcomed back by the family as if he'd never been away. George seemed to have taken a great liking to him; they were talking and laughing outside the registry office like old friends. There wasn't a trace of the boy she'd remembered. Bob was mature, good looking, and obviously a happy man. The only one not there was Bill. That had upset Kate for a while, but her natural enthusiasm for life and any new experience had soon banished her gloom. James appeared quite disgusted with the whole sentimental affair, and Annie grinned to herself. It wouldn't be long before the boy changed his mind about girls and romance. He was at the lanky stage but it was clear that he was going to be a handsome man. As time passed, James was showing signs of his father's quiet temperament, and that was a relief to his mother. Rose had always said that she hoped her children didn't inherit her intolerant, explosive nature. And, as time passed, it looked as if neither of them had.

While the photographs were being taken Annie noticed that Rose was relaxed and clearly enjoying herself. Her sister might have been difficult in her youth, but time, Bill, and children of her own had certainly mellowed her.

'That was a very nice wedding,' Marj said, blowing her nose. 'I thought that son of mine was never going to marry, but he's found a fine girl in Dora. And I might get some more grandchildren now.'

Annie laughed. 'After having nine children I would have thought you'd had enough of babies.'

'Grandchildren are different. You can always hand them back to their mother when they get too much trouble.' Her eyes clouded for a moment. 'All except Bob's children, of course, I don't suppose I'll ever see them.'

Annie squeezed her mother's arm, knowing this was a source of sadness to her. 'I expect you'll have plenty of others.'

After the photos were taken, the boisterous wedding party made their way to Rose's place.

In spite of rationing, Rose and Marj, with help from Dora, had managed to put on quite a spread. The wedding cake looked splendid, until the cardboard replica was removed to reveal a simple sponge. This caused a lot of laughter, but the war had been going on for over three years now, and shortages were accepted without comment. Everyone just did the best they could.

'Annie!' Dora called over. 'Gran wants to have a chat with Rose but she won't stay in one place long enough for Gran to catch her.'

'Come with me.' Annie took hold of the elderly woman's hand and gently walked her over to Rose. 'Sit down for a while, Rose. Dora's grandmother wants to talk to you.'

Annie pushed her sister into a chair and pulled up another one for the old lady.

'My name's Maude,' she told Rose, 'and I've been itching to meet you. I saw you in action once and I've never forgotten it. You were standing for election to the local council, and at one of your public meetings you jumped off the stage, rolled up your sleeves and threatened to flatten one heckler.' Maude slapped her leg in glee. 'I've never seen a man so terrified. Hadn't laughed so much in years. You got my vote all right.'

'I remember the incident.' Rose looked highly amused. 'He couldn't have been much more than five feet.'

'That's right,' Maude chortled. 'You towered over him, and could easily have carried out your threat.'

They both roared with laughter, and Annie, seeing they were getting along well, left them to it.

When Annie returned to camp the next day there was a spring in her step. It had been a long time since she'd felt so light-hearted. It had been wonderful to see Will married to such a lovely girl as Dora. The traditional honeymoon was out of the question, but they had managed to grab a couple of days in a hotel by the sea. Annie smiled to herself. They hadn't said where they

273

were going but the happy couple had disappeared as soon as was polite. The future looked much more hopeful now, because after a fierce battle by the Russians the Germans had just surrendered at Stalingrad. The Germans didn't seem so invincible now and morale was high.

'I'm back, Sam,' she called, as she walked past his open door. A few steps further on she stopped. There hadn't been any response and she knew he was there; she'd caught a glimpse of him sitting at his desk.

Retracing her steps, she went and stood in front of him. She had never seen such a strange expression on his face and it was difficult to decide what kind of mood he was in.

'Is something wrong?' she asked him.

'Hmm?' He appeared preoccupied. 'Did the wedding go well?'

'Yes, it was lovely and we were all sorry you couldn't come. What's happened, Sam?' she asked again.

'I've just finished debriefing one of our operatives who's returned from France.' When he looked up, pain was visible in his eyes. 'He might have come across my sister and she's working for the Resistance.'

'Oh, that's wonderful,' Annie said, knowing just how worried Sam had been about the only remaining member of his family.

He looked ready to explode. 'I've got to find out if it really is her. We were sending someone in tonight, but I've managed to get permission to take his place. Once I've gathered the information we need then I'm going to try and find her.'

'You know you can't do that, Sam. Send someone

else.' The expression on his face was making shivers run through her. This was dangerous.

'No. This is something I must do myself.'

'Then take me with you.' Annie knew from his anguished expression that it would be suicide for him to go in this mood.

'No!' He thumped the desk to emphasize the rejection. 'This is none of your business.'

Annie recoiled as if she'd been struck. She had never seen him this volatile. He was usually a quiet, controlled man; she knew it would be useless to argue. And he'd obviously already cleared it with those in charge.

'Very well,' she told him. 'But if you get caught, then you and a lot of other people could be killed. And when you're knocking on the Pearly Gates, remember that I told you so.' She turned to walk out of the room.

'Wait!' He ran round his desk, caught her arm and turned her to face him. 'I'm sorry for shouting. I know you're only trying to help because you care, but there's more to this. I think there's someone else with my sister. Sit down and I'll explain.' He held a chair out for her.

When they were settled, she waited patiently for him to speak.

'As I listened to the operative talking about the people who had helped him in France, I became convinced he was talking about my sister. The description fitted, right down to the small heart-shaped birthmark on her right arm.'

Sam stopped and gazed into space for a few seconds, then continued. 'In the house with my sister was an elderly woman who was looking after a small boy of

275

about three years old. It was her grandson, she had told him.' His voice became husky with emotion.

Annie didn't interrupt. Sam obviously needed time to compose himself, for something had come as a great shock to him.

He took a deep breath and then cleared his throat. 'There was a girl I'd known from childhood, and as we grew up it was expected by both families that we would marry one day. And if the war hadn't come along that's what we would have done.' Sam stood up and started to pace the room. 'Maria was heavily pregnant, and we were going to be married in two weeks, but the wedding never took place. As soon as the Germans invaded I was off fighting.'

'Do you know if your girl is still alive?'

Sam shook his head in a forlorn gesture. 'I was away for about six weeks, and when I finally got back to my village I was told she had been killed by shellfire during the battle for our village. I got out of France then. If this woman is Maria's mother, then the boy she is looking after could be my son.'

He looked at Annie, searching her face, and there was a gleam of hope in his troubled eyes. 'Suppose Maria had the baby before she died?'

The look he gave her was enough to bring tears to her eyes. Annie knew Sam was building up for some unbearable grief if this turned out to be untrue. She hated saying this, but he shouldn't hope for too much. 'If you were told she had died, then that is probably what happened.'

'I know.' He sat down again and buried his head in his hands.

'Things are very confusing over there,' she felt she ought to point out, although he knew that better than anyone, 'and the grandmother might not be any relation to your Maria.'

'I've got to find out!'

Now Annie understood why he was willing to risk his life. She couldn't blame him for that. 'What are your plans?'

He sat back and sighed. 'I'm leaving tonight, and if it is my son then I'll try and bring him, Maria's mother and my sister back here.'

'That's quite a task,' she told him quietly.

'I know the odds against success are enormous. But what would you do, Annie, if you thought it might be one of your family?'

'Nothing would stop me from finding them,' she admitted with honesty. Sam shouldn't go back to France yet, but she knew that if she were in his shoes she wouldn't hesitate to take the same chances.

He glanced at his watch. 'I must get ready. I will send only two messages, one with the intelligence I've gathered, and the second for transport back here.'

'I understand. Take care, Sam.'

'I will.' He gave a tight smile, and then strode out of the room.

The next three weeks dragged by without a word from Sam and a feeling of gloom began to settle over the ops room.

Annie had remained hopeful for two weeks, but as the silence continued, she began to fear that he had been caught, or even killed. Every intercepted message was quickly decoded in case it gave an indication of arrests, either of Sam or any other operatives. But there was nothing, and the waiting was tearing everyone's nerves to shreds. Dora and Jean had given up trying to coax her away from the camp; even the promise of all that lovely food at the American dances wouldn't shift her. Only those closely connected with Sam knew what was happening, but the tense atmosphere alerted everyone that something was up.

'Get some rest,' Wing Commander Felshaw told Annie. 'If anything comes through, I'll let you know.'

It was two-thirty in the morning and Annie rubbed her tired eyes. 'OK, I'm too exhausted to concentrate, anyway.'

When she arrived back at her hut, Dora was waiting for her.

'It's about time too. If you don't get some sleep soon you'll make yourself ill.'

Annie dredged up a smile. 'Just because you're my sister-in-law doesn't mean you can boss me around.'

'Really?' Dora feigned surprise. 'I thought that was my job now.'

'Where on earth did you get that idea from?' Annie was too tired for the usual banter, and kicked off her shoes, then stretched out on the bed with a groan of relief.

'Have you had anything to eat?' Dora threw a blanket over her.

'Can't remember.'

'That means you haven't,' her friend declared. 'I'll go and cadge you a sandwich and a cup of tea.'

278

'I don't want anything, Dora, I just need to sleep for a few hours.'

'Don't argue with your new sister-in-law.'

Annie peered at Dora. 'Does Will know how bossy you are?'

'No, I'm keeping that as a surprise.'

'My poor brother,' Annie murmured. 'He doesn't know what he's let himself in for.'

Dora laughed. 'Oh, I think he does. We had a riotous honeymoon.'

'That's nice.' Then Annie was asleep.

'Wake up!'

Annie's reflexes surged into action and she sat up, although she was still half asleep. She peered at her watch and saw that it was five in the morning; she'd only had a couple of hours' rest.

Jean stopped shaking her. 'You're needed back on duty.'

'Right.' Annie took some deep breaths to try to clear her head.

'Hurry. They said it was urgent.' Jean was forcing Annie's feet into her shoes and tying the laces. 'Good job you're already dressed.'

Annie was out of the door of the hut and running, then tumbling down the steps to the ops room. There must be news, and she was praying that it was good.

'We've heard from Sam,' Wing Commander Felshaw told her as she erupted into the room. 'He wants transport for himself and two passengers, tonight, if possible.'

'Are you sending in a motor torpedo boat?' Annie asked.

'No. He can't reach the coast. We'll have to get them out by plane.'

Annie was dismayed. 'That's dangerous. Why are you taking such a chance?'

'No choice, I'm afraid. This hasn't just been a mission to find his family; Sam's gathered some vital information for us, and he's got to get out in a hurry. The message was too lengthy for him to send it through.'

Annie nodded, knowing how imperative it was to keep all transmissions short.

'He will be coming through again in thirty minutes and you are to give him these instructions.' He handed her a sheet of paper and studied her through narrowed eyes. 'You look a mess.'

'Sorry.' Annie tried to smooth the creases out of her skirt. 'I fell asleep in my clothes.'

He gave a wry smile. 'Well, when you've finished here, go and put on a clean uniform and meet us in the yard. I want you to meet the plane with the immigration official. Sam might need your help.'

Annie gazed through the window of the control tower and searched the sky. The small Tempsford airfield was only a short distance from Chicksands, and as dawn began to stain the sky with a silvery glow even the field seemed to be holding its breath. There was an eerie feel about the place, and the waiting was agony. Had the plane been able to get in and pick up its passengers?

'Here it comes,' someone said.

'At last!' Annie hurried down the steps and waited for the small plane to taxi towards them.

When it stopped she could see an elderly woman being

lifted out in obvious distress, and Annie stepped in to help. Then Sam eased himself to the ground carrying a small child.

No one spoke until they were inside. Welcome mugs of tea were provided, and Annie concentrated on trying to get the woman to drink some. When she had managed a few sips and seemed more composed, she turned her attention to Sam and the child.

The boy was staring at his grandmother in wild-eyed terror, and fighting to get away from Sam. The breath caught in Annie's throat as she looked at them. They *were* father and son; the likeness was unmistakable.

She knelt in front of Sam and reached for the struggling child. 'Let him go to his grandmother,' she told him as gently as possible.

As soon as the boy was free he threw himself at the elderly woman and buried his face in her skirt.

'Drink this,' Annie ordered, and thrust a mug into Sam's hand.

He gulped the tea down, and she was relieved to see some colour coming back into his face. 'Rough journey?' she asked.

He nodded, not taking his eyes off the child.

'Where's your sister?'

'She wouldn't come.' Sam looked as if he'd been to hell and was not sure if it was possible to get back from there.

'Your son's the image of you,' she told him, reaching out for his hand. When he looked at her the torment in his eyes nearly made her cry out. Whatever he'd discovered on this journey was clearly traumatic.

'He's terrified of me.' His words were barely audible.

It took less than an hour for the forms to be completed, and Sam's son and the boy's grandmother were officially classed as refugees. Then, to Annie's dismay, Sam was whisked off to a debriefing session even though he was obviously at the end of his strength.

Sam paused at the door, gave Annie a beseeching look, and asked, 'Will you stay with them for tonight, Annie?'

'Of course,' she replied giving him a reassuring smile. Then she picked up the child and followed a nurse, who was helping the grandmother to the waiting ambulance.

24

March 1943

Sam had rented a flat in Shefford for Jacques and his grandmother. It was close enough to Chicksands for him to pop round there every spare moment he had, but it was not a satisfactory arrangement, and Annie was losing patience with Sam. She'd walked into the tiny lounge and found him nearly out of his mind with worry.

'Stop pacing around and listen, Sam!' Annie ordered. 'You've been back two weeks now and little Jacques shows no sign of settling down. You can't keep him cooped up in this flat; he's used to the country.'

'I can't dump the problem on your family, Annie.'

'You won't be *dumping* anything on them. They've offered.' Annie smiled, hoping to coax him out of his stubbornness. She was extremely worried about the little boy and his grandmother. The elderly woman was very ill, and Jacques was becoming more withdrawn with each day that passed. She'd talked it through with her mother and Rose, and they'd felt it might help if Jacques lived with a family for a while.

He gave a weary sigh. 'I don't know what to do for the best. I'm out of my depth with this.'

'Sam!' Annie was getting cross with him now. 'Maria's mother is ill and needs looking after; she can't cope with a small, troubled boy at the moment.'

'I'm aware of that,' he growled, his expression a mirror of his irritation and worry.

Rose said that if you refuse she's coming round here to knock some sense into your stupid head.' Annie adopted her sister's determined pose and placed her hands on her hips.

'Ah.' He gave a strained smile. 'I can't risk that.'

'You'd be wise not to. You've never seen my sister when she's made up her mind about something. She's an unstoppable force, believe me.'

'Oh, I do believe you.'

Annie sensed he was giving way so she pressed the point. 'George has managed to get enough petrol for the journey, so Maria's mother will not have to travel by train. Come on, Sam,' she coaxed. 'You know this will be best for your son, and Mum will take good care of his grandmother. If we place him in the middle of a large and loving family it will help him overcome his fears, and I've been given extended leave so I can stay with you.'

Sam nodded, ran a hand wearily over his eyes and conceded defeat. 'Thank you, Annie.'

The journey to Wales was hard on the grandmother, and to make matters worse the boy knew she was ill. He was clearly frightened and clung to the elderly lady for the whole trip. Any effort by Sam or Annie to comfort him was pushed away. Jacques allowed Annie to care for his grandmother during the journey and accepted food and drink from her, but he wouldn't have anything to do with his father. Annie was relieved that George was doing the driving and not Sam. Sam was not a good driver at

284

the best of times, and the poor man was so distracted with concern they would surely have had an accident.

It was a relief when they arrived and Rose strode towards the car, taking charge of everything in her usual, no-nonsense manner. Once the old lady was settled in bed she fell asleep instantly, and the doctor was sent for.

'Come along, young man.' Rose scooped Jacques from the bed. 'Let your grandmother rest.'

He opened his mouth to scream, then looked into Rose's eyes, and the sound was cut to a whimper. Even he recognized that you didn't argue with Rose.

James, Kate, Pirate and Tibby were waiting in the lounge with a selection of toys scattered about the floor. When Rose put the boy next to them he scuttled on to the settee and hugged a cushion in front of him for protection.

'What's wrong with him?' James asked Sam.

'He has been taken from everything he was familiar with, and his grandmother is too ill to help him. He knows no one and is very frightened.'

James nodded in understanding, picked up a small toy train and handed it to the cowering boy. A hand sneaked out from behind the cushion and touched the desirable object.

'You can have it,' James told him, pushing the toy into his hand.

The little fingers curled around it and then it was pulled under the cushion and examined in secret.

Annie heard Sam's sharp intake of breath and she touched his arm. 'It will be all right. Just give it time.'

'What's his name?' Kate spoke for the first time.

'Jacques,' Sam told her.

'Hmm. I'll call him Jack.' Kate went and sat beside him, gave a wide smile, then began to ease the cushion away from him.

At that moment Marj arrived with tea, bread and jam, and even a home-made cake. 'Sit down all of you. We'll have our tea in here today. I've got milk for the youngsters.'

Kate had managed to get the cushion away from Jack, who was staring at her as if fascinated. But he was still huddled in the corner of the settee.

'Poor little sod!' Wally muttered. 'What kind of a life has he had?'

'Not good,' Sam told him, but did not elaborate further. Rose, a glass of milk in her hand, went over and sat on the arm of the settee. 'Here you are, Jack, you drink this. You must be famished.'

The boy tore his eyes away from Kate to look at Rose, his gaze swinging from mother to daughter, and then back again to Rose.

Annie handed Sam a plate. 'It looks as if he's been renamed. Do you mind?'

'No. At least they're getting some response from him, and that's more than I've been able to do.'

'They'll soon have him laughing and running around.' Annie wasn't surprised to see tears well up in Sam's eyes. It was obvious he adored his newly found son, and the strain of rejection must be hard to take.

'I just had to get him out of France, Annie.' He sounded almost apologetic. 'But all I seem to have done is inflict more unhappiness on him.'

'It was the right thing to do.' Annie tried to put herself in Sam's place. She knew that if she'd found a member

286

of her family in such terrible circumstances she'd have done the same thing. It might take time but Jacques would eventually adjust. She watched her sister, and sighed to release the tension in her chest. If anyone could ease his fear, it was Rose.

'There's a good boy.' Rose held up the empty glass and smiled at Jack. 'Would you like some bread and jam now?'

'He can't understand you,' George pointed out, as he came into the lounge after unloading the car.

'He soon will.' Rose cut a slice of bread into small squares and popped one piece at a time into Jack's mouth, waiting patiently for him to chew and swallow.

Annie remembered Rose doing that for her when she had been little.

They were all settling down to enjoy their tea when the door opened and a tall man strode in.

'Daddy!' Kate erupted off the seat and into her father's arms.

Everyone was milling around, greeting Bill and laughing, except Sam and Annie who had seen Jack's reaction to the tall sailor.

'Oh, my God!' Sam rushed over to the settee.

'What is it?' Bill was beside him at once.

Sam explained briefly about his son, then said, 'It's the uniform, he's terrified of them.'

Bill shrugged out of his jacket, ripped his tie off and bent down to look behind the settee. 'Hello, young man.' He spoke in French, his voice calm and gentle, as always. 'Aren't you going to come out and see me?'

Kate joined her father. 'You don't have to be frightened of my daddy, he's very kind.'

Annie listened to a scuffling sound from behind the settee, and then saw Bill surge to his feet holding Sam's son.

'My goodness, you are a handsome boy,' Bill told him as he sat down and settled the child on his knee. 'What's your name?'

'Jacques,' he whispered.

Kate climbed up beside her father. 'I'm going to call him Jack.'

'Really?' Bill ran a hand affectionately over his daughter's hair, and then smiled at the boy. 'Is that all right with you?'

The child nodded and said, 'Jack.'

'The doctor's here,' George announced.

Rose and Sam left the room, and returned twenty minutes later, their expressions grim.

'She's bad, isn't she?' Marj said.

Rose nodded. 'She refuses to go into hospital, so she'll stay here with us and we'll look after her.'

Sam cast Rose a grateful look, then spoke to them. 'She knew she was dying and agreed to come here so that my son could have a better life. But the journey and worry have weakened her.'

'I'm so sorry.' Annie's heart bled for Sam and his son. There were difficult times ahead of them.

During the next few days the March weather decided it was going to have a last winter fling; it was bitterly cold and trying to snow all the time. Jacques followed James and Kate everywhere and became agitated if he couldn't find them. But he still wouldn't go to his father, and it was obviously upsetting Sam.

Twice a day Jacques was taken to see his grandmother, who made a supreme effort to smile and joke with him. She told him each time that he was now with good people who would look after him. He listened solemnly, and clung to James and Kate even more after each visit.

Bill returned to his ship after three days, and a week later the elderly woman died peacefully in her sleep.

'How are you going to tell Jacques?' Rose asked Sam.

'I'm going to let him see her. If she suddenly disappears he will think I've sent her away, and God knows I have enough problems with him as it is.'

'Do you think he will understand if he sees her?' Annie asked him. 'She looks so peaceful, as if she's just fallen asleep.'

'It's the only thing I can do; I think he will understand what has happened to his grandmother.'

'I'll come with you.' Annie held out her hand to Jacques and he followed obediently.

'The boy stood by the bed staring at the body of his grandmother. He was absolutely still and silent, the only movement was a single tear as it trickled down his cheek. Then he ran from the room, down the stairs and into the lounge, throwing himself on to the settee and huddling in the corner, as he'd done the day he arrived. He had made progress, but now it seemed as if that had been reversed.

Annie watched as Sam sat beside his son and tried to comfort him, but the boy screwed himself into a tight ball and ignored him, lost in his own misery.

Kate surveyed the scene for a while, then sat next to Sam and reached across him to take hold of Jacques's hand. She slipped her other hand through Sam's arm and leaned against him.

289

Annie was constantly amazed by her niece's ability to do the right thing at the right time. By her gestures she was clearly telling Jacques that his father could be trusted. The boy seemed to think about it for a while, then slid on to Sam's lap and gave way to his grief, sobbing into his chest.

Annie breathed a sigh of relief; he had turned to his father at last. There was a long way to go, of course, but it was an encouraging step. She was at the end of her special leave and had to get back to Chicksands, but at least she had the comfort of knowing that progress had been made with the boy.

'Blimey!' Dora exclaimed when Annie arrived back at camp. 'You look awful. What on earth have you been doing?'

'It was a rather harrowing leave.' Annie then explained about Jacques and his grandmother.

'Poor little bugger.'

'Yes. It's been a tragic business. Rose persuaded Sam to let Jacques come to the funeral so the boy could see and understand that his grandmother really had gone. I think it worked because he seems to have accepted it now.' Annie closed her eyes as tiredness swept through her. 'I feel wrung out, and would like to have stayed for a few more days, but Sam is on compassionate leave for another two weeks.'

Dora gave Annie a searching look. 'You ought to think about yourself for a change. You're always doing things for other people and you're not getting any younger. It's time you found yourself a husband.'

Annie tipped her head back and laughed. 'And that will solve all my problems, will it?'

'No, but life will be much more fun,' Dora told her.

'Don't you want a family of your own?'

'When the war's over, but I can't say I've given it much thought. Why all this talk about babies, anyway?' She gave her friend a suspicious glance; she appeared extra pleased with life.

Dora looked smug. 'I think I might be pregnant.'

'What! You and Will haven't wasted any time. Are you sure?'

'No, I'm not sure, it's too soon, but I'm hoping.'

If this turned out to be true, Annie knew her mother would be delighted to have another grandchild.

Dora grinned. 'Anyway, we're getting off the subject. You ought to keep your eyes open for a suitable husband and father of your children.'

As tired as she was, Annie couldn't help being amused. Her friend certainly was broody. She placed a hand on Dora's forehead. 'Are you feeling all right?'

'Of course I am, you daft date. I'm trying to be serious here and give you a little sisterly advice, but you're not taking it seriously.'

'And I'm not going to, I'm quite happy as I am.' When they reached the mess, Annie pushed Dora through the door. 'I'm not on duty for another hour, so let's get something to eat.'

'I suppose you could marry Sam,' Dora persisted, clearly changing her earlier opinion that Annie should not consider it. 'You'd have a ready-made family then.'

'That man's got enough problems without adding to them by taking on a wife.'

'I suppose you're right.' Dora sighed. 'You wouldn't make him a good wife anyway. You can be an awkward devil where men are concerned.'

Annie looked at her friend in astonishment. 'When have I been awkward? Come on, tell me!'

'Well, you kept Paul hanging on when you had no intention of marrying him.'

'Now just a minute! Paul hung on to me, not the other way around. I told him often enough, but he just wouldn't listen. And I was too soft-hearted to hurt him.'

'You're not now, though. There's a toughness about you that wasn't there before.'

'From the sound of it, you've been bossing Sam around.'

'So you keep telling me.' They wandered up to the counter to see what was on offer. 'So what else am I supposed to have done?'

'I have *not*.' Annie sighed. 'I like and respect Sam, but he was drowning in problems and I couldn't bear to see it. He just needed someone to push him in the right direction. The man's got a stubborn streak.'

'Hark who's talking!'

Annie went to clout her friend but Dora ducked out of the way. 'Hey, no hitting a pregnant woman.'

They both burst into laughter while they collected a cup of tea and a sandwich, and then sat down. The mess wasn't very busy so they were able to find a table to themselves. All Annie wanted to do was rest her head on her arms and sleep but if she did that then she'd never wake up in time to report back for duty. She sat up straight again and tried to shake off the fatigue. She hoped to goodness that Dora and Jean didn't want her to go out this evening, because she just wasn't up to it. Losing Jacques's grandmother had been distressing for all of them, but at least the boy was talking to his father now.

Annie dragged her attention back to Dora. 'Now you've started to pull my character to shreds, you might as well continue. What else am I supposed to have done?'

'Well, there's the way you've treated Reid. You're being unreasonable, and that isn't like you at all.'

Annie stirred her tea aimlessly. She wasn't too happy about Reid being brought into the conversation, but Dora had a point, things had become rather muddled just lately and it was time she sorted her life out.

'When we were on leave and I met him at your house I had a real good look at him.' Dora sat up straight, clearly warming to her subject. 'I'm good at summing people up, and Reid Lascells is something special, believe me.'

Annie sighed.

'And it's no good you looking like that. You're like a horse with blinkers on, so I'll tell you what he's like. Reid's a strong man, I admit, but he's not uncaring; just look at the way he's keeping an eye on Bouncer. And if you took the trouble to look into his eyes a bit more you'd see he's got a good sense of humour. He's witty, brave, handsome, and so damned gorgeous that I'll bet the girls fall at his feet and beg to be taken to his bed.'

'I'll bet they do!' Annie muttered darkly.

'There, you're jealous!' Dora grinned in triumph. 'I

knew you couldn't be as uninterested as you pretend, and he fancies you as well.'

'I think you've flipped,' Annie told Dora, in disgust. 'We can't stand each other, but you are right about one thing: I have been rude to him.'

'Then do something about it,' Dora persisted, serious once again. 'Don't harbour resentment, it will hurt you more than him.'

'When did you suddenly become so wise?' Annie gave a faint smile.

'Since I fell in love with your wonderful brother. And I'm so proud to be a part of the Webster family.'

'Even if one of them is turning into a bitch?' Annie couldn't help asking.

'I never said that,' Dora protested. 'You're still the same kind girl I met when we joined up, but you've just lost your way a bit. You should go and see Paul's parents the first chance you get.'

'You're right, I do feel guilty about that . . . as well,' Annie added, and then looked at her friend. 'Is that the end of the list of things to do?'

'Of course,' Dora grinned. 'I didn't mean it when I said you'd become hard-hearted. You've got a centre like marshmallow, but you ought to put things right with Paul's family – and that includes his brother.'

'I've already sent him a letter,' Annie was getting fed up with this now. Dora was always going on about her and Reid, and she was too damned tired for another lecture.

'That's no good. Arrange to meet him and look him in the eyes when you tell him you're sorry.'

That was the last thing she wanted to do. The thought

of facing Reid again was rather unsettling, and she couldn't for the life of her understand why she felt like that. He would probably laugh in her face if she tried to apologize.

Dora drank her tea, watching her friend closely over the rim of her cup. 'He's a good man, and just the type you need.'

'Reid!' Annie roared at the ludicrous idea. All they ever did when they met was snipe at each other.

Dora gave a dramatic sigh. 'Well, if he won't do, then I'll just have to find you someone else.'

'Don't you dare!'

As the Spitfire came to a stop Reid eased out of the cockpit and jumped to the ground. He didn't fly as often as he would like to these days, but when he did find the time it was exhilarating. He gave the aeroplane an affectionate pat and examined a small oil leak coming from the engine. 'You're running a bit rough, old girl.'

As he strode towards his office he called one of the ground crew over. 'Get someone to have a look at that plane, please.'

'Yes, sir, Webster will deal with it, he's just finished the job he's on.'

'Right.' Reid continued walking. Webster? Of course, he'd forgotten that Annie's brother was stationed here at Tangmere. He should have taken the trouble to speak to him before now, but his days were so busy, and the mountain of paperwork seemed to grow by the minute, not to mention the interminable meetings.

An hour later he prowled over to the window. The Spitfire had been taken into the hangar. He'd just go and see how they were getting on with it.

He had met Charlie when he'd visited his mother's house and he recognized him at once. 'Anything serious?' he asked.

Charlie scrambled down. 'No, sir, we'll soon have it fixed and you can take her up again in an hour, if you want to.'

'Wish I could.' Reid grimaced. 'But I've got a meeting to attend in a couple of hours.'

'Bit boring after flying, sir.' Charlie wiped his greasy hands on a rag and smiled. 'But safer.'

'True.' Reid looked at him carefully. The family resemblance was clear to see. Charlie had the same colouring as Annie. 'I was pleased to hear that your brother was safe.'

'So were we,' Charlie told him. 'He got married in February to one of Annie's friends.'

'How is your sister?' Reid knew that question had come out with a hint of eagerness when he saw Charlie's speculative glance.

'Fine, as far as I know.'

Reid was pleased to hear he had dropped the 'sir' and was chatting quite normally with him. 'What does she do, *exactly?*'

'She's a wireless operator but she never talks about her work. We've even tried to find out from Sam, but he doesn't talk either. Of course, with her languages she's probably involved in some secret work,' Charlie said, obviously proud of his sister.

'Who's Sam?'

'He's French and Annie works with him sometimes. He's a nice bloke,' Charlie added, looking back at the engine he'd been working on.

Reid could see he was eager to get on with it, and he had wasted enough of Charlie's time. 'Remember me to your mother when you see her again.'

'I'll do that.' Charlie was already climbing on the plane. It was a lovely summer day, and Reid wandered back to his office deep in thought. Annie had obviously taken this Sam home, because Charlie seemed to know him quite well.

He stopped suddenly, surprised by the depth of feeling running through him, and at that moment he wanted the hostility between himself and Annie to be at an end. He was in a strange mood and the thought of all that paperwork waiting for him made him change direction, so instead of returning to work he headed out of the gate; he had a bit of time before the meeting. Once outside he walked along a small lane, deep in thought. When he'd been listening to Charlie talking about Annie he'd wanted to ask what she had been like as a child, what did she like and dislike? In fact, he'd wanted to hear all about her – all the small and large things that made her the woman she was today. Had she had any lovers?

He paused and gazed across a field, watching the birds pinching the farmer's soft fruits and treating the scarecrow with contempt. He was experiencing a feeling quite alien to him – jealousy! He remembered her smile, the way her eyes glowed when she was angry, and how good she looked in her uniform. Her slender figure and shapely legs even the awful stockings couldn't hide. But it wasn't just her outward loveliness; there were hidden depths to Annie Webster that it could take a lifetime to discover . . .

A gust of wind blew the hair into his eyes; he brushed it away and gave a sardonic laugh. Of course, it was obvious. He had fallen in love with her, and that was a damned stupid thing to do!

The next morning Reid tossed his bag in the car. The sun was shining and there were seven peaceful days ahead of him. He needed this break. Being station commander was not an easy job, but Bouncer was right, he was well suited to it, and most of the time he enjoyed the work, but he did miss flying and the friends he'd made in his old squadron. Bouncer was back with them now, and if his letters were anything to go by he was thrilled to be flying again.

The drive to his home in Berkshire was relaxing and Reid used the time to analyse his feelings for Annie. There had been other women in his life but he'd never felt like this about any of them; they had been there for a while and then gone, and he could hardly remember any of them now. But Annie Webster was different; he wanted to be with her all the time, to touch her, hold her, laugh and even argue with her, just so long as they were together. When they'd first met he'd been determined to dislike her, but that hadn't been possible, and he had a sneaking suspicion that he'd fallen for her the moment he'd set eyes on her. He'd fought it, of course, but it was no use denying that he was in love with her. Yet she showed no liking for him. However, he'd never been one to back away from a challenge and by the time he reached home he knew what he was going to do about her.

His mother hugged him as soon as he got out of the car. 'How long have you got?'

'Seven days.' He kissed her cheek. 'Where's Dad?'

'He's at the factory; some sort of crisis. They are struggling to get out an order of nuts and bolts, I think.'

'Shall I pop down there and see if I can help?' he asked.

'Would you? Father would be so relieved. He's always saying that you are twice the businessman he is. Have a cup of tea before you go, though.'

They went inside and she put the kettle on to boil.

'Are you going to stay in the air force after the war, Reid?'

'No. I'll get out as soon as possible.' That was something he was clear about. Paul would probably have considered a career in the air force after the war, but not him, he would be out as soon as he could.

'Oh, that's a relief. Your father isn't finding it easy managing the engineering business again and said that if you decided to stay in the air force then he would sell the factory.'

'There's no need for that.' He stirred his tea and smiled at his mother. 'By the time this lot's over, I'll have had all the excitement I can handle. It will be a pleasure to take over the business again.'

His mother looked at him hopefully. 'Time you settled down.'

That's what he wanted as well, but he was going to have a fight on his hands if he wanted to win Annie.

Reid walked into the factory and found it strangely quiet; one of the machines was standing idle. A middle-aged man came up to him, all smiles, and shook his hand.

'It's good to see you again,' the worker told him.

'And you, Tom. How's the family?'

'We lost our son-in-law, but our daughter's a sensible lass and she's pulling her life together again.' Tom looked sad. 'Damned shame about Paul, he was a nice boy.'

'Yes, it was a shock. I'm sorry to hear about your loss as well, Tom.'

300

'Bloody war. Still, it looks as if things are on the turn now.'

Reid nodded. 'Let's hope so. Now, what's going on here?'

'The machine has broken down and we can't repair it. Your dad's at his wits' end; we've got a shipment of nuts and bolts to deliver in three days, and this has to happen. It's old, of course, and needs replacing.' He gave a helpless shrug.

'Let me have a look.' Reid removed his jacket, rolled up his sleeves and started to examine the machine.

'Hello, son, when did you arrive?'

'Just got here, Dad.' Reid noticed how tired his father looked, and smiled in encouragement. 'This always was a temperamental brute, but it knows better than to argue with me.'

It took him the best part of an hour, but he finally stepped back with a grunt of satisfaction. 'Try it now, Tom.'

The machine coughed, shook, and sounded as if it wasn't going to start properly, but when Reid aimed a kick in the region of the motor it sprang into life with a roar.

His father slapped him on the back and grinned in relief. 'Haven't lost your touch, I see.'

Reid washed his hands in the sink to remove the worst of the grime, said goodbye to Tom and led his father out of the factory. 'I'll be here for a week, so you needn't worry if she goes wrong again.'

'But it's your leave,' his father protested. 'It isn't right to have you working when you need a break. And just wait until your mother sees you. You're covered in oil.'

When they arrived back his mother was sitting in the garden under the old oak tree talking to a girl in uniform.

'Annie!' His father walked across the lawn to greet her.

'How lovely to see you.'

'And you, Mr Lascells. I'm sorry I haven't been able to come sooner.'

'We understand, my dear.' He kissed her cheek. 'How long have you got? Can you stay a while?'

Reid saw Annie glance at him, and as she hesitated he stepped forward, smiled and also kissed her cheek. Though he would like to have done more. She was so lovely and he wanted to keep her here for as long as possible.

'Please stay,' he said.

'Well . . .' She was obviously surprised by his greeting.

'I've only got a forty-eight-hour pass, and I haven't brought any overnight things with me.'

'Don't worry about that,' Mrs Lascells said. 'I have spare toothbrushes and everything else you could need.'

'In that case I'd love to stay tonight.'

'Wonderful! I'll start dinner at once.'

'Can I help?' Annie asked politely.

'No, my dear, you stay here and talk to the men.' Mrs Lascells examined her son. 'What on earth have you been doing? That shirt's covered in grease.'

'He's repaired one of our machines,' her husband told her. 'I swear he's the only one who understands the temperamental beast.'

'You'd better change out of that shirt before dinner and I'll soak it overnight.'

Reid nodded and sat on the grass, leaving the garden

seat for Annie and his father. 'I was talking to your brother Charlie yesterday,' he told Annie.

Her smile was animated at the mention of her brother.

'How is he?'

'Fine. He was working on a Spitfire I had just landed.'

As soon as the words were out he knew he shouldn't have said that.

'Are you still flying?' his father asked, concern showing on his face.

'Whenever I can,' Reid admitted.

'Whatever you do, don't tell your mother. She thinks you are permanently grounded now.'

'I won't say anything to worry her, but I love flying, Dad.'

Just then his mother came back and there was silence for a moment as they stopped speaking. Reid hoped she hadn't heard their conversation because the last thing he wanted to do was upset her. But she was smiling.

'Only an hour to dinner,' she told them.

Annie moved up to make room for her on the seat.

'There's something I'm curious about, Mrs Lascells. Reid is an unusual name; where did it come from?'

'My maiden name was Reidmont, and I wanted to keep something of it, so when our first son was born we named him Reid.'

'I'm glad you didn't call me Reidmont,' he remarked with a slight grimace.

'I was tempted,' she laughed, 'but your father wouldn't let me.'

'Thank heavens for that!' Reid caught sight of his shirt and hauled himself on to his feet. 'If you will excuse me, I'll go and change.'

Once in his room he stood by the window gazing at the garden below. His parents were talking to Annie and they were all laughing. What a bit of luck her turning up like this; it would give him a chance to put things right between them. He felt optimistic about being successful because he hadn't sensed the usual hostility. Of course, she might just be appearing polite for his parents' sake, but he didn't think so. She had very expressive eyes, and they hadn't been glaring at him in contempt.

He whistled as he washed and changed his clothes. Time to put his plans into action.

'Fancy going dancing?' Reid asked Annie later when they'd finished their meal.

She hesitated for a moment. 'I don't think I can do that. I came to see your parents.'

'Don't stay in because of us,' Mrs Lascells smiled at them both. 'You go and enjoy yourselves.'

'Of course you must,' her husband agreed. 'We shall have the pleasure of seeing Annie tomorrow.'

'Well, if you're sure? It would be nice, I haven't been dancing for some time.'

'Then you must go,' they said together.

Reid stood up and held out a hand to Annie. 'Come on then, let's jive the night away.'

'Can station commanders jive?' she asked, looking highly amused.

He put on a hurt expression. 'I'll have you know that I was the squadron expert.'

'This I've got to see.' She laughed and placed her hand in his.

He closed his long fingers around her delicate hand

with a feeling of elation. She had clearly changed her opinion of him and was prepared to be friendly. But he wanted more than *friendly.*

He took her to Newbury Corn Exchange which was situated in the historic market place. Reid told her that the building had opened for trade in 1861 but was now being used as a community venue. The place was crowded when they arrived, and a big band was in full swing. Dancing was a favourite pastime for everyone, but especially young service people. It gave everyone a chance to relax, mix with a crowd and enjoy glorious music.

Reid towed Annie into the middle of the throng and was delighted to see that she was an excellent dancer, and obviously loved it.

'You're good.' He shouted above the sound of the orchestra, as he spun her round.

'So are you,' she told him.

He pulled her back into his arms. 'Something we agree on at last.'

Annie smiled up into his face. 'It took a while, didn't it?'

The music had now changed to a foxtrot so he wrapped his arms around her, and as there was hardly room to move he marked time, enjoying the feel of her close to him. He wanted to bury his face in her silky hair, but resisted the urge. He mustn't move too fast.

'I'm sorry I've been so rude to you, Reid,' she told him.

He held her away from him so he could look into her upturned face. 'I'm the one at fault, Annie. I had no right to shout at you.'

'Why did you?' she wanted to know.

'I was devastated about losing Paul and your composure angered me.'

'That was the second time in about eight months I'd lost someone close to me and I was still hurting,' Annie explained. 'The blow of Paul's death hit me hard, but I wanted to grieve in private. Can you understand that?'

Reid nodded. 'Who was this other person? Not one of your family, I hope?'

'No, he was a dear man and everything possible was done to save him but to no avail.' She smiled up at him. 'This is a very gloomy subject when we are supposed to be forgetting our problems and enjoying ourselves.'

'You're right.' The tempo changed to a quickstep and he swung her round and back into his arms again. 'Now we've both apologized, do you think we can be friends?'

'I'd like that.' Her laugh was exuberant as they started to jive along with all the others on the dance floor. The American dance had soon caught on, and people were finding it a wonderful way to relieve the stress of wartime life.

That was one hurdle over but he was determined to deepen the relationship. It was going to be difficult since they could only meet occasionally; he would have to make the most of every opportunity.

During the interval they took their drinks and went outside for a breath of fresh air.

Annie sighed and leaned against a wall. 'Phew! That's better. It's like an oven in there.'

Reid finished his beer and put the glass down. 'Who's Sam?'

Annie looked startled by his sudden question. 'Someone I work with. Why?'

'No reason, I was just making conversation.'

'Well, I think you'd better change the subject because you know I can't talk about my work or anyone connected with it.'

'Of course. Careless talk costs lives,' he added rather flippantly. 'I should have known better. Would you like another drink?'

'Yes, please.'

He picked up the empty glasses and headed for the bar. He was curious about this man and he would have to see what he could find out about him.

He was soon back with two more drinks. 'How's Captain Freeman?'

'Bill? He's fine as far as we know.' Annie sipped her drink. 'How long is this blasted war going to last?'

'Fascism in Italy is finished, and there's a good chance they will surrender now Mussolini's been ousted.' He took the glass out of Annie's hand, put both their drinks down, and pulled her towards him. 'It's another step in the defeat of Germany but there's a long, hard fight ahead of us still.'

She didn't protest as he wrapped his arms around her, so he lowered his head and sought her lips. When she relaxed in his arms he deepened the kiss, ignoring the whistles he could hear coming from others enjoying the night air.

Suddenly, and with surprising strength, she pushed at his chest. He released her at once and stepped back. If they hadn't been in such a public place he might have been able to find out how much she really did like him, for he felt that her whole attitude had changed, and it was exciting. After taking a deep breath to steady himself, he said, 'I thought we were friends?'

'Not *that* friendly.' She straightened her jacket and glanced at the interested spectators.

'How friendly do you want to be, Annie?' He placed his hands on either side of her face, bringing her attention back to him. He knew he was pushing his luck, but after tomorrow she would return to her post and it might be months before he saw her again. It wasn't any surprise that there were so many hasty marriages these days. There wasn't time for long courtships when you weren't sure if you'd ever see each other again.

'I don't know. You confuse me,' she admitted, ducking away from him. 'The dancing's started again.'

He led her back into the hall. Confused was she? Well, he would settle for that tonight, and he had the satisfaction of knowing that she hadn't pushed him away immediately. In fact it had taken her quite a long time.

As they swung into an energetic dance routine, she was soon laughing again. Reid spun her round and round, feeling light-hearted. One thing he was certain about – *he* wasn't at all confused!

26

Annie smiled to herself as she walked along the country lane, feeling the leaves crunch under her feet. She loved to walk whenever she had some spare time, and autumn was her favourite time of the year, with its riot of colour and nip in the air. She breathed in deeply; the war seemed a million miles away on a day like this.

Dora and Will's baby was due in a month's time. Much to Dora's disappointment she hadn't been pregnant soon after the wedding, but she certainly was after Will's next leave! Annie's family were scattered around at the moment. Her mother and Wally were looking after Dora, Bill and Will were at sea and goodness knows where, Charlie was still at Tangmere, and Rose was staying in Wales with George and the children. Her sister had taken over the responsibility for Jacques, and according to her letters the boy was settling in quite well. Bob was attached to a British unit and was still in this country, managing to see their mother now and again, which made Marj very happy. George was also delighted to have his daughter out of the firing line. Annie knew he had fretted all the time that Rose was in London, for he knew she would be in the most dangerous place she could find.

Annie hadn't seen Reid since the summer, but he wrote often and she looked forward to receiving his letters. She was not sorry to be away from him though, because she found his strong, dominant presence disturbing . . .

Annie carried on walking, lost in thought and enjoying the quiet of the countryside. She only heard the roar of the motorbike for a second –

There were half a dozen requests from the men for special leave on his desk and Reid shuffled through them. Some of the men were quite inventive with their reasons, and he was about to toss them aside to be dealt with later when a name caught his attention. As he read, a cold chill rippled down his spine.

'Jenkins!' he thundered.

'Sir!' The man almost fell into the room in his haste.

'Bring Webster here – at once!'

Charlie arrived out of breath and stood to attention.

'Which sister?' Reid demanded without preamble.

'Annie, sir. An American on a motorbike knocked her down.' Charlie's voice wavered. 'Mum says she's hurt bad, got a broken ankle, broken arm and a gash on her head. The doctors are checking now to see if there are any internal injuries.'

'Where is she?' Reid was already putting on his hat as fear gripped him like an iron band.

'They are worried about the head injuries and they've taken her to Bart's in London.' Charlie's voice shook. 'She's still unconscious, sir.'

'Stop calling me, sir,' Reid growled, as he looked at the address. 'The bloody name's Reid to you and your family.'

'I want to go and see her.' Charlie was clearly agitated

and an erupting commanding officer was not helping his composure.

'I'll take you.' Reid headed for the door with Annie's brother close on his heels.

It took just under two hours to reach the hospital, and every mile was agony to Reid as he pushed the accelerator pedal to the floor of the car and held it there.

The hospital was busy but Reid pushed to the front of the queue at the information desk, ignoring the rumble of protest coming from the other people waiting. To jump a queue was considered a grave sin when standing in line for every small item was the way of life. You waited patiently for your turn, but Reid was not in the mood to obey the rules this time. 'Ann Webster,' he demanded.

The nurse looked down a list of names. 'Ward D4, sir, but you can't . . .'

The two men didn't wait for her to finish speaking; they headed for the stairs, taking them at a run.

Marj and Wally were sitting one side of the bed, and a man Reid didn't know was on the other side holding Annie's hand. He was talking very quietly to her in French.

Reid's whole attention was focused on the girl in the bed and fear gripped him. She was unconscious, there were lacerations and bruises on her face, her left arm was in plaster and there was a cage over her legs. Even in the desperate days of 1940 he had never felt as scared as he was at this moment.

'Charlie, Reid,' Marj greeted them. 'I'm so glad you're here.'

'How is she, Mum?' Charlie asked in a hushed voice.

'The doctor thinks she will be all right, but he'll know more when she regains consciousness.'

'And when will that be?'

'We don't know, Charlie, but the longer it goes on, the more worried I am,' his mother told him, looking at her daughter anxiously. 'There has been some movement and a couple of times we thought she was going to open her eyes, but it seemed too much effort for her.'

Wally squeezed his wife's hand in encouragement. 'I don't think she's far away from regaining consciousness now.'

'What exactly are Annie's injuries?' Reid asked.

'Bad cut on her head, concussion, arm broken in two places and a smashed ankle, but they said there aren't any internal injuries,' Wally explained.

'Thank God for that!' Reid turned his attention back to Annie. The immediate need was to bring her round and the Frenchman would never get through to her like that! His tone was soft and coaxing. He guessed that this must be Sam.

The words began to penetrate Reid's mind and he frowned. His French wasn't fluent but he could understand some of what was being said.

'It will be a long time before you jump out of aeroplanes again. That ankle will never take the strain, but your right hand is uninjured, so you will still be the best wireless operator we've got.' Sam waited to see if there was any response, then sighed and stood up. 'She's still out, I'm afraid. I'll see if I can get us all some tea.'

When Sam moved away from the bed Reid took his place, but he didn't sit down; instead he bent over the

312

inert figure. 'If you die on me, Webster, I'll never forgive you!'

His deep voice, raw with emotion, echoed around the ward, and all eyes turned in their direction.

A nurse hurried over. 'There should only be two visitors at a time, so some of you will have to leave. Miss Webster needs rest.'

Reid tore his attention away from the girl in the bed and fixed on the nurse, who backed down, looking uncomfortable caught in his penetrating gaze. 'She can rest when she's fully conscious again. And see she's moved to a private room,' he ordered.

'Very well, I'll make the arrangements, and you may all stay if you keep quiet,' she conceded, then left to attend to her other patients.

With that interruption out of the way, Reid leaned over Annie. 'Are you bloody well listening to me?'

Suddenly, Annie's eyelids flickered and her mouth twitched at the corners. 'Language, Squadron Leader,' she said faintly.

'Oh, she's awake,' Marj said in relief.

Reid sat down then. This was one time he didn't mind being demoted; it showed that Annie was in full command of her faculties.

'The voice of authority,' Charlie told his mother, smiling for the first time. 'She wouldn't dare disobey him.'

Reid ignored the remarks, took hold of Annie's hand and watched her fingers curl around his. 'Open your eyes,' he ordered. He'd known he loved her but until this moment he hadn't realized just how much. If he lost her the pain would be intolerable.

Annie's eyelids lifted and she gave a tired smile to everyone around the bed, then she closed them again.

'Thank the Lord she's regained consciousness.' Sam had returned with a tray of tea and biscuits.

As soon as Annie had responded to Reid, Wally went in search of a doctor, who examined her. 'Good. She is sleeping naturally. You must all leave now.'

They found a small waiting room and settled in there to enjoy the much-needed refreshments Sam had scrounged for them.

'Now, can someone tell me exactly what happened?' Reid asked.

'I'm afraid it was my fault, sir.' A very young American soldier slunk into the room and shuffled anxiously as he looked at them. 'My name's Warren. I borrowed this motorbike, you see, and took it along a country lane to see what it could do. I came round a bend and there she was . . .' His words tailed off.

Reid managed to resist the temptation to throttle the young idiot, but only because the boy was close to tears and obviously upset.

'I'll never ride a bike again,' he choked. 'I thought I'd killed her.'

Marj took the boy by the arm and made him sit down. 'The doctor said she is going to be all right, Warren. You have a cup of tea, it will make you feel better.'

He took the cup she offered, looked at the pale liquid with distaste and then drank it politely.

Marj patted his arm in approval. 'It was an unfortunate accident, Warren. Were you hurt?'

'No, ma'am, but the bike is a heap of junk now.'

Wally joined in the conversation with the American,

314

so Reid turned his attention to Sam. 'What did you mean when you said she wouldn't be jumping out of aeroplanes again,' he asked quietly, not wanting any of Annie's family to hear.

'Ah, you speak French.'

'Enough to understand what you were saying in there.'

Sam thought for a moment. 'She did a parachute jump once and I think she enjoyed it.'

'Why did she do that?' Reid remembered Annie and Bouncer talking about jumping out of a balloon, but he didn't know she'd jumped from an aeroplane as well. Did that delicate façade conceal a daredevil?

'Because she wanted to. What other reason could there be?' Sam asked in a dismissive tone.

Reid bit back a sharp retort. The man was being evasive, but he knew from his demeanour that that was the only answer he was going to be given. And anyway, this was not the place to cross-examine him. Though his curiosity deepened about Sam. What did he do in this war, and how closely was Annie associated with him and his work? Reid knew they were questions he wouldn't get answers to. His own part in this war was simple – you got your plane off the ground and fought the enemy almost face to face – but there were people in the background doing things no one would know about until this conflict ended . . .

Sam studied him carefully. 'I watched you with Annie. Are you in love with her?'

'Yes.' Reid didn't hesitate with the answer.

'That's a change of heart, isn't it?' Sam gave a wry smile. 'I thought you couldn't stand the sight of each other?'

'We got off to a bad start, that's all. Are you in love with her as well?'

'There are different shades of love,' Sam replied. 'Annie has my love and respect, and the rest of her wonderful family have my undying gratitude.'

'And what *shade* is your love for Annie?' Reid asked.

'Not bright red like yours, it's more of a glowing yellow, but . . .' Sam paused for a moment. 'When this war's over I'm going to need a wife, and I can't think of anyone more suitable than Annie.'

'You'll have to get past me first.' Reid's attitude couldn't possibly leave Sam in any doubt about his determination.

'You could be right because it was you she opened her eyes for, not me. But I shall not give up until she tells me that she loves you with all her heart. The last thing I would want is for her to be unhappy.'

Reid nodded. Now he knew where he stood, and he had no intention of losing her to this Frenchman, or anyone else.

The doctor put his head around the door. 'You might as well all go home. She's sleeping soundly and we don't expect her to wake up until tomorrow morning. She will be in the private room next door when you return.'

'Thank you.' Marj stood up and said goodbye to the American soldier who hurried away with obvious relief.

Charlie came over to Reid. 'Can I stay for the night? I'd like to see my sister in the morning.'

'Of course.'

'If you need a bed for the night, we have plenty of room,' Wally told Reid.

'Thanks.' He looked at his watch. 'It's too late to go

back now, and I would like to visit in the morning as well. We can go back together, Charlie.'

Annie groaned as she woke up, and found a doctor bending over her.

'Are you in pain?' he asked.

'Yes,' she gasped. 'What happened? I feel as if a tank ran over me.'

The man smiled. 'No, it was only a motorbike. Do you remember anything?'

Annie tried to think back but it felt as if she was struggling to recall a dream. 'I was walking along a country lane, there was no one around, and then I heard a roar. After that, nothing.'

'Good, that's excellent,' the doctor told her. 'An American soldier was on a motorbike and hit you when he came round a corner.'

'Good job he wasn't driving a truck.' Annie lifted the sheet with her good hand. 'How badly hurt am I?'

'You have a broken arm and ankle, lacerations and concussion.'

'Oh, Lord, what a mess!' Annie fought back a groan, but she wasn't going to let self-pity swamp her. She was alive and her injuries would heal in time.

'What about the soldier?' she asked.

'He escaped with a few cuts and bruises.' The doctor took her pulse and examined her, then gave a satisfied smile. 'You are going to be just fine, and you remember everything, so the concussion will not be a problem. Plenty of rest and you'll be as good as new.'

As he strode away Annie tried to move and fell back with a gasp. 'Nurse, can you sit me up, please?'

Two of them came over, pillows were placed behind her, and they lifted her up.

'Oh, thank you,' she sighed, 'that's much more comfortable.'

'Your mother's here,' the ward sister told her. 'Shall I send her in?'

'Please.'

Marj hurried in looking anxious until she saw her daughter sitting up and wide awake. 'That's better. You gave us all a scare yesterday.'

'Hello, Mum.' Annie held out her hand and pulled her mother towards her for a kiss. 'I'm sorry I frightened you. Are you on your own?'

'The others are coming later. We got told off yesterday so we thought we'd better stagger the visits. There were too many of us here, and when Reid shouted at you they asked us to be quiet, or leave.'

Annie frowned. 'Reid? What was he doing here?'

'He brought Charlie home. Don't you remember?'

There was a hazy recollection at the back of her mind of a deep, firm voice giving her orders, and after thinking about it for a while she gave a wry smile. 'Ah, yes, he swore at me.'

'That's right, but it did the trick because you opened your eyes then.'

'I expect I did,' she admitted. 'That man has an air of command about him, doesn't he?'

'He's certainly very forceful.' Marj eyed her daughter with interest. 'Not a bit like his brother, is he?'

Annie nearly choked on a laugh. 'Complete opposites! Paul was such a gentle and considerate man, but Reid is tough. He speaks his mind.'

She didn't want to dwell on the man who was causing her so much confusion. She had been able to deal with him when they'd met on bad terms previously, but after the dance he'd taken her to she was no longer sure about her feelings. They seemed to have done an about-face, and that didn't appear to be a good idea to her. He was turning out to be far too charming for her peace of mind. She had been receiving letters, phone calls, gifts of items like scented soap, an unheard of luxury in these austere times, and even a bunch of flowers on her last birthday. The man was showing signs of being a romantic at heart . . . She dragged her thoughts away from Reid. 'Does Sam know about the accident?'

'Yes. He spent some time here yesterday, but he's had to return to duty today. He said to tell you that he will visit as soon as he can.'

Wally walked in. 'Hello, sweetheart, you're looking better.'

'Flatterer.' Annie grinned as much as her sore face would allow. 'I must be a real sight.'

'A bit bruised and battered maybe, but you're still as beautiful as ever.' Wally placed a hand on his wife's shoulder. 'Charlie and Reid are outside and would like to see Annie. They've got to return to camp this morning. I think Reid has stretched the rules by allowing Charlie to stay this long, but it was damned good of him.'

'He's a kind man.' Marj stood up and smiled at her daughter. 'We'll go and see if we can find a cup of tea, then come back after Charlie and Reid have seen you. Mustn't have too many people round the bed or we'll upset the ward sister. Rose and George wanted to rush back from Wales but we told them that you were out of danger, and there wasn't anything they could do. George has insisted that you come to Wales to convalesce.'

When they'd left Annie closed her eyes for a moment. She was feeling very tired, but so grateful for and touched by the love of her family. She was an extremely lucky girl.

'Not going to sleep again, are you?'

'I wouldn't dare!' she muttered, and looked up at the tall figure of Reid standing by the bed. 'He must be one hell of a commanding officer,' she told Charlie.

Her brother grinned. 'Oh, he isn't too bad as long as you stay out of his way.'

'That must be difficult.'

Reid chuckled. 'I thought we were friends now, Annie?'

'Is that what we agreed?' she asked in mock horror.

'You must have caught me in a weak moment.'

'That sounds more like our Annie.' Charlie bent over and kissed her cheek, obviously relieved to hear his sister joking like this.

For the next half an hour they talked, and the men did their best to make her laugh and raise her spirits, but Annie secretly found it very tiring. She ached from head to toe and felt completely drained of energy.

Reid glanced at his watch. 'We had better be going, Charlie. I phoned in to say that we would be back by twelve.'

Charlie stood up and squeezed Annie's hand. 'Being with the commanding officer does have its advantages. At least I won't be put on a charge if I'm late reporting in.'

'You want to bet?' Reid joked.

'Oops! Must go, Sis. You hurry up and get better.'

320

'You make sure you do!' Reid told her. 'As soon as you're on your feet again I'll take you dancing.'

Annie looked at the cage over her legs and grimaced. 'That might take some time.'

'I can wait.' He leaned over, gave her a lingering kiss, and spoke softly, 'I can be very patient when I have to.'

'Really?' Annie opened her eyes wide in mock surprise. 'You could have fooled me.'

Charlie clearly didn't believe that either. 'That will be news to the boys back at base.'

'Really?' Reid feigned surprise. 'I thought I was a most tolerant officer.' Then he kissed Annie again.

Charlie cleared his throat. 'It's getting late . . . and I thought you and my sister were just friends?'

Reid stood up. 'We are, but I'm working on it.'

Annie didn't miss the look of amusement on her brother's face.

27

Annie had been in hospital for nearly four weeks and was bored to tears. The first couple of weeks had been painful and she'd felt too ill to take much notice of what was going on around her, but now she felt fine. As her health had improved the restrictions forced on her by the broken ankle and arm were enough to drive her mad! She had been told not to attempt to move without the nurses' help; she was considering having another go at standing up, when a visitor walked in.

'Will!' Annie exclaimed in pleasure. 'When did you arrive home?'

'Last night. Our ship's in dock to have some new equipment fitted.' Her brother sat on the bed next to her chair. 'And just in time too. Dora had a girl in the early hours of this morning.'

'Oh, how wonderful!' She clasped his hand. 'Congratulations. Are they both all right?'

He smiled proudly. 'They're just fine.'

Annie was sitting in a chair beside the bed and stamped her uninjured foot in frustration. 'When am I going to get out of this place? I'm missing everything, and I want to get back to work.'

Suddenly Sam walked into her room. 'You won't be fit enough for duty until the new year.' He sat beside her.

'Why not?' Annie waved her right hand at him. If she had to endure much more of this idleness she'd go crazy!

'Look, there's nothing wrong with this, I can still operate a wireless.'

'The injury to your ankle is very bad and you can't walk yet,' Sam pointed out. 'And you won't be able to use crutches with a broken left arm.'

Annie felt like screaming, but he was right, blast him. She'd tried walking with a stick and would have fallen if a nurse hadn't been holding on to her.

'You've got to be patient,' Will told her. 'You've had a serious accident and recovery is bound to be a slow business.'

'I'm trying to be patient.' She sighed, laid her head back and closed her eyes. 'What are you going to call your daughter?'

'We haven't decided yet. Dora wants to call her Rose, but I'm not sure about that.'

Annie opened her eyes. 'Why not? It's a nice name and Dora admires Rose very much.'

'I know.' Will frowned. 'But Rose is a unique woman, and I'm not too keen on giving our little daughter the same name. She might be constantly compared with our Rose and that wouldn't be right for her.'

'Hmm.' Annie could see Will's point and it would seem strange having another Rose in the family. 'What about Emily, Rose's other name?'

'What a good idea.' Will beamed at his sister. 'I'll suggest it to Dora when I see her this afternoon. I'm sure she'll like that.'

'I wish I could see her as well.' Annie's mood plummeted into gloom. It was terribly difficult to keep depression at bay when she felt so helpless. 'Give Dora my love and kiss little Emily for me.'

'I think Emily's a lovely name,' Sam told Will in approval. 'What did she weigh at birth?'

'Seven pounds exactly.'

Annie watched Sam's face as he talked to Will about the birth and wondered what he was thinking. He'd never seen Jacques as a baby, or taking his first steps, or heard his first words . . .

She felt it was time to change the subject. 'Tell me what's going on in the outside world, Sam.'

'Well, you know that Italy declared war on Germany three weeks ago.' Sam couldn't contain his excitement. 'And this country is filling up with troops and equipment . . .'

'Ready to launch an invasion?' Annie asked.

He nodded. 'Next year!' It *must* be next year.'

'Oh, damn, damn!' Annie moaned. 'I've got to get out of here, Sam.'

'How does next week sound?' A doctor strolled up to her. 'You've made an excellent recovery and we'll be able to remove the plaster from your arm in a few days' time. However, you will still have to keep it in a sling for another couple of weeks.'

'What about my ankle?' she asked. She could manage with one arm but the ankle was causing her concern.

'That will have to wait a while longer. We want you to come back on January the 3rd and we'll have a look at it then.'

'Thank you, doctor.' Annie's sigh was heartfelt. 'I'm going round the bend being cut off from everything.'

He laughed. 'So I've noticed but you'll still have to take things very easy for a few more weeks.'

As the doctor walked away Will said, 'You can go down to Wales and spend Christmas there.'

'That would be lovely. George has written several times insisting that I come home and be looked after properly.' Then her smile faded. When she thought of the journey on a crowded and cold train, she wasn't at all sure she had the strength to cope with it. She was feeling shaky and weak. 'But how on earth am I going to get there? I'll never manage on the train.'

'I'll fly you there.' Reid strode into the room.

She looked at him in disbelief, and then closed her eyes for a moment. He really was a stunning man: tall, straight, with his dark hair and eyes almost the same colour as his uniform. 'You're joking?'

'No, I'm not. I've still got my own plane and I'm sure I can get permission to use it on this occasion. There's a small airfield near Pontypool.' He shook hands with Will and Sam. 'I can squeeze another one in, if anyone wants to come.'

'Not me, I'm afraid,' Will told him with obvious regret. 'I'd love to see everyone but I've only got a three-day pass, and I want to spend as much time as possible with Dora and the baby. God knows where I'll be at Christmas.'

'I'd like to take you up on the offer,' Sam said. 'I could help with Annie and it would give me a chance to see my son.'

'Son?'

Sam explained briefly and Reid listened, a deep frown furrowing his brow.

'Of course you must come,' he said when Sam had finished talking. 'I'll bring you back as well, if that would help?'

'It certainly would, but I'd like to stay for a couple of days.'

'I think I can wangle some leave,' Reid told him with confidence.

Annie looked at the three men as they made arrangements without consulting her. 'Just hold on a minute. Don't I have any say in this? And what are you doing here, don't you ever do any work, Squadron Leader?'

'Now and again,' he replied, a slight smile on his face at the demotion again. 'I've left Tangmere in the hands of my deputy for a few days.'

'If you don't want to fly,' Sam said with a mischievous grin, 'I could always take you down by truck.'

Annie held up her hand in horror. 'Oh, no, I'd rather fly than risk you behind the wheel again.'

'Good, that's settled then.' Reid noticed the sweets on her bedside table. 'Where did all those come from?'

'I've had a constant stream of American soldiers bringing me treats. Warren said his buddies wanted to cheer me up and let me know how sorry they were that one of them had hurt me so badly.' She gave a delighted grin. 'I've even been given two pairs of nylons.'

Sam glanced at Reid and pulled a face. 'We must definitely get her out of here or we won't be able to get in the door for American soldiers.'

Reid spun on his heel. 'I'll go and find out when we can move her.'

Four days later Reid carried Annie into The Haven and laid her on the settee. She rested her head back and closed her eyes. Although Sam and Reid had done everything they could to make the journey to Wales as quick and comfortable as possible, it had taken a lot out of her. It was a blessed relief to be there.

Rose pulled a stool over and lifted Annie's injured leg on to it. 'We've made up a bed for you downstairs, and there's a toilet and washroom right next door.'

'Thank you, Rosie.' Annie smiled. 'How are the children?'

'They're fine.' Rose turned to Sam. 'Jacques is settling in very well. He's having his afternoon nap at the moment.'

Just then the door was pushed open and Jacques trotted in carrying a toy rabbit by the ear. He stopped suddenly when he noticed Reid, then looked at Sam.

'Daddy?' He spoke the word exactly as Kate did, and it was clear he'd been listening to her very carefully.

Sam knelt down and hugged his son, and Annie was delighted to see that the child did not pull away. Progress was being made.

Annie smiled, holding out her hand to him. 'Hello, Jacques, do you remember me?'

'You're Auntie Annie,' he said in clear English.

He sidled past Reid and stopped by the stool, reaching out to touch the plaster on her ankle. 'What's that?' he asked.

'I've broken my ankle and have to keep that on until it's healed,' Annie told him.

Annie was surprised at how well Jack had picked up the language. 'You speak English very well now.'

'Auntie Rose 'elped me,' he told her as he climbed on to the settee beside her, still clutching his toy.

'That's a nice rabbit,' she said.

'Kate give me.' He squirmed about until he pulled a

small toy soldier from his pocket and showed it to Annie. 'James got lots of these and 'e let me play.'

Sam knelt down in front of his son. 'Are you happy living here, Jacques?'

He nodded. 'Auntie Rose is nice. Grandpa Wally and Grandpa George play with me, and Grandma Marj read me stories. Kate and James say I can be their brother.' He gave his father an uncertain look, then tugged at the ear of his rabbit as a glimmer of tears shone in his eyes.

Sam and Annie were talking to Jacques in his own language now, and Reid watched the scene with narrowed eyes. He could see why Sam wanted Annie for his wife; she would be perfect for him and his son. The boy was obviously still troubled and was holding on to Annie with one hand and gazing at his father anxiously.

Reid's heart ached with pity for this poor little boy; he was so clearly confused and troubled.

Not being able to stand seeing the three of them together any longer, Reid walked out of the room, through the kitchen and into the garden. He leant against the house and lit a cigarette, ignoring the cold wind.

Now he understood how his brother had felt about Annie. Paul had been clinging on to an elusive dream – a dream out of reach. He drew in deeply and blew the smoke out, watching the wind snatch it away. Was he doing the same thing? It had taken him a long time to really fall in love, and now he felt as if his hopes were as insubstantial as the smoke. Oh hell!

'Don't give up.' Rose came and stood beside him, pulling her coat close around her. 'Sam and Annie have been through a lot together, but quite what, only they

328

know. They like and respect each other but I don't think it would be right for them to marry.'

Reid offered her a cigarette, and when she refused he said, 'They look happy together, so why do you say that?'

'Haven't you noticed that Sam hardly ever touches her? Annie wouldn't like that; she's always been very tactile. But there's more to it than physical attraction,' Rose said. 'I believe he only sees her as a suitable mother for his son.'

Reid was angry at the thought of a man using Annie like that. She deserved better. You couldn't just label her as a suitable mother; she had feelings and needs of her own. She was a complex and adorable woman . . .

Rose gave him a speculative glance. 'I've seen the expression in your eyes when you look at her, so don't give up. It took Bill ages to persuade me to marry him, but he won in the end, in his usual quiet way.'

'How did he manage it?' Reid asked. It was unusual for Rose to open up like this and he was hoping she would keep on talking. He wanted to know all about this family Annie loved so much.

'He kept going away, leaving me to get mad with him, then he would return and pick up where we'd left off, as if it had been only yesterday.' Rose gave a quiet chuckle.

Reid grinned, remembering the tall captain who had the respect of all his crew without ever raising his voice. 'He knew what he was doing.'

'Bill always does.' Rose smiled back at Reid. 'But I'm glad he never took "no" for an answer.'

'Why hasn't Annie ever married?'

Rose shoved her hands in her pockets and frowned. 'I've always assumed it was because she had a career she enjoyed and didn't want to be tied down with a family of her own just yet, but I believe the real reason is that she hasn't met anyone she could love with passion.'

'And you believe that's important to her, do you?' Reid asked.

'Yes. As a small child she was always outgoing and affectionate, loving people in a way I could never understand.' She laughed softly. 'As soon as I turned my back she would be sidling up to the men I knew, giving them an appealing smile until they lifted her up. I know she would never marry unless she felt absolutely sure it was right, and in the absence of that special man in her life she has showered her family with love.'

Reid tried to imagine Annie as a small child and it wasn't difficult to do; she must have been a real charmer. And although she was a grown woman now, she had retained an air of innocence that was damned appealing. Whenever they were together he found himself watching the way she responded to people; the ready smile and gentleness he often glimpsed in her eyes. His brother had been right – Annie Webster was a very special woman and he wanted her! He looked at Rose and smiled, dragging his mind away from the girl who was starting to fill his every waking moment. 'Charlie told me that you have another brother who ran away to sea as a boy and ended up in Australia.'

'Yes, Bob.' Rose grimaced. 'He was difficult as a child and he did the right thing by leaving. He's made a good life for himself out there; but at the moment he's in this country with the Australians. We've got two more sisters:

Nancy and Flo. They are settled with their own families and we hardly ever see them now, which makes Mum sad, but that's the way with families, isn't it?'

'Yes.' Reid looked at the tall, beautiful woman beside him, and could understand why Bill had pursued her with such determination. Suddenly he felt better; Rose knew Annie better than anyone else, because she had practically brought her up during those tough years in Garrett Street. He didn't know the whole story but he'd gathered that Annie could have died very young if it hadn't been for Rose's care. If she believed that Annie and Sam weren't in love with each other, then that was good to know. 'Thanks for talking to me, Rose.'

'It was my pleasure.' She walked towards the kitchen door. 'Are you coming in now? It's cold out here and tea will be ready soon.'

Reid followed her into the warmth of the kitchen with its tantalizing smell of freshly baked bread, then on through to the lounge again. The cold air and the talk with Rose had cleared his mind.

Jacques gave Reid a doubtful look when he back came in but Sam told his son, 'He's a pilot and flew us here today.'

The little boy's eyes opened wide and he fired rapid questions at his father in their own language.

'He wants to know if he can see your plane?' Sam told Reid.

'I'll take him tomorrow.'

At that moment there was the sound of children's voices and Jack scrambled off the settee. 'Kate and James home from school.' Then he was off as fast as his legs would carry him.

No sooner had the boy left the room when he was back again, trailing after Rose's two children.

'Auntie Annie.' Kate came and kissed her gently, making sure she didn't knock her arm or leg.

'Can you walk?' James asked as he examined the bulky plaster on her foot and ankle.

'It's difficult, but I can manage.' Annie put her foot to the floor and stood up. 'See, they've put something on the bottom of the plaster so I can stand on it.'

'Tea's ready!' Rose looked into the room. 'I'll bring yours in here, Annie.'

'No, you won't. I'll eat with the rest of you.'

Reid stepped forward as she tried a step, but she waved him away. 'I've got to do this myself. I can't be forever calling for help.'

When Annie reached the table she collapsed on to a chair and gave a triumphant grin. 'Made it! I knew I could do it. And it's no good you looking so disapproving, Squadron Leader, because I'm determined to fend for myself while I'm here.'

'I've been demoted again, have I?' Reid asked, smiling at her dangerously.

'Well,' said George, changing the subject quickly to avoid a row erupting, 'it looks as if we'll soon be ready to invade France. Will you go home after the war's over, Sam?'

Jacques stopped chewing and fixed anxious eyes on his father. 'Home?'

'Yes, Jacques, but not until all the Germans have left,' Sam told him.

The boy swallowed. 'We find *ma mère*?'

'What does that mean?' James whispered to Annie.

'His mother,' she told him, anxious that the little boy should have asked such a question.

Jacques looked at his father. 'I want nice mummy, like James and Kate 'ave got.'

'I promise you shall have one.' Sam's voice was husky with emotion.

'Don't make promises you might not be able to keep, Sam,' Rose reprimanded firmly. 'It isn't right to give the boy false hopes.'

'I'll keep my promise, Rose.' Sam had a look of sheer determination on his face. 'I'll do anything to make my son happy.'

Reid could feel Annie slipping away from him with every word from the grim-looking man sitting opposite him.

The next morning was a Saturday so the three children, Sam, Wally, George and Reid, crammed themselves into George's car and went to the airfield to see the plane. Before the war it had been a private airfield and there were still a good many small planes parked there for the duration. Because of his rank, it hadn't been difficult for Reid to obtain permission for this brief visit. James was soon inside Reid's Lysander asking a stream of questions, but Kate and Jacques didn't seem too keen and only wanted to view it from the field. Reid studied the two children and couldn't help noticing that Kate, at seven years old, was beginning to show a hint of her mother's dark beauty, and Jacques, only three years old, appeared frightened to be out in the open. Poor little devil!

Reid left James in the cockpit and jumped down. The little boy had asked to see the plane, but now he was hanging back, looking rather unsure of himself. He was hanging on to George's hand and glancing nervously around the field. 'Don't you want to have a look inside?' he asked Jacques.

It took some persuading but he eventually managed to entice the two reluctant children inside. Kate was clearly uneasy, but after a couple of minutes Jacques was looking around with interest and chattering excitedly in his own language. Reid couldn't follow the rapid flow of words, and he doubted that the children could either, but they didn't take any notice, and kept talking to him as if they understood every word. He smiled at their antics. It was refreshing to see how they all got along together even if they couldn't always understand the words. Mankind could take a lesson from children, he thought.

Jacques began to shiver with the cold, so Reid scooped him up and put him in the back of the car, tucking a blanket around his little legs, and then everyone else clambered in. He started the car and they made their way back to the house, the children chattering away all the time.

'Are you still flying in combat?' George asked as they pulled up in front of the house.

'No, and I do miss it,' Reid admitted to George and Wally, 'but my mother's relieved. After Paul was killed she was terrified the same thing would happen to me.'

Wally helped Jacques from the car and then looked at Reid. 'You stay on the ground, my boy. Losing one son is enough for any family.'

That was something Reid couldn't argue with. The loss of Paul was still an open wound for them all, and he wondered how many years it was going to take before the pain eased.

As soon as they arrived back everyone went into the lounge and huddled around the log fire. One good thing about living in the country like this was that there was always a plentiful supply of firewood, and fresh food from their kitchen garden.

Marj bustled in with mugs of cocoa. 'I saw the car pull up and thought you would need this. It's perishing cold out there today.'

Reid took one with a smile of thanks. Annie's mother was looking tired and that was hardly surprising; this house was always full.

'Gosh, that was great!' James rubbed his hands and held them out to the fire in an effort to get them warm again. 'I'm going to learn to fly when I'm old enough. Will you teach me?' he asked Reid.

'If you still want to in six years' time when you're twenty.' Reid looked at the silent little boy. 'Would you like to learn when you're grown up?'

Jacques gave this careful thought, and then shook his head. 'You fly us.'

Marj handed round the hot drinks and Reid settled in an armchair. He couldn't help feeling troubled. The more time he spent in Jacques's company, the more obvious one thing was. The child never smiled!

The journey from Pontypool to London had been long, tiring and cold. Annie felt it had all been worth it, though, as she watched her cast being removed, and gave a groan of sheer pleasure. Thank heavens for that! She had hated the restrictions the plaster had imposed on her life.

The doctor examined her ankle and nodded approval.

'That's healed well. How's the head, no bad headaches or dizzy spells?'

'No, none.' She put her foot to the floor, stood up very carefully and grimaced.

'No jiving for a while,' he joked.

'I promise.' After the doctor had left, the nurse helped her on with her stockings and shoes, and then handed her a walking stick. 'Use this for a couple of weeks.'

'Thanks for everything.' Annie hobbled to the main waiting area and nearly bumped into Reid, who was charging along with a scowl on his face.

'Sorry I didn't meet the train,' he apologized. 'I was delayed and the roads are treacherous.'

'That's all right. I got a lift from the station, and I wasn't expecting you, anyway.' And if his thunderous expression was an indication of his mood, she thought, then he needn't have bothered coming.

Reid glanced around. 'Where are Wally and George?'

'They both have bad colds and I wouldn't let them come.' Annie was glad of the stick as she made her way along the corridor. The ankle did not feel at all secure now the support had been removed.

'What?' Reid stopped her. 'Are you telling me you made that journey on your own?'

'Of course I did. People were very kind and helped me all the way.' She continued walking, wondering why he was making such a fuss. It hadn't been a pleasant or easy journey but she'd managed quite well considering the bulky plaster had made movement difficult.

'Why the hell didn't you let me know?' he exploded.

'The weather was too bad to fly you back, but I could have come and collected you.'

'Reid, I am not helpless.' She cast him an exasperated glance. 'My arm is completely healed and I could walk reasonably well, if slowly.'

'Where are you going now?' he asked with a resigned sigh.

'There isn't a train for Bedford today so I'm staying at Roehampton for the night. I'm fit to return to duty as from tomorrow.' She couldn't wait to get back and stuck into the job again. Although Dora wasn't there any more, Jean still was, and the rest of the girls were a lively bunch. Before, when she had spare time, which wasn't often, they had gone in a group to the pub, or dancing. Although dancing would be out of the question for some time, she thought, as she limped along.

'Well, if we get any more snow you'll have a job reporting back on time.' Reid held a door open for her and they made their way to the main entrance.

'I'll worry about that in the morning,' she told him

sharply, suddenly feeling very tired. She could do without this kind of pessimism. 'But I'll get there all right.'

'Can't wait to get back to Sam?' he snapped.

Annie gave him a withering look. 'What's that supposed to mean?'

Reid's sigh was weary and he massaged between his eyes. 'Sorry. I'm in a foul mood. I was concerned about you when the weather closed in, but I thought Wally and George would be with you.'

'I couldn't let them come, Reid,' Annie explained. 'They were both too ill to sit in a freezing train for hours.'

'Couldn't Rose have come with you for support?'

'There's Dora, the baby and her family down there, and with two sick men to look after as well, she couldn't leave.'

Annie stopped when they stepped outside and she saw the air force truck parked right outside the door. 'Did you come in that?'

'My car wouldn't start,' he grumbled.

The expression of disgust on his face was too much for Annie, and she began to laugh. 'Oh, dear, you have had a rotten day, haven't you?'

'I'm glad you find it funny, because I bloody well don't!' He opened the truck door and lifted Annie into the passenger seat, then jumped in himself. 'Is there anyone at home?' he asked as they drove out of the hospital gates.

'No, our houses have been empty since early November.'

'Oh God! I hope the blasted pipes aren't frozen.'

Annie hit him on the arm. 'Will you stop being so gloomy? Of course they won't be. Bill made sure every-

338

thing was properly lagged. Are you coming down with the flu or something?'

'Nope. I'm disgustingly healthy.'

Annie decided it was useless talking to him, so she settled back and the rest of the journey was silent. Something had upset the big, scowling man, and she didn't think she wanted to know what it was.

When they got to Roehampton it was colder in the house than outside, and that was clearly too much for Reid's fragile temper.

'You can't stay here,' he exploded. 'It's like the Arctic.' She rummaged in the kitchen drawer for a box of matches, fed up and with her patience evaporating. 'It will soon warm up when I get the fires going. They are already laid and I've only got to put a match to them.'

He took the matches out of her hand, struck one, and lit the paper in the large black-leaded kitchen fire. 'If you insist on staying, then you'll need hot water.'

Annie was pleased to see that he sounded a bit more reasonable now. 'It won't take long, that fire is very efficient.'

Reid blew on the flames and gave a grunt of satisfaction as the fire caught. Then he disappeared to light the lounge one.

Annie shook her head, bemused by his strange mood, and put the kettle on to make some tea. While the water was boiling she unpacked her bag. Thank goodness she'd brought enough food to feed Reid as well. She dreaded to think what he would be like if he had to go hungry this evening.

'It's snowing again,' he said, as he came back into the kitchen.

'I'll get you something to eat, then you'd better be on your way before it gets too bad,' she told him.

'I'm not leaving you here on your own,' he said in astonishment. 'How the hell are you going to get back to camp in the morning?'

'On the train, of course.'

'Oh, fine!' he said, throwing his hands up in disgust. 'What do you want to do, break the other leg?'

She spun to face him, hands on hips. 'What the blazes is wrong with you? You're treating me as if I was some brainless idiot. I've taken care of myself in worse conditions than this and survived.'

'Oh, when?' Reid was studying her through narrowed eyes.

Blast! Annie thought, that was careless of me, but the man was infuriating, and he was also curious. But what she'd said was true. That trip to France had been cold, arduous and frightening, but it had certainly made her tougher and more able to cope with difficult situations. She busied herself with making the tea and putting soup on to heat, hoping he wouldn't pursue the subject. She must watch her tongue more carefully in the future. Not that she considered Reid a security risk, but her mission to rescue Jack Graham was top secret, and she wouldn't want to put the brave people who had helped her in danger.

'So, why the foul mood?' she asked, changing the subject.

Reid shrugged. 'It's nothing. I'll get over it.'

Annie put two bowls of steaming vegetable soup on the table with chunks of Rose's home-made bread. 'Do you want to talk about it?'

'No.' He sat down and started to eat. 'What's Will and Dora's baby like?'

'Just beautiful, she's got masses of silver-blonde hair, and is a contented little tot. Mind you, she was spoilt rotten by everyone.' Seeing baby Emily had been wonderful. Her mother had fussed over her new grandchild, clearly delighted with the little girl.

'The house must have been packed over the holiday.' Reid finished off his soup and spread margarine on another piece of bread.

'All room was taken up, with camp beds crammed in every space,' Annie said and laughed, 'and because of the bad weather they are all still there.'

'Except you,' he remarked, picking up his knife and fork to tuck into the vegetable pie Annie had brought back from Wales with her.

'I had to return,' she told him, a defensive note in her voice. 'I've been out of action for long enough and can't wait to get back to normal again. I believe 1944 is going to be an exciting year, and I want to be in the thick of it.'

'I know, Annie.' He reached out and placed his large hand over hers. 'I'm sorry I took my bad temper out on you.' He grimaced. 'I'd promised myself I wouldn't do that to you again but when I thought about you struggling on your own I was furious with myself. I should have come for you.'

'I am a grown woman, Reid. I don't need a nursemaid.'

'I have noticed,' he remarked drily.

Annie pulled her hand away from his. Arguing with him made her feel sad. 'Can we go back to being friends again?'

He laughed then, a deep amused sound that Annie found rather disturbing. 'We do seem to antagonize each other, don't we?'

She looked closely at the handsome man, and couldn't help wondering why she always felt so defensive around him. But she couldn't come up with an answer.

He helped clear away their dishes, refusing to let her stand up for too long. After everything was put away Annie opened the airing cupboard and felt the tank.

'Good, there will soon be enough hot water for a bath.' The sooner she could soak her ankle the better, for it was aching badly now. In spite of all her bravado about being fit for work again it wasn't going to be easy.

'It'll be cold up there,' Reid pointed out. 'Have you got an electric fire?'

'There's one in my bedroom but it's only a single bar.'

'I'll put that in there for a while, it will take the chill off.' He headed for the stairs, taking them two at a time.

While he was upstairs, Annie checked to see if there were fresh sheets and blankets in the airing cupboard, but to be honest she didn't feel like shivering in a cold bedroom. The warmth of the fire was seeping through her now and she felt dreadfully tired. She yawned.

'Come on, you look exhausted.' Reid came back and took her by the hand. 'The lounge is warm enough now.'

She didn't protest when he led her to the other room. The settee was pulled up to the fire and she sat down with a sigh of relief.

'You've had a long hard day,' Reid said. He put some more logs on the fire then joined her, gathering her into his arms. 'Rest now.'

Annie tucked her legs up and rested her head on his chest. He was such a thoughtful man when he wasn't snapping and snarling, she mused as she drifted off to sleep.

'Annie!'

She didn't want to wake up. She was so warm and comfortable . . .

'The fires will go out if I don't see to them soon.'

'Hmm?' She sat up and yawned. 'How long have I been asleep?'

'Over an hour.' He stood up, stretched, and then started to build the fire up again. 'The bathroom will be nice and warm by now. I'll remove the electric fire when you're ready.'

Annie flexed her foot and ankle; it was feeling rather sore. Perhaps she had overdone things today.

'A hot bath will ease that.' Reid smiled down at her.

She hoped he was right. 'I think I'll sleep down here tonight, in the warm.'

'I was going to suggest that,' he agreed. 'The beds will need airing before they can be used. You take the settee and I'll sleep in one of the armchairs.'

'Will you be comfortable enough?' she asked. He looked much too large to rest in a chair for the night.

'Sure. When we were flying several times a day I learned to snatch sleep wherever I could, and so did the rest of the squadron.' He gave a wry smile. 'We were so damned tired.'

'They were desperate times, weren't they?'

He nodded, a faraway look in his eyes, and Annie knew he was reliving the struggle they'd had. No one was

343

going to come out of this war the same person they'd been before it started.

'You don't have to worry about me. I could sleep on a clothes line if I had to.' Reid poked the fire into a good blaze again, and then sat on the floor staring into the flames, obviously lost in a world of his own.

Annie stood up and stretched. 'I'll go and have my bath now.'

Half an hour later she was back, dressed in her flannel pyjamas, dressing gown and a pair of Wally's long hand-knitted socks. She threw the pillows and blankets she was carrying on one of the armchairs.

Reid had a glass of whisky in his hand and he held it up to her. 'I found this in the sideboard, do you think Wally will mind?'

'Of course not.' Annie studied Reid's downcast expression. 'I wish you'd tell me what's worrying you.'

He swallowed the drink down and grimaced. 'Well, there's this girl I'm crazy about . . .'

For some daft reason the thought of Reid with another woman disturbed her, but she managed to laugh. This was the last thing she would have expected. Reid didn't seem the type to let a woman trouble him.

Annie sat on the settee. 'Come and tell me about her.' Reid settled next to her and put his arm around her shoulder. 'She's lovely, intelligent, infuriating and she's got another man after her.'

'You're not going to let that stop you, surely?' She couldn't believe he would step aside and let someone else have what he wanted without a struggle. His char-acter was too determined for that.

344

'It's complicated.' He shrugged.

'What's complicated about it? You want her, don't you?' It was hard to understand why she found this so difficult to talk about. After all, if he was in love with some woman, then what was that to her? She was just feeling a bit emotional after finally having that damned plaster removed, she thought, that's all it was. Once she got back to work, she would feel more like herself.

'More than anything I've ever wanted in my life,' he admitted.

'Then go after her, you fool,' she told him. 'If you don't, you'll regret it for the rest of your days.'

'I'm glad you feel like that.' He reached across and started to unfasten her pyjama jacket. First one button, then the second . . .

'Just a minute!' Annie caught hold of his hand. 'What do you think you're doing?'

He gave her a searing look. 'You told me to go after her, so I'm trying to see if making love to her will win her over.'

Annie pushed him away and scrambled to her feet, the sore ankle forgotten. She was deeply wounded by his attitude. 'I will not be used by you to relieve your frustration. I am not a substitute for the woman you love.'

'You've got it all wrong, Annie. You're not a substitute. The only one I'm thinking about is you. It's you I'm in love with!'

Annie was incensed by what she considered a blatant lie. 'Don't you make fun of me, Reid Lascells. And don't try to excuse your conduct by lying to me. I know you're only looking after me to keep the promise you made to

345

Paul. Your mother told me all about it. All I can say is that you can't love this girl very much if you are willing to put someone else in her place for one night. I would not have expected you to take advantage of our situation.'

Reid gave a ragged sigh. 'I'm telling you the truth.'

Annie had had enough of this. If she didn't get rid of him soon she would burst into tears, and she was damned if she'd do that in front of him. The lying devil! She picked up a pillow and a blanket and tossed them to him. 'You can sleep in the kitchen. There's an old armchair in there by the fire.'

It had been a long and sleepless night. Annie had found it difficult to stop her mind from racing. The fact that Reid had tried to make love to her after telling her he was crazy about some other woman was beyond belief, and had hurt dreadfully. Not that *she* loved him, of course, but she objected to being taken advantage of like that. Although they always seemed to fight when they met, she respected him, and to think he would stoop to doing something like this was upsetting – and disappointing.

Reid was already in the kitchen making tea and toast for their breakfast. He gave her a hard stare as she walked in. 'Did you sleep well?'

'No,' she admitted. 'Did you?'

He didn't answer as he spread margarine on the bread and placed it in front of her. 'The weather's cleared a bit so I can drive you back to Bedfordshire as soon as you're ready.'

'I can catch the ten o'clock train.' She bit into the toast and ignored the look of fury racing across his face.

'Don't you argue with me, Miss Webster,' he growled,

346

'because I'm not in any mood to put up with your nonsense this morning.'

She decided it would be best if they didn't speak to each other if they couldn't be civil, and they certainly didn't seem to be able to this morning! The atmosphere between them was positively explosive. They drank their tea and ate the toast in silence. Within half an hour they were on their way.

Annie slept most of the journey, making up for the hours of tossing and turning last night. It was the safest thing to do because if they argued any more she'd start to crumble, as her emotions were raw at the moment. She'd never known anyone who could upset her like this man.

'We're here.' Reid shook her awake and got down to help her out. He lifted her out of the truck and handed her the kit bag. He looked her straight in the eyes for a few moments. His expression was intense and strained. 'I'm not a liar, Annie,' he said quietly, and then jumped back into the vehicle and sped off up the lane.

She stood there for a while as she wrestled with a deep sense of hurt. She was convinced that Reid was only paying her all this attention because of the promise he'd made to his brother. How she wished his parents had never told her about it.

'I'm back, Sam.' She looked into his office and wiggled her foot. 'Look, no plaster.'

'Good. I didn't think you'd make it,' Sam said. 'Are the trains running?'

'Reid brought me back in an air force truck.'

'Did he now?'

'Yes. He collected me from hospital yesterday and we stayed overnight at my house.' Annie wondered why Sam was frowning.

'But your family are still in Wales, aren't they?' he asked. 'Were you alone with him all night?'

'I could hardly send him out on a terrible night like that, could I?' Annie had had enough! What was the matter with these men? She'd had to put up with Reid in a foul mood, and now Sam.

She stormed out and headed for the ops room. Sam and Reid were as bad as each other. She wasn't daft. It was obvious that Sam was looking in her direction as a mother for his adorable son, so he might not like to think there was another man on the scene to spoil his plans, but what was Reid up to? And what right did any man have to make plans regarding her future without finding out if she was agreeable or not?

Annie had always considered that she understood men reasonably well but not any longer. She had been wise to remain single. They were a blasted mystery!

29

The watery spring sunshine filtered through the high cloud and bathed Tangmere airfield in a golden glow. Reid shaded his eyes as he scanned the sky. The invasion of France couldn't be far away now and troops were being moved to various places along the coast. He'd been overjoyed when he'd heard that his old squadron was being transferred here for the next few months. This was just the lift he needed. Since that disastrous night in January, he had stayed away from Annie, hoping this tactic would work as Rose had suggested, but he doubted it. It was his own fault, of course; he should have convinced her, but the truth was he had bungled it. He had been thrown by her disbelief that he could love her, and dismayed to find she knew about the promise he'd made to Paul. It was clouding their relationship and the way she thought about him. He might be a good pilot but he had a hell of a lot to learn about women.

One Spitfire roared over their heads and spun into a victory roll. Reid chuckled, his worries forgotten for a moment. Bouncer. He was tempted to put his reckless friend on a charge for that.

Some of the pilots now landing had been involved in the Battle of Britain, as Churchill called it, and although that phase of the war was over, life was still dangerous for them. One of their many tasks was to escort bombers across the channel, and that meant they were fighting over France. If they had to bale out there, then they were taken prisoner. Reid felt his insides clench when he remembered how close he'd been to that when Dunkirk was being evacuated. He'd have hated to have been locked up and unable to take any further part in the war.

'Hi, skip.' Timber Woods sauntered over to him.

Reid slapped the tall pilot on the shoulder, then he was surrounded by the men of his old squadron. Some he knew; some he didn't; many he missed. 'It's good to see you all.'

They fell silent as they watched Bouncer land. It was always a breathtaking moment.

'Ye Gods!' Reid exclaimed. 'He doesn't get any better, does he?'

'No,' Timber agreed, 'but once he's airborne he's a real demon.'

'I remember. He's always a good man to have with you,' Reid walked over to his friend who was clambering out of the plane. His mobility was still slightly impaired, but nothing to speak of considering how badly he'd been injured. It was five months since he'd seen Bouncer but instead of slapping him on the back in delight Reid kept his expression serious.

'Patterson! You're on a charge for that fancy bit of flying,' Reid used his best command voice.

Bouncer sprang to attention. 'I realized the undercarriage wasn't down so I had to go round again. Took a bit of shaking loose.'

'Is that the best excuse you can come up with?' Reid asked, raising a brow in query.

350

His friend rubbed his chin. 'It worked in the past.'

'Not this time, you're talking to me now.'

'Ah, well.' Bouncer gave a resigned sigh. 'What's the punishment, then?'

'You've got to get the first round of drinks in to-night.'

A cheer rang out from the rest of the pilots. They were in full agreement with that kind of reprimand.

The ground crews were waiting to get their hands on the new planes, and Reid called Charlie over.

'Bouncer, Charlie, Annie's brother, will look after your Spit for you.'

The pilot beamed and shook Charlie's hand vigorously. 'How is the delightful Annie, now?'

'Completely recovered from her accident and back to normal,' Charlie told him.

Reid made a sound that sounded suspiciously like a snort of disgust, and Bouncer eyed his friend.

'Don't tell me you're still fighting with each other?'

Reid's only answer was a wry smile.

'I think you need your head examined, old boy.' Bouncer turned back to Charlie. 'Give her my regards next time you talk to her, and tell her I'll be writing shortly.'

Charlie nodded and hurried off to check over his new charge.

'What are you writing to Annie for?' Reid asked.

'It's nothing to concern you, old chap. I've got a bit of news for her, that's all.' Bouncer watched Charlie clambering over his plane. 'Good, is he?'

'The best we've got,' Reid assured him. 'He'll look after you well.'

His friend nodded. 'Thanks. Wouldn't like to cop it now the end is in sight.'

Reid looked at Bouncer in astonishment. 'When did you start worrying about your safety?'

'Things change.' He punched Reid on the arm and grinned. 'Things change.'

Bouncer *had* changed, though in what way Reid couldn't quite fathom. There was something different about him. The strained, rather cynical look about him wasn't there any more, and his friend seemed alive with happiness, but what could have caused this transformation wasn't clear. He'd have to get to the bottom of the mystery later.

Reid shot back his cuff and checked his watch, then looked at the group of pilots. 'I shall expect you all to be in the Fox and Hounds by twenty hundred hours.'

'Yes, sir!' they chorused.

Reid watched them amble off to stow their gear and settle in, and he felt more uplifted than he had done for many a long week. It was going to be wonderful having them stationed here. How he'd missed the camaraderie, the flying, the exhilaration of touching down after a hard fight, and even the danger. That was when he'd felt truly alive – every moment had been precious and to be lived to the full.

He marched back to his office with a purposeful air to his stride. Now they were stationed here he was going back up with them at the first opportunity, and damn his responsibilities on the ground. When the invasion began he was going to be a part of it!

*

The pub was in uproar by the time Reid arrived.

'You're late,' Bouncer scolded and pushed two pints towards him. 'Get those down you at the double; the next round's on its way.'

Reid complied, then sat back as the table was quickly filled with full glasses again. Timber held one of the glasses aloft.

'Here's to Bouncer. Congratulations, mate.'

'What's all this about?' Reid glanced round at the smiling faces and took a mouthful of beer.

'I'm getting married,' Bouncer told him.

Reid choked on the drink and received thumps on the back from the men. 'You're *what*?' he asked hoarsely.

'I'm getting married in two weeks,' his friend repeated.

'Good God! I never thought I'd see the day.'

Bouncer gave a smug grin. 'I told you things change. Will you be my best man?'

'Of course I will. When did you meet her?'

'It was soon after I returned to Kenley. Jenny's so lovely and kind, Reid, she really bowled me over.'

'I'm very happy for you,' Reid told him with sincerity. He had recovered from the shock now and surged to his feet. 'This calls for a real drink. I wonder if the landlord's got a bottle of good whisky tucked away somewhere?'

'If anyone can get him to part with it, it's you,' Timber encouraged.

The barman was only too happy to help the pilots celebrate and Reid was soon back with double whiskies and beer chasers.

'Oh, well done!' Bouncer complimented. 'That officer's uniform does have its uses sometimes.'

'I should hope so.' Reid held up his glass of whisky.

353

'Let's all drink to Bouncer and his bride. May they grow old together in happiness and peace.'

'That was a fine toast, my friend.' Bouncer looked quite overcome for a moment. 'I'd like as many of you to come to the wedding as possible.'

'We'll *all* be there,' Reid announced. 'I'll fix it. We can't have one of our squadron getting married without a guard of honour.' Although he was no longer a part of this group he still felt as if he belonged, and after the Battle of Britain he doubted that the link would ever be broken.

'Jenny would like that.' Bouncer drained his whisky, quickly followed by the beer. 'My round again, I believe.'

By now they were a very *happy* crowd, and although Reid had drunk as much as anyone else his mind felt surprisingly clear. He had allowed himself to become bogged down with responsibilities and cares. The job he was doing wasn't always easy or smooth running. Then there was Annie. She had tied him up in knots and he was a fool to have allowed that to happen. It would be best if he just accepted that she couldn't stand the sight of him, and that she would eventually marry Sam.

He downed another pint. Yes, that's what he'd do. Much better for both of them, and that decision might help to improve his temper. He would still keep an eye on her, of course. After all, he'd promised his brother, hadn't he?

Annie loved receiving letters and she had had four today. The first one was from her mother and Rose, giving her all the family news, the second was from Dora, and that had her in fits of laughter; motherhood certainly hadn't dimmed her sense of humour. The next was from Charlie and she gave a wry smile as she read the account of Reid's old squadron arriving, and the party they'd had in the pub that night. 'You should have seen them, Annie,' he wrote. 'Those men certainly know how to have a good time.'

She could just imagine.

The last letter was in a hand she didn't recognize, and after slitting it open she gasped in pleasure. It was from Bouncer inviting her to his wedding in six days' time. She had taken a great liking to Bouncer and she was very happy for him. She would go, if it were possible.

Annie went immediately to see if she could have the leave. She didn't think there would be any problem because she was always willing to work extra hours, and often didn't even take the time off she was allowed.

'I can let you have twenty-hour hours only,' the wing commander told her. 'And make the most of it because it might be the last for some time.'

'Thanks.' She stopped on her way out and turned back. 'Do you think the invasion is imminent?'

He shrugged. 'Couldn't say, but if any more troops and equipment arrive this island will sink into the sea from the weight of it all.'

Annie laughed at the thought and went back to her post. The tension and anticipation were building, and Sam was becoming more restless as each week passed. If there was an invasion of France this summer, then she knew that Sam would be right behind the first wave of troops.

Annie had managed to catch a train to Chichester all right, but she'd had to wait ages for a bus to Boxgrove where Bouncer and Jenny were getting married. It was a beautiful spring day, just perfect for a wedding; Annie was looking forward to this very much. Bouncer was a fine man and deserved to be happy. She reached the church just in time; the bride's car was arriving as she hurried inside. Bouncer was in the front pew, laughing at something the man next to him was saying. Of course, Reid would be the best man, Annie thought, as she studied them. An impressive pair, they were great friends who had been through hell together.

The organ burst into tune and the large congregation stood to watch the bride walk along the aisle. She was quite lovely, with chestnut hair, and wearing a flowing gown made of parachute silk. Annie couldn't help smiling to herself: it looked as if Bouncer had made good use of his parachute at last.

It was a touching ceremony but there was a slight ripple of amusement as Charles Algernon Patterson took his vows. Bouncer was going to take some ragging for that, Annie realized, and fought back a chuckle. It was probably the first time any of them had heard his real names. While the register was being signed, the ushers urged everyone outside.

'Charlie!' Annie cried in delight when she saw her brother. 'I didn't know you'd be here.'

'Didn't know myself until the last minute, but Reid fixed it for me. They've chosen this church because it's not much more than half a mile from the Tangmere airfield. Friends can pop along to the wedding, even if they can only stay for a hour or so.'

'It's good to see you.' She hugged him, and then stood back. 'Why have they made us come out of the church?'

'You'll see in a minute.'

Reid strode out, gave an order, and two lines of pilots formed a guard of honour. When Bouncer and his bride stepped through the door they made an archway of swords for the newly-weds to walk under.

'That's wonderful,' Annie sighed. 'And a fitting tribute to a brave man, but where on earth did they get the swords from?'

'Those crazy men can get anything if they set their minds to it. But they're all special, Annie. I watched them through the battles; never knowing if they were going to die that day, and waiting in vain for friends who never returned. They may seem crazy at times but it's just their way of coping with the danger.'

'I agree, Charlie, and there are others working quietly in the background who have that kind of courage as well.'

Her brother gave her a studied look. 'Yes, you would know about that, wouldn't you, little sister?'

Annie merely smiled and watched Reid. Wearing full dress uniform he was enough to take her breath away. How could the girl he was crazy about not fall into his arms? His temper and sarcastic tongue were disturbing, of course, but he had seen and done things beyond the imagination. And now he had a lot of responsibility. She had judged him too harshly.

Bouncer called them over for the photographs. 'Annie, thank you for coming; this is Jenny.'

Annie smiled at the radiant girl. 'I'm delighted to meet you. And you look absolutely beautiful.'

'Thank you.' Jenny smoothed her hand over the gown. 'It made a lovely wedding dress, didn't it?'

Her new husband laughed. 'Much better use for it than jumping out of aeroplanes.'

It was a pleasant late April day and the photographer took his time, ordering them into special groups and different poses.

Once the photos were finished and the bride and groom were on their way to the reception, Reid came over to Annie and Charlie.

'Glad you could make it, Webster.'

Annie, being in uniform, saluted him. 'Wouldn't have missed it for anything, Squadron Leader.'

'Oh God!' Charlie muttered, and beat a hasty retreat. She watched her brother for a few moments then started to laugh. 'He's afraid you might put him on a charge if he associates with me.'

'Not because of his sister's insubordination, I wouldn't.'

Annie looked up at the man in front of her, saw the amused glint in his eyes, and grinned. It seemed as if their argument in January had been forgotten, and she was pleased about that.

'Is the girl you're crazy about here?' she asked, scanning the crowd for a likely candidate.

'I'm afraid you'll have to look in a mirror if you want to see her,' he told her.

It took a few moments for that to sink in, and when it did she shook her head. 'Reid. You really do say the most outrageous things. Are you ever serious?'

'Yes, I'm really serious now.' He gave a long, resigned sigh. 'But of course you still won't believe me.'

'You'd hardly expect me to, would you?'

'Why do you find the notion so ludicrous, Annie? I'd like to know.'

'Well, from the moment we met we've fought, except for a couple of tranquil meetings, and the idea of spending the rest of our lives together is too dreadful to contemplate. We wouldn't have a piece of china left.'

Reid's face broke into a grin. 'Life wouldn't be dull, though, would it?'

'No, it wouldn't.' Annie looked earnestly into his eyes.

'I know you find me physically attractive, and I feel the same way about you, but that isn't enough to build a lasting relationship on.'

He fell silent for a few seconds, and then nodded.

'You're quite right, we've got to stop fighting with each other. I'll work on it and see if I can improve my temperament.'

'You're impossible, do you know that?' Annie couldn't help smiling.

He bent and kissed her fleetingly on the lips. 'Don't marry Sam, he isn't right for you.'

Annie watched him stride away, and felt a mixture of indignation, amusement and confusion. What right did he have to tell her what to do with her life?

'I've cadged us a lift, Annie.' Charlie ushered her towards a car. 'Why do you and Reid always treat each other like that?'

'Oh, it comes quite naturally,' she told her brother.

Charlie watched his commanding officer for a moment then shook his head in amusement. 'He would make one heck of a brother-in-law.'

Her brother ducked as Annie took a swipe at him.

'Don't you start. I thought it was only women who got soppy at weddings.'

He gave her a curious look. 'What has the big man been saying to you?'

'A load of nonsense, if you must know,' she retorted. 'Anyway, you're the one who should be thinking of marriage.'

'Well, I must admit it does seem like a good idea . . .'

'Have you found someone?' Annie asked eagerly. She adored her brothers, and now Will was married to Dora, she would love to see Charlie settled with a family of his own.

'I might have,' he hedged.

'What's her name?'

'Patricia – Pat, but don't go saying anything yet,' he warned. 'We only met a few weeks ago.'

Annie almost danced in delight. 'I won't say a word, and I do hope it works out for you, Charlie.'

'What about you, Sis, are you thinking of marrying Sam?'

'He hasn't asked me, but I know he's thinking about it.' Her sigh was deep and thoughtful, and then she shook her head. 'It might seem like a good solution to young Jacques's future, and I do love the little boy, but we would probably end up regretting it after a while. I'll only marry for one thing, Charlie, and that's love.'

Her brother gave her a speculative glance. 'You're a real romantic at heart, aren't you?'

'Have you only just found that out?' She smiled and walked over to the car, but her brother's remark had given her pause for thought. Had her romantic streak stopped her from finding happiness with a man? Was she looking for the impossible? She'd always joked that she was waiting for another man like Bill, her brother-in-law, but she doubted that another man like him existed.

The reception was being held in a village hall about a mile from the church. Considering the wartime rationing the buffet was quite sumptuous.

'It looks as if someone has been dealing on the black market,' Annie remarked to her brother as they helped themselves to the food.

'Maybe, but I'll bet the squadron had a hand in this spread.' Charlie chuckled. 'Those pilots are an enterprising bunch.'

Reid's speech had the guests roaring with laughter as he related some of Bouncer's funniest exploits. The groom took this all in his stride and sat there with a wicked grin on his face, as if to say, I'll get you later for this, my friend.

A small air force band arrived and everyone began to dance. It was a joyful occasion, and for a short time the war was forgotten.

'Is the ankle strong enough to dance?' Reid stood in front of Annie and held his hand out.

'It's as good as new.' She let him lead her on to the dance floor. The band was playing a slow foxtrot and Annie relaxed in his arms. He really was a wonderful dancer, and this was the only time they never argued. Her smile was mischievous.

'What's amusing you?' Reid asked.

'I was just thinking that the only time we are in harmony with each other is when we're dancing.' She

361

looked up into his face and laughed. 'Perhaps if we danced every time we met we might not fight.' Reid pulled her closer. 'Now there's a tempting idea.'

'Did you enjoy the wedding?' Jean asked Annie the next day.

'It was lovely, but I think I danced too much.' She massaged her ankle and foot before easing her shoes on and smiling at Jean. 'Back to work now, though.'

Annie hurried to Sam's office. It was empty. 'Where's Sam?' she asked Wing Commander Felshaw.

'He's taken a few days' leave to go and see his son while he's got the chance.'

Annie sensed the excitement in his voice. 'Is the invasion close?'

'Not far off,' he told her. 'We're going to be busy. The enemy mustn't get wind of this until it's too late.'

'Let's pray the preparations stay hidden.' Annie wasn't sure how the huge build-up of troops could be kept secret, but the whole operation depended on taking the Germans by surprise. It seemed like an impossible task because this small island was bursting at the seams with men and equipment. Hitler must know!

30

June 1944

It must be on! The orders were that no one could leave the base or make contact with anyone outside. The skies had been black with bombers making their way over to Germany and elsewhere. No one had ever seen such massive formations, and Annie couldn't help sparing a thought for the people who were going to be on the receiving end of these bombardments. Tanks had been rumbling out of their hiding places in wooded areas, and were now heading for Portsmouth and other parts of the coast. Troops and vehicles were trundling through the villages, clogging roads, and all heading in the same direction.

All it needed was one reconnaissance plane to spot them . . . but everyone was holding their breath, hoping that wouldn't happen.

Annie had been at her post for hours but didn't feel tired. The feeling of anticipation was keeping everyone wide awake.

'Take half an hour and get something to eat,' the officer told her.

'I'm not hungry.' Annie didn't want to take a break in case something happened while she was away. She felt a moment of sadness. How sorry she was that Jack Graham wouldn't see this day . . .

'That was an order,' she was told sternly. She removed her headphones and another operator stepped into her place.

Annie found Sam outside glaring up at the leaden sky. 'Your blasted English weather. What a time for it to close in. They can't go in this. The longer this operation is held up the more chance there is of discovery.'

'Maybe not, Sam,' she told him. 'They won't be expecting us to launch an attack across the Channel in these bad conditions.' Annie touched his arm. 'Come and have a meal with me, Sam. You're getting soaked out here and worrying won't change the weather.'

'All right,' he agreed. 'There isn't anything else I can do at the moment.'

Annie didn't even know what she was eating and she was certain that Sam didn't care. They were just clearing their plates because it was the sensible thing to do, but it wasn't surprising because everyone was on edge. Although the mess was busy it was strangely quiet. Men and women were toying with the food, unable to eat, or letting cups of steaming tea grow cold. Waiting, waiting . . .

'I thought you were going to France before the invasion,' she said, breaking the tense atmosphere.

'I wanted to, but it was considered unwise, and I had to agree. We didn't want to take the chance of arousing the suspicions of the Germans. I'm going in as soon as the troops start to move inland.'

'I assume you don't want me with you? I'm completely recovered now, and I wouldn't have to jump out of a plane this time.' She knew it was a forlorn hope, but she would dearly have loved to follow the troops in as France was liberated.

'No, Annie, I will be able to move much faster if I'm on my own. But I'll take a wireless and keep in touch.' He smiled to soften the refusal. 'There won't be any need for a covert operation and this trip of mine will be more personal than military.'

'I understand. The Germans must know we're coming, though, mustn't they?' She watched the distracted man stirring his tea. The tension was so great Annie found it hard to even take a breath.

'They know, but let's hope and pray they haven't guessed when or where the landings will be.'

Annie looked at her watch, knowing that that prayer was uppermost in everyone's thoughts. 'I've got to get back. You won't disappear without telling me, will you?'

The deep worry lines smoothed out for a moment and he smiled. 'No, I'll let you know. Rose has promised me that if I get killed she will adopt Jacques and bring him up as her own son.'

'She's a good mother and Bill adores children, so you need have no fears for him.' Annie smiled and touched his hand. 'But nothing is going to happen to you, Sam.'

'I know, it's just a precaution, that's all.'

June the 6th and the news they'd all been waiting for came. Troops and equipment were pouring on to the Normandy beaches. Annie and many others shed a few tears of relief but there was a great deal of worry as well. Where were the sailors in her family, and was Bob among the first wave of troops to hit the beaches? Would this be the decisive move and the end of the German aggression? How many more lives was this going to cost?

The news coming through over the following couple of days was optimistic, but it was frustrating trying to glean information. They guessed that everything coming over the wireless was carefully edited before it was given out. Annie knew only too well that they couldn't give away vital information that might help the enemy. But some troops were moving inland already and there was cause for hope that this was the beginning of the end.

Three days later, Sam found Annie at breakfast.

'I'm leaving for Portsmouth now,' he told her. 'I've got permission to go across at last.'

'You take care, and please keep in touch. Try to stay behind the Allied lines, and I hope you find your sister again,' she said. Sam was kitted out in combat gear with French badges on his shoulders. He had hardly worn them since Annie had met him, as the nature of his job made him keep a low profile, but now he was a determined man going back to his own country to see it liberated.

'That will be my first task, and then I'll try to see if any of Maria's family have survived.' He smiled at her and then hurried on his way, obviously eager to get going.

Annie realized, for the first time, that Sam was still in love with the girl he'd been about to marry when the war started, and she found that incredibly sad. Not only for the brave, complex man, but also for Jacques, who would never know his real mother. Damn the war, she muttered under her breath as her eyes clouded with unshed tears. It had already caused so much suffering,

366

and there was more to come as the troops poured into France.

She sighed and returned to her work. It was obvious that Sam couldn't wait to return to France, and she wondered what he was going to find when he saw his home again. Annie's heart ached for him and everyone who had been torn from their homes by this madness.

What a night! Reid scanned the sky over Tangmere airfield. Dawn was just beginning to stain the sky with a glimmer of light; they would be able to get airborne soon. One week after the invasion and Hitler had unleashed his latest weapon against them.

'They're not bombers. What are they?' Bouncer tumbled into Reid's office having slept through the night. He was still buttoning his shirt. His hair stood on end and he needed a shave.

'Unmanned aircraft – flying bombs,' Reid told his friend. 'They've been coming over all night.'

'Why didn't you sound the alarm?' Bouncer ran a hand through his hair, but it immediately sprang up again.

'There isn't anything we can do until it's light,' Reid said, and flinched at Bouncer's colourful language.

'I don't like this, Reid, from what I've heard they're dropping all over the place. Doesn't that blasted man know when he's beaten?'

'He's making one last desperate effort to stop us, I expect,' Reid said.

They waited anxiously until light filtered through the clouds; Reid donned his flying gear, then walked out with Bouncer to meet the rest of the pilots. There was no way he was keeping out of this! 'We've got orders to try and shoot some of those things down before they reach our coast.'

They did their best and were reasonably successful, but the flying bombs were difficult to shoot down, and far too many still managed to cross the coast. Once again London and the surrounding areas were suffering death and destruction. The invasion was progressing with parts of France already liberated, and this onslaught of the flying bombs had come as an unwelcome shock.

'There's someone at the gate to see you,' Wing Commander Felshaw told Annie. 'Says she's your sister and it's urgent.'

Annie ran. If Rose had left the children and come here to see her, then it must be something very serious. The last time she'd been called out like this Will had been missing. Was it Bill? No, her sister would not leave the children if that were the case, she reasoned.

'Rose!' Annie stopped and struggled to catch her breath. 'What's happened?'

'I'm on my way to London, Annie, and I thought I'd stop off here and try to see you.'

Her sister's expression gave little away, but Annie knew her too well. Anxiety showed in her eyes. 'What is it?'

'As soon as the D-Day landings were under way, Dad was convinced the war was as good as over and he headed for London to open up his house again.'

Annie's heart thudded. The doodlebugs!

'It's been four days now,' Rose continued, 'without a word from him, and he'd never do that. I wanted to let you know before I go and search for him.'

Annie didn't want her sister doing this on her own. Rose's relationship with her father hadn't been easy, but over the years a deep and abiding affection had grown between them. If anything had happened to George then her sister was going to be devastated. 'I've got some leave coming up; I'll see if I can bring it forward. I've been on duty practically non-stop since the invasion began.'

Rose looked relieved. 'Thanks, Annie.'

Fifteen minutes later, Annie was back with a two-day pass and an air force lorry. 'I've cadged a lift with Flight Sergeant Hargreaves. He's going to London,' she told her sister. 'Hop in.'

They were dropped off about a mile from Bloomsbury and continued on foot.

'I told him not to go,' Rose said as she strode along. 'But the stubborn old fool wouldn't listen, as usual.'

'We'll probably find him in the local pub drinking with his friends.' Annie tried to soothe her sister. It wasn't often anyone saw Rose as worried as this, and the closer they got to their destination, the faster she walked.

'I expect you're right.' Rose scowled. 'And if he is, then it will give me great pleasure to hit him for causing us all this worry.'

Annie grinned in spite of her concern. 'You've done that before, haven't you?'

'The first time we met.' Rose's eyes gleamed at the memory. 'What a fight we had. It was a shock meeting my real father at the age of sixteen, and I hated his guts!'

'But his mother was a lovely lady, wasn't she?'

A smile touched Rose's mouth. 'She was a fine woman, and it was really because of her that I eventually became friends with George.

'Do you remember when you took me to see her?' Annie asked. 'You were frightened to death I was going to break something.'

'We'd never seen such beautiful things in our lives, had we?' Rose gave Annie an affectionate glance. 'You loved looking at everything, and weren't at all jealous about someone having so much and us so little. I could never understand why you weren't bitter. The conditions we lived in were inhuman.'

'I didn't have anything to be bitter about, Rose. You looked after me and shielded me from as much of the squalor as you could.' Annie smiled at her big sister, remembering those difficult years when the whole family had relied on Rose. What a burden they'd placed on her.

They walked in silence for some time, and then Annie heard a strange swishing sound. She looked up and gasped in horror. Following them along the road was a doodlebug with its engines cut, and it was gliding down. Rose spun her to face the way they had just come. 'Run!'

They hurtled back up the road and were thrown to the ground as the bomb exploded.

'Are you all right?' Rose scrambled to her feet and helped Annie up.

'Yes. I thought those things were supposed to cut their engines and then nose dive.'

'So did I, but evidently they don't always do that.' Rose brushed off the dust and swore fluently under her breath as she looked at the devastation at the end of the road.

The street was suddenly alive with people running to see if they could rescue anyone. Annie watched Rose hesitate and knew that her sister's instinct would be to pitch in and help, but concern for George was uppermost in her mind, so she spun around and walked away.

'We'll have to go around that. Let's try and find that father of mine.'

When they turned into the street, Annie gave a cry of anguish, but Rose remained silent, not moving. The house wasn't there. All that remained was a huge pile of rubble.

Rose's mouth was set in a grim line and she grabbed a policeman who was hurrying past her. 'When did this happen?' she demanded.

'About two nights ago.'

'Anyone killed?'

'I don't know. You'll have to enquire at the Town Hall. They've set up an information desk there.'

'Not much left, is there.' Annie's voice was husky with tears as the two sisters stood looking at the place where a grand house had once stood – a house with so many memories for both of them. 'If he was in there . . .'

'He wouldn't have stood a chance.' Rose finished Annie's sentence, then strode away, her face a mask as she headed for the information centre.

Annie hurried to catch her up, too upset to face the facts. 'Perhaps he wasn't there?'

'Of course he was. We'd have heard from him otherwise.' Rose's tone was brisk but she couldn't hide the inner pain she was feeling.

It didn't take long to discover the truth. There had been several people killed that night. They were sent to identify the body.

Annie couldn't bear to go in but Rose took on the unpleasant task without flinching. 'At least we can have a funeral,' Rose told her, after she'd confirmed that one of the dead was Sir George Gresham.

Rose's eyes were dry but Annie knew how her sister was suffering. Being so alike, father and daughter had often fought, but they had loved each other. When George had walked into her life for the first time the arguments had been fierce but he'd accepted her as his daughter, and made no secret of how much he loved and admired her. He had become a loved member of the family and his loss would be deeply felt.

'London was his home,' Rose said, her voice softening, 'so we'll bury him here.'

It was a simple ceremony with only the two sisters present. Rose had chosen the Bible readings herself and Annie felt that George would have approved of the arrangements. His beloved daughter was there and that would have been all he'd have wanted.

'I wish I could come back to Wales with you,' Annie said to her sister. 'But I have to report back now.'

'I know, and thanks for being here, Annie. It has helped a lot.'

'Are you going to try and salvage anything from the rubble?' Annie asked.

'No, Dad moved the most valuable pieces down to Wales, and anyway, I don't suppose much has survived.' It looked as if it took a direct hit.'

Annie thought about the lovely house. It had been George's pride and joy, but now it was gone, like so many homes. 'It was supposed to have been part of James's inheritance, wasn't it?'

'Yes.' Rose gazed into space for a moment. 'But

material things can be replaced; it's the loss of loved ones that's hard to take. They are irreplaceable.'

'We've got our memories, though, Rose, haven't we?' Annie lingered to take a last look at the simple grave before they turned away.

Her sister looked grim as they walked out of the churchyard. 'I'll get a nice headstone when the war's over. Though why the silly old fool had to go and get himself killed when we're nearing the end . . .'

For the first time, Rose allowed herself a few tears, and Annie joined in, for the man they had all come to love. It was going to be difficult telling the rest of the family that George was dead, and she didn't envy her sister the task.

'Any news from Sam?' Annie asked as soon as she arrived back at Chicksands. The tragic loss of George had pushed Sam from her mind for a while but now the worry was back in full force. Ten days and not a word from him!

The officer shook his head. 'Nothing.'

'Where is he, and why didn't he contact us as soon as he landed?'

'Perhaps his wireless set isn't working, or he's lost it.'

Annie couldn't accept that. If that were the case then he would have found another way to let them know he was all right. France was swarming with Allied troops and any of them would have relayed a message for him. Her nerves were frayed. What with losing George so unexpectedly, and now Sam disappearing, she was feeling more than a little edgy. 'He ought to have more consideration! My sister told me his son keeps asking when he's coming to see him.'

'All we can do is wait.' The officer walked away. Annie jammed the headphones on and gave a weary sigh. She wished she'd gone with Sam. At least she'd know what was going on. It was damned frustrating sitting on the sidelines and waiting . . .

31

'Anything?' Annie asked the same question every time she reported for duty, but she already knew the answer. It was the beginning of September and still no word from Sam. She feared the worst by now and her heart ached for his little son. Jacques had settled in well with Rose and the children, but he was constantly asking for his father. He was in a strange country, speaking a strange language, and he'd lost the one woman he'd clung to – his grandmother. Was it any wonder the boy didn't know how to smile? Even James and Kate had been unable to coax a laugh out of him.

Annie sat down, muttering under her breath. When this war was over there would be a lot of adjusting to do, and many families were going to have empty spaces in their lives. There was talk that the war would soon be over, but she had her doubts about that. It was true that Paris had been liberated on August 25th, and this had been the cause of great rejoicing, but now there was a new threat of v2 rockets. These weren't like the doodle-bugs; you couldn't see or hear them, and there wasn't any defence against them. The first anyone knew about them was when they exploded, and then it was too late. How she longed for this dreadful war to be over.

Annie tried to shut off the jumble of disturbing thoughts. She still had work to do but her mind constantly wandered back to Sam. Was he alive or dead? Worry gnawed away at her insides. Was she fated to lose all the men she became fond of – Paul, Jack Graham, George, and now perhaps Sam? Thank heavens Reid was no longer flying.

She sat up straight and frowned. Where had *that* thought come from?

'Take a break,' she was ordered by the officer-in-charge.

Annie glanced at the clock and was surprised to see that she had been at her post for nearly four hours. She stood up, stretched and headed for the door.

The mess was busy but she managed to find a corner table on her own. She didn't feel like talking at the moment. How she missed Dora's cheerful company.

After eating, she cradled her cup of tea in her hands and bowed her head. She was so weary. 'Where the hell are you, Sam,' she muttered fiercely under her breath.

The tap on her shoulder made her jump and the tea slopped over the side of the cup.

'You're needed,' Jean told her.

'Right.' Annie drank what was left of the tea, and hurried back.

'We've had a message from Sam,' Wing Commander Felshaw said and handed her a sheet of paper.

Annie read it and gave a sigh of relief. It said: 'Returning immediately. Await my call.'

For some strange reason an uneasy feeling grew. 'Is this all he said?'

'Yes,' was the brisk reply.

What did he mean by – await my call? And when would he call? Why was the message so short? There wasn't any need for that restriction now. She stared at the paper in the forlorn hope that it might reveal some answers, but of course it didn't.

'I'm afraid we'll have to be patient.'

Annie studied the officer. 'What's going on, sir?'

'Nothing that need concern you at the moment.' His tone was dismissive.

Annie wasn't going to be so easily put off. 'I think it is, sir. My sister is looking after his son, and if something has happened to Sam then I have a right to know.'

'As far as we are aware he is OK.'

'I can hear a "but" in your voice.' Then something became clear. 'This isn't the first message you've had from him, is it?'

'No, we received one at three this morning.'

'What did it say?' she demanded, stung that the news should have been kept from her.

'All I can tell you is that he has been in trouble, but he's out now and coming back on the first available boat. The rest of the information is confidential.' He walked away, effectively putting an end to her questions.

Annie sat at her desk with a stubborn expression on her face. How the hell had he got into trouble? If he'd been behind the German lines she'd kill him herself! He ought to be thinking about Jacques, and trying to stay alive for his son, not chasing off on some mission of his own. She decided she wasn't moving from this spot until Sam's call came through.

It was sixteen hundred hours when she was summoned to the officer's room. 'Sam, he wants to talk to you.'

She reached out eagerly but he held on to the phone. 'Whatever help he needs, you are to give it. You can take

377

all the time off necessary.' Then he released the phone to her and strode out of the room.

Annie's heart was thudding. Something was wrong.

'Sam, are you all right? Where are you?'

'I'm in Dover.' He spoke quickly, as if in a hurry. 'I need to get to Wales. Will you see if Reid can fly us there?'

'I don't know if that –'

Annie!' He almost shouted at her this time. 'I've got to get there. I've brought someone back with me and they can't travel by road or train. I need Reid's help.'

'Please don't upset yourself.' There was a note of desperation in Sam's voice and she didn't like it. 'Is he ill?'

'Yes, and Wales is the only answer. I've already contacted Rose and she has agreed we can go there.'

'I'll see what I can do. If Reid can't help then I'll find someone who can.' Though it was difficult to know how she was going to do that. This request was unusual and highly irregular. Still she had been told to give him all the help he needed . . .

'We can't travel today; the journey has already taken its toll. Sometime tomorrow, if possible.'

'All right, Sam, where can I get in touch with you?'

'We're in a hotel.' He gave her the address, and a ragged sigh echoed down the line. 'I thank God for the day I met you and your wonderful family.'

Reid was on his way out the door on seven days' leave when he was called back.

'Urgent phone call for you, sir.'

'Yes,' he snapped into the receiver.

There was silence at the other end, and he tapped his fingers impatiently on the desk. He was looking forward to this leave and was eager to be on his way.

'Is this a bad time?' Annie asked hesitantly.

'No, no,' Reid assured her, regretting his sharp tone again. 'It's good to hear from you. I hope there isn't anything wrong?'

His brow creased into a deep frown as he listened. 'Give me the address,' he said when she'd finished talking. He scribbled it down.

'Sam said he needs you, Reid, but I'm sure he'll understand if you can't do this. It might be impossible to arrange, but he sounded desperate.'

'It's all right, Annie,' he soothed. She sounded sick with worry. 'As of this moment I'm on leave, and we must move Sam and this other man from Dover. You never know where these v2 rockets are going to land. How bad is this other person?' he asked.

'Pretty bad, I think. Sam said they couldn't travel today because the journey has taken its toll.'

'You go on down there and I'll come as soon as I can.' He picked up the slip of paper with the address on it and shoved it into his pocket. 'You tell Sam I'll be there sometime tomorrow.' Reid put the phone down, his mind already working out the details. He could take his own plane, of course, but by the sound of it they needed something larger for this trip. However, it wasn't going to be easy to arrange. If Sam was taking someone to Wales then this was a private matter. Still, he would see what he could fix up.

After three phone calls he was intrigued. Everyone was falling over themselves to give him anything he asked for. Who the hell was Sam, and who was his injured passenger?

He strode out to one of the hangars, intent on getting all the arrangements in place. Charlie was working on the very plane he wanted – a DC3. 'What's wrong with her?' he asked briskly.

Charlie scrambled down. 'We're changing an engine. It won't take more than another hour.'

Reid nodded. 'Good, I'm taking her tomorrow. Make sure there's a bunk for a sick passenger. I've just had a call from your sister Annie to say that Sam is back from France and has a sick man to take down to Wales.' Then Reid turned on his heel and hurried away, not giving Charlie a chance to ask questions. His mind was set on the task he'd been assigned. There were a lot of arrangements to make. His first stop was the mess where he found the man he was looking for.

'Hi, Reid.' Bouncer said grinning. 'Thought you were on leave. Can't you bear to leave the place?'

'Something's come up and I need a co-pilot. We'll be leaving at eight tomorrow morning.'

'Where are we going?' his friend asked.

'Hawkinge first, then pick up some passengers in Dover, and then on to Wales.'

'Great.' Bouncer's face broke into a wide grin. 'What's this all about?'

'I really don't know much.' He told Bouncer about the call. 'We'll have to see when we get there, but Annie sounded out of her mind with worry.'

'I expect she is.' Bouncer shook his head in concern. 'But can we do this? We can't just take the DC3 without permission.'

380

Reid picked up Bouncer's mug of tea and drank it in a distracted way. 'I had grave doubts so I made a few calls, and it looks as if someone has been oiling the wheels. Anything Group Captain André Riniou wants is to be granted.'

'That's interesting.' Bouncer picked up his mug, looked inside, then put it down again. 'His passenger must be important, but why take him to Wales?'

'Damned if I know. Rose and her family have taken in enough waifs and strays as it is. That house is aptly named The Haven; it's always packed.'

Bouncer smiled. 'Yes, they are a remarkable family. So, how ill is this person?'

'No idea, but I'm trying to get a military nurse to come with us just in case of an emergency.' Reid stood up. 'See you in the morning.'

'Reid!' Bouncer called him back. 'How long can we stay?'

He shrugged. 'As long as it takes, and as my co-pilot you'll have to wait until I'm ready to return. Could take a while and I do have seven days' leave to use up.'

'Right.' Bouncer rubbed his hands together with pleasure. 'A few days in the country will be just the ticket.'

They reached the Bartlett Hotel in Dover at ten o'clock the next morning, and the manager told them which room Sam was in. Reid gave a gentle rap on the door and Sam opened it at once. The first sight of him was a shock and he heard Bouncer suck in his breath. The man was gaunt with exhaustion.

'Reid.' Sam grasped his hand. 'Thank you for coming.'

'I've brought a nurse with me in case she's needed.' The woman stepped forward. 'My name's Gloria Stevens, Group Captain Riniou, and I can stay with your patient as long as I'm needed.'

Sam stepped aside for them to enter the small room. 'I'm grateful. You are needed.'

For a moment, Reid thought Sam was going to collapse so he caught hold of his arm to steady him. 'You've had a rough time by the look of you.'

Sam glanced anxiously towards the bed. 'Not as rough as her.'

Her? It was only then that Reid noticed the other occupants of the room. Annie was sitting beside the bed, holding the patient's hand and talking gently in French. In the bed was a girl.

Annie stepped away from the bed to make room for the nurse to examine the patient. As the nurse pulled the sheet back Reid just managed to cut off a gasp of horror. He had never seen anyone so emaciated before.

'Oh my God!' Bouncer breathed, his words hardly audible.

'You can see why I need help,' Sam told them.

'I've come with a plane equipped with a bunk and medical supplies,' Reid was so relieved that he'd had the sense to arrange this.

Sam gave a ragged sigh. 'That will make the journey easier.'

'We thought the patient was a man,' Bouncer said.

'That was my fault.' Annie spoke for the first time. 'I assumed it was.'

'Who is she?' Reid asked.

Sam smiled at the girl in the bed and looked back at

Reid and Bouncer. 'This is Maria. Jacques's mother.' He put a finger to his lips to stop them asking questions. 'I'll tell you about it later.'

The nurse came over to them. 'She should be in hospital, sir.'

'No!' Maria's voice was weak but determined. 'I wish to be near my son.'

'You will be,' Reid said, disturbed by the anguish in the woman's voice. 'We'll be flying you to him today.'

'I do not wish Jacques to see me like this.' Maria lifted a skeletal arm with difficulty, and grimaced. 'But I want to be near to him.'

'My sister's suet pudding with treacle will soon have you on your feet again.' Annie grinned at Maria's puzzled expression.

'What is this suet treacle?' Maria asked Sam.

He bent over and kissed her. 'You'll soon find out. It's marvellous stuff.'

Reid touched Annie's arm to gain her attention. 'I thought she was dead?' he murmured.

The nurse, now firmly in charge of her patient, ordered them to be quiet. 'That is enough talking. She must rest now, and we shall need a light meal for her before she can travel.'

'I'll see what I can get.' Annie opened the door.

'A thin soup and perhaps a slice of bread will suffice.'

Annie nodded and left.

The nurse turned her attention to the men. 'Now, sirs, if you will leave us alone for half an hour I will prepare my patient for the journey.'

They left meekly and made their way downstairs to

383

the dining room, where the manager of the hotel supplied them with a pot of tea and toast.

Sam rubbed his eyes then sat back and smiled at Reid and Bouncer. 'I hope you didn't have too much trouble arranging this?'

'None at all.' Reid stirred sugar into his tea. 'Everyone was tripping over themselves to be helpful. Now why would that be, do you think?'

'I gathered some useful information on this trip. They sent someone along to collect it last night, and in return for that service they have given me everything I need.'

Reid nodded in understanding. So, he'd been behind enemy lines. 'What the hell happened, Sam?'

'Soon after the D-Day landings I hitched a ride and made straight for my home. While I was there a villager told me that he thought Maria had been shipped to Germany.' Sam paused, a look of utter pain showing in his eyes. 'I dismissed it at first because her mother had said Maria was dead, but then I met a man who'd escaped from a labour camp. He told me Maria was definitely alive but that she couldn't survive much longer. So I went after her.'

'Into Germany?' Reid asked.

'Yes. What had started out to be a visit to my home turned into a mission of great importance. I saw unimaginable things and was able to bring back a lot of useful information.'

'Hell, that was risky,' Bouncer shook his head in amazement.

'I didn't have any choice. If it was Maria, then I had to try and rescue her.'

'How did you manage to find her?' Reid asked. His

384

respect for this man was growing with every word he spoke. And for the first time he began to have an inkling of the things Annie had been involved in. The two of them had worked closely together, and Reid remembered the talk of parachute jumps. Dear Lord, what had she been doing? His love and respect for her grew.

'That was easy enough. The problem was rescuing her. Thank heavens the weather was still warm because I had to wait for three days before she came out with a working party. I remained hidden, and with only a loaf of bread and a bottle of water with me I was damned hungry, but I couldn't leave. If there was the slightest chance that Maria was there, then I had to stay, no matter how dangerous and uncomfortable the conditions.'

'How did you recognize her?' Reid couldn't help remembering the pitiful sight he had seen upstairs.

Sam gave a sad smile. 'We have known each other since children and were about to be married when the war tore us apart, and she is the mother of my son, so I would have known her whatever state she was in.'

'How did you get her away?' Bouncer was sitting forward in his chair, obviously riveted by the story.

'It was dusk when they returned, and as they passed by I shot out of some bushes, swept Maria up and ran like hell. Luck was on my side, the guards never saw me.'

'What about the other prisoners?' Bouncer asked. 'Didn't they make a noise when you dived out of the undergrowth?'

'They were too weak to respond, all except one girl who tumbled into the bushes with us.' Sam grimaced, obviously remembering the sight of those starving men and women. 'When the column was out of sight, we

385

supported Maria and got as far away from there as possible. We moved at night and hid during the day. I don't know what I'd have done without that girl, she was a wonder at finding food and shelter for us.'

'What was her name?' Reid asked.

Sam gave a dry laugh. 'I never found out. We didn't talk much. We were exhausted, and our situation was dangerous, so we focused all our attention on not getting caught. If the Germans had found us they would have shot us as spies for sure.'

Sam paused as if to gather his thoughts, then continued. 'We eventually crossed into France, but by that time we could hardly stand upright. It was too much for Maria and from then on I carried her. We still couldn't take a chance on there not being any Germans around, so we kept to the wooded areas and rough ground where we could move without being seen. Dear God, but it was hard going. Maria didn't weigh much, but I was getting weak by then.'

Bouncer handed Sam another cup of tea. 'There's a nip of brandy in that, it'll do you good.'

'What happened then?' prompted Reid, eager to hear more of this extraordinary story.

'We just kept walking until we met up with some British soldiers. They told us that Paris had been liberated and the girl took off. It was her home, evidently. Maria and I were transported to the coast and on to a ship returning to Dover.' Sam gave a tired smile. 'So here we are.'

Reid could only guess at the horrors of that journey, but it was clear from the condition they were in that it had taken a superhuman effort.

The nurse appeared and addressed Reid. 'We are ready

to leave now, sir. Maria cannot walk so I shall need help.'

Reid was immediately on his feet, placing a hand on Sam's shoulder to keep him in his seat. The man looked as if he could hardly stand up, let alone carry someone. 'I'll see to her.'

Nurse Stevens had wrapped the frail woman in a blanket and he lifted her carefully off the bed. She weighed practically nothing.

Reid had an ambulance waiting outside and once Maria was settled they headed for the airfield. When they reached the plane, and the nurse had made her patient comfortable and secure, Reid and Bouncer prepared for the flight.

Permission was given for immediate take-off, and they were all soon on their way to Wales.

32

Maria was fast asleep. Annie looked at Sam leaning over the bed. Rose had given them the cottage so they could have peace and privacy. Before George had died he'd had an extension put on the stable at the end of the garden and converted it into a two-bed cottage. When Rose had argued against it he'd told her that The Haven wasn't big enough for all the people she kept taking in. He'd won that battle, and now it was going to be very useful as there was room for Nurse Stevens to stay near her patient.

'Sam,' Annie said quietly. 'You'll come and see Jacques as soon as you're ready?'

'I do not want him to see his mother like this. It will frighten him.' Sam gave a lingering look at Maria, almost as if he was afraid that if he took his eyes off her she would disappear.

'We all understand,' Annie said. 'The last thing any of them wanted to do was heap more distress on the child. He would stay in the main house with Rose and Marj until it was right to move him in with his real mother and father. 'You need have no fears on that score.'

'Thank you.' He gazed at the woman in the bed and sighed. 'I have put her through hell dragging her across country like that. She wasn't strong enough.' His hand shook as he swept it across his eyes.

'You've given her a chance of life, young man.' Marj's voice was firm as she walked in with a tray of tea. 'She might not have lived much longer, and who knows what the Germans would have done when they knew defeat was staring them in the face. You have nothing to reproach yourself for.'

'You're right, of course. But I still feel guilty.'

'Now you know how I felt when Jack Graham died after getting him home,' Annie told him gently. 'The feeling passes, and when you look back you'll see you did the right thing.'

Sam merely nodded and sipped his tea.

Marj smiled and patted his arm. 'I'll bring dinner over for nurse and Maria, but you must join us. Jacques will be so pleased to see you.'

Annie and her mother walked back to the house. 'How is Jacques?' she asked her mother.

'He's been unhappy and fretful. He keeps asking if his father has left him.'

Annie could understand that. Jacques would feel very insecure, and his father disappearing must have thrown him into a panic, wondering if he'd been abandoned.

They walked into the kitchen. Wally was peeling potatoes and Rose was busy making pastry. The old black wood-burning cooker was covered in bubbling pans, and Annie breathed in the lovely aroma. This kitchen seemed to have retained the glorious smells of years gone by, and she always loved coming in here. George's presence was greatly missed in the house. The children had been very upset when Rose had arrived back with the news that he had been killed. They had spent most of their time with him since the outbreak of war, and like everyone else in the family had loved him very much.

'Hello, sweetheart.' Wally wiped his hands and gave

389

her a hug. 'It's good to see you again. Are our guests settled in?'

'Yes. It was a relief to get Maria here. She's in a poor way.' Annie smiled at her sister. 'But your cooking will soon have her on the mend.'

'Let's hope so.' Rose dusted the flour from her hands. 'Where's Reid?'

'He's still at the airfield with Bouncer.'

'Auntie Annie!' James rushed to greet her when she walked into the lounge.

'My goodness,' she laughed, 'you're nearly as tall as me.' He allowed her to kiss his cheek. At fifteen he was looking quite the young gentleman, and she could now see his grandfather in him.

He straightened up proudly and measured up against her. 'I'm taller than you now.'

'So you are, and by a good inch.' She smiled at Jacques who was sitting on the floor trying to fit a piece into a jigsaw puzzle.

'And how are you?' she asked gently.

'All right, thank you,' he answered politely, and then picked up the toy rabbit, which was looking quite bedraggled by now, and started to stroke one long ear. James sat next to the child and helped him put the piece of jigsaw into the right place. 'He's worried about his dad.'

'He'll see him soon,' Annie told James very quietly. 'Where's Kate?'

'I'm here.' She came in carrying some more toys, and, when she'd put them down by Jacques, kissed Annie. The children were obviously doing everything they could to amuse Jacques.

At that moment Reid and Bouncer strode in and said hello to everyone. Reid went over and swept Jacques off the floor. 'Hello, young man, I've got a really *big* aeroplane this time. Would you like to see it tomorrow?'

Jacques nodded and began to run his fingers over the wings on Reid's uniform.

'What's up?' he asked, obviously sensing the strained atmosphere.

Rose explained and he shook his head sadly. 'I expect he's been bewildered, poor little devil.'

Marj put down a tray loaded with cups of tea and Wally winked at Annie. 'Do you know that the first thing she did when we met was to give me a cup of tea, and she hasn't changed in all these years. Not even rationing has stopped her making her favourite brew. It's a bit weaker now, of course.'

The little boy had settled himself on Reid's lap and took a glass of milk from Kate. He started to drink, his troubled eyes searching all the faces in the room.

Suddenly Jacques squealed as Sam came into the room. He shot off Reid's lap – Reid deftly fielded the glass when it shot in the air – and threw himself at his father. The child was swung into the air and then hugged and kissed.

Jacques started to chatter in rapid French and wave his arms about.

'What's he saying?' Reid asked Annie. 'I can't keep up with that.'

'He's telling Sam how he thought he'd left him for good, and he likes everyone here but he wants to go home.'

It was then that the full import of Jacques's real mother

being found settled on Annie. There was no longer any question of Sam persuading her to marry him for his son's sake, and she was swamped with a feeling of intense relief. It would have been so wrong for all concerned, and when she looked at the little boy she was not sure she would have had the courage to refuse.

Maria had made remarkable progress in only four days, and Annie guessed that it was her desire to see her son again that had accelerated her recovery. Rose had a tape measure in her hand and Marj was pinning some of Annie's clothes on Maria. Annie, being the smallest, had given her a few garments but they all needed altering.

Sam touched Annie's arm. 'We must talk.'

They left the women to it and wandered outside. It was late September now, but the day was pleasant, and warm enough for them to walk around the garden in comfort. The singing of the birds was soothing, and Annie smiled at a thrush in the tree warbling out its tune. These little birds were quite oblivious of the drama unfolding all around them.

'Maria is looking so much stronger,' Annie remarked.

'Yes, it must be Rose's suet treacle.'

They both laughed at Maria's description. She spoke a little English but it often came out with words missing.

Sam turned his head and looked at Annie, a hint of regret in his eyes. 'I have been very selfish. I thought only of making a family for my son, and I was prepared to use you,' he admitted.

Annie's glance was quizzical. 'What makes you think I would have allowed you to do that?'

'I did not doubt it after you tried to seduce me.' He grinned then.

'I was drunk, Sam.'

'Yes, and very revealing it was too.' His smile faded. 'Nevertheless, I owe you an apology. I gave no thought for your happiness, I saw you as a suitable mother for my troubled son.' He was looking rather embarrassed and uncomfortable.

'Oh, Sam, you don't have to apologize for that. I would probably have done the same thing in your position.'

'I expect you would,' he agreed. 'Family is important to you, isn't it?'

'Yes, I grew up watching Rose fight to give us all a better life, and what we have now is very precious to all of us.'

'She's a very special woman.' Sam sighed. 'I don't know what would have become of Jacques if she hadn't taken care of him.'

They walked in silence for a while, then Annie asked, 'What are your plans now?'

'I won't be coming back with you. My work is finished and I have been discharged on compassionate grounds.'

'I'll miss you,' she told him. It was going to be strange without Sam around. She'd worked with him since 1940 after becoming a wireless operator, and he'd become a part of her life.

'We have shared much in the last few years, but we'll still be friends. Yes?' he asked.

'Of course.' Annie slipped her hand through his arm. 'I want to see Jacques grow up.'

'Rose has given us permission to stay at the cottage

for as long as we need it. I will marry Maria as soon as it can be arranged.'

'Good. That will make her very happy, and speed her recovery, I'm sure.' Annie stopped to cut a late pink rose with a pair of dressmaking scissors she had in her pocket. 'Give her this from me.'

Sam smelt the perfume and smiled. 'Thank you, she'll love it; there hasn't been much beauty in her life for a long time. My home is still standing, Annie. It will need a lot of work, but as soon as the war's over we shall return to France.'

'Oh, I'm so glad you have something to go back to. When are you going to take Jacques to meet his mother?'

'As soon as Marj and Rose have finished making her look nice.'

'Nice?' Annie laughed. 'Sam, she's lovely, and even in her frail state the beauty shines through.'

'Just wait until she has put on some weight and is in full health again.' Sam's eyes shone with love, and he swallowed back emotion. 'I never thought to see her again.'

Annie squeezed his arm. 'I'm so happy for you.'

Sam stopped and turned her to face him. 'I hope I haven't ruined things for you with Reid. I told him that I intended to make you mine, and I warned him off.'

'So? That wouldn't have bothered him.'

'You don't know, do you?' Sam gave a rueful shake of his head.

'I haven't the faintest idea what you're talking about.' Annie tipped her head to one side and frowned. 'I think you'd better explain.'

'The man is in love with you, Annie.'

Her mouth opened in astonishment. 'Where on earth did you get that idea from?'

'He told me.'

Annie gave him a disbelieving look. 'Oh, I've heard that tale before. He was pulling your leg.'

'No.' Sam was adamant. 'We were rivals for your love, but I was determined to win, even though I knew Reid loved you deeply. And for that act of selfishness I am very sorry.'

Annie was speechless. Reid had been telling the truth when he told her to look in the mirror to see the woman he loved. Dismay and shame swamped her. What a heartless fool she'd been, and how she must have hurt him by calling him a liar that night at Roehampton . . .

'Do you care nothing for him?' Sam asked.

'I'm not sure what I feel,' said Annie, confused. 'I find him attractive and I enjoy being with him, even though we argue most of the time.'

Sam waved a hand in a dismissive gesture. 'Take no notice of that. It is just Reid's defences surfacing. He did not want to fall in love, I think.' He gave Annie an earnest look. 'Give him a chance.'

She knew she would. Sam's revelation had been a shock, but now she came to consider it . . . well, the signs had all been there but she'd ignored them. And her own feelings!

'I expect Maria must be ready. I'll collect Jacques and take him to meet his mother.'

Reid stood by the window watching Sam and Annie talking. It was obviously a serious discussion. Were they deciding what to do about the unexpected turn of events?

He clenched his fists. He was certain Sam wouldn't marry Annie now the real mother of his son had been rescued, but if he was hoping to hold on to her in some way then the man would have a fight on his hands. He was damned if he was going to allow that to happen. He loved Annie so much, and if he'd believed that her happiness was with Sam then he would have slipped out of the picture, but things had changed. He would not let Sam ruin her life now!

'What do you think they're talking about, old boy?' Reid jumped. 'Bouncer! I didn't hear you come in.'

'Bit edgy, aren't you?' his friend remarked.

'I was deep in thought, that's all.'

Bouncer looked enquiringly at him. 'How long can we stay, Reid?'

'Another day and then I must get back. I promised my parents I'd see them before my leave ends.'

'Ah, well,' Bouncer sighed, 'I'd better make the most of my time here. I'll see if Wally needs any help in the kitchen.'

Reid chuckled as his friend left the room. He wasn't sure Bouncer had ever seen a kitchen in his life. It was more likely he was after Wally's secret store of whisky. As the door closed he turned his attention back to the garden, but Sam and Annie were no longer there.

He was about to go in search of the children when Annie walked in.

'Hello,' she said. 'Where's everyone?'

'Most are in the kitchen, I think.' Reid studied her face. She didn't look upset, in fact she appeared to be very happy. 'I saw you talking to Sam. Do you know what his plans are now?'

Annie sat in one of the armchairs and waited until Reid was settled opposite her. 'He's out of the air force now, so he won't be coming back with us. Rose is letting them have the cottage for as long as they want it, and he and Maria will be married as soon as it can be arranged.'

'And how do you feel about that?' He watched her reaction carefully.

Her smile was one of genuine pleasure. 'I'm absolutely delighted. He's taking Jacques to see his mother now.'

'Good. I was preparing to fight him for you,' he declared with honesty. He was going to convince her of his feelings this time!

She laughed. 'Spitfires at dawn?'

'Something like that.' His eyes narrowed at her flippant response. 'You don't seem surprised.'

'I am actually. I was under the impression that I irritated you.'

'You do at times,' he admitted, 'but only because I like to be in control of my life, and I don't feel like that when I think about you. The first time we met I came to you to fulfil the promise I'd made Paul, but after that it was for myself. I wanted to be with you, touch you, see your eyes light up with a smile, or cloud with sadness. Whatever your mood I needed to be with you.'

'Now that's quite an admission!' Her eyes opened wide at his frankness.

He leant forward. 'It's cards on the table time, I think. I honestly believed that you would accept Sam.'

Annie looked thoughtful. 'I must admit that the idea was tempting, and I would have done everything I could to help, but I hope I would have had the strength to refuse him. I want love in a marriage, above children.'

Reid stood up and pulled her out of the chair. 'You can have both, right now.' He kissed her, releasing all the passion he'd kept under tight control. 'What do you say? There's an empty bedroom upstairs.'

Annie eased away from him looking flushed from the heated embrace. 'I'm not going to let you rush me. I won't make a decision until this war's over.'

He studied her expression intently. 'Will I stand a chance then?'

She smiled, stood on tiptoe and kissed his lips briefly. 'We'll see, Squadron Leader, we'll see.'

For that demotion, he kissed her again. From behind them came a voice.

'Whoops!'

Through the haze of his desire, Reid heard the exclamation and stepped back from Annie. James and Kate were standing in the room grinning.

'Shall we go away again?' James smirked.

'No need.' Reid drew in a deep breath. Annie had responded and that was the second time he'd felt her passionate nature come alive in his arms. She might back away from commitment now, but he was pretty sure she wouldn't for much longer.

Feeling more in control, he smiled at the children. 'What have you two been doing with yourselves?'

'We've been looking for Jack,' Kate told them.

'He's over at the cottage with his daddy,' Annie said.

'Ah, there you are.' Rose held open the door for Bouncer who was carrying a tray loaded with the ever-available cups of tea.

Soon the room was crowded as Marj and Wally came

in as well. The discussion quickly turned to the progress of the invasion.

'When do you think the war will be over?' James asked. He was growing up fast and taking an avid interest in developments.

'Well, I don't think it will be this year,' Reid said. 'Winter will soon be here, but if things go well then we might see the end around spring next year.' He looked pointedly at Annie. He wasn't going to let her dither that long.

Annie returned the look and her lips lifted at the corners. She'd clearly understood his meaning without him saying a word, and there was a look in her eyes that made his heart soar with hope.

Suddenly Jacques burst into the room, his face alive with excitement. 'Auntie Rose, can we move my things? I'm going to sleep in the other house.'

'I'll do it before your bedtime,' she told him, smiling down at his flushed face.

The little boy grabbed hold of Kate and tried to pull her to her feet. 'Come see!' When she stood up he launched himself at James. 'Come see!'

Reid had never seen the boy so animated and it was obvious the first meeting had gone well.

Rose's children looked surprised at the excited antics of Jacques. The little boy had just turned four, but to Reid he seemed much younger. The poor little devil had had a traumatic time since he'd been born, and it was wonderful to see him laughing.

'I've got a mummy!' He was leaping up and down. 'My real mummy!' He smiled and then turned and tore out of the room, the toy rabbit in danger of losing its ear.

Kate and James glanced at their mother, who nodded to them. 'Why don't you go with him?'

Without further hesitation they ran after Jacques.

'That's the first time I've seen the poor little thing smile.' Marj wiped her eyes.

Wally patted his wife's arm. 'He'll be all right now.'

Marj nodded. 'We did our best for him, but there's no substitute for his proper family is there?'

Maria and Nurse Stevens joined them that evening. The old house had a dining room but it had been turned into another bedroom, and the family loved to gather around the kitchen table. Annie and her mother had gone to great trouble to make it look lovely for a special occasion. The best linen had been brought out, the glasses sparkled under the lights, and a huge bowl of flowers adorned the centre of the table. Annie was pleased to see what a good job her mother and Rose had made of the clothes for Maria. The navy skirt was full and gathered at the waist, the pale blue blouse had long sleeves, and a silk scarf was tucked into the neck, effectively hiding her thin body.

Jacques had been allowed to stay up late to mark the occasion, and he kept close to his mother the whole time. He watched her shyly, and each time she smiled and stroked his hair he grinned and squirmed with pleasure.

Yes, Annie thought as she saw the little touches of love and affection between them, everything was going to be all right now. Jacques couldn't possibly remember his mother, but he'd clearly accepted her without reserva- tion, which was more than he'd done with his father.

Her gaze strayed to Reid, who was laughing with Bouncer. What a fool she'd been not to recognize her feelings for him sooner, but their first meeting had not been a good one, and she had doubted that a relationship between them would work. She had also been too absorbed in her work with Sam and Jack Graham to give much thought to her own life, but now the end of the war was in sight she was starting to think about the future.

After the meal was over they all went into the lounge. A fire was burning in the grate to take the chill off the evening. Annie gazed into the flames, deep in thought.

'You look pensive.' Reid sat on the arm of her chair. 'What's causing that faraway look in your eyes?'

'I was wondering what I'll do when I'm demobbed,' she said. 'I don't think being a fashion editor again will hold enough excitement.'

'Ah.' He sighed dramatically. 'There was I hoping it was me making you look so dreamy.'

Annie smiled but said nothing. There was no way he was going to know that she'd really been thinking about him. Not yet, anyway.

'Have you found your job as wireless operator exciting then?'

'A lot of the time it's routine and a hard slog, but never dull.'

It was obvious from the way he'd asked the question that he was curious about what she did. And now Sam's activities had been revealed, he clearly wanted to find out how involved she'd been with his work.

'And at other times it's exciting?' He persisted in probing.

'It's had its moments.'

Nurse Stevens came over and Annie took the opportunity to change the subject. Perhaps one day she would tell Reid that she had been behind enemy lines, but not now.

'Hello.' Annie smiled. 'Your patient is making a good recovery.'

'Indeed she is.' The girl turned to Reid. 'I am no longer needed here, sir. When will you be returning to Tangmere?'

'Tomorrow. I have a flight time of eleven hundred hours.'

'If you will take me with you, sir, I will arrange for transport to take me back to the hospital in Aldershot.' The nurse returned to her seat and started talking to Rose, when the door swung open.

Bill was greeted with hugs and exclamations of pleasure when he came into the room. Then he saw Jacques and lifted him up.

'My word, you've grown since I last saw you,' Bill told him. 'Not frightened of me this time?'

Jacques shook his head and whispered in Bill's ear.

'Really?' He put the boy down and smiled at Maria. 'It's wonderful to meet you. No wonder your son is looking so much happier.'

Sam shook Bill's hand. 'How long are you home for?'

'Two weeks.' That announcement was greeted with whoops of delight from James and Kate.

Wally put down his cup. 'This calls for a proper celebration. I've got a drop of whisky and sherry put aside for Christmas, but we'll have it now.'

While the glasses were being filled Bill looked at Reid. 'Have we met before?'

402

Reid was immediately on his feet and shaking Bill's hand firmly. He very much wanted to meet this man again, but he'd stayed in the background while his family welcomed him home. 'You brought me back from Dunkirk after I'd been shot down.'

'Of course, I thought there was something familiar about you.' Bill grinned. 'You're a bit cleaner this time.'

Annie watched Reid laugh, and his admiration for her brother-in-law was evident.

'I saw you leave for another rescue trip,' Reid told him.

'How did you manage to repair the leaks so fast?'

Bill chuckled. 'They stuck something in the holes. I didn't ask what it was, but we could only do one more trip. We were shipping too much water after that.'

'Here we are.' Wally handed the women a sherry each, the men a whisky, and lemonade for the children.

'A toast.' Wally held up his glass. 'To Maria, Sam and Jacques, may the future hold much happiness for you.'

Everyone drank to that with pleasure.

'And now to Bill.' Wally lifted his glass again. 'Welcome home and we pray you will soon return to us for good.'

Agreement echoed around the room, but Bill frowned.

'Where's George?'

The silence was total, and Annie could feel the shock running through the room.

Rose was the first to recover. 'I sent you a letter, Bill. George was killed by a doodlebug when he went to London to get his house ready for the victory celebrations.'

'Oh, dear God.' Bill obviously knew nothing about it, and the news had come as a terrible blow. 'I never received your letter, my darling. I'm so dreadfully sorry; we will miss him.' He held Rose in his arms and rocked her gently. 'What a dreadful thing to happen, I wish I'd been here to help you.'

Rose kissed his cheek. 'I wish you had been too, but we managed.'

Bill kept his arm around Rose and turned to face the room. He raised his glass. 'Let's drink to a fine man.'

Annie's eyes clouded as she watched Bill coping with his grief. Her brother-in-law had always had the utmost respect for George Gresham, and she knew he was going to miss him dreadfully – as they all did.

The glasses were soon emptied and Sam stood up, his hand on Maria's shoulder. 'Will you excuse us. Maria must rest now.'

Jacques caught hold of his mother's hand as soon as she stood up and smiled proudly at everyone in the room.

Annie watched them leave. Maria was leaning heavily on Sam. It had clearly been an exhausting evening, but it was a step back to normality for her.

'Annie?' Bill was puzzled. 'I thought Jacques's mother was dead.'

'That was what we all believed.' She then explained what had happened.

'Poor soul.' Bill was silent for a moment, and then nodded. 'But it's good to hear of a happy ending, eh?'

Annie sat back in the chair and silently agreed with that statement. This war had caused untold sorrow and heartbreak, but it had also produced acts of heroism, and a miracle or two.

33

'I'll land her.'

'Oh no, you won't.' Reid glanced at Bouncer and shook his head to emphasize his decision.

'Come on, Reid,' Bouncer complained. 'It isn't often we get the chance to fly something this big.' He gave an evil grin. 'I want to see if she bounces.'

'She won't,' Reid watched his co-pilot eagerly flexing his fingers, and smothered a chuckle. 'Don't forget we've got a passenger. You'll frighten the life out of her.'

Bouncer glanced back at the nurse. 'I don't think so, old boy, she looks calm enough.'

'That's ignorance,' Reid pointed out. 'She's never seen one of your landings.'

'I'll handle her like a new-born babe.' When his friend didn't answer, Bouncer said, 'I think you're the one who's scared.'

'Too right I'm terrified, look.' Reid held up a shaking hand.

'You liar,' Bouncer roared. 'You've never been terrified in your life and that's what made you such a good squadron leader. You haven't got any nerves.'

'You think I wasn't scared?' Reid asked, remembering how he'd been drenched in sweat, as he'd pushed himself and his Spitfire to the limit in those battles. God, but they were wonderful aeroplanes!

'Scared, yes, we all were, but you were never *terrified*.'

The two men were silent then, each with his personal memories of the struggle they'd been involved in. The only sound was the hum of the engines.

'I'll buy you a beer when we get down if you let me land her.' Bouncer had resorted to bribery.

'Huh! I'll need more than that. I might consider it for a double whisky.'

'You're on.' Bouncer turned his head and shouted to their passenger. 'Strap yourself in, we land in about fifteen minutes.'

'I must be mad,' Reid muttered to himself as he gave the controls over to his friend. Just to be on the safe side he tightened his harness as much as he could, then watched the airfield come into sight.

'I wonder what would happen if I tried a victory roll?' Bouncer asked gleefully.

'I expect the wings would fall off,' Reid sighed.

'Ah, not a good idea then.'

Reid's eyes narrowed as they made their approach and he watched every move the pilot made. His friend was one hell of a pilot, but somehow he'd never quite mastered the art of getting down without bouncing along the runway. He braced himself as the wheels touched the field, but the expected lurch never came. When they were taxiing towards the hangar, he gasped in astonishment. It was a perfect landing.

'Don't look so surprised, old boy. I'm not quite as crazy as I used to be, not now I've married Jenny.'

They jumped down, helped a relieved Nurse Stevens out and said goodbye to her. Then Bouncer slapped Reid on the back. 'Come to my room and I'll give you that drink.'

Reid followed him, sat in the only easy chair in the small room, watched Bouncer retrieve a bottle from behind a cupboard and pour generous measures into two mugs.

Bouncer held his mug up in salute. 'Sam and Maria are in good hands. Annie belongs to one hell of a family.'

'She certainly does.' Reid took a swig of the whisky and felt it burn a path down his insides. He couldn't help remembering the shock of everyone when they realized that Bill didn't know about George's death, but the post was very erratic and was often months late. For those at sea it was even worse, and in this case the important letter had never reached Bill . . .

'Pity Annie didn't come back with us.' Bouncer gave his friend a studied look. 'You could have whisked her away for a couple of days on your own. That house was so full it was a job to find any privacy.'

'It nearly always is. I understand that Rose won't turn anyone away who needs help.' Reid drained his glass.

'An extraordinary woman.' Bouncer examined his empty glass and held it up. 'Want another one?'

'No thanks, I'm heading for home right now to see my parents.'

'It would have been more exciting to take Annie away, eh?' Bouncer suggested with a waggle of his eyebrows.

'What makes you think she would have come?' Reid asked drily.

'Because she's crazy about you.' He gave a knowing wink. 'I don't think you're trying hard enough, old boy.'

Reid stood up. 'It's damned near impossible carrying on a courtship when you can only meet a couple of times a year, if you're lucky. Especially with someone as tricky as Annie.'

'Courtship!' Bouncer exploded. 'There isn't time for that kind of messing about. When you fix the target in your sights you've got to go in and conquer, or else she'll slip away to safety.'

'Is that how you pursued Jenny?' Reid asked, his eyes gleaming with amusement. He'd never heard such eloquence from his friend before.

'Of course, she never stood a chance, so stop mucking about, dear chap. Go and get her. Start writing letters and phoning her,' Bouncer advised. 'Show her your romantic side.'

Reid opened the door and glanced back over his shoulder, his mouth set in a determined line. 'I've been trying to do that, but don't worry, she won't get away without one hell of a fight.'

'Oh dear.' Marj's brow furrowed as she read the letter.

'What is it, Mum?' Annie asked. Her mother had been looking rather worn out just lately, which was hardly surprising considering the chaos this house was always in, with people coming and going all the time.

'Bob's been wounded and they've brought him back to a hospital in Folkestone. I must go and see him.'

'I'll go,' Annie said. She didn't want her mother making the long journey at the moment. 'I must return to camp now Sam and Maria are settled. I'll visit Bob first and let you know how he is.'

'Oh, would you, Annie?' Marj smiled gratefully at her daughter.

'Don't worry,' she advised her mother, 'if he was in a

bad way he wouldn't have been able to write the letter.'

'You're right, of course. I never thought of that, and it is his handwriting.' The frown left Marj's face and she smiled in relief.

Annie knew that her mother treasured the few letters she'd received from Bob over the years, and often took them out of her dressing-table drawer to read them again. He had been the most difficult and unruly of her children, but she'd always loved him.

A check on the train times showed there was one in two hours. Providing it was on time, of course. What a shame they hadn't known the day before; she could have returned with Reid and Bouncer. It didn't take Annie long to pack, and she headed for the cottage to tell Sam she was leaving.

Sam and Maria were taking a gentle stroll in the garden and Sam waved when he saw her. It was lovely to see him looking so relaxed and content, Annie thought, as she hurried over.

'I have to leave this morning,' she told them. 'Bob's been wounded and I'm going to see him before I return to camp.'

'Hope it isn't too bad, Annie.' Sam made Maria sit on a seat while they talked.

'I won't know until I get there. He didn't say much in his letter.'

'When will you come back?' Maria asked.

'Not for some time; I doubt if I'll be able to get any more leave until the war is over.'

'That is a shame.' Maria smiled at Sam. 'You will miss our wedding.'

'We are to be married in four weeks' time,' Sam said, 'and we shall be very sorry if you can't be there.'

'So will I, but I'm sure the rest of my family will make a real party of the occasion.'

'No doubt,' Sam said and smiled. 'Bill is going to try and return in time to give Maria away, and Wally will act as my best man.'

Maria became serious, stood up and reached out to kiss Annie on both cheeks. 'I have been told how kind you and your family have been to my son, and now also to me. I am deeply grateful.'

Annie hugged her. 'We are happy everything has turned out so well.' She glanced at her watch. 'I must hurry if I'm going to catch my train.'

'Mind you behave yourself when you get back,' Sam said with a grin.

Annie pretended to be hurt. 'I'm always good, and without your disruptive influence my life will be one of tranquillity.'

Sam tipped his head back and roared with laughter. 'That sounds deadly dull. It has been a pleasure working with you, Annie Webster.'

'And you.' She hugged him also. 'You be happy, Sam.'

'I shall,' he assured her.

The journey back to Roehampton had been interminable, with delay after delay. She'd been sorry to leave so soon after Bill had come on leave. He was over fifty now and she hoped he would soon be free of the navy. Her sister would be relieved as well. She never voiced her concerns but Annie knew she was worried about him – he looked so dreadfully tired.

She let herself into the house. It was too late to go on to Folkestone today, so she'd sleep in her own bed tonight and see Bob tomorrow.

Annie threw her bag on to the stairs. That could be taken upstairs later, but she needed a cup of tea now. Much to her surprise the kitchen wasn't empty, and the girl standing by the cooker turned and glared at her.

'Who are you?' the stranger demanded.

'I think that's my question.' Annie's gaze raked over the girl and certain things about her registered. She was average height, ample curves, very obvious in a tight-fitting red skirt and cream jumper. She had carefully tended blonde hair, eyes green and hostile.

The scrutiny was returned. 'You must be Annie,' she sneered. 'Well, you'll have to sleep next door because I'm spending a few days with Charles – *alone.*' She emphasized the last word.

'Pat!' Charlie was standing behind Annie. 'This is my sister's home and she has every right to be here.'

Annie turned and hugged her brother. 'Charles?' she murmured in his ear, and they both burst into laughter.

'I didn't mean to be rude.' Pat slipped her hand through Charlie's arm and gazed up at him. 'I was just disappointed we weren't going to be alone after all.'

The girl's attitude had changed completely and with imploring smiles she leaned against Charlie. 'You do forgive me, don't you?'

Her act didn't fool Annie for one minute. She might appear to be contrite but the coldness in her eyes could not be disguised. All that Annie had seen and done in the war, and the loss of Paul, Jack Graham and George had hardened some of the soft edges. She was no longer the

411

trusting girl who thought everyone was inherently nice. This girl of her brother's was quite transparent, and Annie didn't like her – in fact her feelings were stronger than that.

Annie filled the kettle and put it on the stove. 'I'm dying for a cuppa. Anyone else want one?'

'Please.' Charlie sat at the kitchen table.

'Charles,' Pat said with a pout. 'You promised to take me out for a drink.'

'After I've had a chat with my sister.' He took the cup from Annie and smiled. 'Now tell me all the news.'

'We've had a letter saying Bob's been wounded and I'm going to see him tomorrow.'

'What!' Charlie exclaimed. 'Where is he?'

'Folkestone, and we only found out this morning. Mum wanted to come but she's a bit run-down at the moment.'

'Has she seen a doctor?' Charlie looked concerned.

'Yes. He said she's been overdoing things and needs to rest, that's all. It's nothing serious,' she assured him.

'That's a relief. How's Sam and his family now?'

'They're fine.' Annie wasn't prepared to discuss this in front of Pat. The girl looked as if she was eating every word.

Charlie drank his tea and dropped the subject. He'd clearly picked up Annie's reluctance to discuss things in front of Pat. 'You know I've only seen Bob once since he came back so I think I'll come with you tomorrow.'

'He'd like that.' Annie smiled.

'Oh, Charles,' Pat wailed. 'You were going to show me Richmond Park tomorrow.'

'It'll have to wait, I'm afraid.' He headed for the door.

412

'Let's leave Annie in peace, and go and have that drink.'

Annie watched them leave, and worry for Charlie gnawed at her. How on earth had her brother got involved with a girl like that?

Pat insisted on coming with them to Folkestone but refused to come in the hospital.

'I'll have a walk around and find a tearoom somewhere.' She smiled appealingly at Charlie.

With only a faint sigh, he pulled some money out of his pocket and handed it to her. After counting it she gave him a quick peck on the cheek and was off.

Charlie watched her for a moment then gave a rueful smile. 'She thinks I'm made of money.'

Annie didn't comment. 'Where did you meet her?'

'It was at an RAF dance. She's a Londoner, but they were bombed out and now she and her family are living near Bognor.'

'What are her family like?' Annie chose her questions carefully. After all, she had no right to interfere in her brother's relationships.

'I've never met them.' Charlie held the door of the hospital open for his sister. 'Grief, look at this place, it's crowded. Do you know which ward Bob's in?'

'No, we'll just have to queue up.' Annie resigned herself to a lengthy wait.

'You don't like her, do you, Annie,' Charlie remarked.

'My opinion isn't important,' she told him. 'You're a grown man and if she's your choice then I'll do my best to get along with her.'

'I know you will . . .' He hesitated. 'At first I was

413

absolutely besotted with her but now something worries me. I think she believes we're rich.'

Annie looked at her brother in amazement. He looked so handsome and a man of the world in his air force uniform, and she couldn't help laughing at his expression. 'But we are, Charlie. We have a great deal more than a lot of families.'

'I keep forgetting that.' He grimaced. 'The hunger, violence and poverty of our childhood made an indelible impression on me.'

'Does Pat know we originally came from Garrett Street, one of the roughest places in London?'

'I told her, yes, but she didn't seem interested. She's asked a lot of questions about Rose, Bill and George but I've been cagey about telling her too much.'

'Why is that?' Annie wanted to know.

'Dunno.' Charlie frowned. 'I suppose I don't quite trust her, and I believe our family business is our affair and nothing to do with outsiders.' He looked at his sister and pulled a face. 'When I first met her I believed she was the one I'd been waiting for but I have some doubts now.'

'Can I offer a little sisterly advice?' Annie asked. Charlie nodded.

'Don't make any hasty decisions. Take your time getting to know her, and if you're serious insist on meeting her family.' Annie smiled. 'You can learn a lot from families.'

'Sound advice.' Charlie looked at his sister with renewed respect. 'You're tougher and a lot more cautious than you used to be.'

'So I've been told.'

They finally reached the information desk and asked where Bob was, then made their way along the corridor. Annie paused outside the ward. Her brother was in the mood to talk and she felt he needed to. He seemed to be having serious doubts about Pat and she found that reassuring. They were a close family and it would be awful if someone joined them that they couldn't stand. But that could happen, as it wasn't possible to like everyone you met in life. Look at the way she'd disliked Reid after their first meeting.

'Why you never married, Annie?'

She thought about this for a moment. 'Perhaps I've been looking for the impossible, but to be honest I don't think I've ever really wanted to. I was quite happy with my life and career before this war started.'

'I know what you mean. Will and I felt the same but things are different now, aren't they?'

Annie sighed and pushed open the door. 'Yes, everything's changed.'

'Annie, Charlie!' Bob waved to them from his bed. 'What a marvellous surprise.'

'We've come to see how you are.' Annie kissed him. 'What happened to you?'

'I was caught in heavy shellfire and got peppered with shrapnel.' He grimaced. 'They've dug loads of the stuff out of my back and legs.'

'Will there be any permanent damage?' Charlie asked.

'They don't think so, but it will take some time before I make a full recovery.'

'Well, as soon as you're out of here you can go to Wales and rest.' Annie sat on the chair that Charlie had pulled up for her. 'Mum was worried about you.'

Bob looked gloomy. 'All I've ever caused Mum is worry. I was a swine of a kid, wasn't I?'

'That's all in the past.' Annie held his hand in comfort. She knew how easy it was to become depressed in hospital. 'And forgiven.'

'One good thing,' Charlie said, 'by the time you're fit the war will be over.'

'God, I hope so! I miss my wife and nippers something awful,' Bob exclaimed.

'You'll be on your way home to Australia before you know it.' Annie felt sad at that thought. Bob had fitted in as if he'd never left and Annie knew her mother was going to be very upset when he went back to his home so far away. She pushed the gloomy thought away, dived into her pocket and produced a small bar of chocolate. 'That's all I could manage to get, but I expect you could do with a treat.'

'Oh, thanks, I'll eat that when nurse isn't looking.' He popped it in the cupboard next to him. 'Now tell me all the news.'

It took quite a time to bring Bob up to date with all the happenings, and they overstayed their welcome and were ordered to leave by a stern nurse. But they came away happy, knowing that although their Australian brother had been quite badly injured he would make a full recovery. Though he'd been separated from them for many years Annie and Charlie felt they knew and loved him.

'Where have you been all this time?' Pat complained when she saw them. 'I've been waiting ages.'

'We had a lot to talk about,' Charlie told her.

'Can we get something to eat?' Pat moderated her

tone and smiled at Charlie. 'I've found a smashing café.'

'Good idea.' He took Annie's arm. 'Our train doesn't leave for another two hours, so we've plenty of time.'

As they made their way to the café Pat chatted away, but Annie noticed that she never once asked about Bob.

The weeks dragged by. Annie was as busy as ever but felt strangely depressed. It was ridiculous, she told herself repeatedly. She still found her work as exciting and challenging as it had always been, but it had been a strange year with many ups and downs. There had been D-Day in June, the liberation of Paris in August, and the steady advance of Allied troops towards Germany. However, the V1 flying bombs had caused damage, including the death of George, and also the V2 rockets that had followed them. But it was becoming clear that the end of the war could only be months away and she should be feeling ecstatic.

'Why the gloomy face?' asked Greg – a bomber pilot who had come to the end of his flying days due to injury – as he sat down at her table in the mess.

'I really don't know and I'm just berating myself for feeling so low.'

'Don't give yourself a hard time,' he advised. 'Waiting is always the worst, as I well know. Before a bombing raid I used to feel physically sick.'

Annie nodded in understanding. 'That's a bit how I feel now. Suppose the Germans launch an offensive and start to regain the upper hand?'

'They won't.' He spoke with confidence. 'They've

taken a severe pounding, and when Hitler's own generals tried to assassinate him, like they did in July, then they know they're beaten.'

'You're right, of course.' Annie sat up straight and smiled. When that bit of news had come through it had caused elation, and then disappointment that it hadn't succeeded. 'I expect I'm down in the dumps because I can't get home for Christmas.'

'Never mind. We'll have a good knees-up here.'

Annie watched him walk away, leaning heavily on a cane, and set about pulling herself together. She had never felt so unsettled in her life. Even if she couldn't spend the holiday with her family that was no reason to act like a sulky child. That was something she had never been.

Rose's last letter had told her that Bill would be on leave for a couple of days; Bob had arrived in Wales and would convalesce there; Sam and Maria were now married, and Jacques was a very happy little boy. Annie was dreadfully sorry she hadn't been able to get leave to go to Maria and Sam's wedding, but they'd sent her some lovely photographs. Charlie would also be in Wales, but they weren't sure about Will. Dora and her grandmother were arriving in a couple of days' time as well, so the house would be crammed full for Christmas. That was just the way the Webster family liked it.

Annie mentally shook herself. It was no good wishing she were somewhere else, she still had work to do. There was a lot to be grateful for and who knew what would happen next year.

Hopefully they would *all* be together.

*

419

'You can have twenty-four hours to celebrate New Year.' The duty officer handed Annie a pass. 'Go out and enjoy yourself.'

She looked at the pass and chewed her bottom lip. What was she going to do with this? It wasn't long enough to travel to Wales and back, and it wasn't any use going to the Roehampton house; she didn't want to see 1945 in on her own.

'You don't appear to be very pleased.'

'I am, sir,' she said hastily. This was unexpected and she didn't want to seem ungrateful. 'I was just trying to decide what to do.'

'I thought that was settled. Your fiancé is waiting at the gate for you.'

Her head came up in shock. 'My what?'

'Fiancé.' He sat back and folded his arms, looking amused. 'Don't you want to see him?'

'I might if I knew who it was.'

'Ah.' He started to chuckle. 'So he lied to get you time off, but there isn't anything I can do about that. He outranks me.'

'Reid!' Annie exploded.

'If his name's Lascells then that's the man, and I suggest you hurry because he outranks you as well.'

Annie left the room, the officer's laugh echoing along the corridor. I'll kill him, she fumed, as she collected her coat. This will be all round the base within the hour.

But her anger seeped away as she walked towards him. Her mouth turned up at the corners, amused now by his audacity. He was leaning against a car, his collar turned up against the cold wind, and a cigarette in his hand. He

420

really was the most attractive man, she thought to herself. She might as well enjoy the evening.

Reid straightened up and ground out the fag with the toe of his shoe as she approached.

'Resorted to lying, Squadron Leader?' she asked.

He grinned and held the door of the car open for her. 'Whatever it takes, Webster.'

'Well, it worked. I've been given a twenty-four-hour pass.' She got into the car and ignored his muttered expletive.

'I asked for forty-eight hours, at least.' He started the car and headed up the road.

'What on earth would we do in each other's company for that long?'

He cast her a quick glance, and there was no mistaking the gleam in his eyes.

Annie sighed. 'Am I going to have trouble with you tonight?'

'Definitely.'

'Ah well, it's a good job I've only been given a short time off. Where are we going?'

'To a party at the Sterling Hotel, it isn't far from here. They've got a big band and I want to see if you can still jive.'

'And where you have, no doubt, booked rooms?' Annie turned in her seat so she could see his face clearly. There was something different about him.

Reid shook his head. 'Only one room.'

'Did you try for two?' Annie was suspicious of his innocent expression – and he was in such a good mood. 'Why would we want a room each?' he asked.

'Why indeed.' Annie managed to keep a straight face

with difficulty. It was going to be an interesting New Year's Eve. He had told her, quite plainly, what he wanted, and he was giving her the chance to object before the evening began. But she wasn't going to.

It was at that moment she knew that she had, at last, stopped running. It was time to take what life was offering – and if that was Reid then it was all she wanted in this world. The sudden realization of the depth of her feeling for him was a revelation to her.

On the stroke of midnight the party-goers erupted with cheers of joy. The ballroom was packed with every branch of the services, a sprinkling of civilians, and many nationalities. And they were all determined to make this the best New Year party of all time. There was so much hope expressed in the sound that it brought tears to Annie's eyes.

Reid wrapped her in a fierce embrace. 'This is going to be the year, Annie, 1945 is going to see the end of this bloody war.'

He kissed her with unrestrained need, and when he finally broke away he asked, 'Will you marry me, Annie Webster? I love you so very much.'

At that crucial moment she was whisked out of his arms by a crowd of exuberant soldiers and drawn into the snaking line of revellers. Reid quickly pushed in behind her. The noise was deafening and he had to shout to make himself heard.

'What's your answer?'

'Aye, aye, conga!' Everyone was singing with legs shooting out from the line in all directions.

'Annie,' he bellowed.

She glanced over her shoulder and mouthed the word *yes*, almost collapsing with laughter at the same time.

Reid grinned, squeezed her waist and threw himself into the revelry with abandon. This was a bizarre proposal, he thought to himself, but it didn't matter; she'd accepted and that was the only important thing. He'd show her how much he loved her later.

After they'd all snaked their way out of the hotel, up the road, returned and made a tour of the garden, then back into the ballroom again, everything quietened down a little.

'Not the kind of proposal I had planned.' Reid gave a rueful shake of his head. Bouncer had told him to be more romantic, and he'd planned to take her outside, go down on one knee, and give her the ring, but he hadn't been able to wait. The whole thing had turned into a farce.

Annie laughed and wrapped her arms around his neck. 'I think it was lovely.'

'So do I.' He kissed her, and then whispered in her ear, 'There's a nice double bed upstairs, or are you going to make me wait?'

'I think we've both waited long enough,' she told him. 'And we've wasted far too much time arguing with each other.'

The speed with which he led her to the stairs left her in no doubt that he heartily agreed.

Reid propped himself up on his elbow and looked down at Annie. She was fast asleep, her hair in disarray where he'd run his fingers through the silky strands, and his heart squeezed with emotion. She was so lovely and she

423

was his now. He wouldn't have believed he could feel so possessive about a woman but she had changed all that. He'd had plenty of girlfriends but had never felt any sense of loss when they'd parted. The thought of losing Annie, though, brought him close to panic.

Annie muttered in her sleep and he slid down in the bed again, drawing her gently into his arms. Their loving had been wonderful. After her first nervous hesitation she had unleashed a passion that had literally taken his breath away. He was damned sure this had been her first time but how she had managed to stay out of some man's bed until now was a mystery. He seriously doubted that many women in their early thirties were still virgins. Not those as beautiful and loving as Annie, anyway.

He kissed her gently and then cradled her head on to his chest. A feeling of utter contentment swept through him. She obviously had a moral code, which meant she had waited for the right man to come along. It must have been difficult in the wartime atmosphere. The fact that she had come willingly to him tonight meant only one thing as far as he could see. She loved him.

There was a burst of raucous laughter from the party downstairs and Annie opened her eyes. 'Sounds like they're making a night of it,' she said with a yawn.

'Did they wake you up?' Reid cupped her face in his hands so he could look into her eyes.

She gave a slight nod and closed her eyes again.

'Look at me, Annie.'

She smiled up at him with an amused expression. 'Aren't you tired?'

'No. I want answers to three questions, then I *might* sleep,' he said, tucking a loose strand of her golden hair behind her ears. Propping himself up he gazed down at her. 'First. When can we get married?'

'When the war's over.'

'Good,' he agreed. 'That won't be long now, so we can start making plans.'

'Have you got a spare parachute?' she asked, and her grin spread. 'Or perhaps Bouncer's got one he isn't using.'

'I'll ask him, but he's a reformed maniac since he married Jenny.' Reid chuckled as he thought about the dramatic change in his friend. 'I'll get you one anyway.'

'Good, because my family are going to want a proper party.' She gave him an uncertain look. 'I hope you don't mind?'

'Not at all; my parents will expect the same.' He ran his hand over her warm body. 'Now that's settled . . .'

'Wait!' She laughingly caught hold of his wandering hand. 'You said you had three questions.'

'Did I?' He frowned. 'Ah, well, I'll think of them later.'

'No, you won't. I want to know what the questions are.' Annie tried to wriggle away from him but he wouldn't allow it.

He pulled her back into his arms. 'Stop squirming about or I'll never think of them. Now let me see . . . Ah, yes. The second question is, do you love me, Annie?'

'Yes,' she told him with a sigh of pleasure. 'I wouldn't be in this bed with you now if I didn't.'

'Do you want children?'

'Yes, please.'

That was just the answer he wanted and he couldn't stop himself from showing her how happy he was.

She gasped when he broke off the heated embrace. 'Not until we're married, of course.'

'I'll try to see that doesn't happen before our wedding, my darling,' he assured her. 'Why have you waited so long to commit yourself to a man?'

'That's four questions,' she pointed out, 'but I'll answer it anyway.' She snuggled closer. 'I wanted love, and I needed to be sure it was a relationship that had every chance of lasting. I couldn't bear to be in an unhappy marriage; it would destroy me. And I had to be convinced that whoever became my husband loved me as much as I loved him.'

'I do.' His voice was husky with desire.

'I know you do, but I don't mind being reminded again.' Her smile was provocative.

Reid was only too happy to oblige but he restrained himself long enough to slip a lovely diamond and sapphire ring on her finger.

'Oh, that's beautiful.' Annie held her hand towards the bedside light so she could have a proper look at the ring. 'You had this all planned.'

'Yes, all planned. Except the conga, of course.'

It had been a blissful twenty-four hours, Reid thought as he jumped out of the car at Tangmere. He'd reluctantly returned Annie to Chicksands, not knowing when they would be able to see each other again. Damn the war, he thought, he would be glad to see the end of it now. Trying to wangle leave at the same time was difficult, but he'd fix it somehow, as he didn't want to be away from Annie for too long – in fact he wanted her with him all the time! But at least he now knew that she was going to marry him! She loved him!

426

Before unpacking his bag he strolled into his office to see if there were any urgent messages.

'Sir.' Sergeant Jenkins rushed through the door. 'One of the returning fighters is in trouble.'

Reid surged to his feet. 'Who is it?'

'Don't know, sir.'

He left at a run and headed for the control tower. The atmosphere was tense and everyone was listening to the faint voice coming over the speaker.

'What's happening?' he asked the officer in charge.

'Spitfire with engine trouble, we think.'

'What do you mean – you think?' Reid glowered at the man.

'We can't pick up a clear message from the squadron. Something's wrong this end, we think.'

Reid ground his teeth. If he said 'think' once more he'd belt him one. 'Get it put right – at once!' he ordered. 'Now tell me what you *do* know.'

'Not much, I'm afraid, sir, but it sounds serious.' The man shuffled uncomfortably under the fierce glare of his commanding officer.

'If it's that bad why hasn't he baled out?'

'His canopy's stuck . . .'

Reid noted the hesitation and silently dared him to say 'I think', but the man obviously wasn't going to risk it again. However, that piece of information made his insides clench. Being trapped in a crippled plane was every pilot's nightmare. He didn't want to ask the next question but he knew he must. 'Any fire?'

'We don't know. He's been trying to tell us but there's

427

too much static for us to be able to understand what he's saying.'

The muttered expletive made everyone in the tower stare at Reid but he just ignored them and took over the radio. 'Tell me your situation,' he demanded.

The sound of static crackled through the silent room. 'Someone talk to me, damn you.'

A faint voice came over the speaker. 'Smoke everywhere . . .'

Reid tried to recognize who it was but it was no use, and to make matters worse the radio seemed to have packed up altogether. He knew every one of these men, had flown with some of them during the Battle of Britain and he didn't want to see one of them injured or killed at this stage of the war. It was nearly over.

At the sound of engines he rushed to the window and scanned the sky. Two planes roared low over the tower, banked and climbed into the clear, cold January sun. That was the signal to let the fire crews know the plane was arriving.

After taking a couple of deep breaths to try to ease the tightness in his chest Reid hurried down the stairs.

'His canopy's stuck,' he told the fire chief, and the man nodded grimly.

At that moment a Spitfire made a slow pass and wiggled its wings.

'Here he comes.' Reid shaded his eyes and watched the plane's erratic descent. Clouds of smoke were billowing out of the engine and staining the clear sky behind it.

The fire and ambulance teams hurtled off, taking up positions just behind the plane as it attempted to land.

The air was rent with the noise of sirens, some Spitfires landing and others screaming across the airfield in support of their colleague. And Reid knew that each of them was urging the pilot on to make it safely.

The Spitfire was now skidding along almost sideways, and Reid could stand it no longer. He jumped in a truck and headed for the plane. He knew the rescue teams were on the scene and expert at the job but he had to be there.

The pilot was being pulled free when he jumped from the truck. The man was coughing and retching but still very much alive if the stream of strong language was anything to go by.

'Stop swearing,' a medic ordered as he held an oxygen mask over the pilot's face, 'and get on the stretcher.'

The tall man pushed the medic away and swayed when his support was removed.

'Timber, take it easy.' Reid rushed to his side and held his arm. 'That was a close call. What happened?'

'God knows.' He ripped the mask off. 'The engine started to make a terrible noise and I couldn't see a damned thing when smoke started to fill the cockpit. If it hadn't been for the rest of the boys buzzing around and guiding me in I'd have crashed for sure.'

Two medics were now urging Timber towards the ambulance, and while this tussle was going on the rest of the squadron arrived.

'You all right, old boy?'

Reid dipped his head at the sound of his friend's voice, giving him a moment to control his emotions. He hadn't dared consider that it might have been Bouncer up there in that smoking plane. And the knowledge that he might have had to tell Jenny her husband had died made him feel physically sick. He'd had to face many unpleasant tasks during the war but the thought of facing Jenny with news like that was too awful to contemplate.

Someone slapped him on the back and he turned to face Bouncer, completely in control again after that momentary lapse. Good job he hadn't been this emotional in 1940 or he'd never have survived. Watching Bouncer's happiness with Jenny and being in love himself had brought home to him just how precious life was.

His friend grinned. 'That was a landing I'd have been proud of.'

Reid surveyed the smoking, crumpled aircraft and grimaced. 'I would have expected this of you, but not Timber.'

Now the drama was over Reid's temper exploded. He strode towards the truck that was now full of pilots waiting for a lift. 'Heads are going to roll for this fiasco.'

Bouncer clambered in beside him. 'Oh, good, can I come and watch? You're ferocious in a rage.'

'By all means,' Reid said dangerously, 'but first we'll see how Timber is.'

The pilot had quietened down by the time they saw him, and had returned to his usual placid nature.

'I'm going to wring someone's neck over this, Timber,' Reid promised.

'Oh, these things happen, you know that.' Timber laid his head back and gave a tired smile. 'At least she didn't burst into flames, and apart from being badly shaken up I'm unhurt.'

'Thank heavens for that,' Reid said. Then he looked

430

at the men crowding around the bed. 'Drinks are on me tonight.'

A cheer rang out and the pilot sat up, looking suddenly very perky. 'Mine's a whisky, and what about some female company as well?'

'I'll see what I can arrange.' Reid strode out of the room, a smile of relief hovering on his lips. He remembered the last time he'd arranged a party for the men, and they deserved another one. Reid's mind went back to New Year 1941 when they'd been sent north for a rest and how they'd needed it after the battle to stop the Luftwaffe gaining superiority of the air. If they'd failed then Hitler would most certainly have invaded. He'd make sure they had one hell of a party tonight!

Bouncer looked around the room and raised an eyebrow at his friend. 'No girls for us?'

'Did you want one?' Reid asked.

'No, but I thought you might.' He drank half his beer in one go. 'Or dare I hope that you've snared Annie at last?'

Reid nodded. 'We're engaged.'

'About time too.' Bouncer grinned with pleasure. 'When did you propose?'

'New Year's Eve.'

'So that's where you disappeared to.' His friend gave a satisfied nod. 'Hope you were in bed at the time.'

'No.' Reid couldn't help laughing as he explained about the dance. It had been the most bizarre proposal.

Bouncer's mouth dropped open and he snorted in disgust. 'Dear me, old boy, couldn't you do better than that? I'm surprised she accepted you.'

'So am I.' Reid's attention was caught by Timber who was dancing. 'That man's all legs, but he's soon recovered from this morning's crash.'

'Thank God.' Bouncer sighed. 'That was dicey, Reid. We've been together a long time and it would have been tragic if he'd bought it now.'

'It certainly would.' Reid's expression was grim for a moment, and then it cleared. 'Annie won't marry until the war's over but I've managed to pin her down to early June by convincing her that it will be finished long before then.'

'I should think that's a safe enough bet.' Bouncer looked over the rim of his glass. 'Who's going to be your best man?'

'You, of course.' Reid sat back to allow more drinks to be put in front of them.

'Smashing party,' the tall pilot told them. 'Aren't you two going to join in? We'll let you dance with our girls.'

'We might take you up on that later,' Bouncer told him. 'We're busy planning Reid's wedding.'

That announcement was all it took for the pilots to stampede to the bar and order what they considered enough drinks to celebrate with. The table was soon crowded with glasses of beer; the squadron was hell-bent on toasting Reid's forthcoming wedding.

Bouncer roared with laughter at the chaos and his friend's look of dismay. 'That will teach you to try and keep this a secret, old boy.'

Reid winced as someone thumped him on the back but he took the boisterous congratulations with pleasure.

'Tell me all the details,' Bouncer asked, when things had quietened down a little.

Reid then related what had happened as he'd proposed to Annie on the stroke of midnight.

His friend was nearly crying with laughter. 'And what did you do then?'

'Mind your own business.'

Bouncer held up his hand. 'Don't worry; my imagination will fill in the details. Tell me what plans you have for the wedding.'

'Annie's asking Dora and Jenny to be maids of honour, Kate a bridesmaid, but James has flatly refused to be a page boy. He'll be sixteen later this year and he wasn't going to have anything to do with it.'

Bouncer choked on his beer and they both burst out laughing, trying to picture the rather serious boy in satin breeches. Reid couldn't help remembering the look of horror on James's face at the suggestion. When Annie had suggested that he be an usher he'd accepted with indecent haste.

'Why didn't Jenny tell me? I spoke to her only yesterday.'

'She'd been sworn to secrecy until I'd told you,' Reid explained. 'So don't go making her pregnant until after the wedding.'

His friend looked smug. 'Too late, old boy, she's three months now.'

Reid's grin spread. 'Congratulations. It's going to be an interesting wedding.'

'Specially if the bride's pregnant, as well.' Bouncer watched Reid's face carefully.

'She won't be,' he replied with confidence.

'Really? You sound so sure, and that makes me think . . .' He paused and frowned, then shook his head.

'No, you're trying to kid me you're waiting until the wedding night and I certainly don't believe that!'

'I can't control what you believe.' Reid's expression gave nothing away. What happened between him and Annie was private and nothing to do with anyone, not even this great friend of his.

'True,' Bouncer agreed, changing the subject smartly. 'Oh, by the way, I've managed to rent a house just down the road from the airfield and Jenny's moving in next week. I'm fed up with being parted from her. Where are you and Annie going to live?'

'Don't tell Annie any of this,' he admonished, 'but I own a piece of land in Berkshire not far from my family's factory in Thatcham, and I'm going to ask Bill to design and build a home for us.'

'I thought he was a professional sailor.'

'No, he's an architect really, and he'll be out of the navy as soon as this war ends, if he can arrange it.' Reid couldn't help remembering how tired Bill had looked last time he'd seen him. To make a man fight in two world wars was asking too much of him, and it had obviously taken its toll on his health. 'Rose and Bill own the building firm of Grant Phillips and they're going to be very busy when this lot's over. Rose told me he'd designed the Roehampton houses they live in.'

'Ah, well, then he knows his job if they are his.' Bouncer studied his friend thoughtfully. 'What do you think your brother would say about you marrying Annie?'

'He told me once that if he didn't make it through the war, then I could marry her.' Reid looked into the distance, remembering that time, and wondered when the pain of losing his young brother was going to heal. It would take a long time.

'Ah,' Bouncer nodded understandingly. 'He'd like to think you were looking after her, then.'

'Yes, he would. He only ever wanted Annie to be happy, and I *will* make her happy.'

Annie closed her bag and glanced at her watch. Reid should be here any minute now. They had decided to make an early start and it wasn't even light yet. Reid had managed to get some petrol so they were going to take a leisurely drive to Wales, lasting most of the day, and snatching the chance of a few hours alone together. It had taken them until the beginning of May to arrange leave at the same time, and even this had not been certain until the very last minute. Things were happening so fast. Hitler had committed suicide a week ago on the 30th of April, and it was expected to be only a matter of days before Germany surrendered.

Annie gazed around the Nissen hut that had been her home for so long and let out a ragged sigh. It seemed as if she'd been shut away here for ever. Sleeping in this hut she shared with fifteen other girls whenever she could grab a few hours' rest, and working the rest of the time. Oh, it had been exciting at times, but mostly plain hard graft, except for the trip behind enemy lines to find Jack Graham. It still hurt her when she remembered how he had suffered on the journey to the Brittany coast, but at least he had died in his own country with his wife and a son by his side. She was glad she'd been able to do that for him. Jack had been a wonderful man and he would always hold a special place in her heart. Her thoughts drifted back to the winter of 1940 when she'd joined the WAAF, and she smiled as she remembered the laughter at their military issue underclothes. She wondered where most of those girls were now. Annie hoped they'd survived because they had been a good crowd. The one friendship that had remained from the start was with Dora, who was now happily married to Annie's own brother. She could never have imagined that one of the girls she'd met on her first day in the forces would end up as her sister-in-law. After she'd completed her training as a wireless operator she'd been transferred to Cheadle and then on to Chicksands, where she had remained, and it was during those years she had faced her most painful and challenging times: the loss of Paul, Jack Graham and George. But there had also been times of laughter and friendships made, like Jean and Sam, with his adorable son, Jacques.

After another quick check of the time Annie picked up her bag and walked towards the gate. Reid had been pulling strings to get them this leave. They'd been able to snatch a couple of days now and again, but at last they could go to Wales for seven whole days. Reid's parents were already there, so a belated engagement party had been organized. She smiled in anticipation at the thought of seeing everyone again. There had been regular reports from her mother and Rose, of course, so she knew that Jacques had blossomed now he had a *proper* family, as he called it, and Maria was almost back to full health. Sam doted on both of them, Rose had told her, and Annie was delighted. That family had suffered so much and they deserved to be happy now.

Reid was already there, leaning on the car in his usual relaxed manner. As soon as he saw her he came towards her and wrapped his arms around her with a groan of pleasure. 'Ah, I've missed you, my darling,' he told her before kissing her as if he'd never let her go.

Then he tossed her bag into the back of the car and they were soon on their way. Annie was looking forward to a leisurely drive, though she didn't know where he'd managed to get the petrol for such a long journey. But quite frankly she didn't care – she was with Reid and they were going home for a few days.

He gave her a quick sideways glance. 'I've managed to wangle Charlie leave as well, and he's making his way by train.'

'Oh, why didn't you bring him with you?' she asked. 'We could have all travelled together.'

His glance was smouldering. 'Hell, Annie, I've hardly seen you since New Year and I want you to myself for a while, you know that.'

Annie saw his point. She was just as frustrated with this long separation, and was yearning for the time when they could be together. How she wished this flaming war were over. 'That's a good idea because once we get to Wales any time alone will be hard to come by.'

'I'm glad you agree. Charlie's bringing his girlfriend, by the way.'

That news didn't please Annie. 'Oh, dear.'

'Ah,' Reid remarked, 'you don't sound as if you like her.'

'Well, I've only met her once but to be honest I didn't take to her. She tried to order me out of my own home.'

Annie gave a resigned shrug. 'Still it's Charlie's life and if he's happy then that's all that matters.'

A deep chuckle came from Reid. 'If she tries to do that with Rose, then she'll really be cut down.'

Annie grinned at him. 'That should be interesting. The house is going to be packed by the sound of it.'

'Hmm. I hope they've given me a room near yours.'

Annie smiled broadly. This was something he didn't know about. She was tempted to wait and let him find out when they arrived but decided against that. 'Rose wrote and asked me if we wanted a double bed.'

He pulled the car over on to a grass verge, stopped and then turned to face her. 'And what did you say?'

'I told her that as the house would be crowded one bed would do, even if it was in the shed!'

He hugged her. 'That's marvellous. At least I'll have you all to myself at night. I hate being away from you and can't wait until we're married.'

'I feel the same.'

Reid started the car and they resumed their journey. Annie laid her head back and closed her eyes.

'Are you all right?' he asked. 'You look tired.'

'I didn't get off duty until three o'clock this morning, so I haven't been to bed.' They'd been so busy and it was a relief to get away for a while. She'd always loved her job as a wireless operator, but now, with the war drawing to a close, she wanted to be free of the stress. She wanted to be married to Reid and have children.

'In that case you rest. I'll wake you when we stop for a break,' he said.

They drove at a sedate pace, stopping by the roadside to watch the dawn come up and eat the food they'd brought with them. They sat there for some time just talking and enjoying the solitude. They did this a couple more times as the day wore on, in no hurry to reach their destination, and each time they resumed their journey Annie slept.

But just after three o'clock Annie opened her eyes and sat up straight. The car had stopped near a pub and there was no sign of Reid. She was surprised to see the place surrounded with every kind of vehicle, including push-bikes. One hell of a racket was coming from the pub. A group of people came along the road, laughing and singing and waving flags, and then disappeared inside. What on earth was going on?

Just as Annie clambered out of the car to investigate Reid came through the door and ran towards her in long, loping strides. She watched his fluid movements and wondered how many times he'd hurtled towards his Spitfire like that? Several times a day in those terrible months of 1940, she guessed.

When he reached her she was swung off her feet as he danced her round and round in excitement.

'Reid!' she gasped. 'What's happened?'

'It's all over!' He kissed her, then said, 'Germany has surrendered. It's official. Churchill has just announced it on the wireless.'

Annie gave a squeal of delight and wrapped her arms around his neck.

'They won't need us any more, my darling, and we can get out of the air force as soon as possible.'

Before Annie had a chance to say anything a crowd erupted from the pub and towed them inside.

'Landlord,' an elderly man in ARP uniform called. 'Let's have some drinks for the pilot and his lady.'

Reid was wearing his best uniform, with its medal ribbons. It didn't take a genius to know what he'd been doing during the conflict; he was a highly decorated pilot, though she'd never once heard him talk about how he won his medals.

A whisky was thrust into her hand, and it was more than an hour before they could slip away and continue their journey. All Annie wanted to do now was celebrate with the family. All the way along their journey there were crowds of people hell-bent on celebrating; it was impossible to drive through some of the villages without stopping to join in. Everyone thrust drinks into their hands; it was obvious that some carefully hoarded bottles were being opened at last, having been saved for this very occasion.

Annie had lost track of where they were but it didn't really matter. No one cared about anything except that the war was over, and the country was one great big, cheering, laughing party. One man had dragged his wind-up gramophone out on to the street, and when the people started to line up for the conga Annie laughed at Reid. 'Oh no, not that again!'

'Come on,' Reid said and dragged her towards the snaking line of revellers. 'Let's join in and remember the night I proposed to you.'

They danced their way up the street, through people's gardens, and back again towards their car. As soon as they reached it Reid lifted Annie off her feet and dumped her in the front seat. 'Let's get out of here or we'll never see the family tonight!'

They were both laughing as they inched their way along the crowded street, and once they were clear Annie laid her head back. The conga would always remind them of Reid's proposal of marriage, and it was such a happy memory.

Reid grinned as another group cheered and thumped on the car as they went past. 'We're going to be a bit late, I'm afraid.'

'It doesn't matter.' Now the first feeling of euphoria was passing Annie began to grasp what this meant to her, Reid and their families. Bill, Will and Charlie had survived . . . A tear trickled down her face as she remembered those who wouldn't see this day. Paul, George, Jack Graham, and his younger son, lost when the ship had been torpedoed . . . And she couldn't even imagine how many friends Reid had seen die.

She felt Reid squeeze her hand and she gave him a tearful smile.

'I know, darling, it's a bitter sweet moment, isn't it?' She was unable to speak. The pain of loss was heightened at that moment.

It was almost dark by the time they reached Wales, but the house was ablaze with lights, just the same as every place they'd passed and stopped at along the way. Obviously the first thing everyone had done was rip down the hated blackout curtains.

As soon as they drew up the front door opened and the children came running out with torches in their hands. They were flashing the beams up into the sky and screeching at the novelty of being able to show a light. After years of trying not to show even a small chink of light this was unbelievable fun for them. There wouldn't be any more need for the air-raid wardens to walk down the street shouting, 'Put that light out!'

Annie laughed and shielded her eyes as Jacques pointed the light straight in her face. Reid swept the small boy off his feet making him squeal in delight.

'The war's over!' Jacques shouted at the top of his voice. 'The Germans gone. We can go home now.'

'That's wonderful.' Reid put Jacques down and watched him hurtle towards Sam and Maria, who had come out of the house with everyone else.

'What a difference in the boy,' Reid said to Annie.

She nodded but didn't have time to say anything as Kate and James hugged them. It was an unusual gesture from James, but this was a special time – a time to let the emotions run riot. And when she saw the happiness of Sam, Maria and their small son it made her almost believe that the terrible struggle had been worthwhile.

Once inside Annie looked around the crowded room and gasped. Will, Dora and her family were there; Reid's parents; Rose, Bill, Charlie and Bob. 'How did you all manage to get here at the same time?' she asked in wonder.

Bill smiled and kissed her cheek. 'This is your engagement party and we were determined to make it a real family affair. After all, we've had to wait a long time for you to make your mind up.'

Annie laughed and slipped her arm around Reid.

Wally arrived with a tray of drinks. 'We didn't expect the end of hostilities as well when we arranged this knees-up, so we're going to have a double celebration tonight.'

Annie raised her eyebrows at her sister. 'Where are you going to put everyone, Rose?'

'It'll be a tight squeeze,' Rose answered. 'James and Kate will be sleeping at the cottage with Jack, so we'll put at least two or three in every room. We've got some bunk beds to put up down here. But I don't think any of us will be sleeping tonight, do you?'

'I doubt it very much.' Annie gazed around at the sea of faces. 'I thought Charlie was bringing his girl.'

'He did. She's in the kitchen helping with the sandwiches.'

Annie gaped at Rose in amazement. 'You're joking.'

'No, I'm not. She seems a nice girl,' Rose said, 'and she pitched in as soon as she arrived.'

'Really?' Annie still couldn't believe what she was hearing. The girl she'd met would never have volunteered for kitchen work. 'That doesn't sound like Pat.'

Rose chuckled. 'Her name's Madge. Charlie must have changed her.'

'Oh, I do hope so.' Annie headed for her brother. 'Introduce me to your new girlfriend.'

'Sure, Annie.' Charlie headed for the kitchen. 'You'll like Madge.'

'What happened to the other one?' she asked him.

'Oh, she found someone with more money. American I believe.'

Annie regarded her brother and saw that he didn't look at all sad about this turn of events, so he couldn't really have loved her. 'Thank goodness for that. She'd have drained you dry, Charlie.'

'I know.' He stopped by the kitchen door and winked

444

at her. 'I'm not daft, Annie, and you needn't worry, I had a good time for a while.'

She thumped him playfully on the chest. 'I bet you did.'

Madge was petite with dark-brown hair and hazel eyes. She was a homely looking girl; Annie liked her at once and was happy to see that she obviously adored Charlie. Mum will be relieved to see all of her remaining children settled at last, Annie thought.

The youngsters were allowed to stay up; but around eleven Jacques was drooping from all the excitement, and James, now looking quite the young man, took Kate and Jacques to the cottage. He stayed with them, leaving the grown-ups to celebrate.

Bill had bought a gramophone and lots of records – Glenn Miller, Frank Sinatra, Artie Shaw, Vera Lynn and many more of the famous singers and big bands of the war. The furniture was moved back so they could dance and sing the night away.

The dawn was throwing golden fingers of light across the sky when Annie and Reid finally managed to slip away to bed.

'This is the first day of peace in Europe,' Reid told her as he gathered her into his arms, 'and our life together is just beginning.'

He made love to her until she was gasping with pleasure. Afterwards, as they drifted into sleep, it occurred to Annie that they hadn't bothered with any precautions this time. She smiled to herself. What did it matter? The war was over and they would be married in a month's time.

*

It was midday before anyone started to wander downstairs, much to the children's disgust. And it was a rather subdued gathering around the kitchen table. After the joy of knowing that the war was over at last there was a much more serious air about everyone, as they all began to think of the future. For five and a half years the only thing to occupy their minds had been surviving the war, but now everyone had to come to grips with picking up the threads of their lives.

Sam was the first one to announce his plans. 'We are going back to France on the first available boat,' he told them, holding Jacques in his arms and smiling down at his wife. 'We shall be leaving early tomorrow.'

'Then we'll be able to travel part of the way together,' Marj told him, 'because we're returning to Roehampton in the morning. I can't wait to get back to my house again.'

'Why don't you and Annie stay here for the rest of your leave,' Bill suggested to Reid.

Reid looked at Annie for her approval, and then nodded. 'We'll do that if you don't mind.'

'What are you going to do with the house now?' Annie asked Rose.

'That's up to James. George left it to James, so it belongs to him now.'

'Oh, that's right.' Annie remembered now. Rose had insisted that her father leave everything to the children, so James had inherited all the Gresham property, and Kate some money in trust as a nest egg for when she married or reached the age of twenty-five — whichever came first.

'We'll keep it for holidays,' James told them. 'Grandpa

George loved this place and I'm sure he would have wanted us to keep it.'

'Good decision,' Bill told his son. 'It's a fine, solid house and with our growing family it will be made good use of.'

James looked pleased with his father's approval and Annie could see that he was growing into a sensible boy. But with parents like Rose and Bill it was hardly surprising.

'We must take Tibby and Pirate with us,' Kate declared. 'They will be unhappy on their own here.'

'We wouldn't dream of leaving them behind.' Rose smiled at her daughter. 'I've already got a cat box for Tibby to travel in.'

So it was all decided. The rest of the day was spent packing as everyone prepared to return to their normal lives. After all these years it wasn't going to be easy; there was still Japan to be dealt with, but the threat to this country was over. The time had come to look forward, and not back.

It was chaos the next morning as everyone prepared to leave. Reid watched Jacques tearing around in a state of high excitement, the toy rabbit once again dangling from his hand by its ear. Although he was five years old now, today he looked like an excited baby. The little boy obviously had no intention of leaving the precious rabbit behind. Kate and James had given him more toys to take home with him and he was insisting that his father find room for them in their luggage. Kate was overseeing the packing of toys, looking very grown up and motherly for a nine-year-old.

Charlie had disappeared soon after breakfast, but he was back now, rumbling up in a large air force truck. When he stopped and jumped out he gave Reid a thumbs-up sign and winked.

'Where did Charlie get that?' Annie asked as the men started to load the cases into the back.

'I've no idea.' Reid's expression was one of innocence.

Annie laughed. 'Don't try to fool me. He couldn't have commandeered transport without proper authorization.'

Reid grinned at her. 'Just look at the number of cases everyone's got. We had to do something. Charlie's going to drive it back and that means the train journey will be more comfortable for the others.'

'But what about Sam's luggage; is that being loaded as well?'

'Bill has persuaded them to stay at Roehampton tonight and make their way back to France tomorrow.'

'Annie.' Maria came and kissed her on both cheeks. 'I thank you for all you have done for us. You must promise to visit soon and bring Kate and James with you. Jacques does not realize it yet but he is going to miss them very much.'

'We'll come to France as soon as we can,' Annie promised.

'Thank you.' Maria gave a sad smile. 'You will enjoy your next visit more. No Germans to hide from, eh?'

Annie gave her a startled look.

'Ah, yes, André has told me all about your brave action.' Maria turned to Reid and stood on tiptoe to kiss him also.

'You will bring everyone to see us?' she asked.

'Of course.' Reid hugged Maria but his mind was

448

racing. What the devil had she meant when she'd told Annie that there wouldn't be any need to hide from the Germans this time?

As everyone else came and said goodbye Reid watched Annie through narrowed eyes as she hugged Sam.

'Should I call you André now?' she asked, giving a little laugh of amusement. 'You were ratty the last time I tried to.'

'Of course, Sam is no longer needed. That part of my life is finished.'

'Well, André, you and your family be happy.' Annie kissed him on the cheek and then hugged Jacques.

Reid put his arm around Annie as they watched the truck drive away with everyone waving from the back. They would all be dropped off at the station, leaving Charlie and Madge to drive back with the luggage and the animals. He waited until they were out of sight, and then led her back indoors. The house was strangely silent now, and he was glad they were going to have a few quiet days on their own. But first there was something he had to find out.

'Tell me what Maria was talking about,' he said, making her sit on the settee.

'Sorry?'

Reid sat next to her and turned her to face him. 'What was that remark about dodging Germans?'

'It was nothing.' Annie tried to stand up. 'I'll make some tea, shall I?'

'No, not until you've explained, Annie.'

She sighed, reached out and ran her finger lightly over his lips. 'I suppose it's all right to talk about it now. After all, Sam . . . sorry, André, has obviously told Maria.'

449

Reid waited, giving Annie time to compose herself. Whatever this was, it was clearly difficult for her to talk about. He knew just how she felt because he had seen things he doubted he would ever be able to discuss.

Annie began hesitantly, and for the next half hour he never said a word as the story unfolded. He saw the pain in her eyes and watched the tears flow unchecked in rivers down her face. And he knew for certain that this was the first time she'd ever taken this experience out from the back of her mind, looked it square in the face, and relived each moment.

When she'd finished she dipped her head as if all energy and emotion was spent, and Reid wrapped her in his arms and held her. She didn't need words at this moment, just someone who loved her and understood.

If he felt a pang of jealousy for this man Jack Graham she had risked her life for, then he pushed it aside. He now knew how special she was and he loved her even more. If that were possible!

36

It was the middle of June before Annie and Reid could arrange a suitable date for their wedding. They wanted as many of their family and friends there as possible, and it had taken a lot of sorting out. In the end they'd had to settle for the 25th, otherwise Bob would have been on his way back to Australia. He had fitted in with the family as if he'd never left, although they had not seen him since he'd run away to sea as a boy. It would please her mother to have him at the wedding, and as he was leaving in two days' time it would give them a chance to include him in just one more family celebration. Once he left again for Australia it was unlikely they would ever see him again. There was another cause for celebration as well. Bill had been out of the navy for two weeks now and already appeared relaxed and much happier.

Annie looked over her shoulder to check the back of the dress and then turned around, admiring the way the parachute silk hung in elegant folds from a nipped-in waist. She had designed the dress and her mother and Rose had made a wonderful job of it, following her drawing with absolute accuracy.

'You look lovely,' Rose told her.

Annie smiled. It was a relief to be out of uniform for a change.

Marj tweaked the veil and gave a satisfied nod. 'Now,

have you got something old, something new, something borrowed and something blue?'

'I don't think so. Does it matter?'

Her mother looked horrified. 'Of course it does. You can't marry without those things.'

Annie shook her head. 'You're too superstitious, Mum.'

'That's as may be, but I'll not have my daughter walking up the aisle without proper preparation.'

'Humour her, Annie,' Rose laughed. 'I had to go through the same routine before I married Bill.'

'And a good job you did, my girl. You needed all the help you could get to make your marriage survive those first two years,' Marj accused her eldest daughter.

'It was Bill who saved us,' Rose pointed out. 'Not some meaningless material symbols.'

'I know.' Marj smiled at her two daughters. 'But let's not take any chances, eh?'

'Right.' Annie touched the veil. 'This was Rose's, so is that old enough?'

Marj agreed that it was, just about.

'Good. The dress is new and so is everything else I'm wearing, thanks to the family pitching in with their clothing coupons. So the next is something borrowed.'

'I know.' Rose disappeared upstairs and returned with a velvet box in her hands. 'Grandma Gresham gave me this to wear on my wedding day and you can borrow it for yours.'

Annie let Rose fasten the beautiful row of pearls around her neck.

'That's perfect.' Marj beamed with pleasure. 'That just leaves something blue.'

'Will this do?' Annie lifted the long skirt and revealed a saucy garter with a pattern of blue forget-me-nots on it. Rose laughed and their mother gasped. 'Where did you get that?'

'Dora gave it to me. She wore it when she married Will.'

'Ah, well, that will do just fine,' Marj said. 'They are happy enough with one babe and another on the way.'

Rose winked at Annie. 'This is going to be some wedding with both the maids of honour pregnant. Let's hope Jenny doesn't decide to give birth during the ceremony.'

'She's promised me she won't,' Annie told them through her laughter.

'Auntie Annie.' Kate walked into the room, followed by Dora and Jenny. 'We're leaving now, the car's here to take us to the church.'

A lump came into Annie's throat as she saw how lovely her friends and niece looked. Their dresses were also made of parachute silk but they had been dyed a pale lilac, except for Kate's, and that was white with a large lilac sash. It was a truly stunning sight in these austere times.

Wally looked in. 'Come on, girls, the car's waiting.'

Marj bustled off to see that everyone left at the proper time and the two sisters were left alone.

'Nervous?' Rose asked.

'No.' Annie shook her head. 'I know I'm marrying the right man.'

'Good.' Rose stood silent for a while, and then spoke softly. 'Don't make the same mistakes I did, Annie. Reid's a good man – show him you love him.'

'I will.'

453

Rose nodded, and then did a surprising thing. She kissed her sister, smiled and walked out of the room.

Annie was touched by the unusual outward show of affection, but Rose had mellowed over the last few years. The tough young woman had disappeared, leaving hardly a trace of the anger and frustration that had driven her. The tight control on her emotions was still there, of course, and Annie doubted if that would ever change. Rose's young life had been too harsh for that last barrier to come down completely, but those who knew her recognized the deep love she had for family, friends and all who suffered injustice and deprivation . . .

'Time to go, Annie.' Wally handed her the flowers and they went out to the waiting car.

The church in Putney was crowded with family and friends. As Annie glanced at the smiling faces she couldn't remember when she'd felt so happy. Her brother Will was there; his ship had docked just the night before. Charlie was serving as an usher with some more of the ground crew from Tangmere. As she looked around at the sea of air force blue uniforms her grin broadened. That airfield must be empty today!

As the organ began to play Wally squeezed her arm to make her start the walk down the aisle. Everyone in the church faded from thought and vision as she concentrated on Reid. He was standing with Bouncer at his side and had turned round to face her as she walked towards him. He looked stunning in his uniform and Annie wondered how she could ever have believed that she didn't like him. It was only with hindsight that she realized she must have fallen in love with him when she'd glimpsed him on the quay during the evacuation of Dunkirk.

She reached his side and he smiled, leaning forward to kiss her gently on her cheek. 'I love you, Annie, and you look so beautiful,' he murmured for her ears only.

The ceremony passed all too quickly for her. After signing the register they walked down the aisle together, husband and wife. Annie felt so proud as she saw the guard of honour waiting for them outside the church. All the pilots were in their best uniforms, sporting rows of medals on their chests, with every buckle and button shining in the brilliant sunshine.

As they started their walk along the line Reid made a pretence of inspecting them. They stood fiercely to attention in true military style, until you looked into their faces and noticed the wide grins.

'You won't find anything wrong with us today,' Bouncer told them as they reached him, which caused a quiet ripple of amusement to rumble along the line.

'I'd better not.' Reid cast his glance over the pilots again and then gave a satisfied nod. 'You're certainly smarter and cleaner than I've ever seen you.'

They were all laughing now, including the man standing at the end of the line, holding up a pair of headphones.

'Sam!' Annie was ecstatic. 'I didn't think you'd be able to make it.'

He kissed her cheek and handed her the headphones. 'Here's a souvenir for you. I wouldn't have missed your wedding for anything.' He then shook hands with Reid. 'I wish you both a lifetime of happiness.'

'Thank you. How are Maria and Jacques?' Reid asked.

'They are both well. Maria is becoming stronger all the time, and although Jacques misses Kate and James he is settling down and making friends. He keeps asking when you are coming over to see him, though.'

'When can we go?' Annie looked at Reid imploringly.

'We'll go as soon as Kate and James are on their school holidays,' Reid promised.

Marj hurried up. 'They want to take the photos now.'

'We'll talk later,' Annie told Sam, as she was hustled away for the wedding photos.

After a great many were taken there was one Annie knew would be her favourite. Reid and Sam were on either side of her, and the pilots of Reid's old squadron surrounded them. It was obvious to Annie that through the perilous times they had formed a bond that would never be broken, just as she had with Sam, and Jack Graham, had he lived.

But this was not a time for sadness. She had just married the man she loved passionately and the future looked bright and inviting.

Annie moved in Reid's arms and he kissed the top of her head. He couldn't remember if he'd ever felt so contented and at peace with himself. Her delicate fingers traced a pattern over his back and he shuddered with pleasure.

'Are you awake?' he asked huskily.

'Yes.' She moved her head back on the pillow so she could look into his face and smiled. 'I've got a special present for you but I haven't had a chance to give it to you until now.'

Reid grinned. 'You mean I jumped you as soon as we reached the bedroom?'

456

A soft chuckle ran through her. 'You were in rather a hurry.'

'Hmm. Anyway what's this present? I thought I'd already been given it,' he added suggestively.

'Not this one; it's a gift of life.' She kissed him, then said, 'I'm pregnant, Reid.'

He thought she was joking until he gazed into her eyes; they were serious and slightly wary, as if she wasn't sure of his response. Then he grinned. 'I don't know how you can tell that so soon. This is the first time we haven't taken any precautions.'

'No, it isn't. Remember VE Day?'

That gave him a jolt. Good Lord, he'd forgotten that night, which was hardly surprising with the amount they'd all drunk. And in the euphoria of Germany's capitulation all caution had gone by the board. The shock of Annie's announcement was rapidly being replaced with one of utter joy. 'Are you sure? It's only about seven weeks.'

Annie nodded. 'The medical officer checked me over two days ago.'

'That's wonderful,' he groaned, rolling on to his back and pulling Annie on top of him. 'But I wish you'd told me before and I would have treated you with more care.'

Annie looked horrified. 'You're a strong, passionate man and that's the way you must stay. I'm feeling fine. So you're pleased about the baby?'

'Pleased? I'm ecstatic. Get out of the WAAF as soon as you can, Annie.' Reid started to make rapid plans in his head. This changed everything. 'I've got a piece of land in Thatcham near my parents' house, where we can have a house built. I'll find a place to rent until ours is ready. The plans are finished; Bill gave them to me yesterday and Grant Phillips can start the work immediately.'

Annie sat up. 'What's all this? Has Bill designed a house for us?'

Reid nodded. 'This was going to be my special wedding present to you – when I had time to give it to you, of course.'

'But when did Bill have time to do this?' she asked, astounded by the news.

'As soon as you agreed to marry me I got in touch with Bill and explained what I wanted. He was all for the idea and has been working on the design during any spare moment. It's fabulous, you'll love it.'

'I know I will.' She started to rain small kisses all over his face. 'Did anyone ever tell you what a wonderful, thoughtful man you are?'

Reid pretended to give this a lot of consideration. 'Not lately, but you can show me how pleased you are, if you like.'

'I like.'

It wasn't until the war with Japan was over in August that Annie was finally demobbed. The terrible force of the atomic bombs the Americans had dropped on Japan had appalled her, along with everyone else, but it was a blessed relief to know that the war was completely over now. She prayed that the world would never do this again; the weapons of destruction were too horrible to contemplate. She wanted their child, and all the others, to be able to grow up in peace.

She put the finishing touches to the table and went

back into the kitchen to check on her roast chicken. This was a luxury given to her by a local farmer, and she couldn't help wondering how long it would be before food was plentiful again. It would be wonderful to go into the shops and buy whatever you wanted but Annie guessed that it would be some time before that happened. This country was going to need time to recover.

She sang contentedly to herself. This was a pleasant house but she couldn't wait for their home to be finished. With luck the house should be ready for them to move into by Christmas. The baby wasn't due until early February, so that would give them plenty of time to furnish the nursery. She had already chosen which room to use and had it all planned.

'Annie.' Reid strode into the kitchen and kissed her like a desperate man. 'I've wangled fourteen days' leave,' he announced when he finally broke off the embrace. 'And I'll be demobbed by October.'

'That's marvellous.' She knew just how much he wanted out, but he was such an efficient officer that the RAF had been trying to hold on to him. However, Reid wouldn't be swayed, he was eager to get back to the family business and let his father take a well-earned retirement.

'I've also arranged with Rose and Bill for us to take the children over to France to see Jacques at the end of the week.' Reid ran his hand gently over her expanding waistline. 'We'll go by sea, and if you don't feel like tackling the journey, I'll take the children on my own.'

'There's no need for that,' she protested. 'I'm disgustingly fit, the doctor told me yesterday, and now the morning sickness has gone, I'm fine.'

'Good.' He looked relieved. 'James and Kate are excited about going, and we'll have a holiday while we're there.'

It was a glorious summer morning with the first faint rays of the sun giving a hint of the heat to come. Annie leaned on the rail and looked out over the calm sea. There was only a gentle swell and the boat seemed suspended in time. Her mind drifted back to the last time she'd been to France; the circumstances were very different this time. The fear and grief of that journey to find Jack Graham had faded now and she could remember him as the laughing, gentle and very brave man he had been. The horror of the experience no longer troubled her nights. She had done her best and he'd known that, and had been grateful to her for seeing that he survived long enough to see his son . . .

She felt Reid place an arm around her shoulder and she looked up and smiled at him.

'Memories?' he asked perceptively.

'Yes,' she told him, 'but they don't hurt like they used to.'

He nodded in understanding. 'We'll never forget, though, will we?'

Annie straightened up and shook her head. 'And we shouldn't. I just hope that the sacrifices of so many are remembered.'

'They will be.' He smiled and dropped a quick kiss on her nose. 'Fancy a cup of tea?'

'Please. And something to eat, I'm starving.'

A deep chuckle rumbled through him. 'You always are.'

'I think the baby takes all my food.'

'And how is my son enjoying the sea voyage?'

Annie gave Reid a quizzical glance. 'You're sure it's going to be a boy, aren't you?'

'Your mother told me it was.' He led her to the refreshments bar where James and Kate were already enjoying an early morning feast of tea and buns. 'We can have a girl next time.'

Annie laughed. 'Has my mother been reading the tea leaves again?'

'Something like that, I expect.'

'Auntie Annie,' Kate called. 'We've saved some for you.'

'Thanks.' She sat down.

'What's it going to be like where Jacques is?' James wanted to know.

'OK.' Reid helped himself to a bun. 'Sam said that the village is recovering and they've repaired a lot of the buildings now.'

'Must have been terrible to be occupied like they were,' James remarked.

'Yes, and thank heavens it never happened to us.' Reid cut his bun and put half on Annie's plate, giving her a secret smile.

'Only because men like you and Bouncer kept them out.' James gazed at Reid with undisguised admiration.

'Everyone played their part, James.' Reid was serious now. 'It's true the RAF held them off long enough for us to regroup after Dunkirk, but without the merchant navy and the ships which protected the convoys we'd have starved. And the way the army recovered after their defeat showed great courage and determination.'

461

'And there were all the ordinary people,' James reminded them. 'We mustn't forget them.'

'Yes, you're right.' Reid smiled at Annie. 'All unsung heroes and heroines.'

When they landed at Calais Reid managed to hire a car, after much haggling with the owner of a small garage. It was not in the best of condition and had a habit of burping then making a sound like fireworks going off. This sent James and Kate into hoots of laughter, but it was better than public transport, which was practically non-existent.

As they travelled the twenty-five kilometres inland to reach Sam's village, great swathes of the countryside appeared untouched until they came across ruined farmhouses here and there. Annie wondered where the owners were now? There were displaced persons all over Europe and it was going to be a mammoth task trying to get everyone back to their homes.

Reid broke through her sombre thoughts. 'This must be it.'

Jacques came running as soon as he saw them, shouting in excitement. 'You came! You came!'

Annie was thrilled to see the change in them. Jacques was noisy and boisterous, not at all like the frightened little boy who had cowered in silent misery. Maria had changed beyond recognition, and standing in front of Reid and Annie was the most stunning woman, vibrant and alive – and finally Sam. Annie studied him carefully and saw a man at peace with himself and content to be with the family he loved. The deep anger that had always lingered in his eyes was a mere shadow now.

462

When he came and embraced her she hugged him in delight knowing that she no longer had to worry about him. He had come home and was happy.

Reid and Annie spent two days with Sam and Maria, then, leaving the children with them, they snatched a belated honeymoon in Paris.

It was a wonderful time for them, and although stifling hot during the day, they walked beside the Seine during the cool of the evening. After three blissful days they returned to pick up the children. Before leaving for home they all visited a small memorial that had been set up by the villagers to record the names of those who had been killed during the occupation.

James and Kate solemnly placed flowers at the site, then they left, promising to return again soon.

37

Annie was spending the day with her mother and Rose. The October sun was casting shadows across the kitchen table as they sat amid the debris of their lunch, enjoying a good chat over a cup of tea.

'I expect Reid's looking forward to leaving the air force,' her mother remarked.

'Yes. Only one more week and he can't wait. Neither can his father who is eager to hand over the running of the business to him again.'

'He'll be glad to be rid of that responsibility.' Rose started to gather up the dishes.

'Here, let me help with that.' As Annie stood up a searing pain shot through her making her double up and gasp.

'What's the matter?' Marj grabbed hold of Annie.

'I don't know.' She groaned as another pain nearly made her pass out.

Her mother and Rose helped her into the other room and made her lie on the settee with her feet up. Annie was by now moaning in fright. 'The baby! I'm only five months. It's too soon to go into labour.'

Rose was already phoning for the doctor and an ambulance.

'Hold on,' her mother soothed. 'Help will soon be here. It'll be all right.'

But it wasn't going to be, Annie knew that, and the tears streamed down her face in speechless agony. She was bleeding. She was losing the baby!

'Sir!' An out-of-breath sergeant raced up to Reid. 'There's a phone call for you. Says she's your sister-in-law, and if I don't find you immediately she'll come here and break my bloody neck.' He stopped to gulp in a couple of quick breaths of air. 'She meant it. It's urgent.'

Reid was running for his office before the man had stopped speaking, his heart crashing against his ribs. Rose. No one else would threaten a stranger like that. And Annie was with her today. Oh God, what had happened?

He skidded through the door and lunged at the phone. 'Rose!'

Reid thought he knew all about the pain life could deal you at times, but as he listened his world of happiness crumbled around him.

'Is Annie all right?' As Rose told him he bowed his head in grief and tears burnt the back of his eyes. 'I'll come to the hospital at once.'

The phone crashed back on its cradle and Reid thought he must be paralysed. He couldn't move.

'Sir?' The sergeant was looking at him with concern. 'Shall I find you a car and driver?'

Reid dragged his screaming mind together and nodded. 'At once, please, Jenkins.'

When Reid saw Marj and Rose's strained expressions he knew things were bad. 'Where is she?'

465

Marj was speechless with grief, and it was Rose who nodded towards a door. 'In there, she's just come back from the operating theatre.'

There was a doctor and a nurse at Annie's bedside but Reid pushed past them to reach his wife. He hooked a chair over with his foot and sat down, cradling her hand in his. She was so still and silent, not at all like his lively, animated Annie.

'Is she going to be all right?' he asked, not taking his eyes from her face.

'She's lost the baby and a lot of blood,' the doctor told him as kindly as possible. 'But we don't think there's any permanent damage. She should make a full recovery in time.'

Reid let the tears overflow then, quite unashamed. She was going to live, and that was the only thing that mattered.

He lifted her hand to his lips and kissed her cold fingers. 'Don't you dare leave me, my darling,' he scolded. 'My life would be empty without you.'

It was about two hours before Annie stirred and opened her eyes. Her gaze fixed on Reid immediately and he saw the moment when realization dawned. Her hand was shaking as it moved down towards her stomach, but he caught it and held it tightly. He felt his own grief fighting to surface when he saw the pain in her eyes, but he mustn't let that happen. Annie was going to need him to be strong, and although she was no weakling herself this loss was going to devastate her. They had both been so excited about the baby.

Silent tears began to flow and she reached out for him.

466

He sat on the bed and gathered her gently into his arms. Her body shook as the sobs came in great heart-rending sounds.

'Why?' she moaned. 'Our baby was conceived at a time of such joy and I was healthy. Why?'

Reid had talked to the doctor while Annie had been asleep. He had the answers and he decided that it would be better if she knew. It might help the grieving.

'She had a heart defect.' He stroked Annie's hair in a soothing motion. 'And she died before you lost her. The doctor said that even if you'd gone full-term, she wouldn't have survived for long.'

'It was a girl?' she whispered.

'Yes.' Reid held her face away so he could look at her. He could give her some hope. 'The doctor told me that there isn't any reason why we shouldn't have healthy children in the future.'

Annie gave a ragged sigh of relief. 'I'm all right then?'

'Perfect.' He tried a smile, and was pleased to see her return it, even though the tears were still coursing down her face.

'I'm so sorry, my darling.' She held on to him tightly.

'It wasn't your fault, Annie. You mustn't believe it was for a moment.'

She nodded, closed her eyes, and sank into blessed sleep again.

Annie fought her way out of sleep but it was a struggle. She could hear muted voices – voices she recognized. Then her mind began to clear and icy fingers of despair clutched at her. She had lost the baby.

Through her whimper of distress she heard Reid call. 'Annie.'

She opened her eyes then. The private room she was in was only small but somehow most of her family had managed to squeeze in. There was Reid, her mother and Wally, Rose, Bill, Kate and James, Will and Charlie. And by the look of it they'd all brought flowers; the room was a profusion of blooms, the heady perfume overriding the antiseptic atmosphere. It was at that moment she knew just how lucky she was to be surrounded by so much love.

She gave Reid a tremulous smile. She was determined to put a brave face on things, not only for his sake but also for her own. They would get through this together, of that she was certain.

'Sit me up,' she asked, 'so I can see you all.' Reid lifted her and Rose arranged the pillows. 'Ah, that's better. You'll all get told off,' she said, trying to lighten the mood and remove their worried expressions.

'No we won't,' Will said and grinned. 'We've bribed Sister with a bar of chocolate. She said we can stay for an hour and not a moment longer.' Then he was serious again. 'We're all dreadfully sorry about the baby, Annie.' She nodded, and dropped her head as the tears started to gather, but she fought them back. A small hand touched hers and she looked up to see Kate was sitting on the bed. At nine years old it was clear just how beautiful she was going to be.

'If you like I can be your *pretend* daughter – just until you have one of your own, of course.' Kate's dark gaze fixed on Reid. 'That's only if you want to, of course. Mummy and Daddy won't mind sharing me.'

468

'I think that's a wonderful idea, don't you, darling?' Reid squeezed Annie's hand.

'We'd be honoured to have you as our *pretend* daughter.' Annie pulled Kate towards her so she could kiss her, and not for the first time she marvelled at her niece's insight. It was as if she knew just what to do in any crisis.

'Uncle Will, I know you've got another bar of chocolate, and I think we should share it now,' James suggested.

The chocolate was produced and as chatter increased Annie reached up to smooth the frown from Reid's face. 'Don't look so concerned, my darling,' she said softly. 'I'm all right now, and we'll have more children.'

She saw him relax, and the words from the Bible that she loved so much came clearly into her mind. 'If I take the wings of the morning.' Reid and his pilots had climbed into the sky not knowing what the future held for them, and that's what she must do. The pain of this loss would probably always be with her but she had learned to deal with grief over the last few years, and she was a stronger person now.

Her gaze swept over her family and lingered on Reid. He smiled at her and kissed her cheek gently, as if he understood her thoughts. The war had brought hardship and grief but it had also given her the greatest gift of all – the love of a wonderful man.

She would take *the wings of the morning*, and with that uplifting thought the future was full of promise.